D1806076

The Borrack Chronicles

THE BORRACK CHRONICLES

Chris Sullivan

Contents

BOOK 3: THE ICE PLATEAU

Acknowledgements

A special thanks to Barry Young who has encouraged me to write and my wife Dena who also encouraged along with my family. Also to Damian Shalks who has designed the wonderful front cover.

The innocent hope of all children is a rite of passage, for they look to those around them to nurture, teach and help them prepare for life on this beautiful planet; and for so many, they receive it abundance.

Yet there are many more that receive only the deceit of hope, for in their naivety they follow their peers with trust in their hearts, only for it to be betrayed by the greedy, depraved, foolish and heartless creatures that call themselves human. To those children I can offer nothing more than my sympathy and my angry rage at those who have taken advantage of your innocence. To that end, I dedicate this trilogy of stories to you, in the hope that it might ease your pain and suffering.

Prologue

It has been just over a year since my friend, mentor, and, more recently, colleague, retired: his name, Professor Conner Flynn, and mine, Professor Maris Ellis.

As a mark of respect to his great achievements, the university has commissioned me to publish one of the many journals that he wrote. He was an exceptional scientist; in fact, probably one of the best of recent times; a man who did not run with the pack, a man who never dismissed anything without researching it first, and because of his diligence and attention to detail, he has made a significant contribution to the world of science.

As I write this introduction, I can't help but remember one of his favourite idioms. I quote: 'The beauty of science is when you have found the answer to a question; it will open the door to another ten questions, it is a never-ending pit of learning.'

I have trolled through hundreds of his journals to find the best, but have been defeated by his articulate abilities to make all of his chronicles sound exciting and interesting. He is not just a master of science, but of expressing his great enthusiasm for his beloved subject. However, after much deliberation, I believe I have found the one.

Most scientists would have ignored this saga as sheer fantasy, but not Professor Conner Flynn. He saw a science that pushed boundaries until they burst open, revealing a whole new dimension.

The journal chronicles the story of a chimera, a being half-man half-eagle, and his battle with a malevolent force. It would be wrong for me to say anymore; it's best left to the master himself, Professor Conner Flynn.

(Case Study 45) The Chimera (Borrack) | Date1-9-2024

It has been fourteen years since I first came across the chimera, Borrack. At the time, I was on a fieldtrip across the Americas, researching the indigenous tribes of that great continent. It was towards the end of my fieldtrip, at a place called Native Bay, Southampton Island, at the north-eastern tip of Canada, that I first came across this unusual character. At the time I was researching one of the most interesting of all the tribes I had studied; the Sallirmiut, who had lived in that area, overlooking Native Bay one hundred years before. I was sifting through a hollow, surrounded by a ring of boulders, which were yielding some interesting artefacts from that period of time when I was then distracted by a large object flying in the sky. I immediately took cover, so I could study the phenomenon without being seen. Within seconds, I realised the object was not man-made, but natural – although it certainly wasn't normal. It was a bald eagle – not unknown in the area, but this creature was something else. It was huge, the size of a man. In terms of size, such a flying creature had only ever existed in prehistoric times; certainly nothing like it had been recorded in recent history.

It swept back its huge wings and landed. Fortunately, the creature had not observed me. I stayed quiet, making notes, when before my eyes I saw the strangest of sights I had ever witnessed, even stranger than the creature's size. In front of me, this huge bird metamorphosed from eagle to man.

As a scientist, I deal with facts and logic – but this creature defied both. Of course I have heard of strange tales about creatures called chimeras and up until now I would have dismissed such strange stories as just fantasies. Yet I had just witnessed with my very own eyes this huge creature metamorphose from a large bird to man – and, as you can imagine, I was intrigued.

Unlike many of my peers, who would have rubbed their eyes and walked away in disbelief, I felt compelled to seek out this strange episode and give a scientific explanation for it. So I approached the now metamorphosed man, nearly scaring him half to death. After introductions, I sat down with him on the hill looking down on the bay.

The creature's name was Borrack, and as I had surmised, he was indeed a chimera. During our conversations I had taken a mental note of his appearance and that of his clothes – I was fascinated by his clothing: they were made up of feathers, in much the same colours as those of a bald eagle.

We talked for some time. I told him of my research in the Americas, which put him at ease. I then asked about his life and he told me the strangest tale about his life, the origins of his birth, and the curse that had plagued him since then. I remember the conversation as if it were yesterday. I have recorded his words so you can see for yourself exactly what was said.

* * * * *

"It's a long story," Borrack said.

"Well I have the time," I replied.

Borrack relayed his story, as he had told it so many times before. The emergence of The Labyrinth of Golden Dreams, his loathing for that life form, of the village he was born in to, that lay at the entrance to the Black Mountains – the home of that malevolent force. He told me of the Ice Blue

Wind who protected The Labyrinth, his parents' journey to that evil place, and his subsequent birth. Borrack then told me of his adoptive father, Zachary, and his own mission to help the young innocents of this world.

I listened to Borrack the man, devouring up every little bit of information that he divulged and soaked it up with relish.

"How absolutely absorbing," I replied, as my thirst for knowledge was only just being quenched. "So what are you doing here?" I asked.

Borrack panned the landscape until his eyes rested on Native Bay that flowed into Foxe Basin.

"There's a young girl, an adolescent, whose name is Mermosia. Her mind is being ravaged by a secret, a terrible secret she cannot remember; it haunts her to the point where she could lose her sanity. She is my latest mission and I fear that I may let her down."

This chance meeting heralded the beginning of our association, although it was for only two weeks, it was a time I so valued with Borrack the man, the eagle – both from a scientific perspective and a personal one. I had agreed to help him with his latest mission (that of Mermosia) which will unfold later in the journal. I might add, it was a most exciting experience that pushed me and my science to its boundaries, but like all good things, it came to an end, albeit a fruitful one.

My time in the Americas was coming to its end, so we went our separate ways. Borrack was flying off to try and trace his parental history, from one of his father's friends who he had managed to track down.

That is, until he told me of the demons that he had been wrestling with for some time. He then mentioned a name, Erigal, and at that moment my brain went into overdrive until I retrieved that very name from the archives of my mind. It was a bad omen for my friend Borrack, although there was no factual substance to this tale other than being in large part fantasy. I felt obliged to tell him of Erigal and that according to the legend, the recipient of these recurring dreams heralded the loss of a loved one by foul means. Borrack took my warning to heart and decided to change his plans and return to his adoptive father and a close friend who was staying with him. That was the last I ever saw of him.

Nine years later, I was owed some time from the university, so I took a sabbatical. I had always wanted to research Borrack's story so set about finding him; needless to say, it wasn't easy, and it took some time tracking his movements. After many months I eventually found a lead: it was information that took me to a small island in the Indian Ocean, a place called Poutia. It was an island I had never heard of before, but one I wished I had discovered many years earlier, a place of total tranquillity and peace – a paradise.

Unfortunately, after much detective work, I was told some bad news. My friend had passed away a year previously. I was devastated, not just because of the valuable research material that was lost, but at the loss of a good friend and a compassionate being.

However, I later discovered that his partner of eight years lived on the other side of the island, with their two children. The news buoyed me up – so while true it was that I had lost a good friend, his partner would be able to provide me with some clues to his past which I could investigate.

I was given directions to her house, so I trudged across the island to meet her. What I found went was far beyond my wildest expectations. Borrack's partner's name was Maley and she, like Borrack, had also been a chimera. I say had been, because as you will read in this journal, you will discover how together these two characters brought down one of the most dangerous and malevolent forces that this world has ever seen.

I spent nearly two weeks with her and her children, a time that was so enriching ; I learned so much about my friend Borrack, the man, the eagle, the chimera, and his past life, from Maley. I hope that in this journal I have included the important details and given you the history of his birth parents, his adoptive father and that of the Labyrinth of Golden Dreams, which he had already disclosed to me, and only added to my conviction that sometimes the unbelievable is possible. It was an enlightening experience, but I had nothing tangible as proof of his existence and his curse until the last day of my stay with Maley, when she handed me a manuscript. It seemed that since the departure of her soul mate, she, as a mark of respect of love and loyalty, had recorded his history. It was a revelation to me, particularly the confirmation that the time I spent with Borrack on the mission to help the girl Mermosia was so accurately recorded, which to me only confirmed the authority of his tale. This spurred me on; it brought legitimacy to a story that would otherwise have been nothing more than a fantasy.

Once back at Oxford University, after reading and rereading the manuscript, I decided to verify the two preceding stories, "Escape from Reality" and "Elephants Live Forever", which I did and was rewarded for my efforts. I traced those affected by this magnificent creature, Borrack, from Jay and Gemma in the first account, including that of Melvin, the king penguin. Although I did not interview him personally, I met someone who had known him and they confirmed his peculiar appearance and eccentric manner. Then I traced Mumbye's family who confirmed the boy's sad story.

At this point I needed no more proof; so I published this strange story; I have yet to verify its science.

However, before I commit you to the journal written by Maley and edited by myself, I have one important detail to enlighten you with. At this stage it is impossible to verify the validity of this element of the story, as there is no science to explain it, although it does fit into current thinking. I mean The Labyrinth of Golden Dreams! I have already mentioned this entity, and as you read the journal, you will hear a lot more of it, which, as you will have realised already, is the malevolent spirit that both Borrack and Maley defeated for the good of all.

During the many hours I spent with Borrack on the Mermosia case, there were times when we openly discussed Borrack's history, in particular The Labyrinth of Golden Dreams. I learned that when he was a young fledgling, after he had overcome the many battles with the Ice Blue Wind and had broken through her defences, he had spent many hours in the company of that evil force. From what he told me, this intelligent life force was not of this world. To this entity, the distinction between past, present and future had no meaning; equally, emotion was another empty notion for it. According to Borrack, the entity had existed long before the material world of time and space; in fact, all that we know and are familiar with. It seems it was part of a cluster of intelligent life forms. Borrack described it as having intelligence and yet barren of emotions; a being of pure lucidity.

The cluster existed within a compact group, all the time expanding in numbers. At this time, according to the entity, there was no such thing as space, and its assorted myriads of stars, planets, black holes, and the many other undiscovered anomalies, or any of the many things yet to be uncovered.

As the cluster grew in size, hemmed in by fixed boundaries, it became more and more compressed, until deep in its centre, one of the lucid lifeforms exploded, creating a chain reaction so large that it forced anti-matter into matter. A tsunami of lucid energy pushed the boundaries of its existence, outwards in all directions creating a wave of space that is forever expanding. This is what we call the big-bang theory.

According to Borrack, it was one of these entities that was in the formation of the planet Earth; this is what he called The Labyrinth of Golden Dreams.

I have since been to the Black Mountains, the home of that entity, to verify this part of the chimera story, and have found many artefacts – mainly human skeletons and some DNA material that matches nothing on our planet. Although, in itself, this is not enough proof of any kind of alien species. I believe at the present, our science has not evolved enough to prove or disprove the chimera's claims, but up until I met Borrack, I did not believe in chimeras.

With that thought firmly placed in your mind, I leave you to read the journal and for you to make your own assessment.

BOOK 1.

ESCAPE FROM REALITY

CHAPTER 1

Jay and Gemma

"Tell them to stop, Jay!" Gemma said, weeping into her pillow.

Jay lay there listening to his parents arguing. For as long as he could remember it had always been the same, and still it sent the chill of fear down his spine. Jay was only eight and his sister less than six, and there they were in the dark, listening to two adults whose only concern was to prove they were in the right; it was criminal!

Of course, the parents loved their children and if they had known the pain and sorrow they were causing they would have stopped. But they didn't, so each night when the children went away to their beds, they would shout and scream at each other, throwing items around the room in fits of rage. Perhaps they thought Jay and Gemma were deaf or asleep. They weren't just scared, they were confused and empty – empty of love.

Gemma pulled the pillow around her head and sobbed relentlessly. "Do you want to come to my bed?" Jay said softly.

"Yes," she said, still sobbing. She plodded over to Jay's bed and cuddled up to him. "Can we go on a magical journey with Borrack?" She asked tearfully.

"Why not?" he said. Borrack was a figment of Jay's imagination, a large bald eagle taller than the tallest of men. He was so majestic, wise, but, above all, loving; he would carry the two siblings on fantastic adventures. It was the children's only escape! Escape from that incessant mental abuse! Escape from that terror; but most of all, escape from reality.

"Gemma, concentrate now, think of Borrack," Jay said closing his eyes tightly, the two of them laid there holding each other's hands.

Then it started. The room began to spin. A vortex opened up below and sucked them through, the wind whipped up and blew wildly around them, messing up their hair and clothes. With an almighty thump they exited the vortex in a heap, the vortex disappeared into itself, leaving them in the middle of a clearing, surrounded by woodland.

The Moon was full and its silver light illuminated the surrounding area like a huge incandescent lamp. They both sat up looking high into the sky! Looking for their friend Borrack – he was nowhere to be seen – just the countless stars…

"Look Gemma, over there – a shooting star!" They watched as the star shot over their heads and disappeared over the horizon.

"When's Borrack coming?" Gemma said.

"He'll be here soon…" but as soon as he had finished his sentence they felt the downwards draft of Borrack's huge wings. And there in front he hovered in all his glory, this magnificent creature, with his huge wingspan, the white head and large talons. Gracefully, he landed. The two children ran to their friend and saviour, wrapping their arms around his legs.

Borrack dipped his head under his chest to see his young wards. His huge, yellow eyes so wise and kind, focused on them. "Well, my young friends," he said with a deep but gentle voice, "what journey have you planned for us all today".

Gemma looked at Jay. "Jay, can't we go to the land of hopeful wishes?" she said earnestly. Jay looked at the sadness in her eyes. He had told Gemma of a land where dreams and wishes come true, and how one day they would make that journey, and wish for peace and love between their parents.

Unfortunately, such a place did not exist; he'd only said it to create hope for his sister, and perhaps in some way to raise his own hopes. It was not really a lie, just a dream – all he wanted was for his parents to once more fall in love, and spread that love and contentment throughout the house; bring peace and harmony to all.

"No," he said as gently as he could.

"Why not?" she retorted angrily.

Jay floundered for words, "Because I made it up! The place doesn't exist," relieved that the lie was exposed.

Gemma began to cry, she felt alone, helpless and scared for the future. "What hope is there for us?" she sobbed.

Borrack watched with surprise. He knew of their pain, but this was the first time they had ever expressed it – and their pain was his pain. At that moment he felt it so deeply. "Listen," he said, "I know of a place where dreams can come true."

The two of them looked at each other and then at Borrack, their hopes raised, both of them blurting out at the same time, interrupting each other.

"Is it true?" Jay said in disbelief.

At the same time Gemma gasped, "Please! Please, take us there!" Borrack could not control their enthusiasm, both of them began to babble and plead for more information.

"Calm down," Borrack said firmly. "Let me explain before you get too carried away! Yes, there is a place; it's called The Labyrinth of Golden Dreams and it's far from here, in the Black Mountains of the North. The journey will be long and arduous, fraught with danger; I have done it a few times, but I must warn you there is no guarantee of success; and there is a price for everything. I will take you there if you wish me to, but heed my warning! "

The two children looked at each other. Their desire for a blissful home life was more compelling than any warning, "Please, please, take us there!"

they blurted out in unison.

Borrack smiled with his eyes.

Then, as if from nowhere, a bolt of lightning struck the woodland floor. They all looked up into the sky to trace its origin. Far above, huge, angry rain clouds began to crowd the sky, and then another bolt of lightning struck nearby. Then the sound of crackling. It grew louder and louder, and an orange haze began to envelop the woodland. They all stood there dumbstruck, then, without warning, a stampede of woodland creatures appeared, travelling northeast away from the flickering glow. Foxes, badgers, rabbits, deer, and every other conceivable beast ran past them in a state of blind panic, chased by flickering of orange flames. Large plumes of smoke rose high into the sky. The fire was now raging out of control and had completely surrounded the clearing; the smoke it created was thick and acrid.

The children began to cough uncontrollably. Borrack lowered his wing to create a ramp for the children to climb up.

"Quick, you two! Jump on to my back!"

The two made their way up Borrack's wing. Jay first, throwing his arms around his saviour's neck. Gemma was next and cuddled up to Jay.

"Hold on!" Borrack shouted. Then he set his mighty wing into action, and they moved up, then down with awesome power. The enormous downdraft they caused created lift, and within seconds they were soaring high into the sky.

Jay and Gemma were still coughing violently. The rain had started, and hammered down. It was torrential. Borrack looked down to see the flames licking high into the sky. The woodland floor was alive with the uncontrollable fire, and Borrack could feel his young wards shivering with cold; he needed to find sanctuary, and fast. Somewhere dry, warm, with food and water. The sky was brighter to the north, so he changed course to accommodate this information. Yet, although he was extremely strong, he found it difficult to fly against the relentless rain, but he would not give up until they were all safe. No matter how heavy the rain and his passengers made him.

As he made his way further north, the rain began to ease and the heavy clouds started to break up, allowing the moon to shine its ethereal rays through, illuminating the earth below with its shards of silver streaks.

The two children were frozen, their teeth chattering. Borrack scoured the earth's surface; it was essential to find somewhere dry. His eagle eyes searched left and right, crisscrossing the land below him. The clouds had completely evaporated, allowing the moonlit sky to flood the earth, illuminating trees, bushes, fences and buildings, making the eagle's search a little easier. To the left he spotted a building, he circled it several times to gauge its suitability. It met all their needs. The barn stood in the middle of a large field isolated from any other buildings, and though it was badly maintained and had no doors, it was perfect.

Borrack swept down straight through where the doors had once stood. Hay was strewn across the floor. He angled his wings so as to slow him down, stretched out his large clawed feet ready to take the impact when he landed. Thump! He was down, "Ok you two, time to get some sleep," Borrack said as he lowered his huge wing to make a ramp. Jay and Gemma dismounted. Borrack was surprised as they looked absolutely bedraggled, both of them dripping wet, cold, with their teeth still chattering.

The eagle realized there was no way they could sleep like that, so he scoured the barn. In the corner there were some old cloth sacks. He hopped over and picked them up in his beak and took them back to his young wards.

"Get out of those wet clothes and climb into these sacks," he said.

Borrack carefully picked up their wet clothes in his beak and hung them on a nearby post. Then he hopped between the two children who were lying on the floor in their sacks and squatted down between them. Gently he opened his wings and covered the two siblings with them, so only their heads were visible. Immediately they felt his warmth and their shivering subsided.

Jay and Gemma now felt safe, warm, and full of hope for the future. Borrack swung his headfirst one side then the other to check that his young friends were comfortable.

"When will we go to the Labyrinth of Golden Dreams?" Gemma asked excitedly.

"We'll start early in the morning," Borrack replied.

"How long will it take?" she urged.

"Maybe a week," he responded.

"Is it very far away?" she pressed.

"Yes, far to the north. Now we must get some sleep," Borrack said firmly.

"Yes," said Jay, irritated by his sister's relentless questions.

"Sleep now," Borrack commanded.

The two children drifted off to sleep. Borrack, on the other hand, was unable to sleep – his mind was full of his past and future. This was not the first time he had visited the Labyrinth of Golden reams. His history was intrinsically connected to the place, and every visit had been an emotional roller coaster. He feared the journey as much as the place; he would have to pass through the Ice Blue Wind that protected the Labyrinth of Golden reams. 'That ice blue wind she is a malevolent sprit, I only just scraped through with my life last time. But now I must challenge her while carrying this most precious cargo of innocents in my care,' he thought, as he looked at the children sleeping. It nagged at him. Borrack was no coward, he just had no desire to involve his young friends in his own personal feud, but he had placed himself in this predicament. He had promised to help his young wards to find a solution to their unhappiness, at the same time knowing he would have to put their lives in danger to do so. He slept little, just kept turning over the same problem again and again.

CHAPTER 2

The Wise, Old Man of the North

A s he laboured away at his chores, he had little idea that later that day he would be reunited with his friend Borrack. Not that he was far from his thoughts, he never could be. To the old man, Borrack was more like a son. He had raised him from a fledgling. There are those that would pose the question, how can a bird be considered a son? Such a thought would be tantamount to lunacy, surely? Yet the old man of the north knew of this eagle's history; to him, he was not a bird, or even a mighty eagle, just a young man trapped in this creature's body. The saddest thing of all was that this trapped soul was more humane than the best of men. This depressed the old man immensely.

* * * * *

Borrack was up and about way before daybreak; his first task was to find some food and water for his two wards. He shuffled around in the old barn to this end. Far over in one corner he found a crate containing freshly picked apples. 'That's the food taken care of,' he thought. He carried on his search. And there, in the middle of the barn, stood a large barrel filled to the brim with water. He dipped his beak in to check its quality – it was fresh. 'It must have collected from yesterday's storm' he mused. He returned to the two sleeping children, gently he nudged them with his beak. Jay and Gemma yawned and opened their eyes. At first, they were a little confused, but soon recognized their surroundings.

"Listen," Borrack said, "there are apples over there in that crate and fresh water in that barrel," pointing with his wing. "Oh, and your clothes are dry. So, get dressed and eat and drink as much as you can, for we've got a long journey ahead of us".

Gemma as inquisitive as ever piped up, "Are we going to the Labyrinth of Golden reams?"

"Not today," Borrack replied. First, we have to go and stay with the old, wise man of the north for a day or two."

Jay looked at Borrack with a questioning expression, "Who's he?"

Borrack smiled with his eyes, "He's a good, kind man. In fact more like a father to me ".

The two children looked at each other very confused, "Father?" they blurted

"It's a long story," the eagle replied. "Now, come on you two! Let's get organized!"

Jay and Gemma followed Borrack's instruction to the letter. They were soon fed, watered, dressed and ready to go.

"Ok," the eagle said, giving his final orders, "Before we depart, fill your pockets with apples, the flight will be a long one and you'll need something to eat. When you're ready, climb aboard!" He lowered his wing for them to climb up. His two wards did as they were bade. They climbed on to the eagle's back, first Jay, hugging Borrack's neck, followed by Gemma, throwing her arms around Jay.

Borrack moved to the entrance, the moon was sinking into the western sky, casting long silver shadows as far as the eye could see; it was a magnificent sight. It seemed that the moon was struggling to hold onto the earth, like it believed it was some kind of God and the planet below should pay homage to its beauty as a true believer should. The eagle began to flap his huge wings; the air beneath was whipped into a frenzy, a cocktail of dust, straw and gases. In no time, they were airborne, soaring high into the sky.

As he headed northeast, Jay and Gemma watched as the moonlit landscape below passed by. The sight was amazing, the fields below were laid out like a patchwork quilt. They flew over hills, lakes; small hamlets with their traditional churches surrounded by little thatched or peg tiled cottages. Over great estates surrounded by beautiful gardens, a memorial of a time gone by, whose owners had grown fat and rich at the majority's expense. It was still early morning and a few nocturnal animals scurried about as if a curfew was about to be imposed. The further east they went, the weaker the moonlight became, yet still jealously trying to hold on to the land below. As the two children looked to the eastern horizons, they were met with the beginnings of the new day. The sky was orange! Glowing with the brilliance of hope, the glow began to spread across the landscape towards them. As it turned from orange to gold, within seconds, a qualitative change took place: the sun punched itself above the horizon. Its glowing brilliance encompassed the earth, and the planet responded! Once again, its life giver had returned. Every living thing, organic and animal, was filled with its energy -, the only exceptions being those creatures of the night that returned to their burrows and lairs to wait for the sun's demise.

The three continued their journey northeast; the sun was a third of the way through its cycle when they reached the suburbs of that most historic of cities, London. It spread out below them, like the anarchic mass of humanity, which it was. As the two children looked on from above, they saw Old Father Thames cutting through the capital. It reminded them of a huge serpent, snaking its way through the city in a desperate bid to escape, only to be pushed back by the surging tide. They passed by the Palace of Westminster, the cradle of one of the world's oldest democracies. There it stood, full of hope, and yet for the masses, its only legacy was despair. Past St. Paul's Cathedral, and on, pressing towards the northeast and their destiny.

The sun was at midday when they reached the wash and the coastline of eastern England. They swept over the North Sea, to the left of them a few oil and gas rigs bobbed up and down like corks in a bucket of water. Further on, they passed over the shipping lanes with their seagoing vessels plying their trade to the four corners of the earth. By the time they reached the fjords of Norway, the two children felt tired and exhausted and its beauty was lost on them. Borrack could sense their fatigue; he had no choice but to press on.

"It will be a few more hours yet," he shouted.

Borrack felt no exhaustion; his strength and resolve would carry him on no matter how far.

The black cliffs of the fjords dropped vertically down into the inlet; the water reflected the same austere colour. Borrack looked at the spectacle with reverence, Mother Nature had once again excelled herself. As they left the fjords behind, the landscape dramatically changed, they were now flying high over pine-clad forests. It was mid-summer and the sun lazily sunk into the western sky. It was in no hurry to leave. At this time of year, it would always be superior to the moon! And the moon? It had no choice but to jealously accept the status quo.

Borrack was in home territory now; he could see the little log cabin nestling amongst pine trees, the smoke drifting upwards out of the chimney pot. This was his home full of memories, both happy and sad. He circled a few times. He could not see his friend, his adoptive father. The eagle began to circle more widely, searching further and further away from the homestead. Then he saw him picking berries for his evening meal. He was dressed in his normal attire, his hat tilted to one side. Borrack smiled with his eyes, it was both a caring and mischievous smile.

"Hold on," Borrack shouted to his young friends.

Both of them, exhausted and tired, realized, by Borrack's tone, that he was about to go into a dive. He had done it with them many times before and they considered it great fun, something akin to a big dipper ride. They held on tightly. Borrack swept his huge wings back and plunged headfirst down! Not a sound could be heard except the rush of air as they passed through it at speed!

The old man was blissfully unaware of Borrack's intentions. The two children gasped with excitement as they rushed head-long towards the ground. Then, before the old man could react, Borrack spread his wings out, pushed his talons out, and gently plucked the old man's hat off. Then he flapped his huge wings and away he flew, back to the homestead. The old man, shocked, looked up to see what had happened, and there he saw his friend Borrack flying back home with his hat in his claws. He smiled, and shook his fist at Borrack laughing, "You devil, Borrack! You devil!"

By the time the old man reached the homestead, Borrack had landed and the two children were sat on the porch step exhausted and hungry.

"Borrack, it's so good to see you!" the old man said, as he embraced his adopted son.

"You too!" Borrack replied, awkwardly trying to emulate the old man's response with his wings.

"You're looking well, son! And who are these two strangers?" he said, peering at the two children.

"Father, this is Jay, and this is Gemma" pointing at each one with his wing. "Children, this is Zackery, my father. We'll be staying with him for a day or two".

"I bet you're all hungry," Zackery said.

Jay and Gemma nodded shyly.

"I've got a delicious venison stew simmering away in the kitchen – it must be ready by now!" With that, the old man disappeared through the door, only to return a few minutes later, carrying a pot, full of steaming meat and potato stew. He placed it down, quickly went out again, and returned a minute later with a ladle and bowls. Being a warm, summer's evening, Zackery had chosen to dine outside on a wooden table he had made with his own hands. Once more he disappeared back into the log cabin, and this time he returned carrying three mugs and a loaf of freshly baked bread.

"Ok! You lot tuck in and enjoy!" he said jovially.

All of them sat down, the two children opposite each other and Zackery next to Borrack, who stood unseated. Borrack, as always, would eat socially with Zackery, but it was not instinctive, no matter how humane his heart and soul were; the fact was, he was a bird of prey, and his normal diet consisted of fresh prey or carrion.

Zackery and Borrack talked excitedly. They had much to catch up on, and the eagle had not been home for nearly a year. In fact, they were so engrossed in their conversation they hadn't noticed Gemma, who had long since finished her meal and had fallen asleep, her head lying on her folded arms. Jay could barely keep his eyes open, but tried his best to keep up with the conversation, for he felt he was no small child like his sister. No! He was almost an adult. Zackery spotted Gemma, "I think the two little ones are tired," he said to Borrack pointing at the young lady.

"Yes, it has been a long day! It's time for their bed," Borrack replied.

Jay obstinately protested, trying to keep his eyes open.

"Come on, Jay," Zackery said, lifting Gemma in his arms and carrying her off into the log cabin. Jay followed reluctantly, kicking the earth with his shoes as he did so. Zackery laid Gemma down on the bed, and Jay climbed in next to her half-heartedly, and the old man covered the two with wolf pelts.

"Sleep well, my young friends, for every new day brings new adventures, and every adventure brings a wealth of knowledge, and knowledge is more valuable than all the gold in the world," Zackery said, gently closing the door.

CHAPTER 3

Borrack's Tale: Part One

The soothsayer languished in her abode, on an island in the middle of a lake far from humanity's gaze. She was waiting for a visitor she knew would call. The soothsayer thought it strange that someone as cynical as this caller would seek her out for a truth he would not believe in, for he did not judge destiny in the same way as she did.

* * * * *

The next morning Zachary awoke to find Borrack preparing for his journey
"I guess you're off looking for that elusive truth?" he said.
"Yes," Borrack replied, as though found-out.
Both of them knew it was a futile task, for truth only comes with the unfolding of time; however, both accepted that the desire to be armed for future events was a prudent one. In some ways, it also kept Borrack sane; as for the old man, he understood Borrack's desire to be prepared. Zackery studied Borrack.
"There is something else on your mind, isn't there ?" the old man said earnestly. "Yes," Borrack said, "It's the journey to the Labyrinth of Golden Dreams tomorrow."
"You've done it before," Zackary replied.
"But never with children's lives in my hands,"
"Gemma and Jay are going with you?" "Yes! But how can I put their lives at risk? It's the Ice Blue Wind; you know she's out for revenge?"
"Listen Borrack," Zackery said wisely, "I have always taught you not to back away from adversity! Face it – your strength and resolution will protect you and the children. Remember, only confidence will win through."
Borrack knew his adopted father was right. He looked at the old man.
"Of course, you're right. Will you look after the children? They need to rest. Maybe you could—?"
Before he could finish, Zackery butted in.
"Yes, of course, I will look after the children, and yes, I will explain the dangers involved in their journey. Now I suggest you get on your way! And good luck. I hope you find the information you're looking for. "

* * * * *

Zachary sat on a bench outside the log cabin, whittling a piece of wood. Borrack had left some time earlier in an attempt to find future truths, leaving the old man in charge of his two young wards. The sun was once again chasing the moon away, as Zachary amused himself with his wood carving. His huge hands looked far too clumsy for such a task, but he had the dexterity of an artist. A silver coffee pot was perched on the table in front of him, when, suddenly, in the highly polished reflection he caught sight of something moving. It was Gemma timidly peeking out from behind the door, intrigued to see what the old man was doing. The wise old man turned slightly so the young girl would get a better view of his handiwork, hoping it would coax her out. It worked, and, tempted by curiosity, she made her way over to be where Zachary was sitting.

"What you doing, mister?" she said.

"I'm carving a small doll for you," he replied gently. "See?"

She smiled shyly, but you could see she was delighted. She thought the doll he was carving looked perfect, and she was going through names for her in her mind, when Zachary's voice interrupted her thoughts.

"Do you want some breakfast?"

Brought back to the here and now, she nodded, when, at that very moment Jay appeared.

"Good morning, young man," Zachary said cheerfully, "would you also like some breakfast?"

"Yes please, mister."

"You and Gemma sit down here at the table, and I'll be back in no time," with which Zachary disappeared into the cabin and the children duly did as they were bidden. A little while later and the old man reappeared, carrying a large pot of porridge, freshly baked bread, mugs, plates and bowls, and then they all tucked into their food.

Half-way through, Jay piped up, "Mister, where's Borrack?"

Zachary looked at him. "He's gone to seek out some proof about his tribe and parents."

"Tribe?"

"Yes tribe." Zachary replied.

"Birds don't have tribes," Jay said, looking rather puzzled, and continued, "They live in flocks."

Zachary looked, first at the young boy, and then at the girl, their eyes were questioning him.

"Perhaps I should explain," he said. "But first, let's clear the dishes away! You can both help."

It wasn't long before the chores had been finished, and they were once again sat around the table. The children looked at the old man, waiting for his explanation. Zachary started with a question.

"When you look at Borrack, what do you see?"

The children looked at each other, the question was obvious, and both said reluctantly, as if the question was a trick, "an eagle."

"Yet things aren't always what they seem," the old man replied, somewhat mysteriously. After a pause, he continued, "Yes, his physical appearance is that that of a bird, but, beneath that façade, is a man! And every bit as human as any of us, you or I! He is what's known as a chimera – have you heard that word before?" he said, looking at the children. They shook their heads. Zachary went on, "It is a creature whose appearance masks its true self; a hybrid, if you will. There are many such creatures within the Black Mountains, but only two outside of them – one being Borrack, and the other, the Ice Blue Wind".

The two children weren't sure if they were hearing correctly. Had they gone mad, they wondered? The look of puzzled bewilderment was clearly evident on their faces, because Zachary laughed, and continued.

"Yes, I know it's hard to believe! But it's absolutely true! Borrack had a human father and mother."

Gemma, using all her strength to summon logic over confusion, asked, "What happened to him?"

Zachary heaved a sigh. "It's a long story, and the truth is, you have to go back to a time beyond time itself, back to when the Earth was at the start of its history. No life existed, let alone intelligent life! Well, not the sort of intelligence that humanity has achieved." The old man pointed to the Black Mountains on the horizon.

"There, deep inside those huge rock formations, in a labyrinth of caves, intelligence was evolving; not organic or living tissue, but deep down, within the heart of the rocks. It wasn't the sort of intelligence that can decide right from wrong, feel pain or understand emotions, no! It was more mechanical, something akin to a computer. Capable of granting wishes without conscience or recourse, without repercussions or ramifications. Yet, it did feel one emotion, but just one: that of self-preservation! So there it lay dormant. For no other life existed, nothing to challenge its immense power! And such power. It passed through the evolutionary epoch of time, through the prehistoric period, to the emergence of the first mammals, and was there during the slow and painful development of humanity. This was its ultimate challenge, and one that was so detrimental to so many poor, unsuspecting souls. This is where Borrack's tale begins."

The children looked up at Zachary, their eyes filled with fascination.

Zachary continued. "At the foot of the Black Mountains, a community of hunter-gatherers settled. At first scraping a living off the land; later, much later, they became farmers. But unlike most farming communities, who were at the mercy of the erratic weather, which, more often than not, led to the failure of their crops and starvation. They were fortunate, for they had discovered a labyrinth of caves, known to you as the Labyrinth of Golden Dreams." He paused, to let it sink in. "Its benefits to the community were immense. When they wished for bountiful crops, they were theirs for the taking. In return, they treated the Labyrinth of Golden Dreams like a god, offering sacrifices of life and death."

"However, like all good secrets, it didn't stay secret for long. This led to catastrophic consequences. An avalanche of opportunistic thieves fell upon the Labyrinth of Golden Dreams, stripping it bare of its valuable minerals, even its natural polished gold mirrors – those very mirrors that would reflect the wishes of its benefactors and bring them to fruition. However, the Labyrinth's desire for self-preservation was too strong and those poor would-be thieves were turned into all manner of beasts to roam the black mountains on their bellies, for an eternity; a living purgatory."

The children sat quietly, listening intently to the old man, taking in every word.

"The Labyrinth of Golden Dreams," he continued, "became overwhelmed by the onslaught of thieves and demanded help from the tribe. The chief was summoned and ordered to sacrifice his own daughter to become the Guardian of the entrance to the Black Mountains, the gateway to the Labyrinth of Golden Dreams. He did as he was bade, with a heavy heart. It saddened him greatly; his beautiful daughter was turned into a chimera, a wind! It was a wind that would cut across the entrance of those Black Mountains. At first, she was warm and gentle, nurturing her tribe, only angered when someone threatened the Labyrinth of Golden Dreams."

"She was always hopeful that one day she would be returned to the bosom of her family. But as the years rolled on, she watched her family grow old and die. Grandparents, then father, mother, brothers and sisters… until, eventually, there was no one left. She became lonely, isolated and, with time, this became anger! Her love and beauty perished, until all that was left was rage. She turned on her tribe, making their lives sad and unbearable. She would punish them with biting northern gales, destructive hurricanes, blow rainclouds until she provoked flooding, and fires from the lightening she would usher over them, destroying their crops, homes and hopes. For generations the tribe stood firm against the Ice Blue Wind, taking everything she threw against them, but her anger knew no bounds."

"But no matter how strong their culture and tradition were, the Ice Blue Wind and time were wearing them down, and like we all do when confronted by an insurmountable problem, they began to question their very existence. The village elders held a meeting, a vote was taken and a decision made – the tribe would move! Move away, far, far away from the Black Mountains and the Ice Blue Wind, which had haunted and tormented them for so long. Yet, one man held out: young, tall and with dark hair; he was a man of principles."

"He asked to talk to the village elders. They agreed, and he laid before them a plan."

The two children were now totally engrossed in Zachary's story.

"What happened?" Jay implored.

The old man smiled, "Well, Jay, they accepted the young man's plea. He would travel to the Labyrinth of Golden Dreams and wish for help. He would take a gift of a sacrificial goat. It was also agreed that his heavily pregnant wife should accompany him."

Gemma suddenly wanted to say something, but unsure of her question, stumbled over her words.

"Had they not asked for hel-help from the Lab-Labyrinth of Gol-Golden Dreams before?"

"Yes," Zachary replied, "But without success. This was to be a last-ditch attempt."

The children wanted to know what happened next.

Zachary cleared his throat and continued, "The two of them set off, taking the track to the Black Mountains. The Ice Blue Wind must have had a premonition of their intentions, for she threw everything at them: wind, snow and hale, but nothing was going to stop them, or their mission. They struggled on against their foe, even though the woman was heavy with child. They went higher and higher towards the entrance of the Labyrinth of Golden Dreams, until eventually they broke free of the evil wind. The two turned to look back over their journey and the village they had just travelled from, which nestled at the entrance to the mountains. The Ice Blue Wind had now turned her fury towards that small community; her rage was more ferocious than ever. The couple felt for their friends and family; this was why the mission was so important. The sun pierced through the clouds, its light flooded through like huge columns of translucent marble. It was as if these columns were supporting the heavy clouds, so as to stop them crashing to the ground."

Zackery relayed the story as he had been told it almost word for word, and the children appreciated it.

"After a while they turned to continue their journey. But they were surprised by the appearance of a large King Penguin. His eyes were sad and full of hopelessness. He held his wing out as a gesture of introduction. 'Hello, I'm Melvin!' he said, in a friendly way; the truth was he was lonely! Lonely beyond imagination.

"Why?" asked Jay, inquisitively. "Ah! My young friend, the penguin is like Borrack and the Ice Blue Wind, a chimera. Do you remember earlier I mentioned about the thieves who tried to rob the Labyrinth of Golden Dreams? Well, Melvin is such a character. His crime may have been a thousand years old, who knows? Maybe more, but he is still being punished for it, and probably will be until the end of eternity."

"So, to continue. The couple talked to Melvin and told him about their quest. To Melvin it was like something from heaven! To have company, to talk and to have a sense of belonging; it was paradise. He insisted that he would guide them to the entrance of the Labyrinth of Golden Dreams, no matter how short the journey there. When they agreed, he was awash with a feeling of well-being."

"As they walked together, they laughed, talked and joked. Melvin could not remember a time when he had been so happy, but like all good things, it was short lived. They reached the entrance to the Labyrinth, and the couple said good-bye and disappeared inside leaving Melvin even sadder and lonelier than before."

"The two entered the cave, feeling both apprehensive, and, at the same time, a sense of great expectation. They pulled their terrified sacrifice behind them; he struggled, perhaps sensing his impending doom."

"They had heard much about the Labyrinth of Golden Dreams, but neither had been there before, but no amount of verbal description could have prepared them for its exquisite beauty."

"As they moved into a huge antechamber, they could see it was the size of a cathedral. In the centre of its huge, domed roof there was an aperture – not large, but big enough to allow a shaft of sunlight to pass through. Its brilliance bathed the huge structure in a golden light. The rays of sunlight bounced from stalactite to stalagmite, providing a path to a portico off the main structure. The couple, with their sacrificial goat, passed through in awe. Once past the portico, they entered a second chamber, this one illuminated by the first, but somehow, the light seemed to be amplified! For its brilliance was superb! As the couple took in the spectacular vista, they saw huge mirrors hewn into the rocks."

"They were no man-made structures – the mirrors had no visible outline ; they seemed to merge from the highly polished mirrors to the vapid red rocks. The light, streaming from the main chamber, provided a rainbow of colours, both crisp and vibrant. Even the sacrificial goat seemed to be hypnotized by its beauty. They all moved to the centre of the structure, and then, from nowhere, a deep voice echoed around the room!"

"'DO YOU COME IN FRIENDSHIP?'"

"'Yes!' the young man replied."

"'FROM WHENCE DO YOU COME?'"

"'The Village,' he replied."

"'WHAT ARE YOUR DEALINGS HERE?'"

"'I have come to ask for the most precious of gifts,' the rainbow colours began to flash with frenzy, for what seemed an eternity for the couple."

"The deep voice once again encompassed the structure:"

"'WHAT IS YOUR GIFT? boomed the demanding voice."

"'This goat, Your Lordship,' the young man replied, pointing to the unfortunate creature. Again, the rainbow lights began to flash."

"'WHAT IS YOUR WISH?'"

"The young man explained to the Labyrinth of Golden Dreams about the problems with the Ice Blue Wind, even pointing out, in the most tactful of ways, how they had petitioned help from him on many occasions without concession. Unfortunately, the problem was now so grave that the tribe were now preparing to relocate to a more hospitable place, far, far from the valley. The rainbow lights flashed furiously, then went quiet, and then flashed again."

"The truth, as I see it," said Zachary, "was the Labyrinth of Golden Dreams was in a dilemma. The whole point of the Ice Blue Wind was to stop unwelcome visitors, which it was extremely successful at doing. However, in the last few decades, even the villagers had stopped coming. I've heard it said from a reliable source that less than three visitors made the pilgrimage to the Labyrinth of Golden Dreams during those years."

Jay butted in, "From what you said earlier, the Labyrinth of Golden Dreams would not have cared. As you said, it had no feelings."

Zachary looked at the children with admiration! It was proof that they had been paying attention.

"Yes, and that's correct, except I believe that the Labyrinth of Golden Dreams had discovered another sense, though not one that showed compassion or empathy. No! A sense of self-obsession; he craved adoration. It had been treated like a god by the villagers for so long, it began to believe it to be true. But what good is a god without its followers? And it would have no followers, if the tribe moved! No, it had to do something."

The old wise man of the north carried on his story word for word as he was told it. "The deep voice reverberated around the structure."

"'I WILL GRANT YOU YOUR WISH. IS YOUR PARTNER WTH CHILD?'"

"'Yes,' replied the young man."

"'THEN IT WILL BE THE CHILD WHO WILL BE THE TRIBE'S SAVIOUR. HE WILL RID YOU OF THE ICE BLUE WIND! NOW, LEAVE YOUR OFFERING AND GO!' boomed the Labyrinth."

"The couple excitedly thanked their god, pouring compliments upon him like veritable sycophants, leaving the goat, which by now was totally calm. And then the couple made their way back to the village."

"What happened to the goat?" Gemma asked.

Zachary frowned. "To be honest, I don't know. All I can tell you is what I have heard from others, who have visited that place: there are a lot of skeletons lying about the floor. My best guess is that the animals starved to death. For what good is a creature of flesh to an inanimate object?"

"Inanimate?" Jay said.

"Perhaps I should put it another way: an intelligent lump of rock. Anyway, the couple returned to their village, and told the elders and the villagers of their great news. The unborn child was to be their saviour. The tribespeople fell to their knees and prayed to the great god who dwelled in the Labyrinth of Golden Dreams; it was a miracle. After that, many presents were left at the door of the young couple's home, to welcome the coming of the great saviour; the village elders organized a great feast, followed by a week of celebrations."

"As for the Ice Blue Wind, she had heard the rumours of the new saviour, and disappeared to the southernly entrance to the Black Mountains, where she sulked. She felt that maybe that the new messiah would sweep her away and she would perish. Even the sun pierced through the clouds bathing the village in its brilliance. The villagers began to see the sun as a good omen; others talked of the time, aeons ago, when the village and its people lived like kings, and those times were on their way back! The mood was of great optimism."

"As the time approached for the arrival of their saviour the villagers became more and more excited. Then, it happened! The midwife was summoned, the young man was sent out of the hut. The village people crowded around him, as he walked up and down in anticipation, waiting for the news. The villagers patted him on the back to congratulate him. The labour seemed to last for hours; the atmosphere was electric."

"Then they heard a scream! The midwife came running out, crying, screaming, 'It's the Devil!' … She was in a blind panic, all she could do was repeat that it was a devil, a spawn of evil, a creature of darkness incarnate!"

"The tribespeople looked at one another in amazement, dumbfounded; there was silence as the young man and one of the elders ran into the hut. They reappeared a few minutes later… The young man was in tears; the village elders tried to calm the crowd, who were by now becoming agitated."

"'It's not what we expected,' he said."

"'Why?' the crowd shouted angrily."

"'It's not human,' he muttered."

"There were cries from the crowd, 'Speak up,' they shouted!"

"He did as they requested. 'It's not human' he replied, almost shouting. The young man fell to his knees in tears."

Zachary looked at the children, his eyes were sad and tired. "You see," he said, his voice breaking with emotion, "Humanity has many flaws, and the worst one of all is hysteria. It is infectious, and nearly always results in violence, and it is always those poor, innocent souls, which the crowd see as responsible for their disasters, that take the brunt of their anger! Unfortunately, the young man took the full force of the crowd's emotions; they beat him and abused him. Then they ran away, far away, taking all their possessions. Even the village elders followed, like the cowards they were. The village was left empty, except for the fatally wounded young man, his best friend who was nursing him, and his partner with her deformed infant. There they were, left to die with no compassion by their so-called friends and neighbours".

Zachary was visibly crying, the memories made him very emotional. This was the reason he had become a recluse, for he could never come to terms with man's inhumanity to man; and this was a classic example. Gemma, who felt close to the old man now, comforted him.

"How do you know all this?" Jay said, stroking the old man's arm gently.

The old man pulled himself together, wiping the tears from his eyes. "Because I found them, yes, it must have been a few hours after the event. I had been to the village a few times before and had found the villagers friendly but not over-welcoming; however, I wasn't expecting what met my eyes that day. First, I came across the young man lying on the ground outside his hut, with his best friend attending to his wounds, which were horrific."

"Then I went inside the hut. There a woman lay weeping, gently cradling a bundle in her arms. I touched her shoulder, she looked up and her eyes met mine."

"'It's my baby!' she cried, 'It's my baby!'"

"'What about your baby?' I said gently."

"She gently moved the blanket to one side, and there, in her arms, half-exposed, was a scrawny fledgling! An eagle, his eyes closed, with only down on his body."

Zachary looked at the children; he could see that they had guessed correctly. "Yes, it was Borrack."

"What happened next?" Jay asked.

"The friend of the young man appeared; he turned and whispered in my ear. The young, wounded man had finally given up his fight for life. His friend's face was awash with tears. We sat by the young lady's bed, comforting as best we could. We didn't need to tell her about her partner; she seemed to have sensed his demise. We sat there for many hours," Zachary said, his hands and voice trembling with emotion, tears running down his cheeks.

"And then she looked up at me, and said, 'Please take my baby and bring him up as your own.' Her bright, blue eyes were pleading for me to say 'yes'. I nodded my confirmation. She gently grasped my arm with her frail lily-white hand, and smiled."

"'Please name him after his father; such a good, genteel man, whose name was, 'Borrack'. I choked up a 'yes, of course'; she smiled once more. It was so serene... and then she slipped away from this world, maybe to join her partner; who knows?"

Zachary forced a smile. "Then the young man's friend and I buried the couple, in a sheltered spot, far away from the grasp of the Ice Blue Wind – and went our separate ways. I took the young Borrack, still wrapped in his swaddling blanket, and followed my route home. I turned back to look at the village only to see the Ice Blue Wind return; her anger was so venomous! She swept the village away leaving nothing but the graves of that brave young couple, Borrack's parents!"

"I sometimes think that the Ice Blue Wind, at that time, deep down in her soul, realized how much the tribespeople meant to her, and that's why she destroyed their habitat! Not out of rage at them, but at herself."

"So, there you have it! Borrack may look like an eagle, but, deep down inside, he is as human as you and me, maybe more so."

"Does Borrack know all this?" Jay said.

"Yes. I raised him as my own, but I always told him the truth! I took him to his parent's graves, showed him the ruins of his village. I did my very best to pass on to him the laws of natural justice, to always show compassion, empathy, and respect the laws of nature. Always forgive, never look for retribution, and try not to be judgmental! If you should judge them, then hold your own council; above all, seek only the truth."

Gemma had lost her shyness some time ago. She found Zachary warm, kind and loving – she missed that so much from her own parents. "Did Borrack ever visit the Labyrinth of Golden Dreams?" She asked.

Zachary smiled "Yes! On many occasions! Mind you, it took him a long time to get past the Ice Blue Wind. In the early days, he would challenge her so he could enter the Black Mountains, but he always returned home defeated, sometimes with terrible injuries. As the years rolled on, and he became stronger and wiser, he succeeded in breaking through the malevolent creature's defences; after that, he made regular visits. He even made friends with Melvin, the King Penguin, and visited him often. Oh! And once he entered the Labyrinth of Golden Dreams, with the express desire to wish for his people back; he was only partially successful."

"What do you mean?" Jay said

"Well, his wish was granted," Zachary looked up; the sun was just beginning to set. "How rude of me, I've been talking for so long, and I haven't offered you anything to eat! Not since breakfast, and it's nearly bedtime."

Zachary went back to the hut and prepared a lavish evening meal. He laid the table and brought the meal out, and they all had their fill.

"Well," Zachary said, firmly, "You have a long, perilous journey tomorrow, and we're all going to be in trouble with Borrack if you do not get some sleep! So, I think it's time for bed."

"Oh, can't you tell us some more stories about Borrack and the Black Mountains?" Jay said playing for time.

The old man looked at them, then, with an assertive voice, "No! My young friends, it's time for bed, come on."

He clapped his hands, and the children ran to the hut laughing, as Zachary chased them, pretending to be the Ice Blue Wind, "SH————-SH——-sh—— sh—…" as he mimicked the wind. They jumped into bed and Zachary covered them in the wolves' pelts. Then from his pocket he pulled out the little wooden doll that he had carved earlier, and gave it to Gemma.

"As I promised," he said, smiling.

Her eyes lit up with delight, and then, without warning, she sat bolt upright, and threw her arms round the old man and snuggled into his chest and said softly, "I wish you were my daddy, Zachary."

Jay nodded in agreement.

The old man felt a lump in his throat.

"Listen," he said gently, "Do not judge your parents harshly! There is no way your parents could not love you; I do already, and I have only known you for a day; the truth is, you are a credit to them. No! They both love you, as time will prove. So, sleep on this thought. You cannot change the past, only the future. So do not dwell on what has happened, but look forward to what is still to come."

The two children smiled at the old man. He was as wise as Borrack had said, and as gentle as a lamb. He kissed them both on the forehead.

"Sleep well, my young friends, for every new day brings a new adventure, and every new adventure brings a wealth of knowledge, and knowledge is more valuable than all the gold in the world."

CHAPTER 4

Borrack's Tale: Part Two:
The Soothsayer

The following day, the Ice Blue Wind could feel Borrack's presence; she raced excitedly up and down the entrance to the Black Mountains. In her wake, she created thunder, lightning and hail – her emotions were not ones of benevolence; for such a feeling had long since died; no, these were of hate, revenge and anger – this was all that was left, of that once beautiful girl. For her only desire now was to hurt, maim or kill; nothing else would satisfy. She knew that this period was not the time for revenge, but the hour was fast approaching… and she would be ready for it.

* * * * *

The eagle cast his eyes up to the skies – the moon was bright and in its first quarter and, as far as the eye could see, a myriad of stars glimmered and glistened in the black emptiness of space. Borrack's journey would take him to the east of the Ice Blue Wind, down across Denmark, into Germany, towards Hamburg, and from there, he would head south.

His destination, the Black Forest, for, nestling in the depths of the forest, a secluded lake existed, and in its centre, a small island, unknown to all, but those who go in search of their future.

The eagle nodded a farewell to his adopted father, and flapped his huge wings, which lifted him high above the homestead. Borrack looked down at the croft, his place of security for as long as he could remember; it was still dark. He wished he could have stayed, and could have abandoned this foolhardy journey, a journey that would lead him to a misguided belief in destiny, 'As if destiny could be predicted or planned,' he thought, 'Where would that leave the belief in freewill?'

He saw the old man waving his farewell s. The eagle smiled, and was filled with a surge of love for Zachary, his adopted father. A man who did not judge, a man whose heart was bigger than the world, a man who had saved him, nurtured him, and it was a debt he would never be able to repay. Borrack flapped his powerful wings and headed south.

The moon was still casting its light across the planet's surface. To the east, he could see the Ice Blue Wind, as she excitedly flitted across her domain. Borrack sensed her malevolent spirit, and knew that they would shortly meet and, no doubt, do battle… it unsettled him. It took another thirty minutes before he was no longer able to see that creature, the Ice Blue Wind; Borrack so despised her, and yet, empathised with her – for she, like him, was a chimera. But, unlike him, she had been ripped from the bosom of her family – to do the bidding of the Labyrinth of Golden Dreams. At least his taste of humanity had been fleeting he had been born an eagle, and from what he had seen of man's actions, it suited him.

From the east, Borrack saw the beginnings of the new day, as the majestic life-giver appeared on the horizon. Its golden light crept across the planet, pushing the dark of night back, as it did battle with its nemesis, the moon. It was a battle as old as Earth itself, and one that would be played out until the planet's demise.

The majestic eagle headed towards the German border; there, he would head for Düsseldorf. An hour later, he reached his objective: The Rhine. The powerful river cut through the countryside, as he followed the Rhine and headed for Cologne.

The sun was climbing ever higher. To the west, Borrack spotted heavy rain clouds building, moving east, and threatening to encapsulate him in their grip, and slow him down. He increased his speed; the eagle only had the day to obtain the truth he was so desperate to know. He reached the outskirts of Düsseldorf as the leading edge of the storm struck. It changed direction and followed him. Its strength was immense – he could feel the wind as it pushed him along, and the mighty eagle heard the rain as it lashed down behind him, threatening to engulf him. He dug into his reserves of strength to stay ahead of the storm; he certainly wouldn't want to be in the eye of it. He cast his vision downwards to see the river was surging under the onslaught of the added water; he flew on, increasing his speed, but only just keeping ahead of the tempest. Below, the river's belly swelled and swelled, until it could no longer cope with the onslaught of rain, sending a tidal wave upstream, which followed the mighty eagle.

Borrack flew ever faster, keeping ahead of the great storm, his vision cast downwards as he cut through the Rhine valley. Either side, the beautiful countryside, the small hamlets and castles huddled by its banks with such elegant beauty. But behind him, the lowlands were being swamped by the tidal wave of storm water sweeping upstream.

By mid-day, the mighty eagle had reached Stuttgart and the Black Forest.

From now on he had little to go on; Zachary had told him of the Soothsayer and of her habitat, but was unable to give the exact location, other than that she lived in the northeast of the forest, on a small island, far away from civilisation. He flew high above the forest canopy, his eagle-eye scanning the terrain below looking for that small, elusive lake. Borrack zig-zagged across the canopy looking for any tell-tale signs, but it was an impossible task at this time of year, when the woodland was in full bloom.

Something caught his attention in his peripheral vision, and, as the eagle circled, something glistened, and he circled again and descended. He hovered just above the woodland canopy, and, as his mighty wings created a downwards draught, so the top of the trees swayed in response, and then he saw a small section of lake. Borrack remembered Zachary's words: that, directly west of the lake, there will be a mountain, the colour of purple rises up from the forest.

At last the Eagle had found it! He flew in expanding circles, looking for an opening in the woodland roof. His eagle eye spotted the very place. He cut down through the opening, and there, in the dappled sunlight, the lake and its island shimmered. He flapped his huge wings and headed towards the small island. He circled it several times, but it seemed to be deserted, although there was a shack and a small jetty protruding into the lake, but no sign of a boat. There the eagle hovered. To the east of the shack there was a small beach, and, a little inland, what looked like a well-tended vegetable garden. The mighty eagle flapped his wings, and then glided down to the beach, landing gently on the soft, yellow sand.

Borrack scanned what he could see of the island, beyond the vegetable garden, and, indeed, as far as he could see, it was covered in thick vegetation, unmanaged by human hand; but someone was living there – the vegetable patch was proof of that.

'Maybe they've gone to get supplies?' he mused, eventually deciding he would wait. Borrack walked over towards the jetty and shack, keeping his eye on the lake, hoping the owners would soon return.

While waiting, his mind wandered back to Zachary and the children. He hoped Jay and Gemma were behaving themselves. From there, he started to ponder over the problems that would surface tomorrow and the journey to the Labyrinth of Golden Dreams, and the inevitable battle with the Ice Blue Wind. In his mind, he went through many of the tactics he could employ to get him and the children past that malevolent spirit; he needed something that would take her by surprise, something she would not suspect. It was a problem that he had to resolve, something that was fool proof and provide one hundred percent safety for Jay and Gemma. His mind raced through the hundreds of scenarios, until he was shaken from his daydream by a voice, the voice of a child.

"Mummy, is that a chimera?"

Borrack turned to see a woman and a child walking along the beach towards him, the child no more than six, and the woman thirty-plus.

'Surely,' the eagle thought, 'She cannot be the soothsayer.' Borrack had imagined her older, a lot older. The eagle was in his thirties, and, according to Zachary, his real father had come to see the soothsayer a little before his ill-fated visit to the Labyrinth of Golden Dreams, which would have been thirty-one years ago. 'It was impossible for her to be the seer,' he thought.

If the mighty eagle looked surprised, it did not register with the lady, for, in her mind, something triggered a distant memory, a bookmarked recollection.

"Yes, dear, it is Borrack the chimera, half-human, half-eagle," she said in reply to her daughter's question, but her mind was perplexed by the memory, a thought that seemed as if it had no foundation. She knew Borrack, the eagle, the chimera would seek her out to establish his fate, even if he didn't believe in destiny. But this thought had been something she had not seen coming, something locked in her psyche, something planted there by her mother. That memory, planted so long ago, played out in her mind, and in that recollection she saw a horror that would unfold in less than an hour; it was of a tragedy that would irreparably damage her family.

Borrack, however, surprised at first by the appearance of the two of them, now began to study the lady's face and in that short time she had gone ashen grey; her stress was obvious.

The lady stood staring, but not looking at anything, her mind playing over and over again that horrific bookmark memory planted there so long ago by her mother.

The little girl peered up at her mother and said, "Mummy, Mummy!" But she did not respond; again, the girl called her and her reaction was the same.

Borrack intervened, "Madam!" he shouted. Still she remained petrified ; the eagle flapped his wings across her line of vision. Her eyes flashed in recognition; she focused on him.

"Borrack!" she bellowed, "You must save my husband, please; he needs your help! I have no time to explain, but in less than an hour he will be caught in a flooded river and unless you help he will..." her voice dropped to an emotional whisper, "... drown."

Borrack replied calmly, trying to alleviate the situation, "What is your name?"

"Beth," she replied emotionally; her daughter, sensing her fear, began to cry. Beth dropped to her knees and took the girl into her arm s, "Shhh, Grace, it's going to be all right; Borrack is here to help."

"Tell me Beth, where is this happening?"

"On the river, heading south, just past the purple mountain."

The eagle looked confused, "Can you be more precise?"

"Yes," Beth replied. She stood up and moved towards Borrack, she then placed both her hands on either side of the eagle' s head. At that moment, the eagle could suddenly see Beth's bookmarked dream; and, instantly, the location was seared into his psyche. Beth removed her hand and went back to comfort her daughter. Embracing the crying child, she looked back up at the eagle and pleaded, "Please, please, can you help him?"

Borrack smiled, flapped his huge wings, and disappeared north in search of her husband, with the aid of Beth's dream firmly planted in his mind.

He traced the river towards the purple mountain, keeping his eagle eye on the wild waters, swollen with the deluge of the passing storm. The mighty eagle dropped vertically down, until he was flying just above the rapid river. His eagle eyes, cast down, looking for the lone figure of a man amongst the detritus that the swollen river had gathered on its angry journey from the Rhine – logs, plastic, branches, to name but a few. Borrack watched the brown, foaming water flooding the banks either side of the waterway, picking up more rubbish and flushing it down stream. He flew on, scanning the river closely mile after mile without success… and, then, something caught his eye … it was a capsized canoe.

The eagle circled; he flew ever closer to the river, looking for a body between the flotsam; he scanned the banks closely, but there was still no sign. In his peripheral vision he suddenly saw something downstream… Borrack turned, and flew towards the object as it hurtled downstream in the raging torrent. It was nothing more than a tree trunk… but there was something clinging to it.

Borrack circled, and then hovered above the object, his eagle eye examining the area – it was a man – lifeless. From upstream, another tree trunk smashed into the first. The man lost his grip and slid below the detritus. The eagle dived down to get a closer look, and hovered above the raging water, hoping the body would surface. He caught sight of him, as the body bobbed up out of the murky depths! Borrack swooped down and plunged his talons gently into the man's body. Then the great eagle flapped his huge wings and lifted the lifeless object from the river and headed back to the small island, in the hope that it was not too late.

Beth and Grace were both looking into the sky anxiously, waiting for Borrack's return.

The little girl saw him first, "Mummy, Mummy, look!" she said, pointing to the black figure on the horizon, moving at speed towards them.

As the eagle rapidly approached them, Beth could make out a limp, lifeless body hanging from the mighty creature's talons. Immediately, what little hope she had evaporated. There was no way her husband could still be alive, she thought, though she tried to hide her thoughts for her daughter's sake.

Borrack homed in on them. The eagle sensed her despair, but was confident that all was not lost. He hovered to one side of the small shack, and gently lowered the limp body to the ground and released it, with a soft thud, while he flapped his huge wings, moved to one side and landed.

Beth ran to her husband, where he lay prostrate on the ground. Despite her emotions running high, she instantly focused. She rolled his body over and placed her ear to his chest, listening for the tell-tale signs of life. Grace stood there shocked, unable to take in the enormity of the situation. Her mother began to pump at her father's chest. Beth was now on autopilot, all other emotions pushed to one side, in an attempt to revive her husband and save her family.

The eagle looked at Grace. In her eyes, he saw confusion and the collapsing of her world. He called her name once, twice and then, on the third time the little girl responded.

"Grace," he said, "Come with me, let Mummy help your Father. Let us fly around the island; please come?" Borrack pressed.

Grace's tear-stained face peered at him, and she ran to him in the hope that the nightmare unfolding in front of her would somehow vanish. She climbed up one of his wings and buried her face into his warm feathers, hiding from the tragic reality that was playing out in front of her.

The mighty eagle flapped his huge wings, and graciously rose into the sky. He circled the island at least four times before he felt his passenger relax. Borrack had spotted a beach on the far side of the small island earlier, where, above it, a steep rock face rose up, of black granite. He gently swept down and landed on the fine yellow sand. He lowered his wing and the little girl climbed down.

Her eyes fell upon the black granite rock, and then, back at the eagle.

"Will Daddy be okay?" she asked emotionally.

Borrack smiled comfortingly, "Yes! I'm sure he will be fine," he replied reassuringly.

She was not so sure, and with that, the little girl's eyes wandered back to the black rock face. She seemed mesmerised by it.

"That's Mummy's favourite place," she said.

"Is it?" Borrack replied.

"Yes, she always goes there when she needs to relax."

"Maybe it helps her to see the future."

The girl felt a shiver down her spine and looked back at the eagle.

"Maybe, but there is something not quite right about that place," she replied.

Borrack sensed that she could see something, something in the future.

"What is it Grace, what can you see?"

She peered at the place again.

"I don't know!" Grace shouted, agitated, "I want to go home, now!"

The eagle lowered his wing and Grace scrambled up and buried her head into his neck, shutting out that black rock and her dark vision. She sobbed, trying to drive away the demons from her mind, feeling unable to tell anyone in case the image became true. Borrack sensed her anxiety; he flapped his wings and they rose vertically, flying across the rock face of black granite. The Eagle stared down at it, wondering what Grace had witnessed, thinking he would mention the incident to Beth when the time was right.

Beth was sat on the veranda of the shack, overlooking the jetty, and saw the return of Borrack and her daughter. The eagle landed and lowered his wing; the little girl slid down and ran to her mother.

"Mummy, Mummy, is Daddy okay?"

Borrack watched Beth's face; she smiled, and at that moment a wave of relief swept over the eagle: her husband was alive.

Beth swept the child up into her arms, "Yes, darling, he's all right, thanks to…", Beth's eye's fell upon the eagle, "Borrack."

"Mummy, can I see him?" Grace pleaded.

"Yes, dear, but don't tire him; he needs rest." She put her daughter down, and the girl ran into the shack. Beth walked over to the eagle and threw her arms around his neck, "Thank you, thank you so much! You've saved my family. How will I ever be able to repay you?"

"Maybe by answering a question," Borrack replied. After a pause, he added, "I know you are a soothsayer, but how did you know where your husband would be, and the trouble he was in? a premonition?"

Beth pulled away from him, and looked into the eagle's eyes, "You have so much to learn. I sense you do not believe in the inevitability of destiny, and it may shock you to know… that neither do I!"

"First, let me answer that question. Until I saw you, I had no idea that my husband, Mark, was in trouble. As far as I was concerned, he had left this morning in his canoe to pick up some supplies and it was business as usual. Now, something else you may not know about mystics, is that they can see the path of general fate in others, but not in their immediate family. It was your appearance that triggered a memory in my mind, which had lain dormant for many years, which was most certainly planted by my mother. I suspect she had seen the events of today played out in her own mind when she first met your birth father, she then placed a bookmark in my memory which would be triggered by your arrival."

Borrack butted in defensively, "You said earlier that soothsayers cannot see the destiny of their families, so how did your mother…"

But, before he could finish, Beth answered his question, "Mark, my husband, was unbeknown to my mother and remained so until she passed away, so he existed outside of our family at that time."

"Now, to answer the second question, the inescapability of destiny cannot be seen by a mystic, we can only generalise on the proceedings that lead to an event. How that event plays out is under the control of the recipient's freewill. For instance, your intervention today could have had a totally different outcome. We were lucky, a few seconds longer, and Mark may have not made it, which also answers the art of prophecy."

The eagle could see her sincerity, and as such he became less defensive.

Beth also sensed Borrack's attitude change, and felt that perhaps she was opening his eyes to kismet. She smiled at him, "My Mother talked much about your birth Father. Apparently, he had spent many months seeking her out to ascertain whether he should journey to the Labyrinth of Golden Dreams to help his village. According to my Mother, he was anxious about the repercussions he and his wife would face."

"My Mother, as I will with you, replied that a mystic can only visualise the journey, not the outcome, which must be left to the recipient; it is their decision, as to the path which they take."

Beth did not flinch from the truth, "In your case, that path has left a legacy that you must live with."

Borrack glanced away, as if embarrassed by her comments and said, "Did your mother highlight any problems that might have occurred after visiting that place?"

Beth smiled sympathetically, "Borrack," she said, "Look at me."

The Eagle did as she requested, and looked deep into her eyes.

"My mother told your father that although she could not predict the future, the Labyrinth of Golden Dreams was a malevolent spirit, a creature that would extract a price for any deed required, and that he, at all-costs, should stay away from it. Unfortunately, she had read your father well; he had a generous nature and a moral code that this world is so sadly lacking. His mind was already set, he would save his village at any cost and so he took along his pregnant wife on that journey, crossing the evil path of the Ice Blue Wind, to reach the Labyrinth of Golden Dreams on that fateful day."

The eagle felt his anger build at his father's actions and its consequences for him.

"It seems that I'm the one who must pay for my father's misguided integrity," he replied, because, ever since he could remember, a battle had raged inside Borrack, for his humanity... and now he felt justified to apportion blame.

Beth felt his anger, his pain and his battle.

"Borrack," she said, "Your humanity is intact, and, I have to say, you are your father's son. You talk of misplaced integrity; there was nothing misplaced about your father's actions. No more than there is anything misplaced about your future forays, with your two young wards that you have taken under your wing. You deem what you are about to do will help those children, as your father believed that appeasing the Labyrinth of Golden Dreams would help his people."

The eagle knew the soothsayer was right, and his anger abated.

"Will this foray, as you put it, succeed? Will the children be reunited with loving parents?" he asked.

Beth smiled, "It is not within my power to see the final, inevitable conclusion of destiny; you must choose that path, as you will, with the two adventures that follow. However, I believe in good over evil and it is a battle you will fight, not just for your humanity but for mankind as a whole."

"I will, however, offer you a word of warning, and I ask you to heed it. If you do not, someone close to you will pay the ultimate price. Watch out for the black shadow."

Borrack looked at her questioningly, "What do you mean?"

Beth became serious, "As I look into your future, I see many journeys, and, as I have already said, I do not see a conclusion to them, but I see one thing common to them all, the black shadow. And there is something else: it has been with you since your birth. It has been watching you. I sense it is malicious. That is all I see, you must be aware of it, it means you and yours, harm."

Just as Beth finished speaking, the eagle saw Grace appear supporting her father. He turned to Beth, "Does Grace also possess your gift?"

"Yes, it runs down the female line of the family; why do you ask?"

"When I took Grace for the tour of the island, we stopped off at a beach over-looked by a steep rock face, which I believe is your place of meditation, is that right?"

"Yes, that's right," Beth replied.

"It's probably nothing, but she became very agitated about the place – it was as if she could sense something evil, something yet to happen."

Beth smiled, "She is still young, and her skills have yet to develop. She was probably spooked by outside forces; it's quite common in young mystics. Grace will eventually learn how to exclude worthless thoughts."

As Grace and her father approached, the girl's eyes focused on the eagle.

"Borrack, this is my father, Mark, he would like to thank you."

"Mark, you should be resting, you've had a traumatic experience," Beth said.

Mark looked at his wife, "Beth, I'm fine now, and I wanted to come and thank my saviour." He fixed his eyes on the eagle, "So, you're my rescuer? I believe you are what they call a chimera, is that right?"

"Yes," Borrack replied.

"Then thank God you are, for I doubt anybody would have been able to pull me from those raging waters, except an eagle. I'm indebted to you."

The Eagle smiled. "Your gratitude should be for your wife. Without her ability to see future events and pass them onto me through telepathy, she would not have been able to warn me of your predicament."

"Even so, it was you who plucked me from that quagmire of near death," Mark said, as he put his arm around his wife's shoulders, "I hope, Borrack, you will join us for a meal – and you must stay as long as you like."

"I so wish I could, but I have a pressing engagement tomorrow and two children who are depending on me."

With that, the eagle looked into the sky to see the majestic sun setting in the blue firmaments of the west.

"Are you sure you won't stay?" Mark repeated. Beth placed her hand on her husband's arm and gave him a knowing look. Mark looked back at Borrack, "It seems my wife knows more than I. But, please, if you're ever passing by, pay us a visit; you're always welcome."

The eagle looked at Mark and said, "Thank you."

Then he turned to Beth, "And thank you for your help."

Beth smiled, "I was pleased to help, but remember, Borrack, be aware of the black shadow."

The mighty eagle flapped his huge wings and climbed high into the sky. He circled the small island, taking a last look at Beth and her family, and then retraced his steps back to Zachary and the children. As he flew, his mind turned Beth's warning over and over; it was a conundrum, but the facts pointed to the Ice Blue Wind as the black shadow. By the time he reached the homestead, he had convinced himself that it was her, the Ice Blue Wind; it was a costly mistake.

A long time after Zachary had put the children to bed, Borrack retuned. He looked tired. Neither of them mentioned the eagle's futile attempt to find future truths.

"Have the children been well?" Borrack asked.

"Yes, they have been smashing. I have told them your story, and warned them about the Ice Blue Wind."

"Thank you, Father," Borrack replied.

"Are you still apprehensive about tomorrow?" the old man asked, as he searched Borrack's eyes for the truth.

"Well, there's no point lying to you, because you know me too well. Of course I am, but, as you said last night, never back away from adversity."

"That's the spirit! So, I think Borrack, you should get some sleep; you look tired! And it's going to be a long day tomorrow," Zachary replied.

"Yes, you're right"

* * * * *

Some weeks after Borrack's visit, Beth the soothsayer needed time to meditate. It was a beautiful, warm morning, which was the best time for her gift.

"Mark, Grace, I'm going to my special place, I'll be back later."

Her daughter ran to her, "Mummy, Mummy, please don't go, please stay with us, please, Mummy!"

Beth dropped to her knees and put her arms around her daughter.

"It's okay Grace; nothing's going to happen; I'm only going to meditate. We are safe here on our island."

The little girl tried hard to get her breath as she sobbed uncontrollably into her mother's shoulder.

Mark knelt down next to them, he looked at his wife with a knowing expression, he said, "Leave her with me," he spoke to Grace, "Come on, love, come with me, Mummy will be fine," and, with that, he lifted the child and carried her off to the shack.

Beth stood up and watched them go, shocked by her daughter's reaction. She walked to her place of meditation, agonising on whether to turn back, but she thought she was worrying unnecessarily, and remained on course.

Beth reached her destination and climbed the steep rock and sat on top cross-legged looking at the horizon with the warm sun caressing her. She drifted into a trance. However, sometime later, she sensed that something had changed. She felt cold, as if the sky had clouded over. Beth opened her eyes and saw that the horizon was still clear and blue, but, for some reason, she was in shadow. She looked upwards and, above her, she saw a black shadow. In Beth's mind, the word Erigal repeated and repeated itself. Suddenly, the black shape descended upon her! She struggled to fight back, but Beth was no match to its superior strength, as it sent her to her fate. Beth tumbled to the rocks and sand below. As she did, Beth saw Borrack's destiny unfold, in all its hope and tragedy, until her head struck a large boulder. There Beth joined those that have lost their battle with life, and then the black shadow melted away, confident that he had protected his master's future.

CHAPTER 5

Our Father's Sins

The King penguin, Melvin, stood on the slopes of the Black Mountains, overlooking the ruins of the village. It was enveloped by the sleet of the Ice Blue Wind. 'If only,' he thought, 'If only I had not come to this God-forsaken place. Why? Why did I have to do such a stupid thing?' He felt so lonely; he tried to remember when it was that he had committed those crimes against the Labyrinth of Golden Dreams – was it a thousand years ago? Perhaps it was even more. His greed had led him to this purgatory and there was no way out. He turned away in despair, his life was ruined and pointless! If he could have cried, he would have! But he couldn't; not that it would've changed anything.

* * * * *

Zackery woke the children before the sun had lifted itself above the horizon. He gave them their breakfast, then he provided them with warm clothing and food for their adventure. All of them remained quiet, contemplating what was to come. As for Borrack, he wrestled with the insurmountable problem of trying to get the children to the Labyrinth of Golden Dreams, across the path of the dreaded Ice Blue Wind. He wished he had never heard about the place. The Ice Blue Wind could so easily put pay to the expedition, and, maybe, fatally wound one of the children, or even both. It was a hellish nightmare for the eagle.

All the children could think about were the promises of a happy home life, with loving parents. Even Zackery's explanations of the Labyrinth of Golden Dreams and the Ice Blue Wind, did not dampen their enthusiasm; this was theirs for the taking. As for Zackery, his was a mixed bag of emotions; on the one hand, he had the same misgivings as Borrack, not that he would ever admit them to his adopted son, and on the other hand, he had become emotionally attached to the children, in the short time he had known them; it was going to be hard to say goodbye.

The time soon approached when Borrack lowered his huge wing, so the children could climb aboard. Zackery hugged both of them as they made their way to their respective place on the eagle's back.

Gemma looked deep into Zachary's eyes, "Will we see you again?" she asked.

"Of course, you will!" Zackery said, lying; he knew he would never see the children again. It saddened him but he could not change what was to be.

Jay, as usual, was the first to board. He swung his arms tightly around Borrack's neck, and then Gemma followed and placed her arms around Jay. Borrack looked into Zachary's eyes; he could see the old man's pain.

"Don't worry, I'll take good care of them."

Zackery smiled, "I know you will Son, and you too take care and come back soon."

The old man lovingly stroked the eagle's beak. Borrack once again flapped his huge wings, creating a whirlwind of dust and debris! Then slowly, but surely, he began soaring upwards. Zachary watched, his emotions were confused; he knew that once Borrack and the children had left, he would feel empty and alone. He told himself that the feeling wouldn't last long, maybe a few hours, perhaps even a day. He consoled himself with the thought of poor old Melvin, the King penguin, whose solitude had lasted for a millennium, maybe more! It helped a little.

Borrack soared upwards, then circled and swooped down to bid a final farewell to Zachary. The children waved goodbye excitedly to their new friend. The old man responded by waving back; he watched sadly as they disappeared into the horizon.

As they flew northeast, the sky again began to glow orange. The sun once again was claiming his rightful role as life giver, and, once again, every living thing rejoiced in its glory. This had been the way since the dawning of Earth's history, and would remain so until the final sunset on this beautiful planet. Nothing could survive without that ball of energy; even the jealous moon was beholden to that sun, the life giver, the only one, true, material God.

As the light clawed its way across the land below, the children watched in awe as the pine clad forest burst into life. When the light finally reached over the horizon, the Black Mountains became visible. To the fore, the children saw a wall of dark blue sky, interspersed with huge white flashes, which travelled from one end of the Black Mountains to the other. It was both magnificent and yet frightening; its power was immense.

They both watched with trepidation, as they got nearer and nearer; this was the Ice Blue Wind and her anger struck fear into their hearts. Borrack flew onwards; he felt no fear, just apprehension for his young wards' safety.

In no time they reached the wall of dark blue sky. Borrack landed on a small hillock, a short distance from the Ice Blue Wind. He turned his head to face the children

"I need you to wait here for me. I am going to see if I can get safe passage for us through the Ice Blue Wind -although I think it unlikely."

The children nodded their acceptance. The mighty eagle flew off in the direction of his foe, his nemesis.

Jay panned the horizon. He noticed, just out of reach of the Ice Blue Wind, two mounds of earth, one marked with a cross – and, a little beyond that, the desolate ruins of a village.

"Gemma, look over there!" pointing towards the mounds of earth, "That must be where Borrack's parents are buried, and look there! Just past the burial mounds, that must be the remains of the village. This is where Zachary stopped with the young Borrack and watched the Ice Blue Wind destroy their settlement – do you remember him saying so?" he asked excitedly.

"Yes," Gemma replied.

They watched as Borrack reached the wall of dark blue sky. He hovered there. He looked magnificent, this huge bald eagle, taller than the tallest of men, with his yellow eyes and his white head. There he was hovering almost stationary in front of this wall of sky with the blinding white flashes shooting across it in front of him and, yet, against this angry sky, he seemed to be dwarfed, helpless, almost insignificant.

The sight transfixed the children, but little could prepare them for what happened next. Directly in front of the eagle, a translucent fluid face appeared, almost four times his size. Its image was three dimensional, although Borrack had learnt through experience that its density was only paper-thin; more like that of a paper mask. The face undulated, like the swell of a storm-ridden lake. It was an angry face, bitter and twisted with hate.

At last she screeched, making the children wince with fear.

"You come to challenge me, Borrack, but if you think you can destroy me, then think again! It's you that will meet your doom!"

At that point, two translucent fluid hands appeared, in perfect proportion to the face. The effect seemed to underline her superior power.

"I do not seek to destroy you," Borrack said calmly, "I merely wish for safe passage for me and my young friends."

"Safe passage?!" she screamed, "Why should I allow such a thing?"

Borrack gestured with his head towards the children.

"I need to take my young wards, to the Labyrinth of Golden Dreams."

"For what reason?" she asked, sneeringly.

"They are tortured by the belief that their parents do not love them."

"They're in good company," she said sarcastically. "Look at us, haven't our parents have set a wonderful example? My father gave me up to become a wind and you? Well! Your parents trapped your humanity in the shape of a golden eagle so you could destroy me."

Borrack could feel the bitterness in her words.

"You're so wrong," he said, "They didn't abandon us, in both cases they were looking to our community, our tribe! Can't you see we are from the same family; we're all that's left from our bloodline. Perhaps it's true that we are paying for our fathers' sins! But not out of any evil, no! But in the pursuance of the greater good."

The ice wind was dumbstruck by Barrack's words.

"If you're right, why didn't my father rescue me?" she said meekly.

"How could he, how could he break the spell of the Labyrinth of Golden Dreams? He was just a mere mortal, a man whose heart was broken; broken, for he had to give up his beautiful daughter."

"How can you know his heart was broken, you didn't know him," she retorted angrily. Borrack looked deep into her eyes, and said gently, "Melvin the King penguin told me. It seems he would watch your father on many occasions, from a distance, sitting in the Black Mountains, looking down on you. He would hear him sob into his large hands, repeating again and again 'My beautiful daughter! What have I done? Please forgive me.'"

The Ice Blue Wind mellowed a little, "We have only the penguin's word for it!" she said, "And that means nothing; there is no proof, just a story from a proven thief!"

Borrack quickly responded, "Tell me, was your Father's name Protness?"

"Yes," She said in surprise

"And yours, Berlice?"

The Ice Blue Wind hadn't heard her name since the death of her parents. She had almost forgotten it. Her ice-cold heart began to melt; the undulating swell became a ripple, gently caressed by a calming wind. Even her colour changed from an angry, deep blue to a much paler blue. The children were watching from a distance and could see the changes. The contorted face that had been full of hate and anger became almost serene, and then the children witnessed her former beauty – even her voice lost that evil edge.

Melvin watched from the Black Mountains. He hadn't seen the Ice Blue Wind so calm for a millennium. He knew it had something to do with Borrack.

The Ice Blue Wind kept repeating and repeating her name interspersed with her father's, over and over again. "Berlice, Protness, Berlice, Berlice, Protness. My dear father, he did love me, he didn't abandon me. Protness… Berlice…" She was in her own world, her past and happier days.

Borrack at that point realized he and the children would not get safe passage. For the Ice Blue Wind could not survive in her past world; it was impossible. She just wouldn't cope. Her only salvation was one of anger, hate. Anything less would allow the unbearable pain of immortality and loneliness flooding in. She would be at best as lonely as Melvin, or mindless like the other poor creatures, that the Labyrinth of Golden Dreams had punished. In a selfish way Borrack wanted her to be angry and hateful. To him it was for the greater good; who else could protect humanity from itself, from its natural instinct for greed, from the Labyrinth of Golden Dreams? No! This way, she would stop those reckless creatures (man, that is) from bringing sorrow on themselves and those that shared their lives. It had to be for the greater good, as the Ice Blue Wind's father, and his own parents, had decreed, that is, the sacrifice of the few, for the benefit of the many.

As Borrack had predicted, the Ice Blue Wind's mood changed, and her anger returned. Her face had once again become contorted with rage, while that calming ripple, caressed by a gentle wind, became a torrent of huge storm-ridden waves. She screamed and spat at Borrack.

"You cannot blind me with your silver tongue! I am no fool; you peddle your lies to win my confidence, so I drop my guard, and then you'll try to destroy me!"

Borrack responded, even though he knew he would not win, "Why should I want to destroy you?"

"Because it's your destiny, as set out by the Labyrinth of Golden Dreams, as mine is to protect the Labyrinth "

"Rubbish," Borrack replied angrily, "How can it be my destiny? For what reason should I want to destroy you? I have no loyalty to the Labyrinth of Golden Dreams, that heartless lump of rock!"

For a second the Ice Blue Wind was stumped. Then, loudly, she railed, "To protect your tribe, your village!"

"What tribe? Look, there is no one, and in your anger you destroyed the village. No, I have no interest in the Labyrinth of Golden Dreams, or its evil manoeuvres for retribution and self-preservation."

Borrack knew the argument was over; he flew off to his young wards waiting for him on the hillock. As he went, the Ice Blue Wind spat out her abuse in torrents. The eagle had tried to provide the children with safe passage; it was always going to have been a long shot, and it had failed. Now he had to look at the other alternative, he would have to run the gauntlet and face the inevitable. The Ice Blue Wind was no match for his speed and agility, but with the children on his back, that was something else! Ever since the three of them had rested at the barn, he had been developing a tactic that would provide as little risk to the children as possible. It was an audacious plan, one that, unfortunately, would humiliate the Ice Blue Wind. But what choice did Borrack have? The children were his priority. After all, hadn't he tried to reason with her? No! He would have to put his plan into action.

He landed on the hillock, next to the children. His eyes were full of concern.

"Listen," he said with a commanding voice, "The Ice Blue Wind will not give us safe passage, as no doubt you will have guessed. So, I am afraid that if you want to go to the Labyrinth of Golden Dreams, it's going to be a dangerous crossing! If you want to change your mind, now is the time, and I can take you home."

Jay looked at his little sister, she returned the look. Then they both looked at the angry sky of the Ice Blue Wind, and, both in unison, as if it were one voice, "No, we wish to go on!"

Borrack admired their tenacity.

"Ok," he said, "Listen carefully, I want you to take your position on my back as per usual, and hold on tight, for this is going to be a very rough ride! I will be diving and climbing steeply more than once. Then, when we cut through the territory of the Ice Blue Wind, she will be hot on our tail, trying her best to catch us. So, make sure you hold on as tight as you can!"

The children looked nervous, but they were resolute. Borrack lowered his wing, and the young children climbed aboard and did exactly as the eagle had demanded.

Borrack flapped his huge wings, and in no time they were airborne again. By the time they reached the translucent face of the Ice Blue Wind, all their fears had disappeared. For the children, their fear had been replaced with the rush of adrenalin, leaving them thrilled and excited.

Borrack's mind was filled with the tactic he was going to employ. Within yards of the translucent face, Borrack swiftly changed direction. He climbed almost vertically, the translucent hand matched his every move, and this was what he was hoping for. The eagle had used this tactic many times and he hoped the Ice Blue Wind would respond in the same way.

Ever since he was a young bird, Borrack had studied the Ice Blue Wind's reaction to his own tactics. Always looking for weaknesses in the wind's defences, and there was one that was glaringly obvious. He had noticed that the Ice Blue Wind's translucent hands never, at any point, crossed her face! This was her Achilles' heel, and one he was about to take full advantage of. Under any other circumstances, Borrack would not have considered this course of action; it was an affront to his sense of fair play – it was wrong, but these were exceptional circumstances, and the children's safety had to come first

Borrack climbed and dropped across the translucent face several times, luring the Ice Blue Wind into a false sense of security. Then Borrack made his move, he flew vertically up, until he was in line with the centre of the face, but at least thirty yards higher than the head. There, he paused, and the translucent hand mirrored his exact position. Then the eagle went into a vertical drop. He knew the hand would not follow him once it had reached the top of the Ice Blue Wind's head. The children were now well accustomed to Borrack's dives; they held tight and could hear nothing but the air rushing past their ears, and it was exhilarating. But both the children and the Ice Blue Wind were blissfully unaware of Borrack's next move. As the eagle reached the middle point of the face, the centre of the eyes, he swooped round until he was in a horizontal line with it.

Then, with lightning speed and agility he homed in on the bridge of the nose, flapping his huge wings to increase his speed. Then, within a second, he punched through the face sending fluid shockwaves to all of its corners. Melvin, who was watching from the Black Mountains, stood dumbstruck. He had never witnessed anything like it in his life. The sight was magnificent, there, in front of his eyes, he saw the mighty Borrack puncture through the fluid face of the Ice Blue Wind, which dwarfed the eagle, and on his back, he carried two small children. As the mighty eagle passed through, he was followed by a waterspout, which in turn fell back to the face, distorting it. It was an amazing sight, and one he would never forget for as long as he lived.

The Ice Blue Wind was in a state of total shock; she could not believe that her defences had been breached so easily; she felt humiliated. She quickly regained her composure, and her inverted face exploded outwards to face her foe. She now seethed with anger, the sky turned dark grey. Flashes of lightning shot all around Borrack and the children. The Ice Blue Wind now tried to plug her defences, by bringing both those translucent hands into play; one from above and the other from below, in a pincer movement. The eagle could see the wind's reaction from his peripheral vision. He drew deeper and deeper into his reserves of strength, flapping his huge wings to get as much speed as he could muster. It was going to be a close-run thing; even Melvin, watching from a distance, began to shout with excitement.

"Quick! Borrack! Quick! Watch out for the hands! The hands!"

Not that the eagle could hear him, but he was well aware of the dangers. Borrack transfixed on the boundary; once over that line, he would be home and dry. He was now moving at incredible speed, but so were the hands. Melvin covered his eyes – it was too close to call; he didn't want to see his friends crushed by those translucent hands. The eagle could see the boundary – it was no distance, he just needed a little more energy… and he needed it fast! For the Ice Blue Wind's hands were approaching at tremendous speed.

Every muscle and sinew now began to ache in the bird's body; he felt exhausted, but he couldn't rest – the children's safety depended on it. He pushed his being to his limits. With a powerful surge of pure determination, at last he crossed the boundary, but as he did so the Ice Blue Wind's hands clapped together with a terrific crash; it sounded like thunder, only ten times louder. It sent a shock wave of sound in all directions!

When it hit the ground, the whole mountain shook, knocking Melvin off his feet. The sound echoed in every cleft, cave and valley around its epicentre.

Borrack, who by now believed he and the children were safe, was about to have a rude awakening. The sound waves created so much turbulence that the eagle keeled and rocked violently from one side to the other, causing little Gemma to be wrenched from Jays waist, only to fall off of the eagle's back.

Melvin, who had lifted himself off the ground, watched the whole thing as if it was in slow motion. He screamed at the eagle, "The girl! The girl! She's falling!"

Not that the eagle could hear him.

Jay, scarcely believing what had happened, but without a moment's hesitation, suddenly screamed to Borrack, "Gemma! She's fallen off!"

Borrack had realized something was wrong, not just by Jay's shouting, but by the way his body was suddenly lighter. Quickly he glanced about below him and saw Gemma falling. Alarmingly, she was falling directly into the path of the Ice Blue Wind and her translucent hand! The eery hand was waiting on the ground outstretched... ready to crush her!

Borrack's reaction was instant; he shouted to Jay hold on tight, and proceeded to go into free-fall

The Ice Blue Wind smirked with joy, as her disaster was about to turn into a victory! In her arrogance, she would allow all three victims to come to her and their final fate. Borrack, whizzing through the air at full pelt, was watching as Gemma tumbled and twisted downwards... he was catching her up fast, but not fast enough!

The eagle needed more speed, although totally drained of energy – his reserves nearly depleted. But he had no choice, and he swept his huge wings back to give him even more speed.

Jay held on so tight that Borrack could feel his feeble arm around his neck and the boy's fingers pressing deep into his flesh. Melvin watched, scarcely able to breathe, willing the eagle to succeed.

The Ice Blue Wind let out a screech of excitement, with the certain and impending doom of her three victims! The piercing sound echoed around the Black Mountains.

The eagle was now gaining on the young girl, but he could see she was falling to her peril in the open, translucent hand! In what felt like minutes, but must have been the next instant, with the air screeching past, the eagle redoubled his efforts.

Suddenly, the hand started to close in on the little girl. The eagle spread his huge wings out and opened his beak to grab the child.

The hand was closing fast; in the next instant, Borrack flapped his huge wings, and with one swiftly executed move, within an inch of the closing hands, he grasped Gemma in his beak and plucked the young girl away. But, as Gemma was jarred upwards, she dropped the little wooden doll that Zachary had made for her.

The hand snapped shut, but without its victims.

Borrack, now with both the children, flew off to Melvin the King penguin and the safety of the Black Mountains. The eagle carefully lowered Gemma down next to the penguin, and then circled round and landed next to both of them.

Gemma, shaking, was inconsolable, she was sobbing to the point where she could not catch her breath. Jay jumped off Borrack's back and ran over to his sister to console her.

The Ice Blue Wind spat philippics of abuse at all of them; victory had once again been snatched from her by the bravery of Borrack. Her anger was now apoplectic – the grey, leaded sky blackened, leaving only the lightning to illuminate the land below. The heavens opened up in a torrent of rain.

Jay put his arm around his younger sister, "Gemma, you're safe now," he said gently, as the pounding rain washed over them.

"It's not that!" she said, catching her breath between sobs, "The doll… Zachary made it for me!"

Borrack immediately scanned the ground where the translucent hand had been, and there he spotted the doll. He turned his head to his young ward, his eyes smiled at her with compassion.

"Don't worry, Gemma!" he said, "I will retrieve it for you".

"But what about the wind?" her sobbing beginning to wane.

"What does the Ice Blue Wind want with a doll? I feel sure she will let me retrieve it" he lied; the eagle knew he would have to fight for the wooden doll, as did Melvin, however, to reinforce the lie, he nodded in agreement. Gemma was a lot calmer now, but shivering as a result of the heavy rain – Jay was also feeling the cold.

The eagle looked at Melvin, "Could you take the children to your cave, Melvin?" he said, "While I will try to appease the Ice Blue Wind and get Gemma's doll back."

Melvin nodded in agreement.

"I will be back before dark," Borrack said to the children, reassuring them of his actions.

CHAPTER 6

Melvin

The Labyrinth of Golden Dreams lived in its own world. Blissfully unaware that it would soon be receiving guests, in the shape of Borrack and the two children. Indeed, why should it care; after all, it felt nothing and sensed even less. It was oblivious to pain, love, compassion, hate. Unaware of right or wrong! Its only desire was self-preservation and the learnt emotion of adoration. For the Labyrinth of Golden Dreams, nothing else existed; its only role was to function, to exist! And that was all it had ever done and would ever do.

* * * * *

Melvin ushered the children into the cave. It was warm; fissures in the rock formations wormed their way down deep into the earth's mantle, and in those fissures, water seeped down to the hidden depths of the earth, where it hissed, gurgled and spluttered as it turned into steam on contact with the red-hot molten rock that swirled around like a liquid in a witch's cauldron. The steam forced its way back through the same fissures, fighting the oncoming trickle of water, in its attempt to break free of the restraint of the rocks that imprisoned it. The steam pushed upwards and upwards through its only escape, a small waterhole in the middle of the cave. There it pushed through the small pond, sending spurts of steam upwards at regular intervals.

Melvin looked at the two children who were drenched and cold.

"Quick!" he said, "Take off those wet wolves' pelts." The ones that Zachary had given them for their journey. Melvin took them and laid them out on an adjoining rock to dry. The cave boasted a ledge that ran in a semicircle around the water hole. In a corner of the cave he had stored some dry grass, for future bedding. Melvin laid the dry grass out on the ledge for the children. This served as seating as well as bedding in the warmest part of the cave.

The cave was not dark; its entrance was large and allowed the natural light to come streaming in. The opening also afforded great protection from the cold wind; all in all, it was a very comfortable habitat.

Melvin invited the children to sit on the newly laid seating, and he introduced himself.

"Hello, my name is Melvin," holding his wing out as a gesture of welcome.

Jay gently grabbed the penguin's wing and shook it.

"I'm Jay, and this is my little sister, Gemma."

Gemma shyly dropped her head as Melvin turned his gaze on her.

"I'm afraid I have nothing for you to eat here," the penguin said, "But I can offer you some water."

In another corner of the cave, fresh water trickled into a small pool.

Jay replied, "Thank you, Mister; we have food, Zachary packed it for us; but water would be most welcome."

Melvin waddled over to the freshwater and carried it back for Jay and Gemma in two small bowls. The children, by now, were quite warm and dry, and they tucked into their food. Gemma watched the penguin. Zachary description had been extremely accurate. His eye s conveyed a sadness that she had never witnessed before.

Timidly, she said, "Do you want to share my food, Mister?"

Melvin looked up at her and smiled, with those same sad eyes, replying with, "No, thank you! I don't eat anymore."

"Why?" Jay asked.

"What is the point? If I eat or don't eat, either way, I cannot die! I am immortal; nothing can kill me, except maybe the Labyrinth of Golden Dreams – but he just wants to punish me."

Gemma looked at the penguin.

"What did you do that was so bad?"

Jay poked her in the ribs, and shot her a look, wishing she wasn't so nosey.

"Please excuse my sister, she's just a busybody."

Gemma squirmed and brushed her brother's hand away.

"I have nothing to hide," Melvin replied, "I made a foolish mistake, and now I'm paying for it. You see, many centuries ago, I cannot be sure how many, but many, I lived far from here in a beautiful land, with my family. It was so lush and green…"

The children noticed Melvin's eyes, which seemed to glaze over as if they were mesmerised.

Melvin continued, "I was so happy. My brother and I would play in the lush green woodland, swim in the river, or just lay in the field soaking up those long, hot summer days. It was wonderful."

"So, why did you leave?" Jay enquired.

Gemma jumped in quickly, "Was it because your Mum and Dad didn't love you, like ours?"

Jay shot her another look of embarrassment. "Gemma, hush!" he said, feeling a pinch of exasperation.

The penguin chuckled at the outburst.

"No, my young friends! My parents loved and cared for me, and, I suspect, young lady, yours are no different! No, it was not them that caused me to leave. If anyone, it was my brother. As I have already said, we were very happy. But, as my brother and I got older – he was eighteen, as I remember, and I a year his junior – we wanted to strike out on our own. We needed our independence and adventure; we just wanted to make our mark on the world. So, one night when my parents were asleep, we packed our bags and snuck out."

Melvin dropped his head; the children could see the pain on his face.

"I so wish I hadn't left them," he said sadly, "For I never saw them again…"

Melvin was tortured by the pain he and his brother had caused his loving parents, by leaving.

"I never even got to say goodbye," he said quietly. He knew they would have worried and fretted about their disappearance; it would have certainly broken their hearts! Melvin would never be able to forgive himself or his brother for that.

"Anyway, we headed north," Melvin said, composing himself, "On the way we met a fellow traveller, and he told us of a land where we could make our fortune; and, like fools, we listened to him. We travelled on towards our destiny, this so-called gold strike and these Black Mountains."

Melvin could not hide his bitterness. Continuing the story, he said, "We eventually reached the village of Borrack's ancestors, nestling in the entrance to these mountains. The people were welcoming and friendly enough, but when we mentioned the Black Mountains, and all the riches they contained, they denied all knowledge of such wealth, trying to dissuade us from entering, telling us stories of dragons, demons and bandits."

"The truth was that we could see through their lies; they had an abundance of food, clothes and wine. I had never seen a tribe so rich; it was clear they were hiding something. However, in retrospect, I wish we had taken their advice, and stayed clear of this god-forsaken place, but we were young and headstrong. So, one night when all the villagers were asleep, we crept away to the Black Mountains, and our fate."

Melvin paused for a moment, clearly reliving the night in his mind's eye. The children regarded him for a moment, until Melvin became aware of their gazes, shook himself and continued.

"We spent many months looking for the hidden riches of this mountain range, looking in every valley, ridge and cave. We searched them all, and yet all we found were strange creatures! Creatures that seemed out-of-place…" The penguin corrected himself, "I mean, that is, not in their natural habitats. Creatures like Walruses, large rats, locusts, alligators, snakes…"

Again, Melvin dropped his head, embarrassed by his own caricature, "And, of course, penguins! It was obvious that something wasn't quite right about the place, but we ignored the warning signs, only focusing on the riches that we would find! It is strange how greed can blind you, but it does."

"Eventually, we came across an opening in the mountain. My brother entered and I followed. We found ourselves in a huge chamber. We stood there for a while, it seemed like hours, just looking up at this huge, vaulted roof. There was a small hole at the top that allowed the light to flood in."

Jay butted in, "Zachary told us of that place, the Labyrinth of Golden Dreams. He said he had never been there, but from what he had heard, it was strange, like it was not of this world... yet, exquisitely beautiful... beyond compare."

The penguin looked at the young boy, his eyes still conveyed a sadness, and, yet, there was a glint of excitement, maybe a thrill from a past excitement, but excitement all the same.

"It is impossible to describe its beauty!" the penguin said, "You need to see it, to appreciate it. I can remember it as if it were yesterday; the place was so magnificent. The light bounced from stalactite to stalagmite, providing an illuminated path. We followed it like lambs to the slaughter – we were totally mesmerised. The light – I can't explain it!"

Melvin struggled with his words. It seemed to him that no words could do such a sight justice.

"It is impossible to explain! It was ethereal. We saw huge, golden mirrors that were impregnated into the rock, and yet, there was no visible joint. This was the gold that was going to make us rich beyond our wildest dreams! It was ours for the taking."

The children were listening intently.

"We did not expect the gold to be hewn into the rock, and we had no tools to wrench such beauty from its housing. I don't know what we were expecting – maybe gold coins in a casket. We had no plans, just a dream."

The penguin's expression changed. He lost that earlier euphoria; its replacement was now one of despair.

"A dream that turned into our living nightmare, our purgatory."

He continued, "My brother noticed some old bones in the centre of the cave; he searched through them until he found a strong, sturdy bone to use as a chisel. Then a heavy stone for a mallet. We proceeded to hack at the golden mirrors, to dislodge them. Then the cave became animated, lights began to flash into a rainbow of colours. A voice echoed around the cave, deafening us."

Gemma interjected, "What did it say?"

Melvin looked up at the children. His eyes conveyed such guilt and sorrow, and if he could have cried, he would have done, but he couldn't. He dropped his head again, as if talking to the floor.

"It said we had violated the Labyrinth of Golden Dreams. The flashing lights stopped; there was a short lull, then a blinding flash of white light engulfed us. Our bodies were immersed in a searing pain; we rolled across the stone floor in agony for hours."

"When we finally recovered, I could no longer see my brother, just a slow, lumbering turtle. I screamed and backed away in fear! As did he! Then… it dawned on us! We had been transformed!"

He appeared to be held by the same shock that gripped him in that moment, all those centuries ago. His voice began to quiver with emotion. The children moved to his side, to comfort him. He turned and looked from one child to the other, absorbing their compassion with such gratitude. He had never shared his story with anyone else except his brother.

"Then," he said his voice still trembling "We were told that our punishment would last an eternity. We would live in the Black Mountains as the creatures we were, like all the other wretches that had tried to steal from the Labyrinth of Golden Dreams. Then, we were exiled from the cave to live out our sentence, our torment… live it out, without end."

"Do you not see your brother anymore?" Jay asked softly.

The penguin cast a gaze at him, "Yes, occasionally, but what's the point?" he said, "We stayed together for maybe fifty years, or even five hundred years! I don't know, time, like food and sleep, becomes irrelevant, when you become immortal. Whatever it was, he started to lose his mind, like all the other poor victims of the Labyrinth of Golden Dreams. I tried my best to snap him out of it, but it was no use. Eventually, he didn't even speak; he ended up like all the rest of them – a crawling zombie."

"Have you seen him since?" Gemma asked gently.

"Yes, but there's nothing there, just a shell."

Melvin looked down at the stone floor, "It's the one thing I fear most, is ending up like those poor creatures out on that mountainside. I would give anything to go back and live as Melvin the man, if only for a year, a month, a day, or just a few seconds. It doesn't matter how long – just to experience humanity once again, the feeling of being a man, and then death, everlasting peace and freedom from this purgatory."

Melvin fell quiet. His story was told, what else could be said? The children felt his pain, and, in some way, it put their problems into perspective; it even made them pale into insignificance.

All three of them remained quiet, each analysing their own problems. That was, until Borrack returned! The moment he walked in through the cave entrance, the mood changed. Even Melvin lifted his head with delight, and smiled with his sad eyes. Borrack dropped the wooden doll that Zachary had carved for Gemma by the young girl's feet.

She picked it up and caressed it with delight.

"Thank you!" she said, clutching the doll in one hand and throwing her arms around the eagle's neck. It was then that she noticed Borrack's leg – it was oozing with blood. She looked up at him,

"Your leg! It's bleeding! Did the Ice Blue Wind hurt you?"

Borrack glanced down at the girl and smiled.

"No, Gemma, I caught it on a rock flying back, it's nothing!" he fibbed.

Melvin could see the lie and shot him a look. Borrack caught his glare, and between them the truth was shared.

"Okay, children it's time for bed! Tomorrow will be another long day," Borrack said.

The children did as they were told and lay on the straw beds Melvin had laid out for them.

Borrack made his way over to them, "Listen," he said, "Sleep well, for tomorrow we visit the Labyrinth of Golden Dreams, and maybe, just maybe, your wishes will come true!"

Jay looked up at Borrack.

"Could we," he said, nervously, "Ask the Labyrinth of Golden Dreams to release Melvin from his imprisonment?"

The eagle was taken by surprise, "I don't know," he said, stuttering and glancing at Gemma.

"Please!" she said.

"We'll see," said Borrack.

'As if the task weren't difficult enough' he thought, and such a request only added to his problems. Nonetheless, he smiled at them. "Could Melvin tuck us in?" Gemma said.

"Of course," Borrack replied. Then, turning to the penguin, he summoned him and he waddled over.

"Melvin," Gemma said timidly, "Would you read us a story, before we go to sleep?"

Melvin was thrown by the request!

"I don't know! No one has ever asked me that before!"

He found the girl's question charming – yet Melvin had been so lonely, for so long, he felt overwhelmed by the request.

"Well, I'll do my best."

And he did, he told them a story from his childhood, and the children loved it.

"Melvin," the little girl said, "Do you know what Zachary says to us before we go to sleep?"

"No," the penguin replied.

Both jay and Gemma repeated Zachary's word's in unison.

"Sleep well, my young friends, for every new day brings a new adventure, and every new adventure brings a wealth of knowledge, and knowledge is more valuable than all the gold in the world."

Melvin smiled with his sad eyes, "I would love to meet him, and he must be a truly wise man."

Gemma threw her arms around the penguin, and said, "So are you!"

At that moment a tear ran down Melvin's cheek, a tear of happiness. He was so overwhelmed by the children's love. For the first time since coming to the Black Mountains, he began to cry; not out of loneliness or pain, but out of love.

"Sleep now," he said, wiping the tears from his eyes with his wing.

He waddled back to Borrack, his eyes were still red and sore from crying, but the sadness they once conveyed had gone.

"What lovely kid s," he said, "How could their parents not love them?"

"They do," said Borrack.

"So, why are you taking them to the Labyrinth of Golden Dreams?"

"That, my friend, is part of the process."

Melvin did not understand. "Anyway, Borrack, what happened with the Ice Blue Wind?"

Borrack turned and faced the penguin, "She was still extremely angry! And vented her wrath with vigour, as you can see, however, I was fortunate; I only suffered a slight injury."

His leg was still oozing blood.

"I have just the thing," with which, Melvin waddled over to the waterhole, soaked some straw bedding in the sulphurous water, waddled back and placed it on Barrack's wound, "There! That should heal by the morning."

The eagle looked at Melvin and said, "Thank you my friend! My good friend."

The penguin felt so happy.

"I think it's time to get some rest," Borrack said, "I must be ready to face the Labyrinth of Golden Dreams tomorrow."

With that, the eagle went off to sleep, leaving Melvin to reflect over the day.

CHAPTER 7

Part One: The Penalty of Life

A man and a lady sat between two beds, a boy in one and a girl in the other. The ward was large and austere, containing twenty beds. The adults sat quietly, holding hands, their eyes red and puffy – their expressions were sad, scared and they were both emotionally drained.

Less than six hours earlier, they had watched the young girl, their daughter, being pulled back from the brink of death. It was an emotional nightmare. At first, she seemed to wake from her coma, she let out a blood-curdling scream, as if she was falling from a high building. At that moment, the parents felt elated; she had regained consciousness! Hope seemed to fill their heart s; then, the machines that she was strapped to, like some kind of android, began to wail and scream. From nowhere medics congregated around her, in an organized panic. Exposing her young chest, they placed the paddles of a crash trolley, there they shouted, 'Stand clear!' and pumped the young body with electricity. The parents watched in disbelief, their bodies shaking with fear, their face wet with tears.

They looked on as the young body arched in a convulsion; it was like watching a film where a claw wrenches a young girl's body from the hand of death! It was bizarre. Her small hand that was clasped shut, opened, releasing a small, carved, wooden doll. A nurse retrieved it and handed it to the mother. The young girl recovered, but only to regain her comatose existence.

The watery sun begrudgingly pierced through the large window straddling the two beds. The lady swung her head around to face the man, her eyes filling up with tears.

"Why did we argue?"

Her voice breaking with emotion, "If I hadn't have thrown that vase at you, it wouldn't have knocked over that candle."

Tears rolled down her face. The man responded, his expression was one of sympathetic guilt as he threw his arms around her.

"There, there," he said, "It was not your fault, it was mine. I started the silly argument."

The lady clenched the small, carved, wooden doll tightly, the one the nurse had given her earlier; the one the little girl had dropped. If she hadn't had been in such emotional turmoil, she would have realized that her daughter had never owned such an object. But she was beside herself with fear for her children. She looked at her daughter and then her son, they lay on their beds like rag dolls, lifeless – almost without hope. She felt the wooden doll clenched in her hand, it dug into her flesh. She saw her daughter's hand open and unresponsive, so she placed the doll in the girl's hand and gently closed her fingers around it. For a second there was a glimmer of life in the young girl, a mysterious smile passed over her lips. But then it was lost, a false, fleeting hope for her parent s.

The lady looked at her husband, her eyes searching for the past and happier times.

"If it hadn't been for that man," she stuttered, "That man, taller than the tallest of men, that man with those yellow eyes. If he hadn't rescued them from that fire, our children would not be here now," she said, and buried her head into her husband's chest, sobbing at the thought. He could do nothing but comfort her, for he, too, was paralysed with despair.

* * * * *

Borrack woke early, the children were still sleeping. The eagle felt the day would be a long one for his young wards, so he let them sleep on. As for Melvin, he was fussing around the cave. Borrack made his way outside, the sun was on its ascendancy. At this time of day, the sun's heat was at its most gentle. Borrack faced it, the warmth caressed his face, it felt so good, and he closed his eyes for a short time in ecstasy. He hadn't felt so relaxed in days.

As he opened his eyes, he panned the horizon. Way down, by the entrance to the Black Mountains, where his ancestor s' ruined village lay. He saw the Ice Blue Wind -she was quiet and brooding, maybe even sullen, over his victory. Borrack felt for her, but it was the way things were, it was, after all, for the greater good. He consoled himself with that belief. The eagle was deep in thought, and didn't notice Melvin waddling towards him.

"Good morning, Borrack!" the penguin boomed, smiling.

The eagle stuttered in surprise, "Why! Good morning, Melvin! You're bouncy this morning!" Borrack said, looking deep into the penguin's eyes. His sadness had gone, and was replaced with a look of well-being, maybe even hope.

"It's a beautiful day," the penguin said.

"Yes, my friend, it is! You seem a lot happier, Melvin."

"Yes," the penguin beamed, "Those lovely children, they made me realise how good it is to be alive!"

Borrack smiled, "Yes, my friend, on a day like this, you're not wrong."

"Borrack," the penguin began, "There's something you said yesterday that has been troubling me."

"What's that Melvin?"

"When you were talking about the children and their parents, and you said that visiting the Labyrinth of Golden Dreams was just, 'part of the process,' what did you mean?"

Borrack looked at the horizon, "Tell me, Melvin, what good has the Labyrinth of Golden Dreams done for anyone?"

The penguin thought for a while and then responded, "Well, clearly, to those who have tried robbing from it, like me, only pain. But your ancestors certainly enjoyed its benefits."

Borrack turned his gaze to Melvin, his eyes burning with anger, "Do you really believe that, my friend?"

The penguin stuttered nervously with his reply, "Didn't they?"

The eagle nodded in the direction of the village.

"Look, Melvin, look at the village! It's deserted, empty, a derelict shell, why do you think that is?"

Before Melvin could reply, the eagle angrily responded, "Because of the Labyrinth of Golden Dreams, my friend! You know the story better than I. That lump of rock that calls itself the Labyrinth of Golden Dreams, who cares for nothing but itself," Borrack was animated with anger.

"Visiting it, is like the kiss of death! Look at you, the Ice Blue Wind, the deserted village, the poor creatures that frequent this god-forsaken hole, and me! What have we all in common? I'll tell you what, Melvin! That heartless lump of rock, and the nightmare it has endowed upon us."

Silence fell upon the pair for a while, after which Melvin timidly said, "Why take the children there then?"

Borrack turned his head to the penguin.

"I'm sorry, my friend," the eagle replied, "I should not have lost my temper. I just get so frustrated by the belief that the Labyrinth of Golden Dreams is some kind of benevolent life force; it's not; I believe it to be evil. But, to answer your question, the healing process for the children started at the beginning of this adventure, not with the Labyrinth of Golden Dreams. The only reason to visit the place, is because the children have talked themselves into believing that it's so-called magic can somehow make everything all right."

Melvin gave Borrack a puzzled look, "How do you mean?"

The eagle smiled at the penguin, "It's a complicated story, my friend."

"Well, if you have the time, I'm good listener," replied Melvin.

Borrack laughed, "For some time now, the children have called for me at night, when sleep becomes impossible, because of their parents' excessive arguing, when those clouds of depression have encompassed them. Like the walls of a dark cell, when the only comfort they can find is in their imagination. That's where they find me. I have taken them on many adventures, to comfort and ease their pain. But this journey is so much more; this is their ultimate test. This time their young live s hang in the balance"

Melvin was shocked by the revelation, "Are they in that much danger?"

"Yes, they are, in there, Melvin," Borrack nodded towards the cave.

"Jay and Gemma lie asleep," Borrack continued, "And yet they are not there at all. They are, in fact, thousands of miles away in a hospital ward, hooked up to machines that monitor their very existence, and between them sit their parents. Emotionally drained, scared, and, above all, blaming themselves for their children's predicament."

"Why?" the penguin asked.

Borrack looked towards the horizon; he saw the Ice Blue Wind – she still remained quiet and sulky. He swung round to face Melvin and said, "There was a fire, my friend, a fire that swept through the house; a fire that was started by accidental anger, a thrown object, a burning candle, that is all it took! It was enough to cause so much pain."

Melvin was shocked.

"How did the children escape?" the penguin asked.

The eagle turned his head to scan the horizon again, "I rescued them," Borrack replied.

"Do they remember the incident?" the penguin asked.

"No, well, not exactly. If you were to ask them, they would remember a fire, but in a forest and caused by lightning; they were in their imaginary world with me. Since that time, I have been with them, accompanying them on their perilous journey, a journey that hangs between life and death for the two of them."

Borrack dropped his head; it was a burden that anguished him deeply. A silence fell between Borrack and the Penguin.

Melvin, who had listened intently, felt uneasy about something Borrack had said, and then it came to him, he blurted it out loudly.

'They are, in fact, thousands of miles away. They are in an imaginary world, with me.' A sudden fear swept over him, as he recalled the words, and he looked at the eagle.

"Are we not real? Are we only a figment of the children's imagination?"

Twenty-four hours earlier, before he had met the children, he wouldn't have cared. He didn't want to live, but now it was different. The young children had given him renewed hope.

Borrack faced the penguin; he could see Melvin's fear. He gently smiled, and said, "Dreams, nightmares and reality are just two sides of the same coin; who is to say which is real? Do you not feel and think?"

"Yes," Melvin said.

"Then you exist," Borrack replied wisely.

Just then, they heard a noise from behind and turned to see little Gemma appear from the cave entrance.

"Ah, you're awake!" Borrack said, "Has Jay roused as well?"

"Yes," she said, sleepily.

"Then I guess it's time for breakfast!"

The girl nodded and waited for the eagle and penguin to reach her. Melvin put his wing around her and ushered her inside the cave. Jay was sitting up on his make-shift bed of straw.

"Have you still got some food?" Borrack asked, to which they both nodded, "Good," he responded, "then I suggest you eat, because today you meet the Labyrinth of Golden Dreams… and maybe your dreams will come true."

It wasn't long before they were ready to go. Borrack, as usual, lowered his huge wing, and the children climbed aboard. First, as was usual, went Jay, and then Gemma followed. Melvin watched quietly, he wished secretly that Borrack and the children would stay with him forever, but he knew that could never be.

The eagle could sense Melvin's thoughts; he smiled, and sympathetically said, "Fear not, my friend. We will be back tomorrow."

Melvin smiled. He looked at the children, and said, "Good luck! I'll be with you in spirit."

The two children waved as Borrack flapped his huge wings and began to soar high into the sky.

The eagle looked at the landscape below; it was barren and arid, and every mountain, valley and crevice looked the same. Such a place was void of providing the necessities of life. 'No one should have to live in such a place,' he thought, but, to the victims of the Labyrinth of Golden Dream's rough justice, this was their living nightmare. Borrack felt a wave of sympathy for them, and he vowed to himself that he would do his up-most to get his friend, Melvin, released from this god-forsaken abyss, this hellhole of woe, no matter what the cost.

The journey was short. The eagle circled the mountain that housed the Labyrinth of Golden Dreams and made his descent. He spread his huge wings out to reduce his acceleration and braced his talons for the impact! Thump! And they were down. The children clambered down one of his wings. Meanwhile, Borrack scanned the horizon; he could see the abandoned village and the Ice Blue Wind; as yet she continued sulking.

He imagined his parents standing where he stood, taking in the same view, just as Zachary had told him so many times. Borrack wondered if it had really happened. He could hear Zachary's words; as he pondered, he could see those shafts of sunlight piercing through those heavy grey clouds, like translucent columns of marble, as if they were holding up those same, heavy clouds. Of course, the eagle knew it was true; Melvin had accompanied his parents on that occasion, and he had confirmed his adopted father's story.

He felt so sad for them – they had given up everything for their tribe, but the tribe selfishly turned on them. The eagle checked himself, 'Perhaps I'm being unfair on my ancestors' he thought. 'Maybe it was just the fear of the unknown, the different.' Borrack struggled with his emotions, 'If only things could have been different' he thought; yet, the eagle knew better. If only, can never be changed, the sequence of events had decreed that.

He turned and faced the cave entrance; the children looked up at him.

Their expressions conveyed so much – fear, anticipation and excitement, he smiled at them, "Well, my young friends, it's time to lay those ghosts of yours to rest, right?"

They both gave him a puzzled look; they did not understand.

"Never mind," he shrugged and ushered them through the cave entrance.

The moment they entered the cave, they were stunned by its beauty. First, the smell; it was sweet, like honeysuckle, on a warm summer's evening. Then, the vista. Both Zackery and Melvin had not done its beauty justice in their description; but no one could. The huge, vaulted ceiling, with its small aperture at its pinnacle – that was to be expected; but the rest was inexplicable – indescribably exquisite in every detail. It was superb; the beam of light flooded downwards with such brilliance, and, as it hit each stalactite and stalagmite, it bounced off, sending shards of light in all directions; creating an array of different colours, and, in its wake, illuminating the rock formations in blues, yellows, reds and indigoes. Between the shards of light, in the space where only the emptiness of black existed, thousands of insects, like fireflies darted around, creating a myriad of specks of light, like shooting stars.

Along the base of the cave, a path of brilliant, white light spread out in front of them, which lead to a portico. The children's eyes were filled with its exquisite beauty. They turned excitedly to face the eagle, but then another miracle hit them. There, in front of them, stood Borrack the man, with his yellow eyes and his shock of white hair, taller than the tallest of men, and across his face was the broadest of smiles. Jay instantly remembered Zachary's words as if he had just been told them.

'Once, he entered the Labyrinth of Golden Dreams with the express desire to wish for his humanity back. It granted his wish... but only in the confinements of the Labyrinth, or in exceptional circumstances.'

Borrack gently grabbed their small hands and led them down the path; Gemma couldn't take her eyes off the new Borrack.

She tugged on his hand. Borrack looked down at the girl.

"Do you like being like us?" she said.

Borrack dropped to his knees, so as to be at the same level as the little girl, "You mean, human."

"Yes," she said apprehensively, hoping she had not caused offence.

"I suppose I do," he replied.

"I like the old Borrack better," she said kicking at the floor with her foot while Jay shot her a look of disbelief !

Borrack stood up and carried on walking, laughing as he went. As they reached the portico, the sweet smell of honeysuckle hung in the air; it was so pungent. There, a climbing vine clung onto the walls with its twines and tendrils. Its leaves were purple in colour, and, nestling between each pair of leaves, a fragile flower bloomed. The petals were plain, but as the chaotic shards of light hit them, they glowered amber, gilded with a crimson edge.

A gentle, warm wind caressed the portico and as it passed over and around the stalactites and stalagmites, it oscillated. The sound was soothing, with a haunting melody like panpipes. Its sheer beauty mesmerized the two children. Gemma looked up at Borrack and said, "It's very pretty."

Borrack nodded in agreement, and yet, deep down in the eagle's heart and soul, he knew that this beauty masked something sinister, something evil. Not that the Labyrinth of Golden Dreams understood evil; after all, it felt nothing and sensed even less. It was oblivious to pain, love, compassion, hate. Unaware of right or wrong! Its only desire was self-preservation and the learnt emotion of adoration. For the Labyrinth of Golden Dreams, nothing else existed; its only role was to function, to exist! Borrack kept his own council, as he saw it, if the children believed in it and it helped resolve their pain, it didn't matter what he believed.

They entered the last chamber. Jay and Gemma stood and gasped! What they had seen before was nothing in comparison to what met their eyes now. The crisp, brilliant light filled the chamber – the round walls yielded a collection of highly-polished, golden mirrors, all hewn into the rich red rock, with no visible boundary, just as Zachary and Melvin had described.

The vaulted ceiling was studded with all manner of precious stones: diamonds, rubies, and emeralds; all highly polished and all set into the rich red rock. The floor was a smooth stone. In the middle stood a platform, six-foot in diameter. It was made up of white limestone and it appeared soft, like cotton wool, yet, as hard as diamonds. Scattered around the platform lay the bones of countless animals.

Jay looked up at Borrack. "Are they the bones of the sac-sacri-sacrificed animals?" he said, stumbling on his words.

"Yes," Borrack said sadly.

They walked to the platform. The cave suddenly became animated; lights began to flash all around them. Gemma became anxious and buried her head into Borrack's legs, clinging to him tightly. Borrack stroked her hair reassuringly.

"Fear not, little one," he said.

A voice boomed out from the rock and echoed around the cave.

"DO YOU COME IN FRIENDSHIP?"

Borrack knew the drill so well that he could have done it in his sleep.

"Yes," he said, sarcastically. He could not help his manner; the Labyrinth of Golden Dreams just angered him so much.

"WHAT IS YOUR BUSINESS?" the voice boomed.

"First," Borrack replied abruptly. "These two children, Jay and Gemma, believe their parents no longer love each other. And they have come to ask for your help to resolve their parent s' differences, and bring harmony back into the family. Secondly, you have, in these hills, a chimera by the name of Melvin, who you have imprisoned for a millennium, and I ask for his release from his purgatory."

The lights began to flash and then stopped. The voice boomed out.

"IS THAT BORRACK?"

Borrack hesitated, "Yes," he said defensively.

The lights flashed again.

"HAVE YOU A GIFT?"

Borrack replied angrily, "What is the point of bringing a poor defenceless beast in here to starve to death?"

The lights flashed furiously, the voice resumed.

"IT IS THE CUSTOM TO HONOUR YOUR GOD!"

Borrack could no longer contain himself. To Borrack the man, the Labyrinth of Golden Dreams was nothing more than a heartless lump of rock. He knew he could not anger the being in front of him, for it was void of any emotions, but he was not able to control his own outburst.

"You are no god, nor king; you are merely a lump of rock that cares for nothing but itself!" Borrack angrily retorted.

The children looked up at Borrack, pleading with their eyes for him to calm down. The lights flashed again, darting around while trying to compute his insubordination. The Labyrinth had never encountered this reply before, and was trying to understand this emotion that was not adoration.

Presently, they stopped. The Labyrinth of Golden Dreams resumed as though nothing offensive had been said.

"YOUR FIRST WISH, I WILL GRANT. BUT YOUR SECOND, I WILL NOT. THIS CREATURE YOU TALK OF – MELVIN – IS NO MORE THAN A COMMON CRIMINAL WHO ATTEMPTED TO DESECRATE THIS SACRED PLACE!"

The children looked up at Borrack, their young faces pleading for Melvin's release. Borrack felt his anger building up at the Labyrinth. He, like the children, could feel the injustice of the situation.

"How can *you* talk of desecration ?! *You*, who have destroyed so many lives?! You, who have allowed so many poor, innocent creatures to starve to death, because you believe that you are some kind of god?! You, who have allowed a village to be desecrated! And don't forget, you changed a sweet, young sweet girl into an Ice Blue Wind, whose sweetness and gentleness have turned into a twisted, angry revenge. Your selfish being desecrates the lives of all those around, and you have the brazen hypocrisy to punish a young man for eternity for the very crimes you yourself commit?!"

Borrack's anger was now at fever pitch. The lights began to flash again, as if attempting to comprehend his words, when, all of a sudden, they stopped. The voice boomed out, filling the cave and echoing around every crevice.

"I WILL GRANT BOTH YOUR WISHES, BUT, IN RETURN, YOU, BORRACK, MUST FULFILL YOUR DESTINY! THE ICE BLUE WIND MUST BE ERADICATED!"

The children looked up at Borrack, their young faces expressing fear.

Jay shouted out, "No! No! Borrack, please! Tell the Labyrinth of Golden

Dreams that we have changed our minds. The Ice Blue Wind will kill you! Please! Please, tell him we don't want his help!"

Gemma nodded in agreement, looking just as frightened as Jay. Borrack looked down at them. He smiled and dropped to his knees so as to be at their level.

"My young friends," he said, "I am afraid the decision has been made; there is no going back! There is a price for everything, nothing is for free. But remember, I am a chimera."

The children looked at him, puzzled. Borrack stood up and faced the golden mirrors and spoke.

"I will do as you wish, but you must honour this pledge to the children and Melvin, whether I win or lose."

The lights once again flashed for a short time, then stopped and the voice boomed out.

"THE PLEDGE WILL BE HONOURED. NOW GO AND LEAVE THIS PLACE!"

Borrack nodded and turned, and then led the children out of the cave. He ushered his two young wards through the cave entrance, the whole time with them remaining very quiet and extremely apprehensive.

Borrack followed, and, as he did so, he metamorphosed back into an eagle. The children swung around to face him, and there he stood, the mighty eagle, taller than the tallest of men. The eagle could see that the children's eyes were full of sadness. They had, in a short time, learned the realities of life; their needs and wants had to be paid for, and the mighty eagle would foot the bill. It was a bitter lesson and one that created so much guilt for the children.

Borrack lowered his wing and the children climbed aboard; first Jay and then Gemma. He flapped his huge wings and they soared upwards. It was a short flight back to the Ice Blue Wind, and they all remained quiet and thoughtful.

The sky was a clear blue, but, as they neared the Ice Blue Wind, they could see a grey wall of mist; with angry flashes of lightning running the whole length of it. The eagle could sense the Ice Blue Wind; she was waiting for revenge, and he knew it.

Borrack landed and the children dismounted, still pensive and preoccupied for the eagle's safety. From nowhere, Melvin appeared. He, too, could sense the impending doom.

"It seems, my old friend, I have to try and eradicate the Ice Blue Wind; apparently, it is my destiny," Borrack said sarcastically to Melvin. "Will you look after the children Melvin?"

"Of course," the penguin replied.

Melvin could see the fear in the eagle's eyes; he said nothing, so as not to upset the children, but it was in vain; Gemma ran to the eagle's leg and threw her arms around it.

"Please, please stay!" she sobbed. "Don't go and fight, please! We can all live in the cave with Melvin. We don't need to go home; Mummy and Daddy don't love us anyway." She sobbed relentlessly.

Jay rushed to her; his eyes were wet with tears as well. He gently pulled her off of Borrack's leg.

"Shush," he said gently. "There's nothing we can do; it is the way it has to be, shh, shh, now".

Gemma sobbed into Jay's chest, mumbling, "But Borrack will get hurt, won't he?"

Melvin took control and ushered the children to him.

The eagle looked down at the child! It was a pitiful sight, but the die had been cast. This was 'make or break' for the children, and if he had to pay the price, then so be it!

He flapped his huge wings, creating a whirlwind of dust and debris. He soared high into the sky to meet his nemesis, and there he hovered in all his magnificence. From nowhere the translucent face of the Ice Blue Wind appeared. All three of the others watched, transfixed.

The penguin noticed something different about the Ice Blue Wind; she exuded arrogance, the belief of a certain victory, in her manner.

She screamed with confidence, "So, you come to meet your fate, Borrack?" Her voice echoed around the Black Mountains like thunder.

The eagle was in no mood to fight; to him it was a pointless exercise. The Ice Blue Wind, in his view, was the only thing that protected man from the worst excesses of his greed, 'It was for the greater good,' he thought. 'She must stay and guard the entrance to the Labyrinth of Golden Dreams.' Even if he wanted to destroy it, there was no tangible way of doing it. He had tried the psychological approach, on his last meeting with her and the effects had been fleeting. To the eagle, there seemed no alternative than to accept defeat.

"Why must we fight?" Borrack asked.

The Ice Blue Wind cackled, "Because it is destiny," she retorted.

"Whose destiny? It is the Labyrinth of Golden Dreams who talks of destiny," Borrack said, trying to appease her.

"The Labyrinth of Golden Dreams is right," the Ice Blue Wind replied. "Destiny exists, and it's mine!" she screamed.

All the time they were talking the Ice Blue Wind was making her moves, leaving Borrack blissfully unaware of her tactics. Her translucent hand was now within striking distance of the eagle's leg. Melvin, Gemma and Jay had watched in horror as the plan unfolded; they tried shouting to their friend to warn him, but it was hopeless.

"Destiny cannot exist," Borrack replied, "If it did, what would be the point of freewill? Our life would be pre-planned, and all our choices would be nothing more than acting out a pre-ordained script."

"Well, I have a plan for your life!" the Ice Blue Wind screamed, "…To end it!" and, with that, she swung her strategy into action. The translucent hand grabbed the eagle's leg and swung him around like a rag doll. Borrack screamed with pain, as he was swung with tremendous force into the side of a mountain. Borrack screamed in excruciating pain. Melvin and the two children stood and watched in terror. They felt hopeless and helplessly watched as their friend appeared to be annihilated by the Ice Blue Wind. Every bone and muscle in the eagle's body ached. He was dazed and confused, his vision was blurred. Yet, in his peripheral vision he could make out an object flying towards him. The eagle shook his head, his confusion cleared! He realized the object was the ice blue winds other hand. It was clenched like a fist. With lightning speed, he summoned every ounce of energy and darted out of its trajectory.

Her fist slammed into the side of the mountain with such force, that rocks and debris splintered off in every direction, like shrapnel from an exploding missile. Unfortunately, the eagle's chosen direction led him straight into the path of the other translucent hand, which grabbed his wing, almost wrenching it off of his body. He screamed again, the pain was sharp, sudden and unbearable. Melvin, Gemma and Jay were stunned by the horror they were watching.

Gemma cried out to Borrack and dropped to her knees. She watched in terror as her saviour was being brutalized. She sobbed, calling out for Zachary repeatedly, as if he could hear, but he couldn't. He was miles away, unaware of his adopted son's fate. The translucent hand swung Borrack around by his wing and then slammed him into the side of the mountain once again. The eagle cried out in pain and the Ice Blue Wind gave a shrill laugh of delight at her victory. Gemma could take no more, she was exhausted and collapsed to the ground in a heap.

CHAPTER 7

Part Two: Reality

The two adults sat between the beds of their children, gripping each other's hand with desperation. Even the machines that were strapped to the children remained quiet and unresponsive.

The watery sun that had earlier passed through the window, which straddled the two beds, had been replaced by grey, dreary skies. To the parents of the children, it was as if the world had left them in limbo. What little hope they had had, had been replaced by despair, and as each hour, minute and second went by, their despair was being replaced by fear and guilt.

As the parent's eyes met, their guilt was replaced by blame, and each, in turn, dropped their head in shame and internally blamed themselves. It had been like running head-long into a brick wall, in a car without brakes. There was just no hope and no way out.

And then… a miracle! A murmur from the young girl, a sound, then another – nothing distinctive, just a sound. The machine that monitored their very existence came to life. At first, a slow bleep, steady and methodical, slowly increasing in frequency and volume. Then the first audible sound from the girl! Repeating and repeating, "Borrack! Borrack! Borrack…"

The Medical staff ran over in response, but the mother was at her daughter's side first, followed by the father.

The little girl opened her eyes and looked into her mother's face. "It's Borrack," she wailed, "The Ice Blue Wind is killing him, and we must tell Zachary! Please! We must help Borrack! We must help him! Please, please…" she sobbed.

The doctors gently pushed past the mother and father, to check on the young girl's condition. They all agreed the girl was out of danger; a nurse remained, removing the wires that had tied the child to the monitor. Both the mother and father were elated that one of their children was back from the brink. Both looked at the boy, he was still in a coma, then they turned their heads to each other. Their eyes met, and, in those few seconds, so much was said, without a word being spoken. Despair was once again replaced with hope.

The little girl was still sobbing and repeating the same words. "Please! Please… We must help Borrack! He's dying, and we must tell Zachary! Please!"

The mother cradled the child in her arms, "There, there, it's only a silly, old dream," she said reassuringly.

The girl protested, "No! No!" she shouted with urgency in her voice. "It's true, Mummy! It's true – Borrack is dying! We must help… please," sobbing uncontrollably.

The mother looked down at little Gemma; she tried to take her mind off the dream. "Look," she said, "look at the wooden doll."

Gemma looked down at her hand and sobbed, "Zachary made it," she said, and buried her head into her mother's chest, sobbing.

The grey skies began to change into something more sinister. It was becoming darker. Thunder cracked in the distance and a bolt of lightning flitted across the skies, spindly, like an electric spider's web. The rain pummelled against the large windows that straddled the beds, threatening to smash the glass.

The parents sat either side of their daughter trying to comfort her, without success. The young boy slowly opened his eyes, but he made no sound. His eyes were drawn to the row of lights in the centre of the ward; he followed the line with his eyes turning his head slightly to the right. It led to a huge pair of swing doors at the end. There was a nurse's station, and, on either side, lay half a dozen beds, each separated by a window. Most of the beds were filled with patients. A vigilant nurse spied the child looking and duly called a doctor; meanwhile, the boy followed the line back and then onwards to the left, and it mirrored the right. His eyes eventually fell on to the bed next to him and there he saw his parents, comforting his sister. The thunder was coming closer and the lightning seemed to surround the whole building, just as the medical staff descended upon the boy. The parents, who had been unaware of the child's situation, were thrown into total panic, assuming the worst.

A nurse reassured them, "He's fine," she said, and the doctor concurred with a nod of his head, and left the nurse to remove the wires that strapped the boy to the machine.

Jay sat up and looked at his parents. He saw tears rolling down their faces, not tears of sadness, but of relief, hope and happiness. The boy dropped his gaze to his sister, and she was fixed on him; her eyes asked the question before she could say it… "Is Borrack…?"

Jay jumped in quickly, lying, so as not to upset her. "No! He's… he's…"

The boy stuttered, tears began to well up in his eyes and his voice broke. She could see through his charade.

"He's dead," she wailed.

"No, no!" Jay responded, trembling and his face wet with tears, "But it's bad," the boy murmured. He needed comfort, he needed security. He wanted everything he had witnessed to go away. But, most of all, Jay needed the love of his parents, so he jumped out of bed and sprung over to them; they opened their arms and he fell into them. He sobbed openly along with his sister; they cried for Borrack and his fate.

The vigilant nurse returned to her station. She had been unsettled by something, something she had never witnessed before; the two children had shared the same dream. She spoke to a colleague about it and they both gazed in the direction of the family. Even the parents hadn't noticed it, but to them, nothing else mattered. They had their children back, and that's all that they wanted. They had made their pact – they would never argue again in earshot of the children. The family was one again, a loving unit.

There was a sudden crack of thunder directly over the hospital, and the whole building shook and the windows rattled. Then there was a flash of lightning that seemed to penetrate the fabric of the hospital. A gust of wind burst through the large swing doors; nurses ran from all directions to try and plug the hole, but the wind was too strong. The wind pushed its way across the ward; it was cold and tinged with blue and on its back, it carried a cackle; a sound all-too familiar to the children. A sound that sent a chill through their souls, a sound that trumped a victory, a victory over Borrack.

Jay and Gemma felt the eagle's pain! They called his name in unison and cursed the Ice Blue Wind. They buried their heads into their parent's flesh to hide from the cruel world, escape from the realities of life; so much had been learned in such a short time.

The rain smashed against the window, sending torrents of water running down the windowpanes of glass. The children sobbed and sobbed at the passing of Borrack – the parents cried too, in relief and in confusion, for they could not comfort their children or take their pain away. The family huddled together, both sad and lonely, while those in the ward watched with an intense fascination.

But then, as Gemma cried, she suddenly began to feel a warm, comforting sensation on her cheek. She turned her head in the direction of the sensation, and, as her sobbing began to abate, ; she squinted her eye s. The clouds were melting away, allowing the sun to penetrate through.

As she squinted, it became clear that a black object hovered in front of the sunlight, "Borrack!" she exclaimed.

Jay turned his head in response, then, as they both turned their heads to face each other, their eyes met and euphoria took hold.

"He's alive!" Jay yelled, with both joy and amazement.

They both jumped up and broke free of their parents' embraces and ran to the window. Both parents followed and stood behind their children, unsure of what to think. Jay and Gemma jumped up and down excitedly, shouting, "He's alive! He's alive!"

The commotion caused such a stir in the ward that all those that could, ran to adjacent windows, and all those that couldn't had to ask what was going on! Everyone at the windows looked up and witnessed something unique, something none of them had ever witnessed in their lives, and would no doubt never witness again. Because there, silhouetted against the majestic sun, hovered the mighty Borrack, in a truly magnificent sight.

By now, everyone on the ward was dumbstruck – silence had fallen on a hushed awe at the sight. Meanwhile, Jay's eyes were drawn to a strange looking character walking on the pavement below. He wore a tailcoat that went to a point behind his knees; his nose was shaped like a beak and he walked remarkably like a penguin. The stranger looked up and waved, smiling! It was Melvin. Jay tapped Gemma's arm and pointed to him, and they both smiled and waved back excitedly.

Borrack looked down at them and smiled. He looked down on the children, laughing and happy with their loving parents. It had been touch-and-go as to whether they would make it back in one piece, but they had. Borrack had loved them, nurtured them, and would never forget them, in the same way they would never forget him. The mighty eagle knew, as Jay and Gemma did, that they would never meet again. They would, however, join his family of children, past and future; those that he had helped and those that he would help, for that was Borrack's mission.

As for Melvin, he felt something bittersweet, with joy and sorrow in equal measure; elated, on the one hand, because at last, he might find true happiness, even though it might be short-lived; and sad, because he had lost a true friend in the mighty eagle; one who had chosen to sacrifice himself, so that he might be human once more.

Borrack watched the children and Melvin wave good-bye. He felt tired, and every muscle in his body ached; he had taken a beating from the Ice Blue Wind, and, yes, he had been defeated, although it was for the greater good.

The eagle knew he could never die, for he was a chimera, and only the Labyrinth of Golden Dreams or the demise of this beautiful planet could do that. Borrack turned and flapped his huge wings, heading southeast and onto his next adventure.

He flew over village churches; thatched cottages and the patchwork quilt of fields, which were the glory of England. The sun was lazily setting in the west. His body felt tired and heavy; it was time to rest. Borrack spotted a rocky outcrop. He circled and landed. He scanned the vista, which was beautiful; the jealous moon was in its ascendancy, but still submissive to the setting sun. Below, a field of wheat swayed tenderly in the gentle breeze, and the eagle's mind reverted back to his past adventure. It had been a great success – the children were now reunited with their parents and he had never felt more confident; the Ice Blue Wind and the Labyrinth of Golden Dreams would never be able to control his future again; his achievements were proof of that.

He was shaken from his daydream by the sound of a sharp, shrill noise; he turned his head and focused on the sound. Far to the right, a pharmaceutical factory was changing shifts. He watched as workers poured in and out of the factory gates, some starting their shifts, others finishing. It was an industry that was financed for profit over people, and with that thought, Borrack felt a surge of anger. He was off to help a child that lived on a continent far to the southeast that had little food, and, more importantly, medicine. If it were not for the aid of a myriad of charities, many more children would be perishing, to the indifference of the rest of humanity. The eagle was glad he was only half-human; the knowledge somehow eased his own guilt.

He watched the sun slowly dip below the horizon, and his anger began to wane. 'Not all humans are thoughtless,' he thought. 'Look at Zachary, that wise, old man of the north, my adopted father! If only there were more people like him, the world would be a better place,' he mused, 'and there are always the children. They are the future; they must be the new hope.'

As the last vestiges of the old day disappeared, and the jealous moon headed towards its zenith, sending out its beams of incandescent light across all corners of the planet under its domain, the animals of the night rejoiced in the sun's demise. Borrack closed his eyes and slept, safe in the knowledge that that ball of energy, that the one, true, material god, the sun, would return the next morning, filled with life and giving optimism anew for the future.

As the eagle slept, he had little idea that the black shadow was watching and planning retribution.

The End

BOOK 2.

ELEPHANTS LIVE FOREVER

Mother Africa, that continent way to the southeast, the cradle of humanity. She was our life-giver. It was her Garden of Eden that we first walked upon. She was the mother that nurtured our ancestors; she was the mother that watched us grow, with pride in her heart. And, as her offspring spawned a tribe and that tribe spawned so many more, and spread across her lands, she rejoiced with hope in her heart. She watched as her offspring spread over every continent on this beautiful planet, and as the tribes became nations and nations became empires; her heart cried out with such pleasure.

Mother Africa, that continent way to the southeast, the cradle of humanity. She was our life-giver. Today, she watches her offspring disappear, for she sees so much wickedness, so much greed, so much pain. She watches as tribe fights tribe, nation fights nation and empire fights empire, and all in the pursuit of power and greed. She looks on with pained sadness as her own people die of starvation, disease and war, and she knows, in her heart, this need not be. She watches with anger as other nations subjugate her children and rape her land, in the name of the free market ; knowing that the 'freedom' of economic forces means greed and the exploitation of the weak. Oh! Mother Africa, that continent way to the southeast, she who was our life-giver. I share your pain and despair, and, like you, I feel nothing but angry contempt and indignation at the lies and hypocrisies.

CHAPTER 1

A Continent Way to the Southeast

A grandmother, mother and child share a habitat made of corrugated iron, plastic and wood. This is their new home; it is a home of fear and desperation, yet they are but one family of so many that share this refugee camp called 'Hell'!

They are the victims of hate, pushed off their land and brutalized. The boy is called Mumbye. He lays on a dirt floor, dying. His bloated stomach, bulging eyes and stick-like limbs are a testament to the world's empathy. He is eleven, and at such a young age, he is nearing the terminus of his life. The mother and grandmother watch as his young life ebbs away, but their expressions are lifeless. They are traumatized by past events; they have watched as their family has been annihilated by so much hate. They have lost fathers, brothers, sisters, cousins and children. They have no more food to share; they have no more tears to cry; they have no more hope to carry them on ; and their story is just one of so many that share this new home called Hell.

Mumbye lies on a dirt floor, now comatose; he is now oblivious to the hunger and despair that he has witnessed in recent times. In his comatose dream, he is by a beautifully lake, calling out for his friend Borrack. He catches his reflection in the lake; he is as he was when life was content, when his family and tribe lived in harmony with nature, when all was well with the world. In this state he has escaped! Escaped from reality – and he waits patiently for his friend to arrive.

Borrack had left the shores of England some time ago. His huge wings cut through the air with such easy grace and yet their power was so immense. The eagle was deep in thought; his mind was on the boy, Mumbye. The child was eleven, going on twelve, yet Borrack doubted whether the boy would even reach that age; he certainly would not live much beyond it. This, to Borrack, was the worst of his chosen path; there was no way out for the child and the eagle would have to comfort young Mumbye to the end. It would be heart-breaking, but it had to be done; there would be no happy endings, just sadness. The eagle's mind went back to the time when he first met the child; it was the time of their great upheavals. The boy's tribe was caught up in a bloody civil war. The war was fought in the name of freedom, but freedom has such a shallow meaning, and is a word so easily twisted for manipulative ends. For freedom did not exist for Mumbye's tribe – just bigoted recriminations. The boy watched as his father, grandfather and the men of the village were cut down like lambs to the slaughter, and it traumatized him. As he needed to escape, he went within himself. His daydreams became hellish; his nightmares were even worse. That was when Borrack heard him calling, and from that night to the present he had watched the young boy deteriorate. His downfall had been slow and painful, with the expulsion from their village, to the long trek to their hellish refugee camp. It had been a deterioration that had encompassed the deaths of his brother and sisters from malnutrition and disease, to his own fight with hunger. Each event was like a hammer blow to the child, and each event crushed a bit more of his soul. Borrack could do nothing but watch with quiet anger – anger at the world's indifference!

The eagle reached the northern territories of Spain; it was all so lush and green. The majestic sun was at its highest, and Borrack could feel its searing heat on his back. As the golden light came down upon the huge bird, on the surrounding land it cast a shadow, a shadow of the mighty Borrack, which followed the eagle and hugged the contours of the land.

It was like the hand of justice, to those beasts of the fields that fell under its spell. They ran in fear and hid. But to those animals of conscious thought, man, that is, their response was so very different! Those who knew of Borrack's work with that most precious of gifts, they rejoiced, waved and smiled. Those who knew not of him, they looked up in awe and wonderment. To those who tormented that most precious of gifts, that is, children, they ran like the beasts of the fields and hid, with fear and guilt in their hearts. Borrack's huge wings cut through the air tirelessly; he knew the journey would normally take three or four days; but the eagle would do it in half the time. It was imperative to reach Mumbye as soon as possible, for every second to the boy was like a grain of sand falling through an hourglass. And every grain of sand was a small part of his life ebbing away.

Borrack followed the coast of northern Spain and Portugal; onwards he flew, never tiring, with resolve in his heart. The further south he went, so the landscape became more arid. He flew over the cities of Vigo, in northern Spain, and Porto, Lisbon and Faro in Portugal, with many small hamlets and fishing villages between. He saw so many wonderful sights; the river Tagus with its magnificent suspension bridge; a monument to man's achievements, and the tower of Belem, all in the beautiful Lisbon. Then, once again, the mighty Borrack crossed back into southern Spain.

The sun was moving to the west, casting Borrack's shadow to the east, distorting it beyond recognition. The eagle knew he would soon have to rest. He hoped he could make it to Gibraltar – that was his target. He was always mindful of Mumbye and his young life ebbing away. Borrack flew on, but every muscle and sinew in his body had begun to ache. He passed over Cadiz, the city whose history was tied to the discovery of the Americas. As the eagle flew on, his target came in sight: Gibraltar.

Borrack could feel the exhaustion saturating his body, but he resisted its effects. The magnificent Rock of Gibraltar was within striking distance; he pushed his body to its limits.

At last, he was within a mile of his nesting sight. The majestic sun was slowly sinking in the west; he summoned every last ounce of energy, until, at last, he was there! He was circling the Rock, scouting for the safest and highest resting place, when his eye spotted the very place. He glided gracefully down. He spread out his huge wings to reduce his acceleration and opened out his talon s to take the impact of his landing... Thump! He was down.

The inhabitants of that rock scurried away to their habitats, in fear of this unwelcome guest, in case he might seek them out and decimate them. The eagle panned the vista, and, as always, Mother Nature had not let him down. He turned and looked west, and he watched as the sun slowly surrendered to the western horizon. It cast a golden path across the Atlantic sea, the sky glowed red, setting light to the clouds, as if the clouds were flaming torches, illuminating a path for those ancient gods of history. He watched in awe until the majestic sun finally sank below the horizon.

Borrack then turned his head to the east, and there he saw the jealous moon on its ascendancy. It was strange how the moon seemed to mimic the sun, for like the sun, it cast a silver path across that sea of antiquity, that sea of so much history, that sea that had seen so many empires come and go, that sea called the Mediterranean.

The sky was dark with the silver light of the moon, and as the incandescent light encompassed the clouds, it distorted them with a ghostly mystery, bringing out the primaeval sense of fear of Borrack's human side. Nonetheless, the eagle marvelled at the beauty that surrounded him. He closed his eyes to sleep; he would make it an early start tomorrow, for Mumbye's life was ebbing away inexorably, and Borrack knew it.

Borrack woke before sunrise; the sky was dark, the moon was hidden by heavy clouds. He sensed a storm, a vicious storm. Under normal circumstances, he would not have taken to the sky, but these were not normal circumstances; a boy's life was hanging by a thread.

The rock was quiet; not a sound could be heard – the inhabitants' fear of that unwelcome guest, Borrack, had been superseded by a new fear, that of the great storm which was fast approaching. There they would stay in their habitats until the new fear had subsided.

Borrack flapped his huge wings, and almost immediately he was airborne. He soared high into the heavily clouded sky. He could feel the storm's atmosphere; it was oppressive and electric. He knew the dangers; no other creature would venture out in such conditions, but what choice did he have? In any case, he was well-versed in such conditions, for Borrack had faced the wrath of the Ice Blue Wind and had survived. This, in comparison, should be a picnic.

The rain lashed and battered him, while the ferocious wind buffeted the eagle. But he kept his course; he was crossing the Strait of Gibraltar. Borrack looked down at the sea, which was grey and unforgiving; his progress was slow but determined. He was almost two third s of the way across, when, bellowing in that grey, unforgiving sea, he saw two shapes bobbing up and down on an upturned boat. They were clearly in trouble, but he did not have time for such distractions; Mumbye's life was ebbing away. Borrack's conscience was in turmoil; did he have time to save these two unfortunates? Could he pretend he had never witnessed the event? The battle raged on in his mind briefly, but, as always, common sense prevailed.

The eagle swooped down and circled the victims; a young man waved one arm in a frenzy; the other was wrapped around a young boy, supporting his weight; stopping him from slipping into the unforgiving sea.

"Help, help!" he shouted.

Borrack went in closer, despite the fact that the rain was pelting down, the wind was whistling, and the sea was crashing down on the two victims.

"Help! Help us, Borrack! Please! Take the boy!"

Borrack shouted back, "I will circle and lift the boy from you; when he is safe, I will come back for you."

"Just save the boy," the young man shouted, "Save the boy!"

The eagle soared upwards – he needed speed if there was any chance of saving the boy; this element alone was absolutely indispensable in saving the child. For with speed came strength, and, as Borrack had learnt from experience, lifting a dead weight from a standing start, particularly with soaking wet clothes, was a formula for disaster. No! He needed speed. When the eagle was at sufficient height, he powered his huge wings and circled. The rain lashed at him, the wind roared and whistled around him, but he pressed on.

He flew around in circles several times, increasing his speed. At last, Borrack felt the time was right! He dived down towards the child on the upturned boat. He opened his talons and grabbed the boy. Once again, he flapped his huge wings, he could feel the boy's weight – it was heavy with those sopping, wet clothes! But with effort, he prized him from that evil, grey, unforgiving sea. He flew south towards land, battling the elements. In the distance, he could hear the sound of thunder, lightning flashed all around him; Borrack now understood its significance. The storm was at its height.

His mind slipped back to something the young man had shouted, he had used his name. 'How did he know who I was?' the eagle thought. 'Most people would have been scared of such a creature as myself… But the young man seemed to know me!' The whole saga kept Borrack's mind off the raging storm.

At last the eagle reached land, and he followed the coast until he found a safe haven for the boy. Borrack had found the ideal spot, one which was a natural shelter; a large open cave. He circled and gently lowered the boy, then circled again and landed by the child. The boy was shivering, which made his speech stutter

"Ple-plea-please, sa-sav- save my ma-mas-master!"

"Of course, I will!" Borrack replied.

The boy looked down at his feet, still shivering.

"He is su-such a go-good maaa-n, a-and he ta-tal-talks of yo-you al-all the ti-tim-time."

The eagle smiled reassuringly, "Don't worry, I will bring him back safely."

The boy looked up at Borrack and was reassured.

"You get a fire started, and I will be back with him in no time. Don't forget to get that fire started!" Borrack said to the boy as he turned and flapped his huge wings and took off.

He soared high into the sky, but his mind was racing now! The boy had implied that the young man had known him, and the eagle was highly intrigued. 'Who was this young man?' he thought.

Borrack retraced his journey along the coast to the point at which he had made landfall. There, he turned and flew straight across the unforgiving sea, at a right angle to the land. The storm was raging like a stampede of a thousand buffalos; the noise was deafening. The rain lashed down, the waves crashed down on the mighty sea and the thunder boomed, and all of this illuminated by the blinding phosphorous lighting.

The eagle scoured the grey, restless sea looking for the young man; and though it was like looking for a needle in a haystack, at last he spotted him! But that was not all. To the young man's left he caught sight of a massive, rolling, impending wave, rushing headlong into him, threatening to drown him.

Borrack swung into action; there was no time to waste. He powered his huge wings – the eagle was moving at incredible speed now! But so was the wave. The eagle knew the young man would be heavy, a lot heavier than the boy. But what concerned the bird more was that huge wave. If he were to wait until the wave had passed, the probable outcome for the young man would be fatal; however, if he reached the victim too late, he too would be swept away by that huge wave. Borrack knew he had no other option: he would have to take a chance and rescue the young man now.

He was directly over the victim. He went into a dive.

The wave was fast approaching; he swept his wings back to give him more speed. The eagle could see he was just about going to make it, but it was going to be a close-run thing. He spread his wings out to reduce his acceleration, opened his talons and grabbed the lifeless body. The eagle flapped his large wings, the young man's body was heavy, and, at first, would not move. His eyes caught the fast-approaching wave – it was nearly on them. Borrack redoubled his efforts, and at last he prized the lifeless body from the restless sea. In a split second, he realised that he needed more lift if he was going to clear the wave, so he instantly mustered every ounce of energy he could; his whole body ached under the strain; but he was gaining height. The crest of the wave broke just below the victim, narrowly missing his limp legs, which would have dragged them both down to a watery grave. The wave then crashed into the unforgiving sea… he had done it; he had succeeded!

The eagle flew towards land with the young man gripped in his huge talons. The storm began to abate, the rain stopped and the wind dropped. Borrack turned his head to the east; he could see the storm pushing further into the Mediterranean. The sun began to break through the clouds; he could feel it on his huge wings, and it felt so good. As he reached landfall, he turned and retraced his journey back to the boy, and there, just below, he saw him, standing over a fire, feeding it with wood. The eagle circled, and gently lowered the young man, then circled again and landed.

The boy rushed to the young man's side, providing comfort and reassurance. As Borrack approached the young man, he recognized him immediately – he was part of his family of children past and present; it was Ishmell!

The man regained consciousness. He saw Borrack and immediately tried to sit up, only to fall back through exhaustion.

"Don't move Ishmell," the eagle said with concern.

Ishmell looked up at Borrack.

"This is the second time you have saved my life; how am I ever going to pay you back?"

Borrack smiled at the young man.

"I do not help for profit, only out of probity and justice. When you first called for me, all those years back, when your master was treating you with disregard and cruelty, I came to you out of natural justice, as my adopted father had once done for me. The only profit that should be gained from such an act is to see the recipient grow up steeped in natural justice and humanity, and you, my young friend, have shown that in abundance. Your selfless action in saving this boy, almost at your own expense, is a credit to you, and more than enough payment for me."

The young boy smiled at the eagle and then at the young man. "Thank you for saving my master, he's a good man."

Ishmell reciprocated the smile, and in a sign of affection, he ruffled the young boy's hair.

"If I go now, Ishmell, will you be ok?" Borrack said.

"Won't you stay for some food? I feel sure we can find something around here, fish maybe."

"Thank you for the offer," the eagle responded, "But I must go. I have a young boy whose life is ebbing away, and he is urgently in need of my help."

Ishmell looked into the eagle's eyes; he could see his trepidation for future events. "Is there no chance for the boy?" Ishmell said.

Borrack dropped his head, "No…" the eagle responded quietly.

The young man looked at the creature with his head lowered, this creature that was taller than the tallest of men, and, in an instant, he saw him humbled; he seemed to shrink in stature. This eagle, who comforted children through their nightmares and sheltered them from demons, would have to accompany this child in his final moments. To Ishmell, there could be no braver thing to do, and he felt nothing but admiration and love for this eagle, this creature, this Borrack.

"Then you have no time to lose, Borrack, you must go! I will be fine. I have my young apprentice to look after me. So, go! Quick! And may Allah go with you," Ishmell said.

Borrack lifted his head and smiled, he nodded to Ishmell and his young apprentice and once again he powered his huge wings, creating a plume of dust and debris, and he was gone.

The young boy looked at his master, and the master answered the question before the boy could ask it.

"Yes, my young friend, that is the mighty Borrack, taller than the tallest of men."

Borrack flew high. The majestic sun beat down on his wings; burning through the feathers to reach his skin and scorching it. The eagle never faltered – he would reach young Mumbye before sunset. He flew over deserts, prairies, mountains, rivers, lakes, villages, towns and cities, and he saw a myriad of wild animals.

By late afternoon, he was flying over Mumbye's new home! And, Lord, hadn't it grown since the eagle's last visit?! Now it spread out like an open, festering wound on the landscape below. Borrack's anger began to build. 'How could these animals that consider themselves so superior to all other creatures, allow such an abomination to exist? Where was their compassion, their humanity?' the eagle thought.

In the distance he could see the lake, his meeting place with the boy, and as he reached it, he could see young Mumbye leaning against a tree waiting patiently for him.

CHAPTER 2
Elephants Live Forever

Lying off of Mother Africa's east coast, north of the equator, in the Indian Ocean, stood an island. An island built like a fortress. On all sides, huge walls of granite sprang from the sea like sheets of black ebony, almost smooth and shimmering in the brilliance of the sun. On its top lay a lush plateau filled with the fruits of the Garden of Eden. This was the home of a peace-loving people. Where equality reigned supreme. Where all lived as one, regardless of colour, creed or religion, where an injury to one was an injury to all. It was a place where all citizens ran their affairs collectively for the good of all. This place was called Poutia.

Its leader, the Matriarch, was an Empathic, and, in her mind, she could predict the arrival of the mighty Borrack. As for Borrack himself, although he did not realize it, he was coming home to the bosom of his family.

* * * * *

Borrack circled, then landed in close proximity to young Mumbye. The light was beginning to fade, taking with it the extreme heat of the day. The boy was lying against a tree next to the lake; it had provided him with shade, shade from that intense heat, that Mother Africa has in abundance. His eyes were closed; the Eagle wandered over to him and called his name:

"Mumbye, Mumbye."

The boy did not stir from his slumber, so the eagle tried again, only louder.

"Mumbye, Mumbye!"

He still did not wake, and Borrack began to fear the worst. He knew well his young life was ebbing away, and, as he looked closely at the emaciated figure in front of him, he could see the heavy penalty that recent events had taken on the child; his bloated stomach, his fragile limbs that could have been snapped like dry twigs, the translucent skin. Borrack's gaze moved up the body to the face, and as he did, young Mumbye opened his bulging eyes. Borrack stepped back in surprise. He looked deep into the boy's eyes – which seemed as if they were about to pop out of his head at any second. It was at that moment that Borrack felt a wave of sympathy wash over him – this child in front of him was a testament to the world's indifference, and it disturbed the eagle greatly. The boy looked up at the bird, smiled, and said:

"Oh, Borrack, you're here at last!"

His voice was weak and trembling.

"Yes, my young friend," Borrack said trying to suppress his sadness and his anger. "I am here to take you on another adventure."

But Mumbye, like the Matriarch was an Empathic, a gift that is both an asset and a burden. To Mumbye, at this moment, it was the latter – for he had read all of Borrack's thoughts and feelings, and in an instant, he knew his life was draining away, like the grains of sand in an hourglass.

The boy's expression changed; he became serious and said, "Am I going to die soon?"

Briefly, at that moment, Borrack wished he could be anywhere else but there, facing this young boy with this inevitable, inescapable truth. The eagle looked straight into the boy's eyes; he was not going to dodge this question. "Yes," Borrack said seriously.

The boy dropped his head and bit his lip; then he lifted his gaze to his friend's face.

"How long have I got?"

"I honestly don't know, Mumbye. maybe days or weeks, I just don't know."

The eagle replied with candidness but gravity. Mumbye dug his skeletal hands into the dirt at the bottom of the tree, allowing the dirt to be sifted through his bony fingers.

"If I am going to die, will you take me to the land where elephants never die?" the boy said, stumbling over his words.

Borrack was taken aback at the boy's request; his mind began to whir into full motion ! Of course, he had heard of the place – but he had always considered it no more than a fictitious land, a fanciful legend or a figment of the imagination. Yet, notwithstanding, he knew there were many natives, particularly in this part of the world, that believed in its existence; they called it the 'Meadow of Tranquillity', he believed.

Mumbye had been watching the eagle and reading his thoughts.

"The place does exist! I know it does," the boy said pleadingly.

Borrack looked at the child. The eagle knew the boy was an Empathic, and his ability to read the thoughts of others was extraordinary.

"Well, my young friend, I will do my best to get you there, but I have no idea where it is! However, there is a place that may give us the answer; the Island of Poutia."

The boy smiled with relief. Borrack was intrigued by the boy's request, but before he could ask the question, Mumbye answered it.

"If I am going to die, I want to be with my friend Bruma."

Who Bruma was, Borrack was about to ask, when the boy interrupted.

"He was a calf elephant. I befriended him in my old home, when life was content, when my family and tribe lived in harmony with nature, when all was well with the world. It was before those bad men came and destroyed all that was good, including Bruma. They cut him down with a machete, in the same way that they murdered my father, grandfather, uncles and brothers.

Tears rolled down the boy's cheeks – the memories were so painful, and they were entrenched in Mumbye's mind like a perpetual nightmare.

The eagle could see the boy's pain and felt for him.

"Well, if we're to find this place, I think we better get a good night's sleep."

The sun had all but dropped below the horizon; the evening was beginning to get cold. The boy lay down and Borrack lay next to him, covering Mumbye with his wing to keep him warm. The eagle felt the young, feeble body close to him; in no time the child was asleep. Borrack's psyche wrestled with the boy's request, because even if he knew where the Meadows of Tranquillity were, young Mumbye would probably not survive the journey. Bearing in mind the fact that he would first have to go to Poutia, to ask for their help in finding the place, only exacerbated the problem.

The eagle's mind was tortured by the whole affair. As the night wore on, Borrack formulated a plan. He would travel to Poutia in two separate journeys. First, there would be early mornings, so as to catch the gentler heat of the day, and then, just as the sun goes down, the second part would catch the warmest part of the evening. This way the eagle felt he could avoid the freezing cold nights, and the extreme heat of that majestic sun, for both ends of the spectrum could prove fatal for young Mumbye ! Well, that was, at least, his plan to get to Poutia – whatever happened after that was in the hands of the Gods. Borrack closed his eyes and slept.

The eagle woke just before sunrise, and he called Mumbye's name until he stirred. Borrack had managed to find some wild fruit for the boy to eat. It was a gesture without foundation – for how can you feed the physical being when reality is a dream away? But, for the eagle, it was a way of lifting the young boy's morale.

"Ok, young man," Borrack said when the boy had finished eating, "Climb on my back, and we'll start our journey."

The huge bird lowered a wing, and Mumbye, with great effort, did as he was bade. The bald eagle set his huge wings into motion, and gently left the ground. As they soared high into the sky, Borrack could feel young Mumbye's feeble arms around his neck. The child was as light as a feather. He knew he would have to strike the correct balance; if he flew too fast, the boy would lose his grip and fall to his death, whereas, if he was too slow, the journey would take far too long, and the child did not have the luxury of time.

As they flew higher, the sun began to appear on the western horizon. To Borrack it looked as if the mountains that had surrounded and imprisoned that golden ball of energy had split asunder, allowing the sun to escape.

The eagle panned the valley below; a dewy mist clung to the valley floor, giving the appearance of a peaceful lake. Yet, within the exquisite minutiae that the mist was hiding, was bursting forth a cacophonous racket of animal sounds, as the land below sprang into life with the arrival of another glorious day, the gift of the sun, that giver of life.

The two flew on for several more hours, before resting. Over the next few days, Borrack and the boy fell into the same routine; an early morning flight for two or three hours, and then three or four hours in the late afternoon or early evening, before it got cold. The eagle had fine-tuned himself into the boy's health, and, although the child was only skin and bones, Borrack could sense every change in Mumbye's metabolism. Indeed, the eagle was like a flying heart monitor! Borrack had got so involved in the boy's well-being, that he had had little time to take in the wonderful vistas he had passed by.

His senses had noticed the young Mumbye becoming weaker, and his concern was well-justified, for on the third day, late in the afternoon, Borrack became aware of a substantial deterioration in the boy's breathing. While it had been shallow recently, now it had become almost non-existent.

The eagle called out his name, "Mumbye, Mumbye!" he shouted.

But there was no response, and he began to fear the worst.

He looked for a safe place to land; it was imperative to check on the boy. Borrack circled the high plateau several times; he needed a place of safety, a place that was flat, but at the same time, hidden from predators. He spotted the very place… He descended gently, coming into land without even a bump.

The boy still clung to his back; the eagle shouted his name again.

"Mumbye! Mumbye!" but again, no response.

He spread one wing, creating a shallow ramp, and then he gently rocked his body towards the lowered wing. Borrack did this several times, and eventually the boy's grip slackened, and he slid off and down the lowered wing.

The eagle turned to check on Mumbye. He was lifeless. Borrack realized the gravity of the situation. If he were to help the child and bring him back to life, he would have to metamorphose into Borrack the man. Only then could he provide the lifesaving help the child needed. This was the greatest concession that he had extracted from the Labyrinth of Golden Dreams, and it had proved its usefulness on so many occasions, not least of which was the rescue of Jay and Gemma from that fire of accidental anger, which swept through their parent's house. Without this ability to become human, those children would have perished.

The eagle closed his eyes and focused on the Labyrinth of Golden Dreams; his body went into a spasm; the sensation was as if his body were being crushed into a container half its size. It was neither painful nor pleasant, but within seconds he had metamorphose to become a man. He stood tall, wearing a suit of dark brown feathers! This was Borrack the man!

He turned and knelt down by the child. He checked his pulse – there was nothing. He pumped his chest with his large hands and checked his pulse again, still nothing. Borrack tilted the boy's head back and opened his mouth. He placed his elbow on the child's chest and pressed his mouth against the boy's lips and blew down his throat. Borrack could feel young Mumbye's chest expand. Then, with his elbow, he pushed the air out. He did this for several minutes, 'till at last the boy coughed and spluttered as he regained consciousness. Mumbye opened his eyes, and there in front of him, knelt Borrack the man. The boy's reaction was slow – he was semi-conscious. Borrack spoke to him.

"Hang on, young man! I need to fulfil my promise to you and take you to the land where elephants never die."

The boy nodded weakly. The child did not know whether he was alive or dead. But something deep in his unconscious mind saw this figure in front of him as his guardian angel, who would take him to see his friend, Bruma, the baby elephant.

Borrack mumbled to himself about getting the boy some water, with which, he propped young Mumbye up against a tree and went in search of the nectar of life; which, as Borrack the man knew, was a gesture without foundation! For how can you feed the physical being when reality is a dream away?

Borrack scrambled down the side of the plateau. He could hear running water in the distance, so he used every sense in his body to track it down. In no time at all, he had fallen upon it and walked into the middle of a babbling brook. Now, all he needed was something to carry it in. So, he looked around, but there was nothing to use as a receptacle, nothing to carry the water back to Mumbye. Then he felt something under-foot. It was a large stone, in the middle of which there was a hollow that had been etched out by the constant running of water, over thousands of years. He prized it free; it was weighty, but not too heavy to lift. He filled it with the nectar of life and began to climb up to the plateau, and young Mumbye.

Suddenly, though, he heard a squawk. He looked up, and saw vultures circling high above. Instinctively, Borrack knew it was the first sign of impending death.

Without spilling a drop, he rushed to the top of the plateau still carrying the rugged bowl full of water. His young friend, Mumbye, was still lying against the tree where he had left him, with his eyes partly open, but far off in his dream reality.

Borrack rushed to the Mumbye's side, and wet the boy's lips with some water, to which he responded. Borrack raised the rugged stone bowl to Mumbye's lips and tilted the receptacle. He poured it into the boy's mouth, though some of it went cascading down his chin on to his skeletal chest.

Just then, however, Borrack heard a noise from behind! He spun around, and there, in front of him, thirty yards away, stood an adult lion. The creature roared, and, as he did so, saliva oozed from his gapping jaw. The lion moved towards the two of them, slowly at first, and then gathering speed. Borrack threw the rugged stone bowl at the creature, in a vain attempt to scare it off. The lion's speed was picking up, and Borrack sensed impending doom; he closed his eyes and concentrated on the Labyrinth of Golden Dreams! As he did so, his body expanded in all directions, and Borrack, now, once more an eagle, opened his eyes to see the lion bearing down on him and the boy!

Without a moment's hesitation, he flapped his huge wings to give himself lift, and as the predator came within reach, Borrack slashed the creature with his talons, smashing him to the ground. The large creature gave a loud roar in shock and pain, and crawled off in defeat, licking his wounds.

With that, the eagle turned to look at the child; he had been blissfully unaware of the confrontation. Of course, it was now abundantly clear to Borrack that this was not a safe place to stay after all; more importantly, Mumbye was hanging on by a thread and time was now of the essence.

At this point, Borrack now doubted that he would ever have time to fulfil the child's wish, but, whatever the outcome, he needed to take the child to safety, and that had to be Poutia.

The eagle would fly non-stop to the island in the Indian Ocean; he had formulated his new strategy. He would carry young Mumbye in his talons, since the child was, by now, too weak to cling on to the bird's back. The midday sun would be unforgiving, but he would cast shade on the boy by holding him so. So, with nothing to lose, he set off.

On the third day, when the sweltering sun was at its peak, the eagle saw the east coast of Africa and the Indian Ocean. Borrack followed the coastline southward; he was still monitoring the child's life signs, which were faint, but no worse than when he left the plateau.

For some time now, the eagle had felt a strange sensation, one which was hard to explain. It felt as if he was going home, exactly like the feelings he would get when he was visiting the wise, old man of the north, his adopted father, Zachary. The strangest thing of all, however, was that this sensation was guiding him to Poutia. After two hours of following the coast, he unexpectedly turned east across the open ocean; there was no logical reasoning, no planning! Just a desire to turn to the east; it was totally inexplicable. It was like an inexplicable force were pulling him in that direction.

Borrack looked down at the sea, which was relatively calm. He watched as huge container ships passed by underneath him, taking their precious cargoes off to far off ports for future consumption. The eagle had been flying for three days and nights without stopping, and he felt tired and hungry, but he never once dropped his resolve. The day was drawing to its close, as the regal sun disappeared below the horizon. The moon made its appearance. It was full and it brimmed with confidence, illuminating the ocean with its rays of sapphirine light. The ocean responded with pleasure, reflecting the shards of light back on the tips of its waves, giving the impression of a myriad of floating diamonds.

In the distance, Borrack could see the outline of Poutia, with its black granite walls springing from the ocean like an impenetrable fortress! And as the moon poured its light upon its structure, it glinted alluringly. Yet, its appearance was deceptive – the island looked like an impenetrable fortress, ready to do battle in its defence, but was it like a chameleon? Its outward appearance so much different from its reality? For this was the home of good people, strong, kind and identical in their vision.

It was very late by the time the eagle flew over the plateau that housed this community. But to his astonishment, it was bristling with people carrying torches! For the good people of that community waved and shouted with excitement at the arrival of the mighty Borrack! One of their lost sons! The eagle, although he was surprised by their welcome, felt he was coming home!

CHAPTER 3

Poutia

I t is hard to imagine a place without time, but time is, like all measurements, an abstract development of humanity. There are no other creatures on this planet that monitor and record age, speed, height, distance and time, and yet humanity could not function without them. Indeed, its survival and success are a direct result of these phenomenon. In fact, there is a place, a place where, perhaps, the first ever measurements were taken, the measurements of lives.

This place sits on the equator in the deepest part of the Indian Ocean. Composed of vast, extinct, under-water volcanoes. The top protrudes out of the ocean, leaving a small, but beautiful, tropical island, which, to all but a few, is uncharted and uninhabited.

But deep in its belly exists a huge cavern, bigger than the biggest city. This place is the Archive of Humanity and is frequented by the Bookkeeper of Time, the Accountant of Lives and his minions of eighty-six thousand, four hundred and two assistants. They have, between them, registered and recorded the births and deaths of every citizen on this planet since the emergence of conscious thought.

*   *   *   *   *

Borrack circled the plateau; he was overcome by the welcome that the good people of Poutia had laid on for him, just a little embarrassed by the fuss. But to the eagle, the only thing at the forefront of his mind was young Mumbye's well-being! His life was hanging by a thread! The eagle gently came close to the land with the boy tucked up under his chest. He spread his huge wings to decelerate, and with the precision of a great engineer, he opened his talons and lowered the boy to the ground tenderly, as a new mother would lay her new baby in a crib. Then, without causing a speck of dust to move, he flapped his huge wings and soared high into the sky, circled, and then landed in front of the waiting crowd. As he did so, the good people of Poutia crowded around him. Borrack looked around; he could see no sign of the boy; he became agitated and addressed the crowd.

"Where is the boy? Where is Mumbye?" he enquired urgently.

The good people of Poutia looked at each other in confusion.

Again the eagle asked, though more earnestly and angrily, "Where is the boy?"

Then a voice from deep within the crowd piped up.

"He is as well as he can be."

As she spoke, the good citizens of that community parted, creating an avenue of people. She walked down the line of citizens, so she could introduce herself to Borrack. For this lady was the Matriarch. She was small in stature, a white scarf caressed her head, she wore a pair of half-rimmed glasses; and, as she spoke, she looked over her glasses like a schoolteacher. Yet, in the hearts of the community, she was their leader, one without portfolio, a leader whose claim to that position was one of respect and admiration. She was one of those people who wished for neither notoriety nor fame, whose natural talents burst forth with sensitivity. The Matriarch did not need to dictate to her people, for she was an Empathic, she could read the will of her people and act in accordance.

As she reached Borrack her eyes met his and within that one glimpse, she had read the eagle's innermost thoughts.

"Welcome Borrack! Welcome to the home of your mother, and, therefore, yours, by birth right," she said.

Borrack, under normal circumstances, would have been excited and surprised by the revelation; but his concern for the boy was paramount in his mind. He began to inquire about Mumbye, but the Matriarch answered the question before it could be asked.

"You know, as well as I, his life is in grave peril, ; but, like me, he is an Empathic. I have travelled deep into his thoughts, and, I can reveal, his faith and hope in you is what sustains him."

"But I have promised him that I will take him to the land where elephants live forever!" Borrack replied.

She smiled sympathetically at the eagle and said, "I know you never break a promise, Borrack, but some promises can never be fulfilled."

The eagle's head dropped, he felt guilty and, though not surprised to hear that the land was merely one of legend, he was nonetheless crestfallen.

"And after we have come so far?" he said.

The Matriarch turned and addressed her people.

"I feel our guest needs his solitude."

And, with that, the good people of Poutia disappeared into the night.

She turned back to face Borrack, "There may be a chance; it's only a remote possibility, but you may be able to fulfil your promise to the boy."

He lifted his head and peered deep into the eyes of this wise, caring lady, with a perplexed look.

"How?" he questioned veraciously.

She smiled, "I will tell you in the morning, for tonight, you need to eat and sleep."

He began to protest; her expression became stern.

"You are in no fit state to help Mumbye at present."

"But what about the boy?" he pressed, "Has he enough to eat?"

The Matriarch smiled again, "As you know yourself, to feed the child is a gesture without foundation, for how can you feed the physical being when reality is a dream away? The best we can do is feed the spirit; he has at least two days left – with luck, that will be enough time for you to extend the course of young Mumbye's history."

The Matriarch sensed something deeper in Borrack's mind, way down in the depths of his psyche. She again looked into his eyes.

"Borrack, may I ask you something personal?" she said.

The eagle was taken by surprise, "Yes," he stammered.

"You are troubled by your humanity, is that correct? I sense a desire in you to become that which you are already, and yet there is something that holds you back. Am I right?"

"What do you mean?" Borrack replied defensively.

"If I am reading your innermost thoughts correctly, you want to be human both physically and mentally."

The eagle looked away abashedly ; her comments had touched a nerve. He responded curtly, maintaining a gaze firmly fixed on the ground.

"It is true what you speak. Deep inside, I yearn to become like my peer s, my family, like my adopted father; but I cannot. The Labyrinth of Golden Dreams has decreed that this is who I am, an eagle, a chimera, like all the other poor wretches in their different forms in the Black Mountains."

"You disappoint me, Borrack; I know that you don't believe in destiny," The Matriarch said, "If you believe the Labyrinth of Golden Dreams is controlling your physical form, then you are a fool."

Borrack could see that she was right! Why! Was it not long ago that he had argued with the Ice Blue Wind about the same thing?

"But how can I change the decree that the Labyrinth of Golden Dreams has laid out?" the eagle sincerely enquired.

The lady looked deep into Borrack's mind, "You have already changed on a number of occasions, and, if I am not mistaken, just recently, with Mumbye."

"Yes," the eagle replied, "But the Labyrinth of Golden Dreams conceded that I could be a man when the urgency of the situation called for it," he said doubtfully.

"Borrack," the Matriarch boomed, "It *conceded* you? You are allowing a heartless, immoral, unscrupulous lump of rock to control your life and your very bodily form! The Labyrinth of Golden Dreams has no interest in you; it lives in its own world. It feels nothing and senses even less. It is oblivious to pain, love, compassion and hate. Unaware of right or wrong! Its only desire is self-preservation and the learnt emotion of adoration. Do you think it is worried about you? Its only hold on you is your own mind."

The eagle knew she was right.

"If you want, Borrack, I can try to help you! But you must decide!"

The bird was in a dilemma; there was an over-whelming desire to be human, yet, in equal measure, a fear of what that meant. Maybe it was a fear that would make him more disappointed in humanity than he was already. He could no longer run away from his demons.

"Yes," he replied timorously, "Yes, I need to be true to myself."

The Matriarch smiled with concern, for she sensed the eagle's anxiety.

"Lower your head," she commanded ; Borrack did as he was bidden. She laid both her hands on the bird's head, and immediately Borrack felt the power of her magic in his mind.

"Now, concentrate on something other than the Labyrinth of Golden Dreams," she instructed.

The first thing that flashed into his mind was his father, Zachary. His concentration was deep and thoughtful; he felt the power from the Matriarch's hands. They sent a pulsating heat throughout his body, and within seconds, his body went into a spasm. His mind went black, then, out of nowhere, he was looking down from above. He could see all the children he had helped and would help, past, present and future. He could see his parents. He wanted to speak, to reach out and touch them, but he felt there was the memory of a boy he needed to help. As he stretched out to wave, he noticed his hand was human. And with that, he was back in the present, reeling from the experience with the Matriarch.

He became aware of his form. He looked at his hands, now real – he had changed from Borrack the mighty eagle to Borrack the man. The lady removed her hands and Borrack the man stood tall. She smiled at him and said, "Now, I can see the likeness of your mother. Come! Come with me; let us share food, and then you must sleep, for tomorrow, Mumbye's life is in your hands."

Borrack followed that petite but powerful lady, and they broke food together. Then, later, he slept in a bed with linen sheets, which he had never done before.

The sunrays pierced through the un-curtained window and, as the minutes went past, climbed their way across the floor, and up and over the bed, and onwards; until they reached the sleeping man's face. The soft warmth made him squint as he opened his eyes. At first, he was confused; this experience was so new to him. He could never remember a time when he had felt so relaxed that all his cares had evaporated! It was then he thought of Mumbye. He had made a promise to the child. He jumped out of bed and dressed in his suit of golden-brown feathers. He rushed through the bedroom door to the main living area; there, the Matriarch was preparing some breakfast for them.

"How is Mumbye?" he asked skittishly.

The lady turned to face him, "He is no worse and no better! He is holding his own," she replied.

Borrack felt a little foolish, as if he had over-reacted.

The Matriarch nodded at the chair, "Please, sit, your meal is ready."

He did as he was commanded. She sat opposite him, and they ate their meal in silence.

After a while, Borrack looked up at the Matriarch, to ask a question. The Empathic answered before a sound could be made.

"Yes! You did hear me clearly yesterday; this was the home of your mother! In fact, her twin sister is still with us."

Borrack began to babble with excitement.

"Can I see her? Does she know who I am?" but before he could finish, the Matriarch waved her hands.

"Yes! To answer both your questions, and, while I can understand your excitement, at the immediate moment you have a more pressing problem to solve: Mumbye, correct?"

Reality quickly dawned on Borrack. He drew in breath quickly, and uttered, "Yes, you're absolutely right."

"When the issue is settled, you can indulge in your family reunion," she said firmly, to which Borrack nodded.

"I believe you said yesterday, there might be an answer to his plight," he said seriously.

"Well, there is a chance. You may be able to extend his life a little, perhaps enough time to get to the Meadow of Tranquillity, the land where elephants live forever."

"Is there no way we can give him his full life back?" though, deep down, he knew the answer… But he had to ask the question.

The Matriarch looked deep into Borrack's yellow eyes and, with her empathic powers, she could see he already knew the answer! 'However, the question clearly comes from the heart' she thought. She answered compassionately.

"You know we can do nothing; even were the child here in his physical reality, and not in his alternative dream reality, we could do nothing; his body is too far down that road, towards death. This perhaps is one case where destiny, fate, call it what you will, must run its course."

Borrack nodded sagely, though, with difficulty, adding, "So what can we do?"

"There is a place, not far from here. A small uncharted island, laying on the equator. It looks like nothing much more than a small, tropical paradise. But, beneath its wafer-thin crust lies a huge cavern, and, deep in the belly of that cavern, resides the Accountant of Lives. He has recorded the births and deaths of mankind for all human history. He is a bureaucrat, and nobody can die without him first recording it. But, like all bureaucrats, he wallows in detail; maybe you can persuade him to give Mumbye a little more time."

Borrack smiled at that wise lady opposite him.

"Clearly, I have nothing to lose! Or should I say, Mumbye has everything to gain. But I would like to see the boy before I go."

The Matriarch nodded.

"I think that's a good idea," she said. "In fact, he's with your aunt, your mother's twin. An opportune moment for your first introduction."

With that, the two of them made their way to the carer's home. As the Matriarch knocked on the door and entered the abode, she called his aunt's name.

"Simmi!"

There was a muffled response. They followed the sound and there they found her sitting assiduously next to young Mumbye. Simmi started to wipe the boy's brow with a cool, damp flannel, in a way that only a carer could. She looked up as both her visitors approached, her eye s bright blue! Focused on Borrack, she smiled in the realization that this man was her nephew, her family, her blood… her Borrack.

Borrack, for his part, regarded this lady, whose existence had been unbeknownst to him, until merely twelve hours previously ! She got up to greet him with an embrace; she was slight, demure and moved with such elegance. She was how he had always imagined his mother! He responded to her embrace, feeling that he was back in the heart of his family.

The Matriarch, with the upmost propriety, coughed and said, "The boy is stable at the moment, but his life is in greater jeopardy with each passing moment; time is of the essence."

Borrack released himself from his aunt's embrace, and heaved a sigh, "Yes, there will be time enough for reunion when I get back."

He walked over to the child, where he was laying, his face ashen grey, his eyes bulging under the closed lids, his body emaciated and his breathing shallow, though regular. He wiped young Mumbye's brow, with his large hand.

"I will do my best to fulfil my promise to you, young man," he mumbled under his breath. Then he raised his head to face the Matriarch and his aunt, "Well, I best be on my way," he exclaimed, and then Borrack, addressing the Matriarch as he walked out the door of the building, asked, "In which direction is the island?"

She pointed in a south-westerly direction, adding, "Maybe five or six hours by boat, it's the only island around for many miles; it shouldn't be too difficult to find," she replied.

Borrack looked in the direction he was shown.

"I guess it will take me about the same amount of time? You successfully showed me how to metamorphose into a man. I hope I can reverse the procedure."

The Matriarch smiled at him. Borrack closed his eyes and concentrated on Zachary, his adopted father, the wise, old man of the north. His body expanded in all directions; the Matriarch and his aunt watched as Borrack changed from man to eagle – it was an amazing sight, and one that would live on in their memories for the rest of their lives. The eagle, as he was now, smiled at them, turned and flapped his huge wings, creating a plume of dust and debris. They shielded themselves from the swirling dust, and by the time it had settled, Borrack had gone. They both looked south-westerly, and high in the sky they watched as the mighty Borrack disappeared into the ether.

CHAPTER 4
Time Waits for No Man

Deep in one of the many jungles of Mother Africa, a tribe of hunter-gatherers exists. Their lives, under normal conditions, were not easy; but, to their detriment they had been blighted by two enigmas: one was man-made, and the other was the embodiment of evil, a demon. One which, by sight, they judged to be the essence of iniquity. But looks can be so deceptive.

* * * * *

The eagle flew on to his destination. He let his powerful wings do the work, while his mind recounted the last nine hours. It was a revelation to him; he had never lived as a human before; not for that amount of time. But this experience was something else; he had never tasted cooked food – it was so much better than carrion! And then there were the sensations of walking, smiling, and that feeling of waking in a bed with soft linen sheets, as the sun's rays kissed his cheeks. From sitting at a table and talking to the Matriarch, to the embrace of his aunt – these feelings were so different, so corporeal! It had been like taking a drug of happiness; and yet, he felt as if he was betraying all that he stood for. He had, on many occasions, despaired of humanity – its weaknesses, its greed, and its self-obsession. But he had found a liking, a desire to be human… he felt so confused.

All the time in which Borrack was mulling over his thoughts, he had been scanning the ocean surface and horizon for the small tropical island that the Matriarch had told him about when at last it came into sight! He circled and saw how its coastline was of a white sand so fine and interspersed with palm trees. Towards the middle of the island stood the pinnacle of that extinct volcano. It was clad in the most beautiful flora, with colours rich and vibrant! But how very different it was beneath that veneer of the earth's crust, as Borrack was to soon find out.

The eagle circled several times, looking for the portal into that deep vault, which lay beneath that small but beautiful island. His eagle eye scanned every crevice, rift, fissure, and hole! Then, he saw something… an entrance, covered by gorse bushes, at the base of an ancient olive tree.

Borrack hovered above the spot; his wings moved up and down in short sharp movements without creating a sound, as if he was stalking his prey. He was certain that this was the portal to the huge vault that held the archives of humanity, and, with it, the person he had come to see: The Bookkeeper of Time, the Accountant of Lives.

He descended carefully and silently. When he was down, Borrack scrutinized the surrounding area; it was quiet, the only noise being that of the ocean. A perpetual, rhythmic sound, lapping up against the beach, pulling back that fine sand, almost white in colour, and returning again for more; as if its mission was to wash that very sand away, and regain that small desert island, returning it to its own watery empire.

The eagle closed his eyes and concentrated on Zachary his adopted father. He felt his body change, and within seconds, his body went into a spasm. He had changed into Borrack the man. He climbed up towards the likely entrance at the base of that ancient olive tree. The gorse was thick and out of control; it was clear to him that no one had used that entrance in many years. He spotted a large stick, he picked it up and set about clearing that which barred his way.

It was hard work, but at last, the heavy gorse yielded to his will. He made his way into the cave entrance; his yellow eyes took time to adjust to the gloom. In front of him lay a passage descending downward, deep into the belly of the extinct volcano. Borrack followed the path; he could only sense the incline of the ground beneath his feet as he passed over it. He had been following the passage for some time then he heard a noise… He stood still in his tracks! There, in front of him, maybe no more than a few yards away, he saw two white lights! As he strained his eyes, he could see the lights were not lights at all, but were, in fact, eyes set in a small round face! They were attached to a body equally as small. A midget! A human midget! The creature spoke. His voice was like his stature – small and squeaky.

"Welcome to the Archive of Humanity. How may we help you?"

Borrack was lost for words for a minute, but then he composed himself and replied.

"I wish to be taken to the Accountant of Lives."

The creature replied curtly, "Follow me, then!" With which, he turned and marched down the passage, Borrack following.

The creature moved swiftly, but Borrack kept pace.

It was another twenty minutes before the passage opened out into a huge cavern, vast in its size. It was dark and gloomy, damp, cold and it smelt musty. On all sides, as far as the eye could see, there were thousands of levels of wooden scaffolds, with a network of ladders connecting them up like a giant spider's web. On each level of scaffolding, stood rows and rows of shelves, sometimes five storeys high, and all filled with parchment files.

At the end of every shelving unit hung an oil lamp, throwing out a pitiful amount of light. Borrack followed the midget. The path was still descending and the lower they went, the more wooden scaffolding, ladders and shelving with parchment files he saw. Everywhere, little people like his guide, ran around in a frenzy of activity. He looked down at the path. It was so worn, that, at either edge, stood a plinth of solid rock, a foot high. The whole structure was a testimony to the diligence and ingenuity of the little people that ran around like a colony of ants. He followed the creature for another hour, until they reached a heavy wooden door.

The midget rapped on it several times until a muffled voice replied: "Come in!"

The midget opened the door; it creaked on its rusty hinges. A man sat at a large desk, his head down, busy writing.

"Yes, five-hundred and six?" he said abruptly, not lifting his head from his work. The midget replied in his squeaky voice.

"There is a gentleman to see you, sir."

"Someone to see me?" the man said looking up from his work.

Borrack passed through the door, the man at the desk stood up. He was tall with a long white beard and a pair of thin-framed glasses perched on the end of his nose. Borrack studied the figure that stood in front of him. His face was wrinkled, almost white; his eyes were pale blue, bloodshot and red-rimmed. He was old by anybody's' standards. His hair was grey and wiry, and his hands were bony and gnarled. The man behind the desk thrust his bony, gnarled hand out as a gesture of welcome.

"Hello!" he said. "I am the Accountant of Lives. What can I do for you? It's such a pleasure! We seldom get any visitors!" he babbled excitedly.

Borrack grabbed the hand and shook it.

"Well, sir, I have come here on a mission of mercy, and wondered if you could help," Borrack said earnestly.

"Please take a seat," the Accountant of Lives said, then, addressing the midget, he said, "You can go now, five-hundred and six."

The midget left, closing the door after him. The Accountant of Lives looked curiously at his visitor.

"I have, in my charge," Borrack began, "A child who is near to death; in fact, I feel his demise is imminent, and reluctantly I made him a promise; a promise that I will not be able to fulfil unless I can gain some more time for him. I am not asking for a great deal of time to extend his life! Maybe a week or so. I was wondering whether it would be possible for you, perhaps, to slow down his paperwork; perhaps put him further down the list, the list that dispatches the being of man from this world."

The Accountant of Lives looked gravely at his visitor.

"Well, this is most irregular," he said sternly. "No, no! Such a situation could throw the whole system into chaos! No! No, it's not possible."

Borrack looked at him. His disappointment was self-evident.

"Is there no way I can make you change your mind?" Borrack replied.

"No, it just can't be done."

"I have come so far as well! Please, at least think about it," Borrack urged, "The child's name is Mumbye, and he comes from a refugee camp called 'Hell', in Africa."

The Accountant of Lives made no comment, but, as with all bureaucrats, he could not help but finger through his ledgers looking for the child's name. It was second nature to check that his accounts were up to date. There was no sympathy for the child's plight! He was just a number, a statistic. But Borrack had subtly introduced Mumbye's name into the bureaucrat's mind, so that he would not forget him.

Borrack scanned the room; on the wall above, the old man had hung thirty portraits. Borrack gave a polite cough to gain the attention of the bureaucrat; he looked up from his ledgers.

"Who are these fine characters?" Borrack said pointing to the portraits.

The Accountant of Lives turned his head.

"Ah! Yes, all these are erstwhile Accountants of Lives. From the very first to my immediate predecessor."

"Only two hundred bookkeepers, to cover such a prodigious period of time? You all must live to a venerable age."

The bureaucrat turned back to face his visitor.

"In most cases, up to a thousand years! I, myself, am nearly seven hundred years old."

Borrack smiled with surprise.

"Since I have come all this way, perhaps you could show me around; it is clearly a most interesting place," Borrack said, playing for time, so that he might be able to persuade the bureaucrat to change his mind.

The Accountant of Lives smiled.

"Why not? Come! Come, follow me!" he said excitedly.

Borrack followed.

The old man was tall, but his body stooped, which made him look a lot shorter than he was. He moved quite fast and was soon climbing the first ladder, to the first scaffold. Borrack followed, but always two steps behind the old man.

"Ah! This is perhaps the oldest part of the archive; this was administered by the very first bookkeeper, to which we owe such a debt of gratitude. To such a fine man, a man of wisdom, a man so well-versed in the art of paperwork. And, it's to his laws of administration that we have always adhered. In each of these parchments, exist the birthplace, origins and the death of every human that has lived, since the emergence conscious thought. Well… that is not strictly true; perhaps I should rephrase that, nearly every human."

"What do you mean 'nearly'?" Borrack said.

The Accountant of Lives stopped and turned to face his visitor.

"Well, you must accept this is a huge undertaking. For there are some people that have had their births recorded, but not their deaths. In most accounting systems there are always anomalies! Strangely enough, when we have investigated this abnormality, the majority seem to be located in one particular region: The Black Mountains of northern Europe. In fact, just recently, a man who went missing, over a thousand years ago, has just turned up in England."

Borrack now saw a way that he would be able to help the Accountant of Lives, and, at the same time, gain help for Mumbye.

"What was his name?" Borrack replied, distracted by the army of midgets dashing around in a frenzy of activity.

The Accountant of Lives looked inquiringly at Borrack.

"A man called Melvin…"

"I may be able to shed some light on this conundrum," Borrack replied.

The Accountant of Lives was surprised, but delighted, and re-joined, "If you know anything that might resolve this problem, it would be a marvellous breakthrough to this quandary. It has haunted us for aeons. In fact, we have dedicated a special section just for that area! Would you like to see it?"

"Of course!" Borrack replied, "Lead the way!"

The old man moved ahead, climbing many ladders and scaffolds that led to the designated section, all of the time, meanwhile, the army of midgets moved at lightning speed, resolving their tasks with the utmost competency. As the Accountant of Lives led the way, he explained to his visitor about each section of the archive, and how it showed such a rich history of humanity's developments. The migration of millions of people, their achievements, their inventiveness and their successes. But it also demonstrated something else, something more menacing; that is, their bloodshed, their avarice, and their hate of their fellow man. They had climbed thirty stories, when the old man stopped in his tracks.

"This is a most interesting epoch," he said, "The twentieth century! You see these racks of shelves."

Borrack followed the old man's hand gesture, and, as far as Borrack could see, there were rack after rack full of parchment files.

These are the names of all those that died, in that so called war to end all wars. Germans, British, Americans, Russians, Turkish and so many more. A tragedy overseen by supercilious fools! And, was it a war to end all wars? No. If you look up, you will see another scaffold, and on that lays the rack full of parchment files from the following world war. Millions of lives lost in that one, both combatant and civilian."

Borrack looked into the eyes of the Accountant of Lives, and he could see he was moved.

The old man dabbed his eyes.

"That war was, somehow, worse! As if it could not be, for that was a war of hate, hate of anyone who was different. Above that rack, there are even more parchment files of death, through the barbarity of war! They superseded that war of hate. I sometimes despair at humanity, and yet, I know, that there are many, many, good people out there."

At that moment, Borrack had seen something in the old man, which he had not expected from a bureaucrat: compassion.

"Of course, you are absolutely right," Borrack said.

The Accountant of Lives smiled at his visitor, and Borrack saw in him his own philosophy, which created a bond between them.

"Come! It's not much further," the old man said.

They walked across half a dozen scaffolds and climbed another five ladders. As they reached their goal, Borrack could not help but ask a question that had been niggling at him for some time.

"These midgets that assist you – who are they?"

The old man laughed, "Oh! Those chaps?" pointing to one of the midgets busy sorting out some of the parchment files.

"They are the 2nd assistants. Originally, they were the local inhabitants of the island, and when the first Accountant of Lives started this project, he employed them. Since then, generation after generation has worked tirelessly to accomplish this undertaking, under our guidance, to achieve what you see today! In fact, there are eighty-six thousand four hundred and two assistants, coincidentally, the same number as there are seconds in a day. And, it has to be said, that without their help we could not have achieved this archive."

Borrack could see the affection the Accountant of Lives had for these small but enthusiastic people.

"Anyway," the old man said, "This is the section I was talking about. All these parchment files are the births of people unaccounted for. It goes back thousands of years."

"Yes," Borrack said. "And they are all still alive, but not one of them is human!"

The old man shot him a look, "I'm sorry, what did you say?!" he said with disbelief.

"Simply, they are no longer human now."

"And how do you know this?" the old man challenged.

"Because I was born in that village that nestled at the entrance of that evil place."

"What was your name again? Oh, 'Borrack'! Yes, that's right," he said bumbling. "Let me check your birth records."

As he searched through the parchment files, he came upon a name that matched his visitor.

"Ah, here it is! No, that can't be right; he's no longer with us. He had a wife called Morraif."

"Did they have a child?" Borrack prompted.

"Yes, you are right, it appears they did – but he died along with his mother in childbirth, and it looks like it wasn't long after his father's death."

Borrack looked at him askance. "The child did not die… Things are not always what they seem. My birth is not registered because on my mother's deathbed, and at my birth, I was only human in spirit. For I am a chimera; neither beast nor human; but simultaneously both."

The old man looked at his visitor with bewilderment; he sat on the scaffold waiting for an explanation. Borrack began his story; he told his audience of one about the Labyrinth of Golden Dreams, its history, its philosophy and its riches. He told how the small village that nestled at the bottom of the entrance to the Black Mountains had found that evil place, and how the people had used its powers to improve their lives. He continued by telling how they had boasted about its new-found wealth, how the word had spread from tribe to tribe, from nation to nation and from empire to empire, until an army of greedy people had fallen upon the Labyrinth to steal its riches. He explained how the Labyrinth had defended itself by turning those would-be speculators into all manner of beasts to inhabit those Black Mountains for eternity.

The Accountant was listening attentively, Borrack continued. He told of how the Labyrinth had summoned the elders of that village of his ancestors and had ordered the chief's daughter to be sacrificed in order to become the Ice Blue Wind, condemned to protect the Labyrinth from those who would defile its beauty.

He recounted how that beloved, beautiful daughter of the chief elder, fulfilled her duty, and protected that evil place, the Labyrinth, and cosseted her tribe. And, as she watched her family dwindle in numbers through the passage of time, her beauty and sweetness of soul became bitter. And, as the last of her relatives died out, her bitterness became angrier and her soul became ugly. She punished her tribe with vengeance for generations; her vindictive, vengeful soul knew no bounds, until at last her tribe could take no more and decided to leave their ancestral home.

Borrack paused. He looked at the old man; his yellow eyes were both angry and sad.

He then related the tale of his father and pregnant mother, who made a pilgrimage to the Labyrinth to plead for the removal of the Ice Blue Wind, and that when the couple returned in triumph to that village the good people exulted at the news that a new messiah would come and rid them of their wretchedness. And when they learnt that that very messiah was within the belly of Borrack's mother, the village rejoiced in hope!

Yet, it came, that fateful day, one when the world came crashing down on so many people; a day when a fatal injury was handed out to those whose only concern had been the well-being of all.

Borrack dropped his head and paused for some time, with tears staining his cheeks. The Accountant of Lives could see his visitor's distress, but he was caught up in the story, and impatiently he pressed for a conclusion.

"So, what happened?" he urged.

Borrack looked up from his emotional chaos.

"The villagers turned on my father and killed him. Then, they ran away and deserted the village, leaving my mother in postnatal distress. In her arms she did not carry a baby, but a fledgling eagle."

Again, Borrack looked pensive.,

"That fledgling eagle was me. If it were not for my adopted father, I certainly would have perished along with my mother. It was only because my mother begged my adopted father to take me and bring me up as his own, which he did; I owe him so much."

The Accountant of Lives looked at this man in front of him, this man with such an incredulous story; and yet, he knew his tale was true – he could see it in his sincerity.

Borrack looked up and said, "Ever since my earliest recollection, the only thing I have ever wanted to do, was to relieve the pain of those who will one day inherit this beautiful planet. That is my goal! Unfortunately, young Mumbye will never see that day. The best I can do for that child is to fulfil his wish; that is why I have come to seek you out, for your help. But if it's not forthcoming, then I had better go and comfort the child as best I can."

The old man studied Borrack's face. He could see his honesty, his concern.

"Would you mind if I walk with you to that world beyond these cavern walls?"

"Of course not!" Borrack said.

The two of them made their way down the scaffold s and ladders to the stone path worn by the passage of time and headed to the portal that would take them from this vast, gloomy bureaucratic world to Mother Nature's mansion. The old man, who had listened to Borrack's tale with interest, had a question of his own, concerning only a minor detail – yet one that was essential to understand, for one whose life is ruled by such elements.

"You mentioned a man called Melvin; where does he fit in to this conundrum, and why did he appear a thousand years later?"

Borrack turned and looked at the old man, "Ah! Yes, Melvin."

With that, Borrack relayed the story, as they walked to the portal, of his journey with the two children, Gemma and Jay, and how he did battle with the Ice Blue Wind to reach the Labyrinth of Golden Dreams. He elaborated on how he had promised the Labyrinth that he would defeat the Ice Blue Wind, as was his destiny, and, in return for accepting that undertaking, he had extracted from the Labyrinth of Golden Dreams several concessions., One of these being Melvin's freedom from his purgatory, and to live what was left of his life, as was his birth right.

As they reached the portal, the light from the early morning sun poured through. Borrack had been awake for over twenty-four hours, and yet he did not feel tired. The old man focused on the entrance and spoke.

"This is the first time I have left the Archive since arriving some – ah! Let's see – ah! Yes! Nearly six hundred and fifty years ago, plus three months and twenty minutes, plus or minus a few seconds."

Borrack turned his head in astonishment, "How long?"

"Six hundred and fifty years, three months and twenty minutes," the old man repeated.

"Why?" Borrack replied.

The old man shrugged his shoulders, as they passed through the portal. The Accountant of Lives stopped and panned the vista and was dumbstruck for a few seconds.

"Do you know? I had forgotten how beautiful it is!"

"Yes," Borrack replied. "It is beautiful; this is some of Mother Nature's best work."

They walked until they reached the fine, white sand that circumnavigated the island where they both stood for a while embracing the view that surrounded them.

It was quiet; the only noise was that of the ocean, in an almost perpetual rhythmic sound; The old man broke their unspoken vow of silence without turning his head from the vista he was enjoying.

"Borrack, your arrival here today has been a great help. No! It has been much more than that. It has unravelled a mystery that has baffled myself and my predecessor for aeons."

He turned his hoary head to face his visitor, "To that end, I am going to go back and try to rearrange young Mumbye's paperwork. I don't know if it will help, so I make no promises, but I will do my best. It is possible that it might give him a few more days; so I will try."

Borrack faced the old man, "Thank you," he replied, and held out his hand in friendship.

The Accountant of Lives grabbed it, and in that handshake a bond of friendship was sealed.

"Well, I best go and uphold my promise to the young boy."

They smiled at each other, and then Borrack ran down that beach of fine, white sand, and, as he did, he thought of Zachary, his adopted father, the wise old man of the north. The Accountant of Lives watched in amazement, because Borrack was changing from man to eagle. It was a sight to behold.

The old man's eyes were glued to the spectacle in front of him, as the head of the man became that of an eagle, as the body changed from that of the man to eagle, with its muscle and sinew, as the legs and feet turned from the creature of the ground to the king of the skies. And, most spectacular of all, was the transformation of those feeble appendages of man, his arms, to those mighty wings that powered the most majestic of Mother Nature's creatures. He watched as Borrack the eagle, taller than the tallest of men, soared high into the sky.

Borrack circled, and swooped down over his new-found friend. The old man responded by waving with enthusiasm, as the eagle flew back to Poutia.

The Accountant of Lives watched with envy in his heart as Borrack disappeared over the horizon.

Judgment Without Knowledge
is Man's Biggest Folly
Part One: Return to Poutia

The Mountain of Fire stood impervious to the world. It stood at the entrance to the Lake of Serenity and beyond that lay the Meadow of Tranquillity. The Mountain of Fire represented the pinnacle of Mother Nature's anger!

Like the Labyrinth of Golden Dreams, it was unable and unwilling to comprehend emotions. It was supremely indifferent to love, hate, right or wrong. It experienced no pain; simply being.

However, in stark contrast to the Labyrinth, there was no percipience or perspicacity. There was no need for self-preservation and no acquired predilection for being adored. For Mother Nature had cast her hand over this land and created this magnificent Mountain of Fire, to be the head stone of her most beloved creature: the elephant.

* * * * *

Borrack had not slept for over twenty-four hours, but his strength had not diminished; in fact, he felt elated and buoyant, because he instinctively knew that he would now be able to fulfil his promise to young Mumbye. Yet, there was another reason for his elation, a reason based on something that had eluded him his whole life. He had found his birth right, his humanity. It was true he had so much to learn! But that would come with the passage of time.

The glorious sun was once again on its ascending path. The eagle squinted as he watched it wax towards resplendence. The sky was blue; not a cloud, not even a wisp of wind, as he looked down at the ocean, which was shrouded in a heavy mist that swirled and boiled on top of the mighty sea.

Borrack felt the upward pressures of a thermal current under his huge wings; he relaxed their movement and glided up on that gift of Mother Nature. It was a far cry from that grey, damp, dingy cavern which housed the Archives of Humanity; this was freedom.

It carried him high as he glided through its magical path. There was no other creature to share his world in that place, at that moment, and he felt so good, like the king of the skies. His mind reverted to his previous thoughts; the Matriarch had released from his inward-looking prison. She had shown him that the Labyrinth had no control over him, she had shown that he, Borrack, was the master of his own destiny. He no longer felt bitterness, contempt and scorn towards that malignant lump of rock; on the contrary, he felt nothing, but pity tinged with indifference for it. He no longer felt ashamed of history and he had seen something else, that he, Borrack the man had been bestowed with a great gift! The gift of flight through Borrack the eagle; it was a revelation.

He followed the path of the thermal, moving nearer and nearer to Poutia, until at last the thermal dissipated. Then he powered up his huge wings, moving faster and faster to Poutia, until, at last, he could see it. That island built like a fortress; on all sides, huge walls of granite sprang from the sea like black shields ; almost smooth and shimmering in the brilliance of the magnificent sun.

Borrack flew high over the plateau; he scanned the terrain below. He homed in on that small hub of humanity; he saw the good citizens of that community going about their everyday business. To one side he saw children playing, and with them he saw young Mumbye. The boy ran and laughed with his new friends. Borrack was elated at this sight. This was confirmation that his action had been successful; his only regret was that this was only a temporary amnesty and not the restoration of normality for the child. The eagle saw it as the last grains of sand passing through the hourglass. If only it could be for that same hourglass to be turned on its head, to start the whole cycle again!

Borrack flew on until he found a place, quiet and without life, so he could land and become Borrack the man in private. He glided in slowly, spreading his huge wings out to slow his descent. He braced his talons for impact, and he hit the ground without making a sound! He swept back his wings and scrutinized his surroundings. Since he saw no one, he closed his eyes and concentrated on Zachary his adopted father, the old wise man of the north. He felt his body change, and, within seconds, his body went into a spasm, and again he felt that crushing sensation. It was impossible to describe, being neither painful nor pleasurable. !

Very shortly, he had changed from Borrack the mighty eagle to the man. And there he stood, taller than the tallest of men, with his yellow eyes, his shock of white hair, and dressed in his suit of golden-brown feathers. He opened his eyes and stepped back in shock! For in front of him was the Matriarch.

"Well, Borrack, your mission was a success."

"Yes, yes, I suppose it was," he stuttered, "But how did you know?"

Before he could finish what he was saying, the Matriarch replied, "You were back? Surely that is obvious; you know I am an Empathic, and I sense that Mumbye is not far behind me."

As she finished, the boy came into Borrack's view, and the Matriarch turned round to face the oncoming child. The boy ran towards the pair of them and stopped a few yards away. He looked at the Matriarch and then towards Borrack.

"It is you?" he said, "You are Borrack?"

"Yes," the man replied.

The child responded excitedly, without taking a breath.

"So, I wasn't dreaming on that plateau when you helped me and gave me water and that creature attacked us, and you turned back into an eagle."

"Of course it was," and with that the boy ran up to Borrack and held his arms out. Borrack the man picked the child up, and the boy responded by throwing his arms around his neck in a gesture of love.

"Thank you for helping me," he said crushing Borrack's neck with his feeble arms. The Matriarch smiled as she watched the two of them.

"Can we go soon?" young Mumbye said, "Can we go to the Meadow of Tranquillity, the land where elephants live forever?"

Borrack was about to respond when the Matriarch butted in.

"No, young man," she said rebuffing the boy. "Borrack must sleep; he's been awake for twenty-four hours, he needs to rest. Besides, tonight the people of Poutia are holding a banquet, and you two will be the guests of honour."

The three of them made their way back to the village, where young Mumbye joined his new-found friends in play. The Matriarch led Borrack back to her dwelling, and there she prepared them some food, where they ate in silence. Borrack asked about the Meadow of Tranquillity, and the lands where elephants live forever, and if she knew of its location.

She smiled at him.

"All in good time, my friend; first, you must rest." With that she got up from the table and made her way to the door.

"I'll leave you in peace now," she said and closed the door.

As Borrack's head hit the bolster, he closed his eyes and drifted off into the unconscious world. Dreams were something he had never experienced as an eagle, but as a man it would be so different; this would be his first of many; it was a world of confusing imagery and narrative, where all his recent memories merged into a cauldron of anarchy and desolation.

He saw Mumbye, Zachary, the Matriarch, the Accountant of Lives, and the Labyrinth of Golden Dreams, a large black bird – a rook or raven, he did not know which. But none were where they should be! But all of them were tugging at his very being, pulling him in a variety of different ways. He felt as though his body would be split asunder, he screamed with the pain that did not exist, he sweated profusely and shouted at the top of his voice 'Get off me, let me go, leave me alone, go away.' And as the last words bellowed from his lips, he sat bolt upright, and opened his eyes into his conscious existence.

He looked around, confused and disorientated; it took a few seconds to accustom himself to his surroundings. His heart was pounding, and in his mind the black bird remained, haunting him; he could not shake it from his thoughts. Then he heard a gentle tap on the door.

"Borrack are you awake?"

"Yes… Yes," he replied shakily. "I'll be out shortly".

The Matriarch had heard Borrack's scream of distress, but she had realised it was nothing more than a nightmare. Borrack appeared at the door dressed in his suit of golden-brown feathers. She smiled at her guest.

"Well, the good people of Poutia are waiting for your appearance at the banquet."

Borrack followed as the Matriarch led him into the main thoroughfare, and to his surprise he saw the very same thoroughfare brisling with a sea of faces. And as he made his appearance, they all got to their feet and welcomed him with a crescendo of clapping hands. The Matriarch led him to the top table where Mumbye and his aunt were already and seated.

The meal was a lavish affair, with four courses, and as the majestic sun was setting in the west, casting long ribbons of gold and orange light across the street. A group of musicians began to serenade the audience; it was a gentle, heart-warming sound. Borrack turned to his aunt, who was sitting next to him.

"What was my mother like, Simmi?"

"Oh, she was so gentle, so caring and she would have been so proud of you."

"Would she?" Borrack said, "Even though I am a chimera, and only half human."

"Oh, yes! She never judged anyone; she only ever saw the good; that's what made her so unique."

"What about my father?" Borrack probed.

"He was such an honest man, and so handsome and tall with striking green eyes, a man of integrity, a man who believed in what is right. He would have made a wonderful elder."

Borrack dropped his head, "Why did the tribe have to turn on them, Simmi?"

She could see her nephew's vulnerability, so she put her arms around him to comfort him.

"Because, like all of us, they were scared of that which is different, that which we cannot understand. And in their case, hysteria took hold! That primal fear that has haunted humanity since the beginning of time."

She spoke so quietly, yet with such compassion to Borrack.

"How did you learn about my parent s' fate?" Borrack asked.

Simmi looked deep into her nephew's eyes, and replied, "I guess it was from Zachary."

"You know Zachary?" Borrack responded with surprise.

"Oh yes, I have known Zachary for many years! Well, anyway, he must have told you what he found when he entered, into that tribal homeland on that fateful day! Your father on his deathbed being comforted by his best friend."

"Yes" Borrack replied.

"Well, sometime after, his friend sought refuge here! That's when I learnt of the terrible details of those awful events, as your father's friend purged his soul to me with that heavy burden of guilt that he carried around with him. At first I could not believe what he was telling me, but as time went on, I learnt to live with that awful truth."

"What happened to my father's friend? Is he still here?" Borrack said excitedly.

"No, no, he moved off to start a new life; he went to the New World far across the seas to the west. You know, he was deeply traumatised by that whole event, which, I guess, we all would be when we see the caustic side of humanity! Anyway, tell me about Zachary, is he well? I have not seen him in many years now."

Borrack smiled at his aunt, "Yes, he's very well! How did you meet him?"

"He lived here many years ago, long before that fateful day."

Borrack noted his aunt's voice had changed, it had become quieter, more emotional; she was clearly still hurt by those terrible events.

"That day your parents were murdered."

"Why did he leave this place?" Borrack asked.

"Zachary is a loner, a man who does suffer fools easily, and while we have a society that is nearly perfect, there are still personality clashes, and unfortunately, Zachary was on the end of such a relationship. I will elaborate no more."

Borrack understood her body language – it was clear that his aunt was a person who would not spread gossip, and Borrack could respect that, and so he did not press her on the subject. As the sun finally relented to the will of its nemesis, the moon, the good people of Poutia illuminated their tables with artificial lights. This sent the moth s into a frenzy of delight, as the creatures sprung from table to table; circumnavigating the tiny lamps, with their feeble bodies into feverish excitement that could not be satisfied. Simmi, who, for the next few hours, told Borrack about the childhood exploits that she and his mother used to get up to. Meanwhile, Mumbye was being entertained by the Matriarch and the good people of Poutia.

The banquet took on a party atmosphere, the musicians upped the tempo, and couples began to get up and dance. Borrack watched in amusement; it was something he had never witnessed before. The Matriarch smiled at Borrack and, with the forthright confidence that she was known for, she said bluntly to her guest:

"Are you not going to ask me to dance?"

Borrack became flustered. "No! I don't know how," he said.

She got up from the table. "Do not be embarrassed, if you want to be part of humanity, you must do what humanity does."

Borrack reluctantly got to his feet, and followed her lead; at first, he was clumsy, but, as time went on, he improved. While they were dancing

Borrack raised the question about the whereabouts of the Meadow of Tranquillity and the lands where elephants live forever, and if she knew of its location.

The Matriarch smiled. "To be honest, I do not know. But I do know where the answer may be obtained, and it would be better if we talked in a quieter place. Follow me!"

The Matriarch took Borrack away from the festivities, to a quiet secluded place. The moon was once again bristling with confidence as it sent its shards of incandescent light across the landscape. The night was warm, almost humid. The two of them sat down in silence, listening to the sounds of the night, staring at the black horizon. The Matriarch turned her head to face Borrack and spoke.

"This information I give you is only hearsay, thus it may have no foundation; so I make no promises. Deep in one of Mother Africa's jungles lies a valley, and in it exists a creature, a creature beyond imagination. It bears no resemblance to anything else that exists on this planet. From all accounts, those that have seen it describe it as that which they most despise; some say it looks like a snake, some liken it to a dragon, to others a huge spider. The truth is this creature is beyond their imagination, beyond anything that is corporeal on this planet. And because no one can describe it, the best they can do is describe it as their very worst nightmare. But according to that same hearsay, this creature is the font of all knowledge. And with that knowledge, it should be able to tell you if the place you seek for young Mumbye exists or not and if it does, then its location."

"Is it far from here?" Borrack asked.

"I only know that which I have been told and to that end I will do my best to describe its location. The place lies just off the east coast of Mother Africa, to the north of here. If you fly west from here until you reach the mainland coast and follow it north; eventually you will come to a rock that shoots upright out of the ocean. It is brilliant white, and as the sun hits it from any angle, it glows like a beacon."

"At that point, turn west into the interior of Mother Africa, and fly until you come to three peaks; peaks to your left and right, and the third directly in front of you. This is where, according to my information, you will find a tribe of hunter-gatherers. A tribe who has been blighted by two enigmas: one man-made, and the other, the creature beyond imagination; to them it is the epitome of all evil and only they know of its location. And because of the fear they have of this creature, they may not tell you how to find its lair. But you will have to face that problem if it occurs."

Borrack looked at the Matriarch with a perplexed look, ready to ask a question, but the Matriarch replied before the words could leave his lips.

"No! You are right I can't guarantee this information; it is no more than I have been told."

Borrack smiled, "Well, at least it's something to go on. I just hope, for Mumbye's sake, it's enough."

The Matriarch replied with concern, "I hope so too. I feel we should return to the festivities, for the good citizens of Poutia must be missing their guest of honour."

As the night wore on, the party reached its crescendo, and, as with all good parties, to some it lingered on until the small hours of the morning. Mumbye had fallen asleep some time earlier on, on Simmi's lap, and she had carried him off to his bed.

Borrack turned to the Matriarch, "I think it is time I turned in for the night, for tomorrow will be an early start."

"But the good people of Poutia will wish to see you off tomorrow," she replied.

"No," Borrack said graciously, "I feel it would be better for Mumbye, if we forgo any more excitement."

The Matriarch nodded with confirmation, but she also sensed something else. She sensed that Borrack did not want to make an oddity of himself, and she understood his concerns.

"Would you mind if your aunt and I come to see you off?"

Borrack smiled, "Of course not."

"What time will you go and from where?" she asked.

"Just as the sun appears, and from where I landed earlier today," Borrack replied.

"Well you had better get to your bed, for that time is not far away," the Matriarch said laughing.

Borrack's sleep was deep and restful, and yet there was something that had made him uneasy. Deep in the back of his psyche, a dream he could only just recall; he was certain that he saw the same black bird that had haunted him in his fist dream. He shrugged it off.

He dressed in his suit of golden-brown feathers and looked out of the window. The morning sun had not yet made its appearance, so he made his way to his departure point. As he arrived, he was surprised to see the Matriarch, Simmi and Mumbye already there. His aunt was cradling the boy in her arms, trying to keep the morning chill away from his frail body. She had grown attached to young Mumbye and found it difficult to believe that his young body would soon be spent and no more of this world.

The Matriarch approached Borrack. She spoke quietly to him, but she already knew the answer.

"You will do your best for the boy. I hope his journey is peaceful and without pain."

Borrack replied quietly, "I have made a promise to the child, and I will do my very best to fulfil it."

The Matriarch smiled at him and nodded at his confirmation.

"I think it is time to go!" Borrack said.

"You will come back to see us, won't you Borrack?" Simmi asked. His aunt was still cradling the child, but then she made her way over to Borrack and, after standing the boy up on the ground, she hugged her nephew, and said, "You are, without doubt, my sister's son. Please don't forget us."

Borrack smiled with honesty and sincerity, "How could I forget you? You are my family."

And as a glow of golden orange appeared on the eastern horizon, Borrack closed his eyes and concentrated on Zachary, his adopted father, the wise, old man of the north. And by the time he had opened them as Borrack the mighty eagle, the majestic sun had risen, casting its rays of hope across the landscape, imploring its worshipers from the simplest to the most advanced life form to pay homage to the life giver! The one, true, material god: the sun! And, as always, it sent a chill of excitement down the eagle's back. Borrack lowered his wing.

"Come on, young man, let us be on our way."

Simmi begrudgingly let the boy go, and Mumbye ran and climbed on to the eagle's back, threw his feeble arms around his neck. Borrack was amazed by the child's strength; it was a far cry from that day when they first arrived at Poutia, when Mumbye was poised on the edge of death! Even though Borrack knew it was only a temporary reprieve, it was good to see.

The eagle turned his head, smiled with his eyes at the Matriarch and his aunt, and said, "Thank you for all your help."

The boy nodded in agreement, and, with that, the mighty eagle flapped his huge wings, leaving a plume of dust and debris as he took off.

The Matriarch and his aunt watched with sadness in their hearts, for it was hard for them to accept that they would never see young Mumbye again. For this would be his last adventure, in this reality. Although they did not show their sadness to the boy, and, instead, waved excitedly as Borrack and his young ward disappeared into the horizon.

CHAPTER 5
Part Two: The Monster Beyond Imagination

Borrack flew high, with the child clinging to him with a strength that the eagle did not recognise. It was the grip of a child that was healthy, certainly not one that was near to death; he knew it was only temporary, but it inspired him to be a little more courageous.

After they passed over Poutia's huge walls of granite, Borrack's eagle eye spotted a school of dolphins springing from that blue ocean like the gazelles of the seas.

"Hold on tight," the eagle shouted to the boy and then he went into freefall, sweeping back his huge wings to give him less drag and more speed, he plummeted towards the ocean. The boy screamed with excitement, the sound lost as the rushing air superseded it. Mumbye watched in awe as the ocean began to get closer and closer and still they travelled downwards and downwards, closing in on that school of dolphins. The speed of Borrack's decent was astonishing; the boy could not see how the eagle could avoid hitting that mighty ocean. Then within a few yards of that mass of water, the mighty Borrack spread his huge wings out; the effect was incredible. The two of them came to an almost stop, the eagle tilted both wings and the creature swooped round until he was parallel with the majestic ocean, brushing the water with his clawed feet. Borrack powered up his huge wings, while, on either side of him, the dolphins sprang from the sea like playful gazelles. To one side of them, a fisherman watched in disbelief at the incredible spectacle, dolphins jumping from the sea, and between them, a huge eagle with a child perched on his back. The fisherman had to rub his eyes and shake his head to prove what he was seeing was true.

The two of them travelled for some time with the school of dolphins. Mumbye was so excited he shouted and laughed at the whole experience. The last time the boy could remember being this happy was when life was content, when his family and tribe lived in harmony with nature, when all was well with the world. Eventually the school of dolphins dived into the depths of that mighty blue ocean and Borrack tilted his huge wings and flew upwards, where they travelled until they reached landfall.

As directed by the Matriarch, they turned north and followed the coast;

until at last they reached the rock that soared upwards out of the ocean. The eagle circled several times. The rock was white – almost translucent; and, as the rays of the sun hit it, the light bounced off, shooting in a thousand different directions. Borrack flew into the interior of Mother Africa. On the horizon, he noticed the gathering of heavy grey storm clouds. He moved towards them. They were some distance away, but even so, he could hear and feel the thunder! Then he saw the lightning as it straddled the skies like a streak of white-hot molten metal. Borrack was mindful of young Mumbye; although he was a lot stronger than he was when they first set off, it would not be good for him to get too cold and wet. The choice was straightforward, they either

took shelter and waited for the storm to pass, or they flew on, clutching the boy in his claws, pulled in under his belly to keep him warm.

As time was the one thing that there was precious little of, the latter was the only option. The eagle scouted for a good place to land and headed for it. His decent was gradual, he spread his huge wings out and braced his clawed feet for landing, it was smooth and without incident. He lowered his wing and the boy slid down it, and Borrack explained to Mumbye his actions and reasons. The eagle flapped his huge wings again and gently hovered above the boy. He lifted the boy in his claw and powered up his wings and climbed higher. He retracted his clawed foot, the one holding the boy into his underbelly, then, when the child was warm and safe, he increased his speed.

He was moving fast now towards the oncoming storm. As the first drops of rain and gusts of wind hit him, Borrack noticed the three peaks exactly as the Matriarch had described, one in front and the others on either side of him. The storm's intensity increased, the thunder boomed, and the streaks of lightning plunged to the ground at ferocious speeds. Borrack's visibility was now shrouded by the violent storm, so he dropped his altitude, so that he could scan the terrain below, looking for the tribal village that the Matriarch had told him about.

As he peered through the murky cloud, he could just make out a narrow tributary. He followed it; it was heading in the direction of the mountain directly in front of him. The eagle was now being buffeted by the wind and rain that accompanied the storm. He was glad that he had taken the decision to tuck the boy into his underbelly, for the child would not be able to survive these conditions, he thought. He flew tirelessly on fighting against the elements that prevailed. Then, as he made something out, he dropped his altitude again and there it was... he had found it! The village. It nestled on the banks of the tributary and it contained about two dozen huts; as he got closer, he could see they were all built on stilts. This was clearly the man-made blight that haunted the village; it was built on a flood plain.

From one of the huts he could just make out raised voices, and, as he got nearer, he could see that a young woman was in a state of panic. Two other people were holding her back from the veranda, which surrounded the building. He flew nearer and the eagle heard her screams.

"Swalley, my daughter! She will be killed! Please, help!" she cried.

Borrack watched as the woman sank to her knees in distress, pointing to the bank of the tributary; and calling her daughter's name.

"Swalley! Swalley! Please! Please, help her!" she sobbed.

Borrack looked in the direction she was pointing, he focused his eyes and there he saw a small child. She was running towards a small animal, a cat or dog, he could not be sure, the visibility was still very murky. Then he looked beyond the girl. At that moment, a flash of lightning cut across the skies, illuminating the whole area, and there he saw a wall of water cascading down towards the child. It was close, too close for comfort.

The eagle flew into action; he had no time to drop young Mumbye off, as he knew this action would reduce his efficiency and would leave him only one clawed foot to retrieve the girl. He quickly assessed the situation, there was no way he could dive down and pluck the child from the impending danger! The wall of water would be on top of them before he could clear it, and then, would both the children perish? No! He would have to fly to the crest of the wave, turn and fly below its leading edge; grab the child and accelerate upwards.

There was no doubt with the monster wave, rain and wind behind him they would all stand a better chance of survival! He flapped his huge wings and began to increase his speed. It was hard going, for the headwind and rain slowed his progress, but he had no choice; he would have to summon up every ounce of energy. He dug deep into his reserves – his speed now had increased. As he approached the wave, he could sense its ferocity; nothing would stop that wall of water! He flew slightly beyond the crest of the wave and turned, and, as he did, he felt the wind push him along as he predicted. He powered up his wings a little more, it was enough to take him just beyond the leading edge of the wave. He could see the girl. She was frozen with fear, clutching the creature she had retrieved, watching the huge wave that was about to devour her.

Borrack dived down; he could feel the air pressure from the wave pushing him along. He had only one opportunity at saving the child; so he knew he had to get it right first time, for there would be no second chance.

He lined himself up, and poured his power into his wings, while the wave was chasing him fast. He opened the one-clawed foot that was free, and, as he reached the girl, he snapped the talon shut; gently gripping the child. Borrack could feel the wave on his tail. He summoned up even more energy, flapping his huge wings even faster; he could feel the pain of every movement of those magnificent appendages. Nonetheless, slowly but surely, he started to gain more distance between himself and that monster wave, first just a few yards and then by ten yards and then by twenty; until he felt he could safely ascend gradually until he was clear of that wall of water. As he looked down, he watched as that massive wave turned that small tributary into a raging torrent of water, with the power to sweep away anything in its path.

The storm began to abate; he turned and flew back to the hut that housed the distressed mother. There, with the help of the other occupants of the building; he lowered the young girl; still clutching her pet and then young Mumbye.

Then the eagle shouted, "I'll be back when the storm has passed!" With which, he flew off to safer ground.

As the raging storm moved down the valley, the majestic sun appeared, and began to pound its healing rays on the land around the village; leaving the bank as dry as it was before the storm. The villagers poured out of their stilted huts; they began removing the debris from around their buildings and clearing the site. This, as always, was the trademark of their kind of storm, and it was a habitual event.

It was a good hour before Borrack returned. One of the villagers had been taking a short break from the heat and exertion of his labour and was leaning against one of the supports of the stilted huts. It was while doing this, he noticed a black object. He focused on it; it was a bird, a large bird which he watched as the creature descended. He noticed that the lower it got, the larger it became. He began to panic, for this was no ordinary bird; it was some kind of huge eagle. He shouted a warning! All the citizens armed themselves against the evil intruder; they picked up sticks, pitchforks, and clubs, and then they began to prod the sky with them; shouting at the unwanted visitor.

Borrack became alarmed, he could see their hostility; he circled and ascended a little. His eagle eye focused on young Mumbye and the little girl he had saved from that wall of water; the mother and an old man carrying a large stick. They walked towards the crowd and the old man slammed the stick down onto the ground until it cracked with the confidence of a leader. The villagers turned, and, on seeing the old man, they ceased their activities and listened to his words with reverence and obedience. For he was their leader, their wise man, their elder.

Mumbye ran and waved his arms at Borrack, beckoning the eagle to land. Borrack plunged down, and as he neared the ground, he spread out his huge wings to slow his descent and gently landed. Mumbye ran up to him and the boy quickly gave his friend a quick outline of the conversation he had with the elder. It was enough for Borrack to prepare himself for their introduction. The old man approached the creature with his entourage. The eagle studied the old man. He was, without doubt, a leader; a proud, forthright man. But as Borrack looked deep into his eyes, he could see that he was a leader who was under pressure.

The elder spoke with quiet confidence, "Hello, my friend! Please forgive my people for their reaction! The only excuse I can make is that we have very few friends; indeed, we seem to have many enemies, both natural and supernatural. May I also extend to you our profound gratitude for saving my granddaughter's life? The boy tells me," the old man nodding in

Mumbye's direction, "That you are a chimera? Please, excuse my ignorance, but I am not familiar with the word."

Borrack smiled, "It simply means that I am both human and a creature of the sky, and, if it will not alarm you or your people, I will show you."

The old man turned to his people and told them, with an air of authority, to stand their ground, and then he turned back to face the eagle.

"I feel your suggestion would certainly allay the fears of myself and my people."

Borrack closed his eyes, and concentrated on Zachary, his adopted father, the wise, old man of the north. Then, within seconds, he changed from Borrack the mighty eagle to Borrack the man, and there he stood, taller than the tallest of men with his yellow eyes and shock of white hair, dressed in his suit of golden-brown feathers.

The villagers watched in disbelief and sighed at the sight in unison; the young children hid behind their parent's legs nervously. The elder approached Borrack the man, his people watching anxiously, concerned that this creature that stood before their leader would somehow devour him. But when the old man held out his hand to greet Borrack, and Borrack grabbed hold of that hand and shook it, there was a sudden cry of relief from the villagers!

"I hope you and the boy will join us in our communal meal this evening," the elder said, to which Borrack nodded.

The majestic sun disappeared behind the western horizon and the jealous moon made its appearance. Shrouded by a silver mist that stifled its shards of incandescent light, allowing a myriad of heavenly stars to shimmer with nobility. The villagers, along with the elder and his guest, sat on the ground around a blazing open fire, watching, as the offering of wild boar was being cooked slowly over the fire's heat. Borrack, who was sitting next to the elder, turned his head to face his host.

"I wish to ask a question. However, it is a question that I know will offend you."

The old man looked at his visitor, "How do you know it will offend me?" he asked.

Borrack replied, "Because it is in regard to one of your enemies; but, before I ask, let me explain why this question is so important to me."

The old man nodded at Borrack's request.

"I am on a journey. A journey which will take young Mumbye to his final resting place from this reality."

The old man looked shocked, as Borrack relayed the boy's story, from when tribal jealousy, and greed, decimated the family, killing his father, uncles, brothers, and his friend, Bruma the baby elephant, to the expulsion of his tribe or what was left of it! The story continued to the refugee camp called 'Hell', to his fight with malnutrition and disease and his decision that if he was going to die, then he wanted to be with his friend Bruma the baby elephant, in the Meadow of Tranquillity, the lands where elephants live forever. This subsequently had led them to this place. The old man listened intently to everything, and, at the end of the story, the old man spoke:

"So, what is your question?"

Borrack looked deep into the elder's eyes and said, "Could you tell me how to get to the creature beyond imagination, the one you call the demon; the epitome of evil?"

The old man's eyes went cold at the very mention of the creature; even the villagers who heard the visitor mention the demon turned their heads and stared at Borrack with fear in their eyes. The elder dropped his head and looked at his large calloused hands, his mind deep in thought, pondering his response to his guest.

To Borrack, it seemed like an age before the old man spoke, the elder lifted his head and looked into Borrack's eyes.

"Under normal circumstances, I would not help you! Quite honestly, I would not wish that evil on anybody. But in view of the information you have divulged and the fact you saved my granddaughter, I will send a guide with you tomorrow to show you where the lair can be found."

Borrack smiled, "I know I have asked much of you and your people, so thank you on behalf of myself and the boy."

The Elder said, "Tell me about Borrack; the story, the chimera?"

Borrack duly obliged. He told the old man about the village at the bottom of the Black Mountains, the Labyrinth of Golden Dreams, the Ice Blue Wind, and his parents, and of Zachary his adopted father, the old wise man of the north… he told him everything.

Not long after, the meal was served up to the villagers and their guests and was enjoyed by all.

"Can I ask another question?" Borrack said, addressing the elder.

The old man nodded.

"Why do you live in this place, you have a tributary that turns into a raging river that is rampant and clearly dangerous, and on the other side of you exists the Demon, the creature beyond imagination?"

The old man's expression changed, his eyes conveyed sadness.

"My people have lived here for generations, our fathers before us and theirs before them; this is our home."

The Elder dropped his head and examined his hands.

"Do you know its beauty was unsurpassed? The land provided all that a community could want; but in recent years, things have changed; where the Demon now presides, a couple lived, they moved in there about twenty-five years ago; they kept themselves to themselves, but they did us no harm. Then, about ten years ago they disappeared, and the Demon moved in; I suspect the creature devoured them. Then, to the north, the Government built a dam and when it gets filled to saturation point, they open a runoff which floods our village. I'll be honest, my friend, I don't know what to do for the best."

Borrack sympathised with the old man; he could see his dilemma.

"Clearly, you have thought of moving," Borrack said, knowing it was probably uppermost in the old man's mind.

The elder lifted his head to face his visitor, "Yes, yes, but where? We can't go to the other side of the river, because the jungle there is too thick. We cannot take up residence with the Demon, and if we leave the valley, I don't think the community will survive!"

Borrack could see it was a huge responsibility for one man, but he was the elder, their leader, and he would have to make that decision, right or wrong.

"Well, I'd better turn in for the night. Tomorrow, I will organise a guide for you. Good night, my friend," the old man said and disappeared.

Borrack and Mumbye went not long after. The little girl's mother gave them hospitality, as a thank you for saving her daughter's life.

The morning was a dull, grey affair. The clouds were dark and hung heavy in the sky. Borrack guessed there could be a re-run of yesterday's storm; he could not help but feel sorrow for his hosts; this was no way to live, but this was their plight, and it was helpless. The old man was true to his word and provided them with a guide, a strong, fit, young man and they all said their good-byes. Then the three of them set off. The path was overgrown from its lack of use! But then the villagers had no desire to be confronted with that Demon, the monster beyond imagination. The guide hacked his way through Mother Nature's reclaimed jungle with his Machete. The sight of which sent a chill through young Mumbye's spine; it brought back so many vivid memories! And those memories flooded back into his mind, of his village, when the bad men came and killed his father, brothers and uncles and then there was the baby elephant. The boy's eyes welled with tears, but he made no noise, he just walked behind Borrack; to keep as far away as possible from that machete, that blade of death, that symbol of hate.

After some time of cutting their way through the jungle's reclaimed path, they came across two stone pillars that had, at one time, served to hang huge gates upon; they passed through them, still cutting at the undergrowth, for Mother Nature always takes back that which is rightfully hers. Borrack had noticed that, as they approached the area, it was void of any animal noises; in fact it was deadly quiet.

Just ahead they could make out a derelict building, they approached it with caution and, as they did, a noise fell upon them. It was a drone, continuous and without a change of pitch. The closer they got the louder the drone became and then before them stood something. The guide screamed in fear and dropped his machete! He could not explain what he saw in front of him, for it was unimaginable, but it invoked a fear in him, a fear that related to his worst nightmare; he shouted, "Dragon!" screamed, and ran back into the jungle from the unimaginable creature.

Borrack stood perfectly still, petrified with fear. He, like the guide, could not explain what lay in front of him – it was indescribable, and, like the guide, it invoked his greatest fear and hate; and yet Borrack reasoned it could not be! For the Labyrinth of Golden Dreams was thousands of miles away and whatever else, that mountain which housed that malevolent being could not possibly move! This, in front of him, was not the Labyrinth of Golden Dreams; he stood firm against his own insecurity and concentrated on the unimaginable creature! It was like nothing on Earth, it resembled nothing tangible and yet everything tangible. Mumbye moved forward, past Borrack; Borrack tried to stop him, but he was paralysed. He tried to shout, but no sound emerged; he was struck dumb! He could do nothing but watch as the boy moved to the strange something, which was nothing and yet everything. As Mumbye reached the creature, he turned round to face Borrack and shouted,

"Look beyond your fear! Look beyond your hate."

Borrack did as the boy said, and the more he concentrated on Mumbye's words, the more the unimaginable creature took on form. At first it was a haze, a mist, and then it took on shape. And the more he concentrated, the more the shape became pronounced, it was human – it was a young girl, unkempt and wearing ragged clothes.

Mumbye, the young Empathic, placed his arms around the girl's shoulders to comfort her. Borrack moved forward, and as he got nearer, he could see her distress; tears rolled down her face. Her hair was dishevelled, her clothes ragged and dirty and yet her beauty was absolute. Borrack reached the girl, and, like Mumbye, he put his arm around her, to console her. She looked at him with her crystal blue eyes, as if they were questioning her very existence.

"I am so lonely," she said feebly. "I wish I was dead, and then I could be with the people that loved me, that did not judge me, that did not hate me, but loved me for who I am and not the way I look; my parents."

Borrack and Mumbye followed the girl's eyes, which focused on two stone clad graves.

"How long?" Borrack said gently, nodding towards the graves.

"I don't know," she said sobbing, "But many seasons! Why did they have to leave me? Why could they not take me with them?" She bellowed.

Borrack and the boy tried to comfort her.

"What's your name?" Borrack asked.

"Maley," she replied emotionally.

"Maley," Borrack said, "How have you ended up with this curse?"

The girl looked at him with her crystal blue eyes. "My parents were explorers," she said, her voice still shaking with emotion. "They travelled the world seeking out legends and myths, looking for their truth. They were very successful and financial reward followed. Then, one day, they were commissioned to look for a cave filled with the most precious of minerals, silver, precious stones, but something much more valuable than the latter, something unique, walls of polished gold mirrors."

Borrack's face altered. Mumbye the Empathic could sense Borrack's mood had changed; he could feel his anger building.

"Come, Maley, let's get you cleaned up," the boy said. "I saw a waterhole down there."

The boy knew Borrack would not turn his anger on the girl, but at this point in time she was very sensitive and vulnerable, and it would not take a lot to tip her over the edge. The girl turned her head to look at Mumbye, with a questioning look in her eyes.

"Come on," he said, encouraging her to leave Borrack to his own devices. The two of them walked off to the watering hole.

Borrack's mind was full of Maley's words; he knew the story so well! He had heard it so many times, her parents had tried to steal from that malevolent lump of rock, the Labyrinth of Golden Dreams. Borrack had tried to fool himself that this life form, this evil lump of rock, was nothing more than egotistical, something that could no longer haunt him! But he was wrong; the Labyrinth of Golden Dreams would always haunt him. If he could destroy it, he would do, but that was impossible. He kicked at the ground violently to relieve his frustrations, but it didn't help!

Mumbye sat Maley by the watering hole, he tore the sleeve off his tatty shirt, and dipped it in the water.

"What are you doing with your shirt," the girl said.

"Well, where I am going, I won't need clothes."

"What do you mean?" Maley replied. The boy looked at her and began to bathe her tear-stained face. She looked up at him with her crystal blue eyes, waiting for his reply.

"I am going to die," he said casually.

"What?" she said shocked.

"I am dying; I am going to join my friend, Bruma, the baby elephant. Borrack is taking me there and that's why we searched for you."

The girl was stunned. "What do you mean, you're dying?"

Mumbye smiled at her, "It's all right, I am not scared."

"But how do you know you're dying," she said earnestly. The boy finished bathing her face, arms and hands and sat next to her and told her his story; by the time he had finished, her face was once again tear stained; he wiped it again with his makeshift flannel.

"So why have you come to me?" she said gently.

"Because the Matriarch told Borrack that you would know where the Meadow of Tranquillity, the lands where elephants live forever, could be found."

She looked at him puzzled, "Who's the Matriarch?" she said.

Mumbye smiled at her and told her of Borrack's quest to get him to the lands where elephants live forever, he told her of his flight from his home (Hell), to Poutia, Borrack's journey to see the Accountant of Lives, to extend his life. And their journey to the village that sat on the banks of a tributary, of saving a little girl's life from the raging torrent, of the water that cursed the village. He told her about the people of the village who had been blighted by the river and by the creature beyond imagination! And then stopped abruptly; embarrassed by his last statement. She looked at him, her eyes suddenly welled up.

"Is that how they see me?" she said.

Mumbye sifted the sandy soil through his bony fingers, unsure of what to say. Borrack had just approached and heard the last part of their conversation.

"Yes!" he said, crouching down by Maley, to which Mumbye shot him a look.

"There is no point pretending they don't," Borrack said confidently. "Maley is like me and has been cursed by the Labyrinth of Golden Dreams. If she is to survive, she must first come to terms with her affliction; only then can she rebuild her life."

"But how can I?" the girl said defensively.

"Look at your reflection in the watering hole, what do you see Maley?"

"The same as I have always seen," she said.

"Yes!" Borrack replied, "And you're beautiful."

The girl coloured a little, slightly embarrassed.

"Unfortunately, that heartless lump of rock, the Labyrinth of Golden Dreams has created an illusion around you. But as Mumbye has shown me, if you look beyond your fears and hate, that illusion is shattered, and you become what you have always been: beautiful."

Again Maley coloured a little and dropped her gaze to the ground; hoping no one would notice her embarrassment.

"You are wrong, you know?" Maley said.

"Wrong about what?" Borrack asked.

"About the Labyrinth of Golden Dreams. It does have a heart – it lies behind the second golden mirror to the left. My parents found out, realising that it was its weakness, its Achilles' heel. The Labyrinth of Golden Dreams cursed their unborn child, me, for its own defence and told them they would never be able to tell anyone because no one would come near them, because of me."

Maley dropped her head into her hands and sobbed, mumbling, "That's why they died alone, because of me."

Borrack put his arms around the girl, "It's not your fault: just remember you're not alone – there are many of us who have been cursed by that malevolent lump of rock."

The girl looked up at Borrack, "Mumbye said that you and he were looking for the Meadow of Tranquillity, the lands where elephants live forever?"

"Yes," Borrack said.

"I will tell you of its location, but can I come with you? I am sure Mumbye would like me to come," Maley said anxiously.

Borrack looked at the two of them; it was as if they had conspired this plan in secret.

"I don't know," he said, "I was going to suggest that if we could get the villagers to move here you could stay with them."

"No, no!" Maley said, "They will never accept me! Even if you could get them to look beyond their prejudice."

Borrack looked at the beautiful girl in front of him, with her crystal blue eyes, "You are right, they are an insular bunch, they don't seem to welcome newcomers and I don't think they are flexible enough to look past their fears, their hate. So, yes, is the answer! Perhaps you can stay with Zachary, my adopted father, the wise, old man of the north?"

For the first time since her parents had died, she smiled, "Thank you, thank you!" she said excitedly.

"Now, tell me where the Meadow of Tranquillity is, the lands where Elephants live forever, and how far it is."

The girl told Borrack and Mumbye exactly what her parents had told her. It was not far from where they were. It lay due west; the entrance was through the side of an active volcano. It was a difficult passage, wide but fraught with danger. Once they had negotiated that, it would be necessary to pass through a wall of water, that dropped down across the exit. After that, they would have to walk around the side of a stunning lake! The Lake of Serenity. Only then would they come across the Meadow of Tranquillity, where once a year the elephants of times past, welcome those elephants that have left this world to join them, in the land where elephants live forever, with which, Maley finished speaking.

"You said the elephants visit once a year, when?" Borrack said earnestly.

The girl looked puzzled, she racked her brain, her parents had told her, but they had told her so much. They had told her about all their exploits, for they believed that her curse would not allow her to leave this place; she struggled with her memory.

"It is important, Maley," Borrack urged.

"Yes, yes," she said, frustrated by the pressure! And then it came to her. "Yes, it's when the rainy season finishes."

Borrack looked up at the leaden, grey sky, the cloud cover was still heavy and threatening; but it had come to nothing.

"I guess about now," she said.

The day was still quite young. Borrack thought of Mumbye; he looked at the child. He was still quite well, although time was wearing on him. Borrack's mind slipped back to the hourglass, and the sands of time slipping through it.

"I feel we had better make a move now then?"

Maley nodded in agreement. Mumbye looked down at the ground, it had finally hit him; this was his last journey, in this reality, "I'm scared," he said quietly.

The two of them looked at young Mumbye. Borrack felt for the child; Maley put her arms around the boy to comfort him.

"We don't have to go, Mumbye! But I cannot change your fate. I really wish I could!" Borrack replied kindly.

Mumbye looked up, tears streamed down his face. He wiped them away with the back of his hand, "I know you can't change what is to be, and I am so thankful for your help! I'm just being silly," the boy said bravely, forcing a smile.

"I think we had better go, but Maley, with your permission, I would like to go back to the village and offer them your land. But you will have to come to reassure the elder that the land is no longer haunted by…" Borrack stopped short of the words 'the demon', and 'the monster beyond imagination'. She understood his pause and was thankful for it.

"I would be pleased to!" she said, "For the last ten years, this place has held nothing but sorrow for me! My only request is that if they do decide to move here, that they tend my parent's graves as they would their forebears."

Borrack the man noticed a clearing big enough for him to change and become Borrack the eagle.

"Let's go," he said, as he moved to the clearing and the others followed. Borrack closed his eyes and concentrated on Zachary, his adopted father, the wise, old man of the north. He felt his body change and within seconds, his body went into a spasm. The sensation was neither painful nor pleasant. He had changed from Borrack the man, to Borrack mighty eagle. The eagle lowered his wing and Mumbye and Maley climbed on. He flapped his huge wings, creating a huge amount of downdraft lifting him and his passengers vertically, until they were clear of the jungle. Then he circled. Maley looked down on her home; in the most part she was glad to be leaving. But as she saw her parent's gravestones, she remembered happy times and a bead of water ran down each cheek; it was a moment of regret!

Borrack headed towards the village; the sky seemed to lighten – perhaps as a symbol that the rainy season was drawing to its close? The eagle saw a clearing away from the village, far away enough not to spook the villagers, but near enough to meet with the elder. He circled and descended, spreading his wings out to reduce his speed, he braced his clawed feet for landing and, as he touched the ground, the impact was minimal. He lowered his wing and his two passengers disembarked. He swung his head around to face Mumbye and said commandingly:

"Tell the elder that Borrack wishes to talk with him alone; do not alert anyone else."

The boy ran off to fulfil his mission.

"Maley, could you hide behind that tree and keep out of sight! I know it's unfair on you, but I don't want to scare the elder off before I have told him about our plan."

Maley did as she was bid. Mumbye returned soon after with the old man, Borrack smiled at him with his eyes.

"I think I have a solution to your problem, regarding your village."

The old man looked at him with apprehension, "I am listening," he said curtly.

Borrack told him about Maley and her curse as the creature beyond imagination, and of her parents and that they had died naturally, and that since their death she had lived alone, with only her curse to keep her company. He told of her decision to leave and let the people of the village to settle on her land, with the proviso that they keep her parent's graves as well maintained as they would their own forebears' graves. The old man listened intently; he looked down at his large hands and began to play with his fingers, while mulling over the information.

"How do you know all this is true? And can you prove it?" he said sternly.

Borrack again smiled with his eyes, "Yes! But first, I must ask you to stand firm and look beyond your fears and hate, OK?"

The elder nodded. The eagle called for Maley. She came out from behind the tree she had been hiding behind. The old man stepped back in shock, but then he did as he promised and slowly he saw beyond that very desire that had haunted him and his people for the past ten years. And slowly but surely, he saw the girl emerge from deep within her curse and his fears were reconciled. He smiled with sympathy.

"I am so sorry for mine and my people's prejudice, if we had only looked with our hearts and not with our fear! Your pain and suffering could have been averted! I am so, so sorry. I thank you for your kind offer, and yes, we will tend your parent's graves with the reverence they deserve."

With that the old man turned, smiled at Borrack and walked back to the village, and in his mind, he was planning the great move.

Borrack lowered his huge wings. Maley and Mumbye climbed aboard; within seconds they were climbing high into the sky and, as they did, the majestic sun burst through those grey, leaden clouds of menace, melting them away as if they were nothing more than the fears of fools, melting away those very grey, leaden clouds, which had brought so much destruction to that village and its people.

CHAPTER 6

The Mountain of Fire and Life's End

Agrandmother, mother and child share a habitat made of corrugated iron, plastic and wood. This is their new home; it is the home of fear and desperation and they are just one family of so many that share this refugee camp called 'Hell'! They are the victims of hate, pushed off their land and brutalized in the name of freedom. As they watch their chid dying, a slow, agonising death; their hopes are raised as the child becomes lucid and slips from coma into a semi-conscious state. But in their hearts, they know this is only a false hope, a hope without foundation, and a hope without hope; and in their eyes their tears are ready to flow. As they will for Mother Africa, as another one of her children dies, in the name of freedom! That shallow word without substance! Which humanity holds in such high esteem!

* * * * *

The eagle flew high with his passengers holding tight to his back. Maley looked down at how the planet lay below! It excited her; it was so different from her previous, sheltered existence and her loneliness. Mumbye remained quiet and apprehensive. Borrack headed due west, which took him high above the mountains at the end of the valley. He scrutinized the terrain below, where he saw the dam, that manmade enigma that had blighted the village. In front, he could see several small ranges of mountains, each as a prequel to the one behind and beyond all of them he saw The Mountain of Fire and, from the crater on its pinnacle, a plume of smoke bellowed high into the sky, pushing those obnoxious gases upwards, almost vertically into the atmosphere, beyond any living creature.

As the majestic sun moved to the west, the three intrepid travellers followed it. By the time they had reached the volcano, the sun was lying low in the sky. Borrack circled the huge mountain, looking for the large entrance that led to its interior. He scanned the terrain at the bottom of Mother Nature's gravestone (The Mountain of Fire), looking for the magnificent waterfall and the Meadow of Tranquillity, the lands where elephants live forever, that vast meadow where the two realities would meet.

The eagle saw it as a portal between two worlds, a door from one dimension to another. But he could see nothing except the products of this world, field after field, forest after forest, village after village. He scanned the mountainside and there he saw the cave, and next to it, a small plateau. It was big enough to land on, but difficult to reach. It was set between two shear rock faces. His approach would have to be almost vertical.

He shouted to his passengers, "Hold on tight!"

He felt Maley's arms wrap themselves around Mumbye and his neck, pinching the boy into his flesh and holding him securely. Borrack positioned himself above the two pillars of rock and went into a dive; he swept back his wings and cut through the gap with ease. Maley and the boy could hear nothing except the wind rushing past them. As the eagle neared the plateau, he spread his wings out to slow his descent. Then he twisted them horizontally and braced his clawed feet for landing, thump! He was down. He lowered his wings, and Maley and Mumbye dismounted. Borrack looked up at the sky through the two pillars of rock; the day was fast disappearing and being replaced by the darkness of night.

The eagle closed his eyes and concentrated on Zachary his adopted father, and within seconds he had changed from Borrack the mighty eagle to Borrack the man. He turned to his two fellow travellers, "Will you stay here while I survey the cave?" They nodded in agreement.

Borrack the man made his way to the entrance. The moment he entered the cave, he could smell the obnoxious gas; he covered his nose and made his way inside. Directly in front of him, no more than thirty yards away, he saw his first obstacle; it was an arc of fire from wall to wall that discharged up from the floor every thirty seconds. Beyond that, he could just make out another one; as he squinted his eyes, he could see that the second ark of fire was a little more erratic.

He got as close as he dared to the first; the heat was extreme; the fissure that allowed the escape of fire from the bowels of the Earth was over five yards wide! Certainly too wide to jump! Borrack scrutinized the size of the cave. It was more than adequate to fly through; it had both the height and width, even with his two passengers on his back. The thirty second gap between the arks of flame would allow just enough time to pass through safely, but beyond that he could not judge. The truth was that he would have to take a chance! It was in the hands of the Gods, what other option did they have? What was certain, was that both Maley and the boy would have to be securely fixed to his back, for the flight was bound to be erratic.

To that end, Borrack looked for some kind of vine or something that could be used to tether them to him. In the corner he saw some old rope. 'It was dusty and frayed, more than likely left by some other explorer; maybe even Maley's parents?' he thought.

Borrack returned to Maley and Mumbye, with the rope in his hands; they were sitting on the plateau waiting for him. Maley looked up at him, her eyes said it all; Borrack did not need the question.

"I don't know," he said, "It might be possible to get through, but we will have to fly, at least the first section! And you will have to be tethered to me and wear some sort of face mask."

Maley looked at the bottom of her ragged dress, she tore two strips off, one for Mumbye and one for her.

"Well, these will do for the face masks," she said.

Borrack smiled, "Well, at least that resolves one problem. But getting back the same way is anybody's guess."

Maley butted in quickly remembering her parent's words, "No! We won't need to! My parents told me that no one leaves the Meadow of Tranquillity, the lands were elephants live forever, the same way as they enter."

Borrack looked at her puzzled.

She shrugged her shoulders, "That's all they said, and they obviously made it back!"

"We'll worry about that at the time," Borrack replied, "Ok, my young friends, it's decision time. Do we go now or wait for morning?"

Mumbye dropped his head; he did not want to admit his fears. Maley looked at the boy; she could see his anguish, but time was fast running out to catch the annual migration of the elephant's march to their alternative reality.

"If we're going," she said, "It must be now."

Borrack looked down at the boy; he was still looking down, "It's up to you, Mumbye," Borrack said. "If you prefer, I can try and take you back to your home, Hell? But I cannot change the sands of time. I have done my best with the Accountant of Lives; it's now your decision."

The boy looked at Borrack and Maley, "I just don't want to die," he said, "I want to go back to when my family and tribe lived in harmony with nature, when all was well with the world."

Borrack and Maley looked at him with sympathy, "I too wish that could be the case," Borrack said, "Oh! I do wish that was that the case, but that time has gone."

Mumbye knew that what had been said by Borrack was true, that there was no way back; he would have to be brave and go forward. He was certainly more fortunate than most, at least he had two good friends to go with! And what good friends they were.

"We had better go then," he said sadly.

Borrack thought of Zachary, his adopted father, the wise, old man of the north. He felt his body change, and within seconds, his body went into a spasm, the sensation neither painful nor pleasant! He had changed from Borrack the man to Borrack the mighty eagle. The eagle lowered his wing and Mumbye and Maley climbed aboard, the girl then proceeded to tether the rope around Borrack's neck and themselves until they were secure, and then each of them placed their makeshift face masks on.

Borrack would have liked to have flown high, circled and then headed for the entrance, but with the two pillars of rock in the way, that was impossible. He would have to fly from a standing start, so he flapped his wings just enough until he had lift; then he powered them a little more which took him to the entrance of the cave. He calculated that with the right acceleration he could make it to the first ark of fire in less than forty seconds! But he would have to time it to coincide with the collapsing of the flame. He watched the flame recede back into the bowels of the Earth, he powered his wings slowly at first, and then he counted to ten.

The flame then shot upwards, like a comet of fire. He increased his speed as he neared, the flame weakened, a prequel to its collapse. But he was still too far from it to make it safely across. The eagle increased his speed to make up the difference. The wall of fire began to collapse, he was still a little behind schedule, but it was too late to abort the attempt. He poured more power into his huge wings. The flame receded back into the bowels of the rocks; it would be another three seconds before he reached the edge of the fissure, which only left him five seconds to cross that fiery cavity before the flames retuned.

As he reached the edge, he looked down; he could see the molten fire building below, ready for its next incursion. Borrack summoned up yet more energy; he knew he had to get clear of the reach of the wall of fire, or they would all perish.

He watched the flame! It was about to blow, the eagle was nearly at the edge of the fissure; suddenly the wall of flames shot up vertically, just missing Borrack and his passengers. But now he was going too fast, and there was no way he could stop in time for the second wall of fire; it was almost on top of him! He was heading straight for it; Borrack could do nothing; he closed his eyes, waiting for the pain that would sear through his body. He prayed and hoped that Maley and the boy would be safe, and then, as if by a miracle, the wall of fire disappeared into the bowels of the Earth; only to rematerialize as soon as the eagle had passed, just singeing his tail feathers.

Borrack opened his eyes. In the depths of the tunnel he could see an orange glow; he headed for it. Then from nowhere he heard and felt a whoosh of hot air; it hit his underbelly sending him upwards.

The eagle had to act fast, he was heading for the cave roof, and his passengers felt the pressure from below and instinctively ducked their heads. Borrack twisted his wings to correct his course; it was a fight, but with strength and quick thinking he was back on track. The pungent smell of sulphur hung thick in the air. The eagle scrutinized the cold stone rock faces – they were charred, as if at some time in its history the hot gases from the belly of the planet had been excreted through these very tunnels.

Eventually, he reached the end of the tunnel. It led into a vast cylindrical chamber; he was at its very top, and above him was solid rock, so his only exit was down. He looked down into the pit. He could see the molten rock bubbling and swirling at its very base. He scanned the walls, and there were no visible exits; he had only one choice: downwards?

The chamber was big enough for him, Maley and Mumbye to spiral down in, and, as he went lower into the depths of the chamber, he scanned the stone rock face for an opening. He was over two thirds of the way down, when something took his breath away; the molten rock was now being pushed up at speed; from pressure within the Earth's mantel.

Borrack knew there was no going back, he had to press on. He widened his search and then he saw the entrance. It was at least fifteen yards from the rising, molten rock. It was big enough to fly into; but he would have to reach it before that liquid rock.

He shouted to Mumbye and the girl, "Hold on!" then he swept his huge wings back and went into freefall; his two passengers watched in fear as they saw the molten rock climbing to meet them. The eagle was at least thirty yards away from the opening. It was a race between him and that inferno of liquid rock! Who would reach the opening first – the molten rock or Borrack with his passengers?

There could be no contest; he had to win! The alternative did not bear thinking about. He increased his speed and he was making good progress; but so was the molten rock. He was now less than ten yards away and that hot cocktail of liquid rock and hot gases was about the same. He summoned up every bit of energy he could and it was working; he was now less than two yards and the molten rock, he guessed, maybe five. He spread his huge wings and tilted them, he was now going at tremendous speed; his only fear was to glide straight through the entrance, without reducing his speed; it was a dangerous manoeuvre. But there was no alternative.

He aimed at the opening; Borrack could feel the searing heat from the molten rock. Its speed had also increased, the eagle swept down, his clawed feet just inches away from the liquid rock and gases.

Borrack swept through the opening, only to be faced by another wall of fire; he could not slow down in time! Then from behind there was a deafening Whoosh! Hot gases forced their way through the opening, the prequel from the rising, molten rock. The hot gases pushed him along, but, at the same time, forced the wall of fire to spread its flames across the cave floor, allowing Borrack, Maley and the boy safe passage.

The eagle was now being swept along by the hot gases, but, in front, yet another obstacle? A lava flow spouting up from a fissure in the cave floor, it was covering almost two thirds of the tunnel! Again, the eagle could not slow down, the pressure from the hot gases would not let him; he and his passengers were going to be swept into the lava flow, unless he acted fast and decisively.

He twisted one wing in one direction and the other in the opposite direction; his whole body twisted. He straightened his wings; he was now flying sideways – one wing to ceiling one wing to floor; his clawed feet close to the cave wall. He shouted to Maley and Mumbye.

"Duck your heads!"

They did as they were bade and pushed them as tight as they could to Borrack's flesh. The eagle was travelling at incredible speeds, being pushed on by the hot gases. He approached the lava flow and twisted both wings to take him closer to the cave wall; he felt a pain shoot through both clawed feet as they scraped along the blackened cave wall; they only just cleared the lather flow.

Borrack levelled himself up, still being carried along by the hot gases. He saw an orange glow in front of him, but unlike the others, it was duller and inconsistent; one second vibrant, the next dull. He strained his eyes to get a better look, 'It certainly isn't flame or molten rock?' he thought. As he got nearer, he could hear a deafening, gushing noise! It was the waterfall at the exit of the mountain; that led to the Lake of Serenity. He approached it at unbelievable speed, he shouted to Mumbye and the girl:

"Brace yourselves!" and he swept back his wings to reduce the drag! Then they hit the gushing waterfall.

A roe deer was busying itself drinking the water from the lake. There was a noise far above; he looked up and watched as the majestic eagle burst through the fast-flowing water, on his back carrying two people. The deer dipped his head and carried on drinking, he felt no fear or interest, for in this land where elephants live forever, there were no predators, no creatures that would harm one another! For it was a land of peace, a land set aside for Mother Nature's most beloved and treasured animal, the elephant, where they could live for an eternity, in peace and without fear.

Borrack exploded out of the waterfall; he spread out his huge wings and powered them up and gained height. The eagle, Maley and Mumbye could not believe the beautiful vista that surrounded them. The sky glowed orange with streaks of gold, which highlighted the colour. The light was neither dark nor dowdy, but bright and vibrant; the lake was like a mirror and reflected the sky's beauty.

On either side of the lake, trees grew in abundance and so varied – cypress, olives, evergreens, the mighty oak, so many and so beautiful and beyond them the grey, purple mountains that were caressed by the forests. There were waterfalls in abundance, that poured their content into the lake without disturbing its serenity. The eagle looked up for the majestic sun, but it was absent. 'Where was the vibrant light coming from?' he thought, and then he looked down at the tranquil lake and, as his eagle eyes looked beyond its fluid surface, he saw the orange glow of the volcano.

"This must be the source," he mumbled. Then he realised that the sky was a reflection of the lake. They were in a reality, within a reality, a world within a world. Where positive and negative could exist in harmony, where the word contradiction, was a contradiction in and of itself. This was the land where elephants lived forever. He flew on across the lake; he was amazed and humbled by the surrounding beauty. Then the eagle could see a clearing ahead.

"Is that the Meadow of Tranquillity?" Maley shouted and pointed in the direction of the clearing.

Borrack headed for it and circled; there was nothing! Not a single elephant? He circled again and landed; he lowered his wing. Maley untied the rope that tethered them all together, and she and the boy dismounted. Borrack looked at Mumbye, he looked tired and pale, his eyes had dulled; the eagle knew the last grains of sand were now passing through that hourglass. Maley looked at the eagle and her crystal blue eyes seemed to say what he was thinking: they were too late! The elephants of time past had been and gone and would not return for another year; it was too late for the boy!

Mumbye the Empathic had sensed their thoughts.

"No, no!" he shouted and dropped to his knees, put his head in his hands and sobbed.

Maley rushed to his side and put her arms around him. Borrack could do little as Borrack the eagle, so he closed his eyes and concentrated on Zachary his adopted father, the wise, old man of the north, and with that he changed from Borrack the mighty eagle to Borrack the man. He rushed to the boy's side to comfort him.

Then Mumbye shouted, "Borrack, the light has gone! I can't see; why has everything gone dark?" And then he went quiet and stared blankly ahead.

Borrack and the girl tried to shake him from his stupor, "Mumbye, Mumbye," they shouted, but he did not respond. Both feared the worst; but they tried again. "Mumbye, Mumbye, please answer! Mumbye, Mumbye!" But again no response. Tears began to well up in Maley's eyes.

Then the boy said, "Look, look, can you see them?" Mumbye pointed in the direction of the Meadow. Borrack and the girl looked in the direction he was pointing. Then they looked at each other; they could see nothing! Mumbye said it again.

"What can you see?" Borrack said.

"There," the boy said, still pointing. "You can't see them, can you?"

"No," Borrack said reluctantly.

"Let me help you," Mumbye the Empathic said. "Lower your heads."

They did as the child suggested, and then the boy placed one hand on Borrack's head and the other on Maley's head; as he did, they felt a searing heat flow through their bodies. Then everything went black, as they travelled the same journey as the boy did! They felt his fear, his isolation and his loneliness in the blackness of nothing. Then they saw a glowing white dot and, as they travelled towards it, it became a glowing, white hole, and then a glowing, white aperture! Their fears began to abate, and as the glowing, white aperture became a glowing, white window, and as the glowing, white window became a glowing, white entrance, a feeling of euphoria fell upon them. And as they passed through that entrance the glowing, white light dissipated, and as it dissipated, a formless shadow appeared. And, as those formless shadows gave way to material shapes, they could see what the boy was pointing at. And there, in front of them, were thousands of elephants of all shapes and sizes. Some old, some young, many with wounds; many more with their tusks hacked off – the product of humanities greed.

"Look," Mumbye said, "Look! We're not too late!"

Borrack and the girl looked at each other and then at the boy and laughed with delight.

"No, Mumbye you're not!" Borrack said

Then the boy jumped up and down excitedly, "Look, look, over there, Bruma! My friend, the baby elephant!"

Maley and Borrack looked in the direction the boy was pointing in, and next to a huge bull elephant stood a small calf, with a huge scar down one side that had been caused by a machete. The boy called the calf's name.

"Bruma, Bruma!" the calf turned his head, lifted his trunk and trumpeted, then ran in the direction of Mumbye, followed by the bull elephant. The boy ran off in the direction of his friend! Then stopped. He turned and ran back to Borrack and the girl. Then he threw his arms around Maley and kissed her.

"Thank you!" he said. Tears of happiness and sadness began to roll down Maley's cheeks. Then Mumbye turned and faced Borrack, who was already on his knees, and threw his arms around him.

"Thank you so much, but will you do one more thing for me?"

"Yes," Borrack replied, choking back his emotions.

"Will you tell my mother and grandmother that I am happy?"

"Of course," Borrack said, fighting back his tears, which were welling up in his eyes.

"Thank you!" the boy said, "Oh! And, I love you!"

Then the boy turned and ran off to join his friend.

Maley put her arms around Borrack, and they watched Mumbye jump on the back of the baby elephant, who turned and followed the huge herd as they migrated towards the horizon. The two of them carried on watching as the boy and his friend disappeared into infinity.

Borrack could not move, he was so tired both emotionally and physically; he just sat there staring at the horizon, long after the last of Mother Nature's favourite creatures had disappeared! He had never witnessed mortality before, he had never thought about it; but why should he. Borrack the man, the eagle was immortal, so why had this event struck such a nerve so deep down in his psyche? He did know, but it brought clarity to his past, something that he had denied, something that was more obvious than life itself. He had mourned his parent's death and yet he did not know them. It was true that they were good people, but he did not know them. It is true that they would have loved him, but he did not know them. He only knew what he was told about them, but what was true, was the one person who had given him life, who had taught him right from wrong, who had taken him in, when all others would have cast him aside, was

Zachary, his adopted father.

And yet, this adopted father was the only father he knew! That was not to say he did not love his birth parents, because he did; but he did not know them. But he did love Zachary! And, at that moment, a rush of guilt and shame fell upon him – this man had not just been his father, but his mother as well, and he, in all that time, had never shown the love and respect that Zachary had deserved. He had been too wrapped up in his own quest – that of his parents and their memory, but they were gone, and nothing could bring them back. But Zachary was still here. But mortality was short! Borrack felt an overwhelming desire to see his FATHER – Zachary.

Maley had sensed Borrack's distress and his fight with mortality. She had seen and felt the devastation of death; she had watched her parents die, as she nursed them in their last days. The one thing that hurt more than anything else was knowing that she could never die; for, like Borrack, she had been cursed with immortality by the Labyrinth of Golden Dreams!

Borrack stood up, gently removing the girls' arm from his shoulder.

"It's time to go now! It's time to leave this place. I need to see my father; but first, I must fulfil my promise to Mumbye."

She looked at him, and she could see his desperation, his need to see Zachary, his need to right so many wrongs. She nodded submissively.

Borrack closed his eyes and concentrated on Zachary, his father, the wise, old man of the north. He felt his body change and within seconds his body went into a spasm, the sensation neither painful nor pleasant! He had changed from Borrack the man to Borrack the mighty eagle. The eagle lowered his wing, and Maley climbed aboard. He flapped his huge wings, creating a whirlwind of dust and debris. He concentrated on the orange sky and climbed steadily; he was so taken with his own thoughts, that he did not notice the change of colour in the sky. It was true that its change was slow and subtle, and it wasn't until he cast his eagle eyes downwards that he noticed, that the landscape had changed; below, he only saw field after field, forest after forest and village after village; he looked up at the sky and there he saw the majestic sun at its zenith. Gone was the reality within the reality, the world within the world, and gone were the elephants of times past; along with their new arrivals and Mumbye. Both Borrack and Maley felt a twinge of sadness, but at the same time such humility. For they had witnessed Mother Nature's shrine to her most loved creature, the elephant.

The eagle flew west for many hours until he reached that festering wound on Mother Africa's landscape; Hell. Borrack circled; he spotted a small group of people mourning the loss of one of their sons. This was Mumbye's funeral. He landed a distance away, where Maley disembarked. It was agreed that she would wait there until Borrack had passed on the boy's wish, to his mother and grandmother. She would like to have gone, but her curse would not allow it. Borrack changed from eagle to man and there he stood, taller than the tallest of men, with his yellow eyes and shock of white hair, wearing a suit of golden-brown feathers.

He approached the small group of people; he did not wish to disturb their grief. In all, there were three people and himself. He listened to the words that were said, they were short and to the point with little ceremony, for this was commonplace in this large, festering community of plastic sheets and corrugated iron. He placed his large hand on the mother's shoulder; she turned. Borrack could see nothing in her eyes except the dullness of pain; her tears had long since gone, gone with her hope. The grandmother turned as well, to face this tall stranger with his yellow eyes and shock of white hair, and, as Borrack turned his gaze upon her, he noticed her eyes shared the same fate as her daughter's. Borrack said gently and quietly:

"Mumbye is happy now; his pain and suffering have gone."

The mother smiled and, in her eyes, Borrack saw a flicker of light, of peace.

"You must be Borrack," she said, feebly.

"Yes," he replied with surprise.

"He mumbled your name so many times in his last few days! Thank you," she said, "Thank you for your help and the comfort you gave him."

She placed her bony hand on his arm, as did the grandmother, "Will you come back and share our hospitality?"

"No, thank you," Borrack replied, "I have someone who I need to see."

She looked into his eyes, "Yes, your father is waiting."

Borrack walked away, back to Maley, his mind full of that short conversation. It was clear that Mumbye had inherited his Empathic powers off his mother and maybe his grandmother. Yet, there was something much more profound that had touched him; these people had nothing, but what little they had, they would share. It was remarkable, and it was this generosity that raised Borrack's hope for humanity. When he reached Maley, he told her of Mumbye's funeral and the warm welcome he had received. Then he changed from Borrack the Man to Borrack the mighty eagle, he lowered his wing and the girl scrambled up it. Then the mighty eagle flapped his huge wings, creating a whirlwind of dust as he did so. He climbed high into the sky. The eagle had already decided and informed Maley that they would not stop until they had reached home and Zachery. It would take two or three days, but they were both chimeras, and, although they would both be tired and hungry, it was something that was well within their capabilities.

Borrack needed, more than anything else, to see his father – he needed to rectify so much hurt that he had inflicted on the wise, old man of the north, Zachary, his father. The eagle flew across Mother Africa towards Tangiers, and then across to Gibraltar, through southern Spain into Portugal, then again through northern Spain, across France and Belgium, until, at last, he entered the pine-clad forest that had been his home from fledgling to adult eagle.

To the west, he could see the Black Mountains; they brought back so many bad memories! And deep, down inside him, a loathing, that bordered on obsession. He had been part of and witnessed the evil of the Labyrinth of Golden Dreams, and it irked him greatly.

In the distance he could see the little log cabin nestling amongst the pine trees, the smoke drifting upwards out of the chimney pot. This was his home, full of memories, both happy and sad. He circled a few times. He could not see his friend! His father. He increased his circle into a spiral, searching further and further away from the homestead. Then, he saw him picking berries, for his evening meal, dressed in his normal attire, his hat tilted to one side. Borrack smiled with his eyes, it was both caring and mischievous.

"Hold on!" Borrack shouted to Maley.

She was tired and exhausted but realized by Borrack's tone that he was about to go into a dive. Borrack swept his huge wings back and plunged head-first downwards! Not a sound could be heard, except the rush of air, as they passed through it at speed. The old man was blissfully unaware of his fate. Maley watched with excitement as they rushed head-long into the ground. Then, before the old man could react, Borrack spread his wings outright and pushed his talons out and gently plucked the old man's hat off! Then he flapped his huge wings and away he flew, back to the homestead. The old man was shocked! He looked up to see what had happened, and there, he saw his friend, his son, Borrack, flying back home with his hat in his claws. He smiled and shook his fist at Borrack, laughing at his son's audacity.

"You devil, Borrack! You devil!"

Zachary made his way back to the homestead, to meet his son, who he hadn't seen since his last visit with his two young wards, Jay and Gemma. As he approached the homestead, he noticed two figures; one sent a chill down his spine. He stopped and stepped back, a fear deep in the recesses of his mind came flooding back. He knew the fear was irrational! He looked beyond it, beyond that absurd thought and, as he did, he saw a beautiful, young woman, and next to her stood a man, taller than the tallest of men, with yellow eyes and shock of white hair, wearing a suit of golden-brown feathers. The man swung Zachary's hat around in his hands. The old man knew instinctively who he was; it was his son, Borrack. He stood still for a few seconds devouring the information that his eyes were telling him. He had never seen Borrack the man – he had only ever seen him as a fledgling and then an adult eagle. The old man smiled, and walked towards his son, slowly at first, then quickening his pace. Borrack held out his arms and Zachary moved towards them; they embraced. A tear of joy rolled down the old man's face. Zachary grabbed hold of his son's arms and pushed him away.

"Let me look at you, my son!" he said with love and pride in his voice, "So this is what my son looks like?"

Borrack looked down at the old man.

"Yes," he said, choking back his own emotions. Borrack so wanted to tell Zachary how he felt, about how he was, without doubt, his real father and how sorry he was for any pain he had caused him, and that it was only with Mumbye's death and the mortality of life that he had seen his failings.

But Zachary did not need him to tell him; he had already sensed it! He could see his son's love.

Zachary looked at the girl, "And who is this?" he said.

"Oh, sorry," Borrack said, flustered, "This is Maley. I was wondering, would you mind if she stayed with you for a while? Her parents have died, and she is all alone."

"Ah! She is, like you, a chimera?" Zachary questioned.

"Yes," said the girl, embarrassed by his frankness.

"Yes, of course, you can stay with me! I could do with some help, now I am getting older!" the old man replied, "Please sit, let me fix you some food! You both look tired and hungry."

Maley looked at the old man, with her crystal blue eyes, "Please, let me help! It's Borrack who needs the rest; he's been flying non-stop for several days to see you."

Zachary looked at his son mockingly, "What was the rush?"

Borrack dropped his head, feeling slightly uneasy. The truth was the old man knew why his son had returned in haste! He knew he was gaining the wisdom of age. Zachary and the girl disappeared into the homestead for some time, and when they returned, their arms were laden with food and drink.

The majestic sun had long since set, leaving a jealous moon to fulfil its role in providing only half a job. But, as the shards of incandescent light fell across the landscape and the three of them had finished their meal, Borrack told his father about his adventures. He told him of the journey with Jay and Gemma, the battle with the Ice Blue Wind, the deal with the Labyrinth of Golden Dreams, the safe return of the children to their parents and Melvin's release from purgatory. His journey to help Mumbye and to take him to the land where elephants live forever, the adventure with Ishmell and his apprentice; the journey to Poutia and then to the Accountant of Lives, then back to Poutia and his first dream; the appearance of a large, black bird in that very same dream and in subsequent dreams. He told him about Maley and her curse! He told his father about the Fire Mountain and Mumbye's last journey. Zachary listened with interest! But so much more than that, he listened with pride and love in his heart at this young man's story, his son who he had nurtured from such a young age.

The old man turned his gaze to Maley, her crystal blue eyes were firmly fixed on Borrack, and he sensed a kindling, the beginnings of love, perhaps? Not that Borrack had recognised it. The old man looked back at his son, as Borrack told him of his next adventure in the New World. A young girl who was teetering between sanity and insanity, as nightmares ravaged her mind, and of the voice she hears, that crowds out reason and reality.

The End

BOOK 3.

THE ICE PLATEAU

Mermosia

To every square inch of land that is inhabited by humanity, a history exists so rich that its spiritual legacy lives on in the very material elements that encompass this globe, that circumnavigates that majestic sun, and none more so than in the Americas, where the tribes of that great continent lived as one, in harmony with Mother Nature, and where their wisdom perpetuated that paradise until that fateful day, the day the white men arrived, when that paradise was annihilated by the cruelty of avarice and disease. Yet, deep within that land, exists the spirit of those tribes of native America; for their history can never be eradicated from that land; for that land is theirs.

* * * * *

Mermosia sat on the hill looking down over her hometown and, beyond that, the Hudson Bay. She sat there in her dream reality, her unconscious world; a world that was all too short in time. For sleep and her dream reality were her only escape from the conscious world, and that door with its voices that crowded out sanity and reason, which had haunted her for so long. In recent times, those voices had become more prolific, and they echoed around her mind almost continually. Her only respite was sleep, her escape, her escape from reality. But even now as she sat there, her dream world was disappearing, for she had not seen her friend, and confidant, for more than four weeks. He had told her he would be back to help take her away from the ghost voices that had haunted her. Yet again, however, he was still absent, and as with each dream a night passed, a bit more of her sanity was eaten away, and her hopes began to fade. If he did not arrive tonight, all would be lost; she would give her sanity up for insanity, Mermosia could no longer hold on, the voices were too strong.

Borrack made landfall just before midnight. The moon was no more than a crescent and yet its radiant light illuminated the coastline of Southampton Island with reverence. The eagle looked down at the Hudson Bay; he followed the small inlet that led to the port of Coral Harbour. The only settlement on the island, its humanity reached no more than seven hundred souls, most of them employed within the fishing industry. As he flew over the small town, a few lights shimmered and flickered, from one or two of the dwellings, but most were shrouded in the blackness of night, as if hiding from the primaeval fears that lurk within the depths of all humanity. The eagle could see the outline of the hills that enclosed the settlement, of Coral Harbour, and in particular his meeting place with the young girl, Mermosia. His eagle eye scanned the hillside for life, and as he did, he could make out the silhouette of the adolescent girl; she was rocking to and fro; Mermosia was certainly in a state of distress.

Borrack felt and knew that he was in part responsible for her present state of mind; for he had promised he would be back within ten days and nights; unfortunately, as with so many well-intentioned plans, they had been blighted by the anarchy of life and death. His journey with Jay and Gemma and, subsequently, with Mumbye had taken so much longer than anticipated, and Mermosia had suffered as a result. To Borrack, this was a difficult case. The girl's sanity was at stake. She was on a precipice, a tight rope. If she fell one way she could be saved; if she fell the other, all was lost. It was a difficult balancing act made all the more difficult because, unlike Jay, Gemma and Mumbye, she was not in a coma, but in a state of normality; just that her life was split between the waking hours of reality where the door and its maddening voices gave her no respite, and her dream reality which was her only escape from that nightmare. The eagle had made a conscious decision not to transmute into Borrack the man; he felt such an act would push the girl's mental state beyond the point of no return.

The crescent moon was at its summit. This time of year, in the northern hemisphere, the nights were short and the days long; to Borrack, it seemed to be an age-old battle played out by these two spheres; on one side, the majestic sun, on the other, the moon. Each in its own way trying to dominate the Earth; the truth was, there was only one, true, material God, and that was the sun; but the moon would never be subservient to that superior body. So the battle would be waged first in the northern hemisphere and then in the southern and this story would be played out until the demise of that majestic sun, that golden ball of energy.

Mermosia looked up into the clear skies; the crescent moon seemed to pulsate with silver light that embraced the animate and the inanimate objects that it came into contact with, its fluid light resembled quicksilver. The girl's face glistened with silver tears, which rolled down her cheeks and fell onto her arms that cradled her legs, as she rocked to and fro in desperation. Her hope was all but gone, leaving a vacuum, that could only be replaced with fear. Her eye caught sight of an object, her heart missed a beat. She strained her eyes, and there in the darkness of night, she saw the silver silhouette of her friend, the mighty Borrack. Mermosia jumped to her feet and brushed her silver tearstained rivulets from her face. The eagle hovered above for a while, showing his splendour against the quicksilver-light of the crescent moon, then he swooped down and landed next to the girl, creating a whirlwind of dust.

Mermosia stepped up to meet him and threw her arms around his powerful neck and then, as if from nowhere, her emotional anxiety was released with a vengeance. The laughter of relief, the tears of hopelessness, the pounding of anger as her fists pummelled down on his body; all of the emotions mixed up in a cauldron of chaos. She fell to her knees and sobbed, both with relief and anger. As Borrack looked on, he was not surprised by her reactions, or even shocked. He said nothing, just watched with empathy and guilt. The eagle would have loved to have been able to have changed the course of events; maybe if he had left Jay and Gemma to their own fate or even left Mumbye by that lake, waiting for him to take that child to his final resting place. These were all maybes, but the path of events had run its course, and nothing could change the past.

In his own defence, although Borrack was two personas, he was only one creature, and he could only achieve that which was realistic. He would offer no excuse to the girl for there was no point. Mermosia looked up at him from her pitiful squat position; she wiped away the tears that straddled her face.

"Why did you not come back sooner?" she pleaded.

Borrack's eyes met hers and he replied softly, with a forthrightness that could not be countered, "The actions of the past cannot be changed, I am here now, and we will see this problem to its conclusion together."

The girl said nothing; what could she say? The past had gone and, by inference, this was the start of her future. The eagle knew by the look in her eyes that she had accepted the status quo. He smiled gently with his eyes and said:

"Tomorrow evening we will start your fight back, so with what is left of your dream world tonight, let me show you just one reason why your fight and its victory is so important to you."

Borrack lowered his wing, and the girl climbed aboard, the eagle flapped his huge wings, soaring high into the sky.

Casting his eye on the community of Coral Harbour below, he saw those few lights that shimmered and flickered from those dwellings that had fought back the darkness of night and that remained on. Perhaps their occupants were working, or perhaps those occupants were hiding from humanity's primaeval fears? Whatever their excuse, if they had glanced out of their windows, on that night, which was graced by that crescent moon, they would have devoured a sight, which would have lived with them for an eternity. For high above their heads, Borrack the mighty eagle flew with a young girl on his back, silhouetted against that crescent moon, as if that moon had shed quicksilver over the two of them, bathing them in its luminous light in the blackness of that night.

Their journey was short, no more than an hour, and although at that time of year the Ice Plateau was bathed in light; the majestic sun would not cast its golden rays on that magical place for at least half an hour after their arrival. Borrack could feel the young girl clinging to his neck, he could feel the tremble that ran through her body. It was a tremble of fear, a fear of her waking day. He had sensed this fear in her before, but never as bad as this. The eagle understood that the time was fast approaching, a time when her very existence, her sanity, was to be tested, a time when she would have to face her demons or surrender to their power.

Borrack knew that if he were to save her then he would have to stand with her and fight for her sanity no matter what the cost. As the two of them travelled to their destination, they turned their gaze to the terrain below and there they were met with a multitude of wonderful sites. As the great land of Southampton Island, with its magnificent Mathiasen Mountain and Hansen Lake located to the north gave way to Foxe Basin, and onwards, over Winter Island, which was soon followed by the imposing Arctic Ocean, with its huge icebergs. Some were as big as mighty ships or floating landmasses, which had broken free from their captive state, where the chains of winter had held them with such strength. Within the great ocean they saw Mother Nature's creatures; seals, birds, the king of the seas, the gracious whales, and, in one case, a polar bear climbing on to one of the many icebergs.

As they neared landfall, the darkness of night surrendered to the light of day, for they were entering the land of the unending day. This was the artic circle and the material god's kingdom. A kingdom that he, the sun, flourished in for half a year; but, as with all benevolent leaders, he would share his glory with all his subjects, from the lowest form of life to the highest, he showed no favouritism and asked nothing more than that they should pay homage to his great omnipotence. So, in accordance with his ethos, the great sun god would move to the Antarctic for the second half of the year.

They arrived, as the eagle had predicted, half an hour before the great ball of energy cast its golden rays on the Ice Plateau.

Borrack shouted to Mermosia, "Welcome to the Ice Plateau!"

As the girl cast her eyes across the landscape below, she become speechless, for, as far as the eye could see, a huge plateau lay before her and, spaced at ten-yard intervals, were huge ice columns, each at three yards high and with a circumference of a yard. It was an amazing sight. As they flew across this gigantic ice plateau, which could only be likened to a field of huge stalagmites, Mermosia became in awe of Mother Nature's power.

For the next twenty minutes, they flew across the mighty plateau, until at last they reached a small hill on the eastern peripheries. Borrack circled and landed. He lowered his wing and the girl slid down to the ground. She looked across at the huge field of ice columns and turned her head to face the eagle. In her expression he could see her disbelief at such an incredible sight, and, something much more, the fear of her waking hours had been pushed to the back of her mind; he had never seen her so calm.

"It's beautiful," she said.

Borrack smiled with his eyes, "It is, but this work of art is only half finished, you are about to see something special. For, in front of you, lies the power of Mother Nature and when she joins forces with the magnificent sun, that ball of energy, the powerhouse of this planet, then and only then, will you see and marvel at the ultimate beauty."

As the eagle finished speaking, the sun made its appearance, and its golden rays spread across the plateau, and as the first rays struck an ice column, piercing it with its golden light, the light sprung out the other side in a rainbow of colours, and as it did, the column groaned as it expanded with the heat. Then the rays struck the second, the third, the fourth and so on, and, every time, the golden light was diffused in to so many different colours, and each time the columns groaned with expansion. The sun rose higher, and the golden light fell upon the plateau of ice columns, affecting them with its awesome power, and each column responded to the sun's majesty, like a bud on a camellia, a rose, a magnolia, a rhododendron or any of the millions of flowering species that exist on this beautiful planet. They would open up and blazingly show off their beauty, to pay homage to the life-giver, only that the ice columns reproduced that peculiarity a thousand times more. Borrack and Mermosia watched in utter amazement as the Sun poured its golden light rays downward and a tidal wave of colour followed its progress across the Ice Plateau, and behind it, that crescendo of groaning columns as they expanded under the heat of that ball of energy.

The eagle turned to the girl, "Shall we ride the wave of colour?"

She smiled and nodded with excitement. Borrack lowered his wing and Mermosia climbed aboard. The eagle flapped his large wings, creating a plume of soft, white snow, sending it into a frenzy of chaos, and then he rose up above the Ice Plateau, and dived down between the columns. There, the two of them darted forwards, chasing the wave of coloured light. Mermosia was mesmerised as the kaleidoscope of colour oscillated across her body, as they flew through the ice stack chasing the leading edge of that wave of light. Within minutes, they were riding the crest of the wave.

The eagle poured more power into his wings, taking them beyond the crest of light wave by a good distance.

Borrack shouted to the girl, "Hold on tight!" and then he angled his wings and climbed almost vertically upwards for two hundred yards or so, turned, and plummeted to the ground. Mermosia took in a huge gulp of air; all her fears had evaporated into the excitement of the moment. She watched with bated breath as the Ice Plateau came speeding towards them, the eagle swept back his wings and their speed increased. Then, within yards of the compacted snow and dead centre of two ice stacks, the eagle spread his wings out; bringing them to an almost stop and turning them parallel with the ground. To the girl, the whole manoeuvre seemed to have become static in time, in reality, it was less than a fraction of a second.

He powered up his wings, they were now heading towards the tidal wave of light. His huge wings created a vortex under each, which radiated outwards hitting the columns and resonating, creating a humming that was regular and melodic. Mermosia was captivated by its sound. They were fast approaching the wave. Within seconds they hit it: the colour washed over them in a spectacle that could never be duplicated. Then Borrack dived in and out of the stacks at random. Mermosia excitedly responded in rapturous laughter – she could never remember a time when she had been at one with herself; she was in a state of euphoria.

The eagle sensed that Mermosia's dream reality was close to its climax, so he tilted his huge wings climbing out of the ice columns and returned to the small hill on the eastern peripheries of the plateau. He circled and landed. He lowered his wing, and the girl slid down to the ground. She looked excitedly across the plateau; she could still see the sun's rays as they moved across that magical place. She turned and looked at the eagle – in her mind, time no longer existed.

"Can we do it?" she asked, but then she saw Borrack's eyes; there were no words necessary.

"No!" she screamed and threw her arms around his neck. "Please let me stay here! Please, please!" she pleaded, "I can't go back there! Please, please!"

Borrack responded gently, "Mermosia, we will fight this together. I will be at our meeting place tomorrow night. I cannot change the here and now, but I promise together we can change your future. Just hold onto these magical memories and…" but as the last words left his lips, she began to vacillate between the two worlds, her reality and her dream reality. He watched as every single cell in her body began to randomly disappear into the abyss of emptiness.

Chapter 2

The Ghosts of History

Mermosia rocked to and fro in her bedroom, her daydream nightmare ravaged her mind. Her memory played out the same story, time after time. She was maybe five or six, dressed in a nightdress and descending a staircase; however, it was not one she recognised. At the bottom, she reached a door – the voices were loud and angry. The door was dark green; her small hand gripped the glass handle. She began to turn it and the voices turned into screaming; it became unbearable. She clamped her hands over her ears to block out the screams, she couldn't! The voices and the screams were in her head. She cried out, pleading for them to stop, to leave her alone, but they wouldn't. Mermosia's mother listened as her daughter wept alone in her bedroom. Her mother could do nothing but listen with despair; the child's illness was getting worse and something would have to give.

Borrack felt exhausted. He had left the homestead over four days ago, and he had had very little sleep since then, and on top of that, he had to fly back to Southampton Island. True, it was only just over an hour away, and the day was still young; but nevertheless it still added to his fatigue. He looked across at the Ice Plateau. The sun was still sweeping across the ice columns, providing such an unparalleled sight.

The eagle spread his wings out and powered them up; the soft white snow reacted to the huge downdraft created by those powerful appendages, chaotically flying about as if a snow blizzard had hit the area. He soared upwards, circled, and flew southwest. Below, he could see the giant ice stacks, those on the eastern periphery had returned to their dormant state, waiting once more for that ball of energy – that majestic sun, to once again bring them to life and show off their true splendour.

He flew on across the tidal wave of colour and its beauty resonated deep within his soul. His mind reverted back to Mermosia. He had promised her so much and yet he did not know where to start; he knew very little about her. True, he had known her for some months. But her history was a complete mystery, a mystery that was all the deeper because her memory was limited, and, on top of that, the eagle had no contacts in this part of the world. He was on his own. Borrack's mind was too busy to notice the drama being played out in the Artic Ocean below.

A pack of killer whales hunting their prey, as only killers know how, and as for their prey, the seals, they were baying to get into the middle of their collective – so as they would not be the sacrificial creature on the periphery of this scrum of life and death. It was a violent act, but one that was played out the world over. It was simply the natural order of things, survival of the fittest, which every creature on this beautiful planet does instinctively – with the exception of one; man! For their cruelty transcends that of instinct, transcends that of sustenance, and transcends that of natural justice. For men only see the sport of death and trophy. Yet, out of all of Mother Nature's creatures, man has the conscious ability to see beyond cruelty and pain and choose to ignore it in favour of the latter.

The eagle reached Southampton Island by mid-morning; he felt exhausted. It was a warm, beautiful day. The sky was a deep blue, paling into a lighter blue, as it merged with the horizon. The majestic sun was climbing to reach its crowning glory.

Borrack knew the exact location for his rest. A quiet, deserted and yet, somehow, spiritual place, it was a place void of humanity. He had sensed that, at one time, it had been the home to a peace-loving tribe, who had long since been lost in history. It overlooked a bay that lay on the southeast coast and flowed into Foxe Basin. As he flew towards it, he could feel the magical powers pulling him towards its serenity, and, as it came into view, he marvelled at its passive nature. He spread his huge wings out and gently landed.

Unbeknown to Borrack, high above him, in a cauldron of rocks, a man, small in stature, was busy surveying the area. He cast his eyes downwards and saw the magnificent beast land and watched with utter disbelief and interest.

What the eagle needed, more than anything else, was to return to that which was new to him, and at the same time, much more natural to him, his humanity. He felt so much more comfortable sleeping in that medium, even with the dreams and that particular dream about the large black bird that seemed to have haunted him since his first meaningful introduction to humanity. Borrack closed his eyes and concentrated on Zachary his father. The eagle then changed from eagle to man, and there he stood taller than the tallest of men, with his yellow eyes and shock of white hair, wearing a suit of golden-brown feathers. He opened his eyes facing the bay that flowed into Foxe Basin. Borrack the man inhaled the beautiful view into his lungs, sending it to every part of his humanity. He felt so calm, relaxed, and alone, as if he had no cares in the world. It was wonderful, until his daydream was shattered by a voice, a voice from behind him.

"So, you're a chimera?"

Borrack turned his head in shock to locate the sound, and there, in front of him, stood a man! Small in stature, it was a man wearing a tweed jacket and trousers, a clean, white shirt and tie, while on his head perched a trilby hat and he was carrying a briefcase. His face, like his stature, was small, his eyes conveyed his character; they darted up and down Borrack's body and then to his face, boring deep below the surface, looking for information and questions, devouring them and then retuning for more. It was a look that was hungry for answers, which could never be stifled.

"Oh, please, forgive me! How rude of me! My name is Conner Flynn, Professor Conner Flynn."

The man moved round so that he could face Borrack, so as not to cause Borrack any discomfort. He held out his hand in a gesture of introduction, while Borrack, though still shocked, reciprocated.

"Please forgive me, I clearly have shaken you; if you wish to be alone, perhaps?"

"No, no!" Borrack replied, "It's fine, and, to answer your question, yes, I am a chimera."

"How fascinating," replied the professor, "Of course, I have heard much about your sort, but never have I met such a creature."

Borrack smiled and sat on the ground, the professor followed suit and sat next to him. Borrack found the man that sat next to him fascinating, his forthrightness and his lack of protocol made him quite refreshing.

"I have to be honest," Borrack said, "I wasn't expecting anyone to be here, and your appearance here has certainly surprised me; it is normally deserted here. Are you lost?"

"No," the professor smiled. "I am on an archaeological survey, funded by Oxford University and the World Heritage Organization, as I have been, for the last two years. I started in South America and have worked my way north. My remit is the tribe of this great continent both past and present. Oh! And what a fascinating and informative study it has been. Did you know, there is a tribe of Red Indians in Nebraska or, perhaps, I should say, the remnants of a tribe who can recite and dance an enchantment, which can bring their ancestors back from the dead. They even showed me how to perform the enchantment."

Borrack concentrated on Conner's words with interest and found the professor was so calming to listen to. He had a slight Irish dialect that had been corrupted by an English education, which gave his voice a mellow sound.

"Did you manage to bring any Red Indians back from the dead?" Borrack said smugly.

"No," Conner replied, "But I know it can be done, I saw it with my own eyes! So, don't you worry, I will do it one day!" Borrack laughed.

"It's beautiful here isn't it?" the professor said as he cast his look to the bay in front of them.

"Yes," Borrack replied, as he did the same. For a while, they both sat in silence, looking out over Native Bay towards Foxe Basin.

"This place was the home to a tribe called Sallirmiut – long since gone now. A very insular people, they did not take kindly to visitors," Conner

Flynn said, "Do you know what killed them?"

"No," Borrack replied.

"A virus, a simple virus, brought in by the white man. It makes you realise how fragile we are, doesn't it? Something as small as a virus could destroy a whole community; I find that so intriguing."

"Is archaeology your field of expertise?" Borrack asked.

"No, I have doctorates in many things, archaeology is but one. You see, I have a great thirst for all knowledge, and it has been that way ever since I was a small child. I suppose it's a need to chase the truth, to discover the ways of the cosmos and its many, many dimensions. Of course, no sooner do you find the answer to one question, than another ten questions arise from it! In some ways, it's an addiction. It's like you, I watched you fly in, this huge majestic eagle; you landed, and within seconds you changed into a man. There are no physical laws in our knowledge that allow for such a phenomenon and yet it has happened in front of me! I cannot deny it, you are the living proof."

Borrack laughed, "What will your colleagues say when you explain to them what you have witnessed?" he ribbed his new-found friend.

Conner crooked his head to face his companion, "To be honest, they would not believe me! They would think I had been drinking or I was on drugs or something, and if they had witnessed the event, they would have denied it. Unfortunately, their minds are closed to that which falls outside the boundary of the so-called laws of physics; their system and the established order have seen to that. They're happy to bumble along on the laws of metaphysics."

"And you?" Borrack inquired.

"Oh, I look at any problem from a dialectical position, the proposition that everything is in a state of flux, that everything is somehow connected, no matter how tenuous. Anyway, tell me about yourself, your history. I would be so interested to find out how a chimera is created."

"It's a long story," Borrack said.

"Well, I have the time," Conner Flynn replied.

Borrack relayed his story to the professor, as he had told it so many times before – about the emergence of the Labyrinth of Golden Dreams, his loathing for that life form, and the village at the entrance to the Black Mountains, the Ice Blue Wind and his parent's journey to the Labyrinth of Golden Dreams and his subsequent birth. He recounted about his adoptive father Zachary and his mission to help the young innocents of humanity. The professor listened, his eyes focusing on Borrack, devouring and soaking up the information like a sponge.

"How absolutely absorbing," Conner Flynn replied as his thirst for knowledge was being quenched. "So what are you doing here?" the professor asked.

Borrack panned the landscape until his eyes rested on Native Bay, that flowed into Foxe Basin.

"There's a young girl, an adolescent, whose name is Mermosia. Her mind is being ravaged by a secret, a terrible secret she cannot remember; it haunts her to the point where she could lose her mind. She is my latest mission and I fear that I may let her down."

"Why?"

"Simply because I don't know where to start: there is no help I can call on here, and I don't know anyone," Borrack dropped his gaze to the ground. He picked up a stick that lay next to him and began to doodle in the dirt. The professor could see Borrack's concern.

"Look, I have gone as far as I can with my research. Would you mind if I lend you a hand? I have some contacts in Coral Harbour. If you wish, I could make some inquiries after the girl and perhaps get some background information on her. At least that would be a start," Conner said, "Anyway, pleases excuse my bluntness but you look absolutely exhausted."

"Yes, you're right," Borrack said, "I haven't slept for over three days and nights."

"That's settled then. I'll gather as much information as possible and I will meet you here tomorrow morning, OK?"

Borrack smiled, "Yes, thank you, I appreciate your help."

Professor Conner Flynn marched off in the direction of a single-track road, where he had parked his transport which was, like himself, eccentric. The vehicle was a nineteen-sixties Morris Minor. It was his one indulgence; he took it everywhere with him at his own expense. Clearly, there were some expeditions that were not appropriate for that mode of transport. But where he could, the Morris Minor went with him; it was his lucky charm.

As he marched down to his vehicle, his structured mind was busy cataloguing and compartmentalising all the information he had gathered that day and storing it in the labyrinth of pigeonholes that was his ordered mind. He had a photographic memory, and his mind was, without doubt, the most brilliant in his field. Yet, because of his reluctance to submit to the established order, he would never be invited to join their clan. In truth, Connor Flynn saw them all as dinosaurs, out of touch with reality. Their belief in the certitude of science made his blood boil. There was no finality, only the infinitude of science, and his science was based on that. A science without boundary, without restrictions; this was his freedom, and he would never give it up, even if his life depended upon it.

The professor reached his car and sat in the driver's seat. After the third pull on the starter control the engine sprang into life and he drove down the dirt track. The journey to Coral Harbour, as the crow flies, was no more than five minutes away, but because of the terrain, it would be at least forty-five minutes before he would reach the settlement.

Borrack lay on the grass, the gentle sun caressed his face and he slid from the conscious world to the unconscious world, where once again he would face the confusing imagery and narrative that was his dream reality.

Professor Conner Flynn approached the settlement. It contained no more than two hundred timber-clad buildings, all of them home to the local inhabitants. There were also the remnants of a few structures that had at one time served a purpose to the community, which had now become surplus to its needs. On the outskirts of the settlement, a small but well-equipped research laboratory with dormitories attached stood, financed by the Canadian Government for the purpose of scientific and international development. The professor rarely used such places, preferring the comfort of the local Bed and Breakfast establishments.

His reasoning was simple, if he stayed in the research department facilities, he could be forced to meet those that shared his vocation, and he couldn't stomach that. He would be forced to listen to their metaphysical claptrap, which would undoubtedly lead to an outburst by himself, souring the whole atmosphere. No! He was better off in a Bed and Breakfast.

His Morris Minor came to a stop outside his transient home. The landlady of the establishment was the most motherly, bossy and overbearing woman, but this one had a talent that far outstripped anything he had come across before; she had a loose tongue. She was one of the professor's contacts; there was nothing in the community she did not know about, or did not have an opinion about. If you could stomach her incessant babble, it was truly a great source of useful information. Professor Conner Flynn entered the door to the Bed and Breakfast.

"Good afternoon, Professor," the landlady bellowed, "Only half a day then?" she blabbed.

"Yes! I have a pressing engagement in town," the professor lied.

The landlady's eyebrows rose, hoping that a snippet of gossip was coming her way.

"Ho! Yes," she replied, trying to coax the information from Conner Flynn's lips.

The professor knew exactly how to play her.

"It seems a colleague of mine has had an altercation with a young girl in the town, a Mermosia something or other?"

The Landlady crossed her arms under her heavy breasts and looked candidly at Conner Flynn, "You mean, Mermosia Luka?"

"Yes! That's it," the professor said.

"Strange family, moved here about ten years ago. Moved here from Regina, a bit of a mystery surrounding their move if you ask me. The girl, Mermosia, she's a real odd ball. You know, she's got mental problems – should have been locked up in one of those mental hospitals. It's wrong to have someone like that walking the streets; you never know what she might do to honest tax paying citizens like us. Strange you should ask about her though. Someone else was asking after her about a month ago."

"Who was that?" Conner Flynn pressed.

The landlady's expression changed; her mind was not used to changing tack, halfway through one of her tirades of gossip. "Yes, he was a tall man, very smart; probably a policeman or…"

Conner Flynn butted in before she could start another tirade of character assassination, "What did he want to know?"

The landlady lifted her eyebrows again, confused by the professor's bluntness.

"What did he want?" she mumbled to herself, as if the words somehow focused her memory. "He was looking for Mermosia Bassinger not Mermosia Luka."

"How did you know it was the same girl?" Conner Flynn jumped in.

The landlady was flummoxed again by the professor's brusqueness, "Well," she said nervously, in case the professor cut her short again, "His description of the girl, it was as if he had known her all her life. I mean, I pride myself on my memory, and I can remember, as if it were yesterday, when the family first moved here. But his description of the girl was uncanny; he even described the Teddy bear the girl had as a child. I have to be honest, his description brought those memories of mine flooding back to me."

"What did you tell him?" Conner Flynn asked with concern.

"I told where they lived and mentioned the child was not normal and, with that, he thanked me and disappeared."

"Where does she live?" the professor urged.

"If you go down the street to the harbour and turn first right and carry down on that road until you come to the first dwelling with a green door, it faces the harbour; that is the Luka household."

"Thank you for your help," the Professor said and marched out the door, turning in the direction of the harbour.

As he walked, he collated the information he had coerced from of the landlady and stored it in his tidy mind. He reached the harbour; he crossed the road and walked next to the sea wall.

The sea was restless and pounded the wall encroaching on to the road. He stood opposite the green door dwelling; it was small and split into two levels; on the first floor, an uncovered window lay bare. There he could see the sadness of life, the girl Mermosia had her head in her hands; rocking to and fro, and every now and again, he could hear the muffled sounds pierced, as she screamed out in pain.

The professor moved on up the road. At the top, he turned and walked back on the pavement that served the tiny dwellings. As he approached the entrance of the Luka residence, a lady rushed out of the door – her eyes were red-rimmed, her face pale and her body slender. Conner Flynn focused on her face for a second, but in that short microcosm of time his brain had analysed her very being and categorized it into his well-ordered mind. Her tortured brown eyes expressed her frustration, anger and distress at her daughter's illness; her brow, creased into a multitude of furrows, showed her exhaustion and her body language was like that of a trapped animal unable to escape from a predator whose power was awesome.

Professor Conner Flynn carried on walking past the lady while his mind was busy drawing the relative information together. He did not feel pity for the family's dilemma; that was not in his nature. But he saw in them a problem that his analytical mind could not ignore – a problem that raised a question and a question that he was compelled to answer. He moved on to his next contact, Doctor Erick Ashoona the local GP, a friend who was sure to shed more light onto the girl's history.

CHAPTER 3

The Door: Part One

To be aware of your past is the key to your future. It gives you the
benefit of hindsight, to examine and re-evaluate your mistakes, to put
into perspective, that which is right and that which is wrong. To
understand those natural laws that govern you and yours. Without your
history, life has no foundation and a life without foundation is like a
structure without a base; its destruction is assured.

The Sallirmiut of Southampton Island had learnt that lesson aeons ago,
and in their infinite wisdom had discovered the reflection of personal
history in a crystal pool attached to the Hansine Lake. It was a reflection
that had served them well for many thousands of years. It had shown them
their past mistakes, and the most potent of all was the deceit of newcomers,
whether consciously or unconsciously, it had shown they could not be
trusted, so they stayed segregated. Until that fateful day when the white
man arrived, and that powerful lesson was lost. On that appalling day, their
destiny was sealed; old, young, strong and brave, all perished to that virus
brought in by the white man that laid them to rest in the history of time.

* * * * *

The sun was moving to the western horizon and lazily hovered in the
sky, refusing to surrender to the moon. Borrack woke with a start. He looked
around confused and disorientated. He had woken from a dream. It had
been both sharp, in-focus, and with a narrative, and yet he could remember
very little of it; it unnerved him. It was a dream so much stronger than
anything he had had before, and in its wake, it left two visual imprints, as
if the imprints had been seared into his optic nerve. The first, an object: a
black bird, a raven, sinister and menacing, the second, the word Erigal,
repeating itself time after time.

Borrack shook his head, confused, trying to bring back sanity to his
existence; slowly, he regained his composure. The girl Mermosia came to
the front of his mind. He looked up at the sun as it was sinking into the
western horizon, 'I am not too late' he thought. 'It can only be eight, eight-
thirty. The girl would not materialise until ten – maybe later?'

Borrack stood up. He needed food and drink. He scouted around. There above him he heard the sound of running water. He moved towards it and knelt down by a small brook, cupped his hands and scooped the freshwater to his lips. It was cool and refreshing, especially after that strange dream when his pallet had felt as though it was on fire. Borrack savoured the water – it was so good. All that was left was food. He surveyed the terrain. He looked for berries or root crops but all he saw was the carcass of a caribou. His dual personality was in conflict with itself; on the one side, his humanity was disgusted at the sight of the carrion and the thought of chewing at its rotting flesh, but the eagle in him saw it as a good source of food, and one that should not be wasted.

Ever since the Matriarch had introduced Borrack to his humanity, he had found that this half of his personality was becoming stronger and the more he stayed human, the less he wanted to be that other creature; it was a battle that was being waged within him.

He thought of the girl and her plight, he pushed his personal conflicts to the margins of his mind. He closed his eyes and thought of Zachary, then, within seconds, he changed from Borrack the man to Borrack the mighty eagle. The eagle saw the carcass and hopped over to it and pulled at its rotting meat with his powerful beak, ripping the flesh from the carcass and devouring it.

When he had had his fill, he flapped his huge wings and soared into the sky. He flew over Native Bay, which flowed into Foxe Basin, turned, and headed for his meeting place with the girl, on that hill overlooking Coral Harbour.

Although the sun was low, it would not relinquish its grip on the planet. For the majestic sun would jealously guard that which it yearned for. It had given life and, in return, it asked for nothing more than its deserved homage. The eagle spiralled his way down to his meeting place with Mermosia. He could not see her. He scanned the sky as he went down – there were a few clouds, insignificant in size, their tops white and fluffy but their undersides glowed orange and gold from the reflection of the sun, amplifying that ball of energy's magnificence.

As Borrack spiralled around to the east, he could see the crescent shaped Moon on the horizon, the Great Pretender was waiting in the wings for the sun's demise. It was pale, barely visible, almost ghostly, but it hung there, waiting to take the crown from its superior. The eagle spread his talons out for impact – thump! He was down.

No sooner had he landed, than he caught sight of an image, an image randomly materializing in front of him. At first, its form was gaseous, shapeless. He watched as it slowly took on structure and, there, he saw Mermosia wavering between her nightmare realities, to her escape, her refuge, her dream reality.

As she became constant in matter, Borrack noticed her eyes; they were dull, almost lifeless. Mermosia looked up at her friend and confidante and spoke, her voice, like her eyes, seemed distant and quiet with exhaustion, "Can we go back to the Ice Plateau?"

The eagle was speechless for a second.

"No," he said sympathetically.

Her eyes welled up, a tear rolled down her cheek, she collapsed onto the ground. Borrack waddled up to her side and lowered his body down next to hers; he stretched his wing out and rolled it around her. She lifted her head to face him.

Gently, he said, "This is the start of your future. We will fight this illness together, and then when it is all over, I will take you back to the Ice Plateau."

She smiled, though it was half-heartedly and uncertain. The eagle sensed the uncertainty and knew she had all but given up. He tried to rally her.

"Come on, Mermosia, let's fight back. Tell me about your past, the recurring daydream?"

The girl turned her head away. The sun had all but disappeared, and the crescent-shaped moon brimmed with its quicksilver light, defusing the brilliant light across the small static clouds, turning them from white to silver.

"Mermosia, look up at me," the eagle said sternly.

The girl turned her head to look at Borrack. The running tears stained her face. The eagle knew the pain he was causing, but if they were to resolve the problem, he needed as much information as possible.

"I can't," she sobbed.

Borrack gently smiled with his eyes, "Come on, please try,"

The girl spoke, her voice shaky and unsure, as she relayed the story that had haunted her for so long. She told Borrack of the staircase, the green door, the screaming and, as she spoke each word, it was like a red-hot bar searing through her very being. She told of the hand dripping with blood from a wound diagonally across the palm. Then she dropped her head and stared at the ground, as her tears fell on to it, creating small rivulets that disappeared into the coarse grass.

"Is that everything you can remember?" Borrack urged.

The girl nodded reluctantly.

"Except..." she said.

"Except what?" the eagle pressed. Mermosia lifted her head to face Borrack. She looked exhausted.

"Except what?" Borrack said again with compassion.

"Well, the black bird. The raven, Erigal. He has started to appear in the last few months."

The information jarred the eagle, "Black bird, raven?"

"Yes," the girl replied, and once again dropped her head.

In a selfish way, this was a great relief to Borrack. The dream he had had of the raven had unsettled him, but now the motive was clear. It was to do with Mermosia, he obviously had become so involved in the girl's psyche that he had begun to sense her living daydream.

Mermosia's eyes remained firmly fixed on the ground, with her voice barely audible, she mumbled, "I don't think I can hold on anymore. I am so tired. "She looked up at Borrack, "I just can't go on."

Her eyes were bloodshot and brimmed with tears. The eagle looked down at the girl below him, he felt nothing but compassion for her, and he smiled gently with his eyes.

"You must fight! Don't give up! We can beat this – I know we can, please, just trust me."

She nodded her agreement but without commitment.

"Listen," Borrack said, "Tonight, just forget about your day reality, lie here against me and look up at the stars and moon and I will tell you of my adventures."

There they sat the two of them, the girl exhausted, quiet, her mind drained of all emotions, while the eagle relayed his adventures in a calm, interesting way.

As daylight broke, Mermosia watched the sun rise above the horizon. She felt no anxiety about the day ahead, just an acceptance of her fate. She had lost the will to fight and felt compelled to surrender to the darkness in her mind.

The eagle had studied the girl's body language and knew she would be lost to her insanity. He felt helpless, guilty, and at a loss to know what to do.

The sun was a quarter of the way towards its meridian; Borrack sensed that Mermosia would soon wake into her nightmarish world, so he tried one more attempt at rallying the girl's survival instinct.

"Be back here tonight at our meeting place," he urged, "Trust me! We will beat this illness together!"

As Borrack finished speaking, the girl started to vacillate between her two worlds, every cell in her body began to randomly disappear and, as she finally evaporated into her nightmarish reality, the eagle knew that his last words to her had fallen on deaf ears.

The professor had reached Native Point early and waited for Borrack's return. His well-organised mind was busy collating all the information he had gathered about the girl Mermosia, from his contacts, the landlady with the loose tongue and the local GP, who he had known for some time and with whom he had struck a bond of friendship that was unshakable.

They were so much alike, in fact, that he, like the Professor Conner Flynn, saw beyond the boundaries of certitude to the infinite possibilities of science, particularly in the fields of medicine, and, on more than one occasion, he had gone beyond the boundaries of ethical medicine to cure his patients – and was rewarded more often than not by their miraculous recoveries.

As the professor gathered all the strands of information together from the many thousands of pigeonholes that were part of his well-ordered mind, he began to get excited about the future questions he would answer, and in doing so, lay bare the young girl's demons, and in its wake, provide a path for Mermosia's recovery and rehabilitation.

He was deep in thought when he was disturbed by a sound emanating from the sky above. He looked up and there, far above him, he saw Borrack, the mighty eagle. He took a deep breath; the sight was far in excess of anything he had ever seen or could imagine; it was breath-taking. The mighty eagle spiralled his way down, and, as he reached the ground, he spread his huge wings out to slow his descent and stretched out his talons for impact… thump! He was down.

Conner Flynn walked over to Borrack. The professor began to prattle on excitedly over the information he had assembled about the girl, until he looked into the eagle's yellow eyes, and from them he deduced a problem.

"I take it thing's did not go well, then?" the professor enquired.

"No! They didn't. Mermosia, I sense, is giving up; her fight has gone. I feel she will very soon slip into the world of insanity and will be lost forever."

"How long?"

Borrack frowned, "Hours, if not sooner! I have let her down."

Professor Conner Flynn's well-ordered mind went into overdrive. He marshalled as much information as possible, from the thousands of pigeonholes that stored a plethora of knowledge in his well-ordered mind, to resolve the new question he was faced with, and, within milliseconds, he had a plan, one that might just save the child's sanity.

"Listen, Borrack, I have an idea. A way of saving the child's sanity; well, at least until we have finished our research on her."

The eagle looked puzzled.

"You must trust me, Borrack. I'm going back to Coral Harbour to buy us some time. I'll be back as soon as I can, and then we will be going on a long journey."

The eagle still remained confused. Professor Conner Flynn disappeared over the hill to his Morris Minor car.

As the professor drove back to the town, he refined his plan. First, he would stop off at the research facility. There, he would pick up a drug, a drug that he knew was there; for his photographic memory had flagged up a picture of it in the pharmaceutical cupboard. It was a drug used in research on animals – a tranquilliser, but a tranquilliser with a difference. Its effects were stunning. It would send its recipients into a sleep, a sleep void of dreams, a sleep that suspended the creature between life and death, a state of limbo. Once he had the drug, he would drive straight to Dr Eric Ashoona – he could picture the doctor in his well-ordered mind. He, like himself, was a man small in stature. He maintained a small tash, and, like the majority of the inhabitants of Coral Harbour, he was of Inuit decent. His clothes, as usual, would always be immaculate and always the same, a black three-piece suit, white shirt and tie, a black trilby hat and, if wet, a long, black trench coat and carrying a black umbrella.

He was a friend that Conner could rely on, and, in this case, the professor's faith was well-rewarded. After they had accomplished their mission, Conner Flynn drove the doctor back to his surgery and then made his way back to Native Point and his meeting place with Borrack. He had been no more than two hours. After parking the Morris Minor, he walked up the hill to meet the eagle, and there he observed Borrack the man; he had already metamorphosed from Borrack the eagle.

Borrack was looking over Native Bay to Foxe Basin and beyond, taking in its natural beauty. The sky was a deep blue, with fast-moving clouds, and as each cloud passed over the gently rippling sea, it cast a dark, grey shadow that matched the size and speed of the moving clouds. Borrack heard a noise from behind and turned to see the professor marching up the hill; he was still confused as to the professor's endeavours. As Conner Flynn approached, he wore a look of achievement.

"Well, my friend," he said to Borrack, "We have about five days' grace."

Borrack looked bewildered, "What do you mean?" he replied.

"My good friend, the doctor, and I have managed to give the child, Mermosia, a drug. It's a drug that will suppress her daytime reality and her dream reality for up to five days; however, after that time, she will need the antidote, which will then drive her into her dream reality. But, hopefully, by then, we will have some answers to the child's history, which may possibly lay the grounds for her recovery.

The professor then outlined the information he had gathered. He told of the family's arrival at Coral Harbour some ten years earlier, of the man who was looking for the child and knew her like family, but had mistaken her surname, and of the suggestion that the family had moved from Regina, although the professor could not be sure of this piece of intelligence; it was no more than hearsay from the landlady. He told of the doctor and how his records of the family only went back as far as their arrival in Coral Harbour, as if their history before that time had been eradicated. After Conner Flynn had finished speaking, he probed Borrack's eyes with his own, looking for Borrack's contribution to the gathering of intelligence.

"Well, my friend, what did you find out from the girl?" he asked firmly.

"Not a great deal," Borrack replied, "She told me of her living nightmare."

He relayed the information as Mermosia had told him.

"Oh, and there was one more thing, she told me that in her living daydream she saw a hand, a hand with blood dripping from a wound that was cut diagonally across the palm," Borrack did not mention Erigal, the black raven – he felt the information was immaterial; however, as future history was to prove, such an omission would have dire consequences for Borrack.

"So, what now?" Borrack the man asked.

"I am afraid it is a tenuous lead, but it's all we have. It looks like we have to go to Regina. It's going to be a long journey – the best part of thirty hours by car. So, we had best make a move."

With that, the Professor marched off towards his mode of transport, and Borrack followed. They approached the car, and Borrack looked at the vehicle; his face said it all.

"Are you sure that this thing will get us there?"

Conner Flynn turned around.

"What do you mean? That's my lucky charm."

Borrack smiled, "Lucky charm! And you, a scientist? No! We had better fly, at least – that way I know we will get there."

The professor smiled. He was hoping that Borrack would offer.

"Sounds good to me," Conner Flynn replied, trying to show surprise.

Borrack closed his eyes and thought of Zachary, his father. His body expanded in all directions, until he became Borrack the eagle, taller than the tallest of men. Conner Flynn watched the transmutation from man to eagle, assimilating the visual images, processing and dissecting the information and storing it in his well-ordered mind.

CHAPTER 3

The Door: Part Two

The eagle lowered his wing.

"Well, Professor, we had better get going; I hope you know which way to go?"

Conner Flynn smiled.

"Southwest, fly southwest. If you fly low enough, I am sure I will be able to pick out the points of reference."

With that, the professor climbed aboard and held on tight. The eagle flapped those mighty appendages, creating a vortex of dust and debris and lifting them into the sky. Borrack hugged the contours of the land, flying low, as requested by the professor.

The regal sun was rising fast in the eastern sky, almost reaching its crowning glory and discharging its golden rays down over the eagle and his passenger; casting a shadow that the eagle and his passenger chased. To anybody who had caught sight of the two of them, they would have been mesmerised by its sheer grandeur and absurdity. For above them flew Borrack the mighty eagle, and perched on his back, a man small in stature. A man wearing a tweed jacket, and trousers, a clean white shirt and tie and on his head, perched a trilby hat while carrying a briefcase.

As they flew to their destination, the professor's well-structured mind was working on four levels; such were his unique abilities.

On the first level, he was scanning the topography below and collating the information from his photographic memory, so as to guide Borrack the mighty eagle to their chosen destination, Regina.

On the second level, his peripheral vision was taking in the beautiful vistas that lay either side of their journey, dissecting them and collating them into his well-ordered mind.

On the third level, he was thinking about those that shared his vocation and their reaction to seeing him riding on the back of an eagle, a chimera, and how they would cope with such a sight, with their closed minds limited to the boundaries of metaphysics. To the professor, this was what his science was about -infinite possibilities and the knowledge that, no matter how tenuous, all things were connected in the material cosmos.

On the fourth and final level, his well-ordered mind was accumulating all the information about the girl Mermosia, formulating many hypotheses, to unravel the girl's secrets, ruling out the most bizarre, allowing him only three alternatives; one of which he was sure would be the answer. But, as with all science, it needed irrefutable proof, and this journey would open the way to satisfy that question, he was so eager to answer.

As for Borrack, he saw the expedition as his last chance to save the girl from her demons. He had been given a window of opportunity – all too short, but he would do his best for Mermosia.

As the majestic sun continued its journey from east to west, so Borrack's shadow moved from the front of him to the back of him, lengthening as the one, true, material god finally settled in the west, and gave way to the Great Pretender.

The moon's quicksilver light diffused itself across the darkened landscape, bathing in its glorious beauty. The mighty eagle had flown for well over eighteen hours, carrying his passenger, without stopping, and at last, they reached the outskirts of Regina – the capital of Saskatchewan.

The professor who was as sharp as ever, even after eighteen hours, directed the eagle to a safe haven to land and change back into Borrack the man.

It was in the McKell Wascana Conservation Park, wetlands set aside for Mother Nature to nurture, that which was so important to this beautiful planet. It was early morning, just before the sun would once again cast its omnipotence across this part of the planet, and enjoy the reverence it was so entitled to.

The eagle circled a few times until he sought his refuge. He glided down quietly, so as not to disturb that which lay dormant in the primaeval blackness of night, and landed without a sound. He lowered his wing and the professor dismounted, Conner Flynn turned and watched as the eagle mutated from Borrack the eagle to Borrack the man and, as always, the professor was amazed at the manifestation.

The golden ball of energy began to make its appearance on the eastern horizon. The two of them looked at it.

"Well, my friend," the professor said, "I think we should both get some rest, before we start foraging for the truth about Mermosia, don't you think?"

"Yes," Borrack replied.

"There's a small B&B near the University. I used it last time I was here."

Borrack looked at the professor, "So that's how you knew the route here?"

Conner Flynn smiled at his friend, "Yes! I was here for about three months, studying the tribes of Saskatchewan. There are six tribes that inhabited this area, even the name Saskatchewan is an Indian word from the Cree, meaning Swift River; and it is a most interesting place."

By his very nature, the professor could not stifle his enthusiasm. To him, all information was relevant no matter how insignificant. They both walked off to civilisation and the B&B, with the professor babbling on about the six

Indian tribes that at one time laid claim to this land. It was a good hour before they reached the establishment; Borrack stopped Conner Flynn before they entered the B&B.

"I have no money to pay for the room, Professor."

"Don't worry about that my friend, I am sure Oxford University and the World Heritage Organization won't mind paying. I'll just put it down to expenses; they will never know," and grinned. It was a mischievous look. Both of them made an agreement to meet in reception in four hours and went off to their separate rooms. Borrack lay on the bed, and within seconds he was asleep.

Professor Conner Flynn sat at a small dressing table and began to scribble a programme, for the forthcoming investigation. First, they would go to the office of the local newspaper and scroll through the archives looking for the name Bassinger. He was sure this was Mermosia's real surname, and if he was right, it would be the first step in proving his theory correct. Secondly, they would visit his old friend, at Regina University. A professor of criminal science and formerly a detective in the Regina C.I.D.

If Mermosia had been caught up in some kind of crime, he would be sure to know. For he had been in the Regina Police Force for well over thirty years, both as a rookie and later as a detective.

If the professor was right, and both these clues fitted into his theoretical puzzle, then what followed would be the first steps towards proving what his well-ordered mind had already contrived, and, in doing so, answer that question he was so desperate to resolve.

Conner Flynn could not sleep; his mind was too active. He was desperate to start the investigation, as was his need to satisfy that quest for knowledge. After three hours, the urge overwhelmed him. He got up from the small dressing table and made his way to the neighbouring room. He rapped on the door assertively.

"Borrack?" he said quietly; there was no response. "Borrack?" his pitch a little higher, but still no response. This time his frustration got the better of him, "Borrack!" he shouted and banged on the door loudly.

Borrack woke with a start! He was confused and disorientated. His dream still rattling around in his head. The black raven, Erigal, was at the front of that confused imagery and narrative and yet no matter how strong the dream had been he could not remember its content, just the black raven and its name.

"Yes?" he replied, confused.

"It's time we got some work done!" the voice from behind the door said.

Borrack's clouded mind cleared with the recognition of the voice; it was the professor.

"Yes! OK, I'll meet you down in reception," Borrack said, shaking his head, to wake himself from his dream reality.

It was ten minutes before Borrack appeared. Conner Flynn looked at him.

"Are you all right?" he said, "You look dreadfully pale?"

"Yes, I'm fine, just a little tired."

He said nothing about the dream; it was clearly to do with the girl. Somehow, he had become so involved in her problems that he had become empathic with her thoughts.

"So, what now?" Borrack said.

"We're off to scroll through the local paper's archives," the professor replied.

They reached the local paper's office just after one p.m. and were shown into a rather shabby, square room. It was void of any natural light; around three of the walls were desks each containing two microfilm data machines and, by each, a seat was provided.

Both the professor and Borrack sat next to each other adjacent to the door. Between them they scrolled through the bi-weekly issues of the newspaper, from eight to twelve years earlier. It was some three hours later that Borrack came across something relevant.

"Professor! It's here! Yes! This must be it!" Conner Flynn moved over to Borrack's machine, and there it was, in black and white. This was the first proof of the professor's theory:

Dated 29th September 1998

Loving Couple Murdered While
Their Five-Year-Old Daughter Watches

At five a.m. yesterday, police broke into the residence of Mr and Mrs Bassinger, to find the couple lying dead in the lounge, after what the police describe as a frenzied attack. Next to them their five-year-old daughter was reported to have been sat, traumatised. Police have cordoned off the area and are treating it as a major crime scene. The young girl has been taken into care for her own safety and protection.

The rest of the report was taken up with Mr and Mrs Bassinger's history – when they moved to Regina, where they had come from, when they were married and so on, which ran for the rest of the page. As always, Conner Flynn absorbed all the information. no matter how trivial, in his well-ordered mind.

Both the professor and Borrack sifted through the latter copies of the paper, over the next five issues, where it remained the leading story, but still with very little information. After that, the story was downgraded, until the tenth issue, where it was relegated from the paper. The professor looked at Borrack.

"Clearly, from this information, the police never even had a suspect?"

"Where do we go from here?" Borrack replied.

Conner Flynn smiled, "Well, my friend, I have an ace up my sleeve!"

Borrack looked at the professor with an expression of confusion.

"There's a friend of mine at Regina University, a professor of criminal science. An ex-C.I.D. detective; if anyone knows the full story, he will."

Conner Flynn looked at his watch, "If we go now, we should just catch him."

It took a full hour before they reached Regina University and his friend.

Conner knocked on the door. A voice echoed from behind it, "Come!"

The professor marched in, followed by Borrack. The man behind the desk stood up to greet his visitors. He was a stoutly figure – not small, but certainly not tall, bald and of about fifty years of age. His face was jolly, warm and friendly, and Borrack felt at ease with him.

"Conner!" he boomed, as the two of them approached the desk. "How wonderful to see you!"

He held his hand out, and Conner Flynn grabbed it in a way that suggested they had a deep-seated respect and friendship with each other. The stoutly man turned his gaze to Borrack; Conner quickly gathered his thoughts and followed the dictates of etiquette.

"Joshua, this is Borrack, a colleague of mine."

"How very nice to meet you," the stoutly man said.

"Borrack, this is Professor Joshua Thurgood."

"Likewise," Borrack replied.

Joshua could not help himself; he could not take his eyes off of Borrack's face.

"Please excuse me, I suppose it's the policeman in me – but your eyes?"

Professor Conner Flynn butted in quickly, lying to divert Joshua Thurgood and his inquisitive mind from Borrack's real history.

"They're yellow! My colleague has undergone a very experimental operation to restore his sight, which he had unfortunately lost in an accident."

The stoutly man was satisfied with the explanation, particularly as it had come from his friend, Professor Conner Flynn, a man with such integrity.

"Please sit," Joshua said, waving his large hands in the direction of the chairs. "How may I help you?"

"I am hoping you will be able to resolve a riddle for us."

Joshua looked at Conner Flynn inquisitively.

"You see, Joshua – Borrack, well he's a doctor; in fact, the local GP for a place called Coral Bay, Southampton Island…"

As Borrack listened, he was amazed at how quickly the Professor was able to manipulate the facts to deliver a question. He, for his part, kept a straight face to add credence to Conner's lie.

"Well, to cut a long story short, he has, in his charge, a young girl who is suffering from Post-Traumatic Stress Disorder. He feels that, unless he can understand her history and confront her with it, she will withdraw into insanity and be lost in the darkness of her own mind. The girl's name is

Mermosia Luka, but we believe it to have been Mermosia Bassinger."

As the professor mentioned the surname, Joshua Thurgood's expression changed.

"We have gone through the local papers."

Joshua waved his hands in the air.

"There's no need to say anymore," he said. "This is very difficult. What I say to you must not leave these walls; that girl's life depends on it. You see, I know who you are talking about, and you are right, it is Mermosia Bassinger. She is on a witness protection list, not that she was ever a witness, she was too traumatised. The girl could not even remember her own name, let alone the perpetrator of that abhorrent crime. No, she was placed on the register for her own protection. As you have obviously surmised, there were officially no suspects, although that's not strictly true; there was one – Mrs Bassinger's brother. Unfortunately, his alibi was watertight, even though his DNA was found at the crime scene."

"Surely," Conner began to speak, but was stopped in his tracks by Joshua.

"I know. If his DNA was at the scene, then his guilt is assured, and you're right, except the CPS would not go with it. The truth is, the man knows too many powerful people! I am more concerned about visits to the offices of the local paper. Did you mention to anyone what you were researching?"

Borrack looked at Conner Flynn, and the professor reciprocated. Each in their own minds confirming that they had never mentioned the girl or their research to anyone. Professor Conner Flynn jerked his head around to face Joshua Thurgood.

"No, we never mentioned anything at the newspaper offices."

But, at the same time, his well-ordered mind had retrieved some vital information.

"Although, when I was enquiring after the girl's history with one of my contacts in Coral Harbour, the landlady of the local B&B, she mentioned that a man had asked after the girl, and had used her real surname. The irony is that this man's information of the girl's suggested previous surname has led us here."

Joshua's facial expression changed; he became much more serious.

"Did your contact notice if the man had a scar across the palm of his left hand?"

"No, nothing was mentioned," the professor replied.

Borrack shot Joshua a look.

"A scar on his hand across the palm?"

"Yes," the stout man responded.

Borrack chose his words carefully. Professor Conner Flynn had laid down a fictitious character for him to play out for obvious reasons. Borrack's real history was not a rational option when dealing with the likes of Professor Joshua Thurgood.

"When in counselling sessions with Mermosia," Borrack said, "Although her recollection of the events is scant, they are always the same, and one of the things that haunts her is seeing an open hand with a diagonal wound across it, bleeding profusely."

"That is interesting!" Joshua replied, "It is clear that some of those awful events are returning to her memory."

"Maybe, but, unless we can unlock all of those memories in her head, and fast, her destiny is sealed. She is no longer able to take those nightmarish daydreams. That is why we are here."

"Yes," Conner butted in, "So any information would be a great help."

The stoutly man nodded his agreement.

"Well, the information you retrieved from the newspaper archives is more or less true. As I have already said, there was, no, there is, a suspect: Mrs Bassinger's brother, Raymond Le Clec, and he is well-connected – I mean, well-connected. He is the owner of the local paper, and, at one time, Mayor of the city. A nasty piece of work and as corrupt as they come. We know Mr Bassinger was about to blow the whistle on a building scam that Le Clec was involved in; normal things, backhanders and so on for lucrative contracts etc. On the night of the Bassinger's murders, several high-ranking politicians and establishment figures provided him with a watertight alibi. The fact that his blood was found at the crime scene and buried under a mountain of bureaucracy shows his power. No! He is guilty of the crime."

Joshua looked at Borrack, "And your information regarding the wound across his palm is the final piece of the jigsaw. Sadly, because of the girl's mental state, we still can't bring him to justice."

"Do you think he was the man asking about the girl at the B&B?" Conner Flynn asked.

"Undoubtedly! He was checking to make sure she was still no longer a threat to him, and all the time she is unable to remember anything, he is prepared to let her live."

"Surely, he would not go that far; she's his niece?" Borrack said.

"I wouldn't put anything past this guy, he's a psychopath! He didn't think anything about murdering his sister!"

Joshua Thurgood looked at Borrack, "You look a little perplexed."

"Yes," Borrack replied. "You have created a dilemma. If I help the girl to retrieve her memories for that time in her life, there is a strong chance that this Le Clec character is going to come after her to silence her. But if I don't help her, she will most certainly lose her sanity."

"Yes! It's an unenviable position you're in!" Joshua replied.

Conner Flynn looked at Borrack, "I don't think we have a choice."

Borrack turned his head to face his friend.

"No, you're right, there is no other option. We must save her sanity."

Conner nodded.

"I would have made the same decision," Professor Joshua Thurgood confirmed. "Of course, if you need any help, Conner, you have my number. I still have contacts in the Regina police force."

"Well, there is something," Borrack said. "Is there any chance of visiting the crime scene? I know it's some ten years, but I would like to get the feel of the place."

Joshua smiled, "Let me see what I can do. If you contact me in the morning, I will have an answer for you."

Conner Flynn and Borrack thanked Joshua Thurgood for his help and made their way back to the B&B.

The morning daylight broke out grey and overcast, and behind a heavy overcoat of cloud, the majestic sun poured down its life-giving energy, with the surety that most of its power would filter through that heavy cloud to feed and nurture its subjects, and they would once again rejoice in its omnipotence and pay homage to that ball of energy.

Borrack and Professor Conner Flynn woke early – both had slept soundly. Even Borrack's haunting dream about Erigal, the black raven, did not appear, which he wondered if was due to Mermosia's history being unravelled, and perhaps opening the way for her cure. Whatever the reason, he was glad of the respite from that dream.

The professor had contacted Joshua Thurgood early and learnt that he had managed to get access to the crime scene of ten years earlier. He provided Conner Flynn with the address and the time for their meeting; it was less than two hours away.

As they all reached the meeting place, the heavy, grey overcoat of cloud broke under the awesome power of the sun as it burnt at it, evaporating it into the ether of nothing.

Professor Conner Flynn scrutinized the residential area, the dwellings were large detached houses built for upper middle-class families. This, plus all the other facts that he had gathered about the girl, Mermosia, fitted into his theoretical puzzle with such clarity that the question he was so desperate to answer was almost resolved. Borrack looked at the stoutly man.

"Joshua, how did you manage to get access?" he said inquiringly.

Joshua Thurgood smiled

"It pays to know the right people! I contacted a friend in Environmental Health, who owed me a favour. Apparently, they told the residents of the house that because of the risk of gamma radiation in the area, it was necessary to do a full health and safety check on the property, and for their own protection they should evacuate the building while the assessment was under way."

The three of them went into the house.

"Would it be possible to start in what was the girl's bedroom?" Borrack asked.

"Of course," Joshua Thurgood replied. Borrack, the professor and Joshua made their way to Mermosia's old bedroom; it was small, but more than adequate for a young child.

"It has had a makeover since the criminal investigation, as has the rest of the house," Joshua said.

Borrack and Conner Flynn nodded. The professor, as always, took everything in, collating and organizing the optical information into his well-ordered mind. He turned to Borrack.

"Let's walk through Mermosia's last visual memories."

Borrack agreed and they retraced the girl's steps.

"She wakes and hears screaming."

Borrack walked to the door and opened it.

"She states that she descended the stairs, the screams were loud and she felt frightened."

Borrack passed down the stairs, the others followed.

"Mermosia reached the door at the bottom of the staircase, the one that leads to the lounge. It was dark green; it has obviously been painted since then. Her small hand grabs hold of the glass handle."

As Borrack said that, he too took hold of that glass handle and it was as the girl described it. This, to him, was confirmation of Mermosia's sanity.

"She turns that glass handle, the screaming becomes louder, interspersed with shouts, and that's all she can remember. Oh! Apart from the open palm with a cut diagonally across and blood dripping from it."

They all walked into the room. Immediately, Professor Conner Flynn scanned the room taking in the visual images. It was a large sitting room. It had two windows and the majestic sun blazed through them. In his mind, sharp with clarity and focus, he visualized the heinous scene that had taken place ten years earlier in that room.

Conner Flynn began to draw the relevant information from that vast oracle that was his mind, and he knew instantly what had happened on that dreadful day and how it had played out. All that was left for him now was for the girl to confirm the story. Then, that question that he was so compelled to answer would be laid prostrate out in front of him, baring the facts that he had already concluded. It would be a victory in the quest for the truth, and one he would savour.

CHAPTER 4
The Crystal Pool

Deception runs through the strands of all life on earth, no matter how insignificant or lofty, and Mother Nature encompasses this philosophy with open arms. It is never done out of malice or greed, but in the survival of all creatures, it is the food cycle of all life and the key to its very existence. Yet, of all of Mother Nature's creatures, man has the ability to live above deception, for he has conscious thought and the ability to determine right and wrong. Unfortunately, there are those who have the desire for greed and power. It is this emotion that drives them to commit the most abhorrent of crimes in the pursuit of their desires, at the expense of so many innocents.

* * * * *

Borrack and Professor Conner Flynn arrived back at Native Point, Southampton Island, mid-morning on the following day. The flight had been long and arduous. Borrack's mind had been focusing on how they would explain to the girl her history. He was convinced that Mermosia would not accept the word of himself or the professor in the explanation of her past life; it was a dilemma.

The eagle spread his wings out to slow his descent and landed. Borrack lowered his wing and Conner dismounted; the professor could sense that the eagle was worried about something. Borrack looked across the bay; it was calm, a few gulls darted across its surface looking for food. His mind was still trying to unravel the dilemma he had set himself.

"A penny for them?" the professor asked.

"Sorry?" Borrack replied, confused.

"A penny for your thoughts?" the professor reiterated.

"Oh, it's Mermosia. How are we going to tell her about her history? I guess if we had the cuttings from the newspaper, with the photographs… Mind you, those pictures were a bit graphic and probably would have driven her into insanity."

Professor Conner Flynn nodded in agreement.

"Unfortunately, you're right. The problem with photographs is that they only tell the story of that moment in time: they do not lie, but nor do they tell you the whole truth. Like you, I have been considering this puzzle and I think I have a solution…"

As always, Professor Conner Flynn searched deep into the thousands of pigeonholes that stored a wealth of information, which was his well-ordered mind. He drew the relevant strands of information together to provide a plan.

"Do you remember I told you about the Sallirmiut that used to frequent this land? Legend has it that aeons before their demise they use to visit a magical place. It was an oracle, for it told of their past mistakes, and from it they learnt the wisdom of life, which, according to their fables, lies high up on a plateau with a secret entrance that only the Sallirmiut know. And, unfortunately, that secret has died with them."

"The plateau's location is on the northeast shore of Lake Hansen. I have, in my research, visited the place and there is a chain of mountains that resemble a huge citadel, impenetrable, with escarpments, leading to a plateau. That is where I believe the crystal pool of personal history lies. If the legend is correct, and we take Mermosia to the crystal pool and persuade her to look into it, I believe it will force her mind to retrace her history and release her demons."

Borrack turned to face the professor.

"As you have implied, the crystal pool of personal history is probably no more than a legend – and if it is, the whole journey will be for nothing more than a waste of time, which will leave Mermosia even more stressed than before. It is strange that you, a scientist, should fall back on something that has no scientific basis."

The professor frowned.

"Listen, my science is not tied to boundaries. With all legends there is always an element of truth. As I said when I first met you, there are no physical laws that allow you, a chimera, to exist, but you do. So, trust me. I'm sure there is something in the legend. After all, we took a chance on Regina and we came up trumps."

The eagle could not argue with the professor's logic. In truth, he could not think of an alternative, so he nodded reluctantly.

"How long do you think it will take to get to the lake?" Conner Flynn asked.

"It takes just over an hour to get to the Ice Plateau, which is beyond the Hansine Lake; so, I guess, forty-five minutes, give or take."

The professor shot the eagle a look.

"Ice Plateau?" his mind ready to devour this new snippet of information, for future exploration.

"Yes, it's on the peripheries of the Artic Circle, it is uniquely beautiful. I have promised Mermosia that I will take her back there when she's better. Maybe, if things work out, I can take you as well."

Conner Flynn smiled with delight, "In which case, we had better get her back to normal. So, if we leave Coral Harbour at seven p.m., we should have enough light to search for the crystal pool?"

Borrack nodded.

"Well, that's agreed. I'll get Doctor Erick Ashoona to give the girl the antidote at six-forty-five, which should drive Mermosia into her dream reality, and I will meet you where?"

The eagle replied confidently, "Just above Coral Harbour there's a hill. It overlooks the harbour and beyond that the Hudson Bay. I will be there at six-thirty p.m."

"That's settled then. I guess we both should get some rest."

Borrack agreed, and the professor walked off to his mode of transport, his lucky charm.

The eagle closed his eyes and concentrated on Zachary, his father, and in seconds he changed from eagle to man. He cast his eyes across the Bay and he took in a deep breath of its serenity; it was so good. Borrack the man laid down on the grass, the majestic sun caressed his face, its warmth spread through his body soothing it until he slipped into his unconscious world.

His dream world, as always, was both confused in narrative and vision. He was Borrack the eagle, high above the homestead. Below, he saw Zachary and Maley beckoning to him. He dived down to greet them, but within the confusion of the dream, where the boundaries of reality no longer exist, he found himself lying prostrate on the ground at Native Point looking up. The sky was blue, but hemmed in by heavy, dark grey clouds, and in the centre a black shape. He watched as the shape dropped towards him at speed. The nearer the object came, the better he could make out its form. It was the black raven – its physical size matched his own. In his mind, the word 'Erigal' rattled around in his head.

The creature was dropping fast without slowing. It was almost on him; he could see the massive bill and the ruffled throat. Then the raven was on his face, pecking at his eyes. He screamed in agony with a pain that did not exist and brushed his hands across his face, defensively pushing the creature away.

He rolled to one side and struck a rock, his eyes flickered open and he sat up, and looked upwards and saw nothing except the blue sky that stretched to the horizon where it merged with the blue sea.

Borrack rubbed his eyes – he was confused and disorientated. He shook his head, and the realization of his dream fell upon him. The whole episode unnerved him. Borrack again rubbed his eyes. He looked behind him – the sun was sinking, but still hung there confidently knowing it would be another five hours before it would relinquish its hold on this part of the planet.

Borrack the man got up and made his way to the small brook; he cupped his hands in the fresh cold water and splashed it across his face. He took a sharp intake of breath as the ice-cold water ran down his face. Then he cupped his hands again and drank from the small brook. It cooled his parched throat and calmed his nerves.

His mind wandered back, searching the memory of that dream; he was convinced it was connected to Mermosia. As the name flashed through his mind, he remembered about the girl's trip to the crystal pool and the saving of her sanity.

He looked up at the sun; he had probably no more than an hour before his appointment with the professor. He needed food. The carcass of the caribou still lay on the ground, although it had almost been picked dry by an army of creatures, both large and small, whose desire for survival was instinctive.

Borrack's humanity was once again disgusted at the thought of devouring that raw, rotting flesh. But he did not have the luxury of time, to seek out something more acceptable, so he closed his eyes and thought of Zachary, then, a few milliseconds later, he saw through the eyes of an eagle. Borrack the mighty eagle hopped over to the rotting flesh and gorged on what was left, picking the bones dry. Then, he spread his huge wings and powered them up, until he was soaring upwards. Borrack flew out over Native Point, and then turned and followed the coast, until he reached Coral Harbour. There, he headed inland until he reached the hill overlooking the town.

Borrack circled a few times. Below, he could see a lonely figure standing up; it was the professor. The mighty eagle glided down. He tilted his wings to slow his descent, and braced his talons for impact, and he landed within a few yards of Conner Flynn.

Borrack looked at the professor, his huge yellow eyes searching for an answer. Conner Flynn answered before the question was even posed.

"Yes! Doctor Erick Ashoona should be giving Mermosia the antidote just about now; it will take a little time for the drug to work," the Professor said, while he looked down on the Harbour community. It was quiet, not a soul could be seen on the streets. He lifted his head to the horizon and watched a small flotilla of fishing boats returning with the day's catch, followed by a flock of gulls squawking and swooping over the small crafts, scavenging for cast offs.

From Borrack's peripheral vision he could make out a disturbance to one side. He called to the professor, and they both turned to witness Mermosia vacillate between her two worlds, her drug induced sleeping death and her dream reality. They watched as every cell in her body randomly materialized until in front of them stood the girl.

The professor was fascinated by the whole event; it was another image he could pigeonhole in his well-ordered mind. He began to theorise on how such an event could occur, and perhaps, in a future time, he would pose that question that he had witnessed and with his inquisitive mind would answer it to its conclusion. But that was for another time.

The girl looked at Borrack, her expression was confused. Something was wrong. To Mermosia, she had only just left him, she could remember his last words, she muttered them: 'Trust me! We will beat this illness together!', so it made no sense; she had not returned to her daytime nightmare.

Mermosia turned her attention to Conner Flynn, he was familiar, and she had seen him before! Then, it came to her, he was with Doctor Erick Ashoona the morning after Borrack had said those words. Tears ran down her cheeks, she started to shake violently. The professor ran to her side, he took off his tweed jacket and wrapped it around the girl.

"What's happening to me?" she sobbed.

"It's okay, Mermosia. You have been in a dreamless sleep for a few days," Borrack said kindly. "We have discovered the cause of your illness."

The professor gently wiped the tears away from Mermosia's face. The girl looked up at the eagle; her eyes still conveyed her confusion.

"Your illness is the result of something that has happened in your past and we are going to go somewhere that will help you unlock those memories and release you from your daytime nightmare."

Her voice trembled as she replied to Borrack, "Where?"

The professor took hold of her hand; she turned to face him.

"We're going to a magical place. It's a crystal pool, a beautiful place, a place that the forebears of this great land used to use to protect them from future events. When you look into the crystal pool it reflects your past life, good and bad, and provides you with the path of wisdom. I'm going to be honest with you; it is not going to be easy for you to look into that small part of your personal history that has haunted you with such ferocity. But trust me, when you have seen it and have come to terms with it, your life will change and your illness will be gone. So are you ready to go?"

Mermosia nodded reluctantly. Borrack lowered his wing and the girl climbed aboard followed by the professor. The eagle powered up his huge wings, lifting them high into the sky.

They flew northwest towards the majestic sun. The ball of energy hung low in the sky, with a ribbon of cloud that cut through its middle. The sun poured its golden rays above and below the ribbon of cloud, and as the light struck the cloud it sent shards of golden light in all directions, setting the sky and the land on fire with its beauty.

It took no more than forty minutes before they reached the southern shores of Lake Hansen; its vastness spread out in front of them. The fluid surface rippled under the influence of an easterly breeze, and as the sun began to sink lower in the sky, so it cast a golden path down the centre of the lake leading to the crystal pool. Borrack flew towards the golden path, turned west and followed it.

Far above, Erigal, the black raven, watched Borrack as he had done, since Borrack's first experience of humanity at Poutia. He looked down at the eagle and could not help but marvel at the creature's strength and resolve. The girl looked up and saw the sinister Erigal. She shivered with fear, and said nothing, in case her mind was playing tricks on her.

The eagle and his passengers carried on following the golden path to reach their destination; Erigal knew that the girl's daytime nightmares would soon reach their climax. The black raven was an advocate of fate, and in the certitude of his faith, he knew it would be another success for Borrack the mighty eagle. He considered his work here finished; it was time to move on to the final stage. The black raven dropped like a stone, gathering speed as he plummeted towards the lake and with the acrobatic prowess that ravens are famed for; he angled his wings, turning a full one-hundred and eighty degrees, and flew west.

As they travelled down the golden path that lay across Lake Hansen, Professor Conner Flynn kept his eyes firmly fixed on the horizon; at last he could make out the hazy image of a chain of mountains. He shouted to Borrack.

"Dead ahead!"

The eagle acknowledged the statement. The mighty creature increased his speed, and with every flap of his huge wings, so the citadel of black mountains came nearer, until they were flying across the top of them. Borrack circled and hovered high above them. Both he and the professor scrutinized the plateau looking for the crystal pool. Every now and again, the huge bird would swoop and fly on a little further and hover, while again they would scan the surface – this went on many times. It was a manoeuvre that was instinctive to the eagle and one that he had used on many occasions when hunting for food. Something to the left of the eagle caught his attention, and he flew towards it.

The professor also spotted it.

"Yes! Borrack, that's it! I told you it was here!"

Below them, a small pool, caressed by a gentle wind rippled as the sun's rays caught it. The golden light was reflected upwards in an amazing display of grandeur. The eagle circled several times, looking for a suitable place to land. He swooped down, angled his wings to slow his descent and readied his talons for impact. He landed gently and lowered his wing and his passengers dismounted. The professor, with his insatiable appetite for knowledge, marched straight over to the crystal pool; Mermosia backed away from it. Borrack looked at her, he could see her distress.

"It's time you faced your demons," he said.

"No, no," she mumbled quietly, as tears began to roll down her cheeks.

The eagle knew he would have to lead by example. It was something that he did not want to do, but if he was to save the girl from herself, this was the best chance. Borrack would have to tell the girl about his humanity, his history. The eagle's first action would be to change to Borrack the man.

"Mermosia," he said, "We all have demons in our lives and I'm no different. Have you heard of a chimera?"

The girl shook her head. Borrack called to the professor.

"Yes, Borrack?" he replied.

"Could you explain to Mermosia what a chimera is?"

Conner Flynn looked surprised.

"Yes! But why?"

"I want to show Mermosia that we all have demons, and that we have to challenge and face them."

The professor immediately understood the eagle's motives, and with the vast wealth of knowledge that was his mind at his disposal, he explained to the girl very concisely about chimeras. After he had told her, as much as was relevant, he held Mermosia's hand for reassurance and said, "Borrack is such a creature."

He looked at Borrack, and the mighty creature thought of Zachary, his father. Within seconds, the eagle turned from the creature of the skies to Borrack the man, taller than the tallest of men, with his shock of white hair and yellow eyes, dressed in his suit of golden-brown feathers. Mermosia at first backed away, her eyes widened, and her heart began to race with fear. Then she looked into the yellow eyes of the stranger and there she saw Borrack the eagle, the man; they were one and the same, and her fear evaporated.

Borrack held his hand out, Mermosia took it. He smiled broadly at her.

"Let's see what my past shows us in the crystal pool of history. Then, when you are ready, you can do the same."

He led Mermosia to the side of the crystal pool.

The sun had surrendered to the night and made way for the Great Pretender. The moon rose, hovering between its first quarter and its whole celestial body, leaving one half hidden by the shadow of Mother Earth. The hazy, silvery light fell upon Lake Hansen, providing a silver path across it, where once the sun's golden path had lain.

Borrack and the girl knelt down by the pool. Borrack the man peered into it – his image was distorted by the gentle rippling by the wind. For a few seconds, the pool remained the same, then a small area became still, and Borrack's image was no longer distorted. His reflection mirrored himself, in the motionless area. At first, the reflection merged almost without boundary from Borrack the man to Borrack the eagle. All three sat in front of the crystal pool and watched as Borrack's history was revealed, his life was rolled out in front of them in reverse. The first visual images were slow; they saw the journey backwards from the crystal pool back over Lake Hansen back to the hill overlooking Coral Harbour.

As each image flashed in front of them, so its speed increased to a point where it became nothing more than a kaleidoscope of shape and colours as day merged into night, weeks into months and months into years. The small inert piece of crystal pool rippled once again and became calm. They were all taken aback by what they saw next.

The reflection was that of a small village nestling at the foot of the Black Mountains, and as the visual imprint moved forward into history so Borrack's first moments on this beautiful planet were played out. The images became animated and almost tactile, as it showed people milling about with anticipation and excitement outside a small hut. Many had crowded around a man shaking his hand and patting him on his back. The man was tall, handsome with striking green eyes; Borrack immediately recognised him from his Aunt Simmi's description – a tear rolled down his cheek. This was his first ever sight of his birth father and one he would always treasure.

Then, as the visual reflection rolled forward, they saw a lady come running out of the hut, and heard her scream and cry, "It's the Devil! The baby is a devil!"

She was in a blind panic, all she could do was repeat, "It's a devil, it's a devil, that thing's evil! It's the Devil!"

The tribespeople looked at one another in amazement. The young man and one of the elders ran into the hut. They reappeared a few minutes later. The three of them watched the young man, he was in tears, the village elder tried to calm the crowd without success. The crowd by now were becoming agitated.

The tribe turned to violence, as hysteria took hold like a contagious disease. They set about Borrack's father without mercy, leaving him for dead and ran away, taking all they could carry, leaving the village desolate and at the mercy of the Ice Blue Wind.

Borrack, Mermosia and Conner Flynn saw the arrival of Zachery in the crystal pool. He arrived to witness the young man lying on the ground outside the hut, with his best friend attending to his wounds, which were horrific. Then, the visual images moved inside the hut with Zachery's arrival. Borrack, by now, was emotional – sick to his stomach by the inhumanity shown by the tribespeople towards his father; his face was wet with tears. Mermosia looked at her friend and confidante and felt nothing but empathy. Her own history seemed to have disappeared into the emotion of the moment. She put her arm around Borrack's shoulders to comfort him.

The reflected images still kept coming, running the course of Borrack's personal history. The woman lay there weeping, gently cradling a bundle in her arms. Borrack's eyes fixed on the lady's face, and he saw his Aunt Simmi in her. This was his mother and the bundle in her arms was he. Zachery touched her arm; her eyes met his.

"It's my baby," she cried, "It's my baby!"

"What about your baby?" he said gently.

She moved the blanket to one side – and there, in her arm, half-exposed, was a scrawny fledgling! An eagle, his eyes closed, with only down on his body.

The young man appeared from the doorway and whispered in Zachary's ear that Borrack's father had finally given up his fight for life. His friend's face was awash with tears at the terrible loss of his friend. They sat by the young lady's bed, comforting her as best they could. They didn't need to tell her about her partner, she seemed to have sensed his demise.

They sat there for many hours. Then she looked up at Zachary and said, "Please take my baby and bring him up as your own."

Her bright, blue eyes were pleading for him to say 'yes'. He nodded his confirmation. She gently grasped his arm with her frail lily-white hand and smiled.

"Please name him after his father! Such a good, genteel man"

Zachary choked up a, "Yes, of course."

She smiled once more, and then she slipped away from this life. Borrack's composure broke as he let out a cry of emotional distress. Even Conner Flynn, who by his very nature did not feel sympathy, but only the cold facts of logic could not help but feel for this creature, this chimera, this Borrack. The last visual image was of Zachary carrying the young fledgling wrapped in his swaddling blanket, looking down at the village as the Ice Blue Wind laid waste to it. Then the crystal pool retuned to its natural state, as the water rippled across it by the gentle wind. The three of them sat quietly, each in their own way coming to terms with Borrack's personal history.

The moon was halfway through its course. The sphere was like a split personality – one side bright, with its shards of silver light, the other hidden by the shadow of Mother Earth. The silver light no longer hazy, but sharp and crisp. The quicksilver light spread its beams across the terrain below, and as the light hit the rippling, crystal pool, it reflected back up, giving the illusion of fireflies darting across its surface.

Borrack turned to the girl, his face still contorted with emotion.

"You have seen my demons, those skeletons I have had to come to terms with; are you ready to face yours and take control of your life?"

Mermosia looked into Borrack's yellow eyes, and deep inside them she found the strength she was looking for.

"Yes," she replied, confidently.

The girl moved so she sat between Borrack and the professor. They each took hold of Mermosia's hands; she felt safe and secure. The girl stared into the crystal pool of personal history. She watched her distorted reflection, and then, as it was with Borrack, a small area became still, and her reflection was no longer distorted.

Her past life, slowly at first, began to reveal itself, starting with her most recent memories and then speeding into a frenzy of colour and visual images until the imagery came to rest.

It was early morning. Mermosia saw her reflection as a child lying in a bed, a voice familiar and reassuring echoed from somewhere outside the small bedroom.

The little girl answered, "Yes, Mummy.",

The door opened and a lady walked in. She was tall with dark hair and strikingly beautiful. Somewhere deep in Mermosia's psyche there was a stirring, a memory trying to break loose of the chains that had held it for so long.

Tears ran down Mermosia's cheeks. She mumbled, "Mummy."

The visual images moved forward. The little girl held her mother's hand, as she was led down the staircase. Mermosia recognised the nightdress; they were in her daydream nightmare. The mother took the child into the kitchen. At the breakfast bar a man sat.

The little girl ran to him, "Daddy, Daddy."

The man turned, stooped down and picked up the child.

Mermosia recognised him. She mumbled, "Daddy."

Her memory was activated, but still shackled by the trauma that haunted her. She squeezed Borrack's and the professor's hands with her own. It was an unconscious call for help. Both responded as best they could. The little girl looked at her father.

"Daddy can we play tonight, when you get home?"

The father pulled a sad face, "No, my little dumpling, not tonight. I have a meeting with Uncle Raymond."

As the name echoed from the crystal pool, Mermosia shivered with fear, but still the memory stayed chained to that deep-seated fear that would not allow that heinous secret free.

The visual imagery moved on, and as the day progressed, Mermosia felt at one with the little girl. She empathised with her happiness, her carefree attitude, which comes with love and security. Yet, every time Mermosia saw that dark green door in the crystal pool, with its glass handle, she sensed the need to run, to run as far away as possible, away from that dark green door with its glass handle and its monstrous secrets.

Borrack could see her anxiety; he gently squeezed her hand and whispered, "It's okay, Mermosia, we're here for you, stay strong."

She turned her head to face her confidante. Mermosia smiled, it was a smile that was reluctant and unsure, but she knew if she was ever to be normal, she would have to face her daytime nightmare. Mermosia turned back to face the crystal pool. The images flowed through the day. The little girl was happy, unaware of her mother's anxiety, an anxiety that amplified as the day progressed.

As evening drew near, the mother changed the child's routine – it was necessary to accommodate her husband's meeting with her brother. She looked at the little girl.

"We're having tea early tonight, so I can get you to bed before Uncle Raymond comes."

The girl looked up, "Can I stay up and see Uncle Raymond?"

"No, not tonight, darling. We have some very important things to discuss."

"Please Mummy, please?"

"No! Mermosia, not tonight!"

Her response was curt, a little angry; her anxiety was beginning to wear on her. Mermosia watched herself as a child, in that crystal pool of personal history. She watched as the child was put to bed and fell asleep. Then the crystal pool went dark as the child was lost in her dream world.

The crystal pool suddenly sprung into life after a noise from below woke the child with a start. The little girl looked around the room. The night-light was on, reflecting exaggerated shadows on the walls. Mermosia the child felt scared, she needed her mother's comfort. Another noise from below sent the child into tears. She got up from her bed, opened the door, and made her way downstairs. The noises from below echoed their way up the staircase. She reached the bottom and moved towards the dark green door. She put her small hand on the glass handle. Screams and cries carried through the door.

Mermosia turned her head from the visual images in the crystal pool. She looked at Borrack, her face, pale and running with tears, her eyes, red and puffy and full of fear.

"Be strong, Mermosia! Face that hateful truth and then you can be free," Borrack urged.

Reluctantly, she returned her gaze to the crystal pool. The little girl turned the handle and the door swung open. The child screamed, and, as she did, Uncle Raymond Le Clec turned in shock. In his hand he held a large, heavy object dripping with blood. To one side the child's father lay on the floor lifeless, his head cracked open. Her mother was on her knees in front of her brother, bleeding from the side of her face.

While her brother was distracted by the child's appearance at the door, the child's mother stood up and picked up a paper knife lying on the writing table next to her. The brother caught sight of her in his peripheral vision; he held his left hand up in a defensive motion. The blade came down and slashed across the palm of his hand and blood oozed out. The little girl screamed again as her Uncle brought down the heavy object onto her mother's head. She fell to the floor, lifeless. He looked at the little girl, she was sobbing relentlessly. Raymond Le Clec picked up the paper knife and, along with the heavy object, ran from the house.

Mermosia murmured her mother's and father's names, and, as the fog of fear lifted, her memory flooded back beyond that dark green door with its glass handle.

She watched the crystal pool as the last vestige of the saga played out and then the pool once again returned to its natural state. The girl lifted her head and faced Borrack. He studied her eyes – he looked deep into them. The fear that had once paralysed her mind, tipping her almost into insanity had gone and was replaced with a question. There was no malice, anger or hate in her look, just one question! 'Why?'

Borrack looked at the professor and he looked at Mermosia and he saw the same questioning look. He gently picked up the girl's hand and answered the question she so wanted to ask.

"We do not know why your uncle did what he did; only he can answer that. All we know is he was involved in some corrupt practices and that he could not be brought to justice without a witness and you! Well, you were too traumatised to testify."

Mermosia's face remained straight, solemn, her eyes narrowed a little,

"And now?" she said confidently.

Borrack answered, "If you're up to it, I feel sure the professor's friend, Joshua Thurgood, can arrange something."

At the mention of Joshua Thurgood's name, a bit more of her memory flooded back.

"He's a policeman?"

"Yes," replied Conner Flynn, "Well, he was."

"He was kind to me."

As she spoke, images shot through her mind of that moment in her history.

"He drove Mum, Dad and me to Coral Harbour," then she paused and mumbled, "Mum and Dad," and at that second, reality hit home, she looked at Borrack and at the professor, a tear rolled down her cheek. "But Mum and Dad are dead?"

"No!" Borrack said assertively "Your birth parents are no longer with us, but your adoptive parents, who have looked after you and loved you through the most challenging part of your life, are still with you."

The girl nodded reluctantly. Borrack looked at the eastern horizon; there he could see the beginning of the rebirth of the new day. He held his hand out.

"Come, come with me."

She did as she was bidden, and they walked to the edge of the cliff and there they sat.

Professor Conner Flynn stared into the crystal pool; he would come back here soon to investigate the fate of the Sallirmiut. The professor looked around for the secret entrance that would lead him to this magical place. He was pleased with himself, for he had answered the question he was so compelled to answer about the girl's personal history and the verification of her story had confirmed his own theory, it was another small victory for his science.

Borrack and Mermosia sat on the cliff edge, looking east over Lake Hansen. The silver path that ran down the centre of the lake had all but disappeared as the Moon started to slip behind the horizon. High above them, the sky was still dark, and the stars shone brightly – to the east, the new day began to encroach on the landscape, bringing with it the renewal of life.

Mermosia looked at Borrack, "Thank you," she said. "You did not abandon me to my own fears but fought for my sanity. I can never repay you for that."

Borrack smiled.

"I suppose," she elaborated, "We share a similar heritage? I mean, we both have lost our parents."

Borrack the man's expression changed, "No! You knew your mother and father, no matter how short a time you knew them for. Unfortunately, I did not know mine."

At that moment, for the first time in ten years, maybe for the first time ever; she felt the anxiety and the suffering of another, and she felt humbled. Again, tears welled up in her eyes. Mermosia threw her arms around her friend, her confidante, and kissed him on the cheek. She tucked her head into his chest and there they sat and watched as the majestic sun, the one, true, material god made its appearance, in all its glory on this part of this beautiful planet, and all life bowed to its omnipotence. Borrack looked at his young ward.

"Don't forget, tonight, as I promised, I will take you back to the Ice Plateau."

She smiled. It was a smile of confidence, a smile that welcomed life, so very different from times past. He watched as she fluctuated between her dream reality and the threshold of her new life, as every cell in her body randomly disappeared and he knew her hopes and aspirations had returned.

CHAPTER 5

The Deceit of Life

As we pass through life, from birth to death, we make decisions and judgments that affect the course of our personal history. Sometimes these decisions and judgments are logical or the only path to travel. Other times, these decisions and judgments are more of a guess or a gamble, a crossroads with no obvious sign to guide us. It is these decisions and judgments that have the greatest influence on our lives, for their outcome may be beneficial or detrimental to our journey through life and those who share it.

Both Borrack and Mermosia have been victims of such judgments, but only Borrack has been the perpetrator of such an action. It is true that he was unaware of such a judgment, but it was an action that he would come to bitterly regret for the rest of his days, for its outcome would change his life and those close to him in ways he could not have imagined.

* * * * *

Borrack and the professor arrived back at the hill overlooking Coral Harbour, just over an hour after Mermosia had returned to her day reality. Both the eagle and the professor were pleased with the outcome for different reasons. Borrack, because he had released the girl from the chains of history that had tethered her to those terrible demons, and the professor, because he had answered that question that he was so compelled to answer, even though it had thrown up a catalogue of questions, which he knew time would not allow him to seek the answers to.

The eagle spread his wings out to slow his descent and braced his talons for impact… Thump! They were down. Borrack lowered his wing and the professor slid down. Borrack looked at his friend.

"Thank you, Professor. Thank you for your help. I could not have achieved the girl's recovery without you."

The Professor smiled, "It was a pleasure to help."

"Will you contact Joshua Thurgood with the new information?" Borrack questioned.

"Of course, I will, and hopefully, Raymond Le Clec will be doubly convicted for his terrible crimes."

"Oh, there's one more thing," Borrack said, "Tonight, I am taking Mermosia to the Ice Plateau, would you like to come?"

The professor beamed, "Yes, I would love to."

"We'll meet here about midnight," Borrack replied.

With that, the eagle flapped his huge wings, creating a vortex of dust and debris, Conner Flynn covered his eyes to protect them, as the huge bird soared high into the sky.

The eagle flew directly to Native Point. The creature scanned the skies as he looked out over the bay that flowed into Foxe Basin. He saw clouds rolling towards him, they were way out over Foxe Basin, maybe fifteen, twenty miles away. The clouds were heavy with a dark blue to the centre, paling to a dark grey on the outer edges. A yellow light flashed across it, deep in the eye of the monster storm, almost masked by its foggy appearance.

Borrack circled Native Point, angling his mighty wings to slow his descent, bracing his talons for impact and landed. The eagle looked out again towards Foxe Basin. The monster storm was rushing towards him. The grey underbelly of the monster churned up the placid sea into a frenzy, sucking out its energy to feed its momentum. High above the heavy grey cloud, a rumbling echoed around the menacing skies, louder than anything that Borrack had ever heard. Within the dark blue eye of the storm the white-hot yellow flashes angrily announced its approach. As far as the eye could see, both to the right and left, the monster storm approached, as if its tactics were to surround and conquer its victims.

The eagle was mesmerised by its magnificence, he knew he could not stay at Native Point, but he would have to seek out a more secure shelter. But, for the time being, he watched the splendid monster approach. He watched it for more than forty-five minutes, and, as the monster approached, the louder and more frightening it became. The storm's first line of attack began: large raindrops fell, at first slow and intermittent.

From behind, the eagle heard a noise. He turned around grudgingly, not wanting to take his eyes off the monster storm, when there, running up the hill, throwing his arms in the air, he saw Professor Conner Flynn. He was agitated; the eagle could not make out what he was shouting. He moved to intercept his friend and as they met Borrack spoke.

"What's the problem?"

The professor tried desperately to get his breath back.

"It's..." hu- hu- he panted, "It's Mermosia! She's," hu-hu- "been kind-... " hu- hu-...

"OK, slow down," Borrack replied.

The professor bent down and put his hands on his knees, to get his breath back.

"It's Mermosia, she's been kidnapped."

"What!?" Borrack said in astonishment.

"She's been kidnapped! I had just got back to the B&B, and Doctor Erick Ashoona was looking for me. It seems he had gone round to the Luka residence to check on the girl, and, as he got to the sea wall and looked up the road, he saw a commotion outside Mermosia's house. He ran to help, and a man was pushing the girl into a black Sedan car. The mother and father tried desperately to wrestle her free, even the doctor tried to help, but he was much too strong and pushed them away. The doctor did notice one thing in the struggle; the man had a scar across the palm of his left hand."

"How did he know about Mermosia's recovery? Surely he doesn't think he can get away with kidnapping her?" Borrack responded.

"To answer your questions, as to the first, I have no idea! And, the second, don't forget he has friends in high places."

"How long ago did it happen?" Borrack asked.

"Just over an hour ago, I believe."

"Have you spoken to Joshua Thurgood?"

"Yes, he said he would get on to his contacts. But he's extremely concerned that they will be too late to help!"

The eagle understood the implications by the professor's expression. Borrack looked concerned.

By now, the first attack of the monster storm was well under way. The rain became heavy, so heavy that they had to shout to each other to be heard. Professor Conner Flynn smiled; the eagle knew by that look that the professor had a plan.

Borrack cut to the chase, "It is obvious you have a suggestion of what to do."

"Yes, but we don't have a lot of time."

The eagle listened as Conner Flynn outlined his plan. Borrack was not convinced, but the other two courses of action had not convinced him either. First, the trip to Regina, and secondly, the crystal pool of personal history, both had been successful.

"How long before we get off the island by road?" Borrack asked.

"The way the only road snakes around, I would guess anything between two to three hours, if we leave now."

The professor scrutinized the oncoming storm and pulled a face.

"If that storm doesn't slow us down, we might just catch them."

The eagle smiled with his eyes at the professor, "I hope you're not nervous about thunderstorms?"

The professor returned the smile, "It's every scientist's dream to ride high through a precipitation like this," as he gestured to the on-coming storm with his hands.

Borrack lowered his wing and the sopping wet professor climbed aboard the eagle, flapped his huge appendages, creating such awesome power that lifted them into the drowning heavens.

As they flew northeast, the monster storm rushed past, enveloping them and the land below in its dark grey underbelly, still sucking and absorbing every little bit of energy to fuel its momentum.

Professor Conner Flynn held as tight as he could to the mighty eagle's neck, as the wind and rain lashed down on them. As for Borrack, he discharged all his power into his huge wings, and, despite the raging storm pummelling him, he would not relinquish his resolve; the girl's life was at stake and he refused to let her down. He flew blind for some time, seeing nothing but the curling fog and rain of the dark grey light. He flew by instinct, an instinct so interwoven into his genetic make-up so as to take him in his chosen direction without deviation. Every now and again a white-hot line bounced across the horizon, illuminating the whole area in phosphorous light followed by a rumbling so loud that the land shook.

To his right, Borrack spotted the only road that served the island. It resembled a snake as it curled upwards into the northern horizon around the rugged landscape only to appear four hundred yards later coming south. Then the road would disappear again as it curved around a rock the size of a mountain to reappear again a few minutes later. He pressed on, flying northeast, his magnificent wings beating up and down with limitless energy.

His eagle eye spotted something to his right, two beads of light a good distance away, moving south. A flash of phosphorous light shot across the skies, illuminating the whole area, and Borrack could make out the outline of the black Sedan, moving at speed down that snake shaped road. The vehicle followed the road and disappeared north as the highway accommodated another rock the size of a mountain.

The next time the eagle saw the black Sedan he was right above it. Another streak of lightning shot across the skies filling it with phosphorous light, followed by the awesome rumbling of thunder. As the light flooded the area, Borrack caught sight of Mermosia in the passenger seat cowering towards the car window looking up and pleading for help. The Sedan disappeared as the highway took it north.

The professor too had been watching as the events unfolded. He drew from his vast photographic memory of the highway and knew that the next time they saw the road, that was the point they would have to make their stand. For after that, the highway was straight, and that straight highway led directly to the bridge and Le Clec's escape. He shouted to Borrack; his voice was barely audible over the monster storm. The professor raised his voice.

"Land next time you see the highway."

The eagle acknowledged his command, and as the road once again came into view, the mighty Borrack summoned every ounce of energy to battle the monster storm and landed as near to the road as possible.

The professor clambered off and shouted to the eagle, raising his voice to make himself heard.

"Leave me to it. I am sure I can do this!"

Borrack flapped wings and slowly but surely flew upwards. There he hovered, battling against the ferocious winds looking down on the professor, and watching as this man of science danced and chanted in his tweed jacket and trousers, white shirt and tie, and on his head perched a trilby. Soaked to the skin and covered in mud.

Borrack looked on as the professor tried to raise the ancestors of the Lowa (a Native American tribe of Nebraska). The eagle found the whole sight ludicrous and had little confidence that Conner Flynn could pull it off.

At that moment, the black Sedan came racing down the road. Borrack looked ahead where this miracle was supposed to take place, but nothing was happening. He had no choice, if he were to save the girl, he would have to dive at the car and scare Le Clec into stopping or crashing. He powered his huge wings up, moved a short distance... then stopped and hovered. For, there in front of him, at a distance of about half a mile the majestic sun's translucent rays burst through the raging storm, creating a circle that rippled outwards, and, in the middle of that circle, stood an army of Indian braves on horseback, proud, strong and ready to do battle.

Raymond Le Clec, with his foot pressed hard down on the accelerator, one hand on the steering wheel of the black Sedan, and his head turned towards the girl Mermosia. Trying to quieten her down and keep her in check, entered the ever-widening circle of the translucent sunlight.

The windscreen wiper scraped across the dry screen distracting him from the girl. He looked forward at the distraction and slammed his foot on the brakes.

"Shit!" he exclaimed, as the army of Indian braves came into view.

He wrenched the steering wheel to the left and the black Sedan veered off the road into a ditch colliding with a boulder. Steam poured from the front of the car, he looked to where the tribe of Indians stood and watched them vanish into the ether.

The sun poured its majestic power downwards, pushing the circle of light outwards, pushing the monster storm into retreat. The sunrays pushed the boundaries of sun light past Borrack and the professor, across the terrain of Southampton Island; in all directions, until the great storm conceded its defeat.

Raymond Le Clec tried several times in panic to start the car without success. He climbed out the driver's door and ran round to the passenger's door, opened it and dragged Mermosia out. She kicked out at him and he slapped her. Mermosia bent to his will.

Borrack watched, ready to go to the girl's aide. He flapped his wings and dived towards the two of them. Le Clec dragged the girl towards the interior of Southampton Island, the girl did her best to fight him off, but his strength overpowered her, he held her tight with his right hand.

The mighty eagle hovered above them, casting a shadow that left them in the darkness. He stretched out his talons and dived towards Le Clec, who looked up, and in desperation he swung his free arm around in frenzy. Borrack clamped his talons closed but missed Le Clec's arm. The eagle flapped his wings and climbed a little and dived again his talons outstretched.

Le Clec again fought the creature off and did not release his clutch on the girl. Borrack flew even higher and then he went into a dive! As he approached the back of the man, he spread his wings out, clenched his talons and drove them into him. Le Clec dropped to the ground and let go of Mermosia, who ran but was trapped by a ring of rocks. The man jumped up and grabbed out at the girl, but the mighty eagle swung around in mid-flight and placed himself between Mermosia and her kidnapper. Le Clec tried desperately to get to the girl, but, every time, Borrack thwarted his attempts. In the end the kidnapper ran towards the interior in a futile attempt to escape.

The eagle hovered above the girl and gently plucked her from the semicircle of rocks and flew back to Professor Conner Flynn and safety. The eagle lowered the girl; she was shaken and scared by the whole episode, but unhurt.

Borrack shouted to the professor while still hovering, "I'm going after Le Clec! I hope the police will be here when I get back to arrest him! Oh! And don't forget to be at the hill overlooking Coral Harbour at midnight with Mermosia for our trip to the Ice Plat——."

As he flew away, his last words faded into the abyss.

Borrack soared high into the sky and flew in the direction of the assailant's escape. The sky was clear and blue, as the last vestiges of the monster storm had been eradicated. He flew high, hovered and scanned the terrain for movement, angled his wings, swooped, and moved further on.

His eagle eye was examining every crevice and boulder looking for Le Clec; he did this for over an hour. He knew the assailant could not have got far. Then something caught his attention. He stayed hovering, concentrating his vision on one spot. Again, he saw movement. He dived down to the location, and, as he did, he spotted Le Clec.

Borrack went into freefall! Spread his wings to slow his descent, his talons open, ready to snap shut, but the kidnapper saw him coming. He darted out from his position, running upwards to the crest of the hill. The eagle powered up his wings and went into pursuit.

Several times Borrack unsuccessfully tried to catch the man, but he remained elusive. The eagle flew vertically up, then swooped down into a dive heading for Le Clec's back. As he approached, he spread his wings and clenched his talons and drove them into the kidnappers back, pushing him over a rocky outcrop. Le Clec tumbled, freefalling to the ground, knocking himself unconscious.

Borrack hovered above the limp body, closed his talons around it, and carried him off to Conner Flynn.

As the mighty eagle approached the professor, he could make out a line of red and blue flashing lights. There were at least four squad cars parked just off the highway. Two officers were talking to the professor, and Mermosia was sitting inside one of the cars with another police officer. Another officer spotted the eagle carrying the limp body of the kidnapper in his talons. He shouted and pointed! They all turned and looked at the sight, totally dumbstruck.

Borrack lowered the limp body at the roadside, flapped his huge wings and flew off in the direction of Native Point. All the officers looked at the unconscious figure, then up at the eagle as he flew away, then they looked at each other, then they all turned their attention to the professor, waiting for an explanation. He smiled at them meekly and shrugged his shoulders.

The mighty eagle arrived at the hill overlooking Coral Harbour just before midnight. To his surprise, both the professor and the girl were already there. The great creature glided in and landed close to his friends.

The moon shone with such brilliance, it was both full and confident, casting its silver light across the landscape, bathing the whole area in its grandeur. As the silver light spread across Fisher Strait towards Hudson Bay, the great fluid mass responded by reflecting its splendour back upwards in a display of exquisite beauty.

Borrack smiled with his eyes at the two of them. Mermosia threw her arms around the creature's neck and buried her head in his golden-brown feathers; and then she lifted her head to face his.

"Thank you!" she said, happy, and with so much hope.

Borrack looked down at her.

"You did it, Mermosia! You saved yourself! The professor and I only helped."

Then the great bird turned his head to Conner Flynn.

"What happened to Le Clec?"

"They have arrested him for kidnapping and assault. I talked to Joshua Thurgood this evening and he believes, with Mermosia's testimony, they can open the murder case surrounding Mermosia's birth parents, and he is confident they will get a conviction. However, the arresting officer faxed him a report of Le Clec's apprehension, mentioning an extraordinarily large eagle, who single-handedly caught the kidnapper and brought him back, clutched in his talons. In particular, referring to the creature's yellow eyes. He then said, and I quote, 'Dr Borrack had yellow eyes, didn't he? I don't know what's going on, but it seems a remarkable coincidence?'"

"Well, Professor, I will let you talk yourself out of that problem; after all, it should be easy for a man of science?"

Conner Flynn laughed.

The eagle lowered his wing, "Well, are you ready for our expedition?"

And the two of them scrambled up. First, the girl, followed by Professor Conner Flynn, wearing a tweed jacket and trousers, a clean, white shirt and tie, on his head perched a trilby hat, and carrying a briefcase.

The great bird flapped his huge wings, creating a downdraft, propelling them high into the sky. They flew north. Borrack's huge wings slicing through the night air. Their journey was short, no more than an hour, and although at that time of year the Ice Plateau was bathed in light, the majestic sun would not cast its golden rays on that magical place for at least half an hour after their arrival. As the great land of Southampton Island, with its magnificent Mathiasen Mountain and Hansen Lake located to the north gave way to Foxe Basin, and, onwards, over Winter Island, which was soon followed by the imposing Arctic Ocean, with its huge icebergs, some as big as mighty ships or floating landmasses.

As they neared landfall, the darkness of night surrendered to the light of day, for they were entering the land of the unending day.

They arrived as the eagle had predicted, half an hour before the great ball of energy, the majestic sun cast its golden rays across the Ice Plateau. Mermosia excitedly pointed.

"Look! Look, Professor," she shouted. "Look! The Ice Plateau."

The eagle swept down across the first line of ice columns. Professor Conner Flynn looked in utter disbelief, his well-ordered mind analysing all the visual information, storing it and categorizing it, as was his way. As far as the professor could see, there was row upon row of ice stacks away to the horizon and beyond. Borrack tilted his wings a little more, until he was flying between the huge columns.

As his huge wings flapped, it created a vortex under each, which radiated outwards, hitting the columns and resonating, creating a humming that was regular and melodic. The professor listened and immediately equated the frequency of the sound, adding it to his stored knowledge.

Mermosia laughed excitedly as the mighty bird swept in and out between the stacks of ice. The professor said nothing; he had never seen the like before and knew that no words could do justice to its beauty. They flew, weaving in and out between the huge stacks, mile after mile. The girl giggled; she was so happy. Then, as they neared the small hill on the eastern peripheries of the ice field, Borrack tilted his wings, giving him lift. He climbed, turned and spread out those great appendages to slow his descent, and gracefully landed on the fine, white snow.

The professor and the girl dismounted. All three stood, looking across the huge plateau with its thousands upon thousands of ice stacks.

Conner Flynn turned to face his companions, "This is magnificent!"

Mermosia spun around to face him, and repeated Borrack's first word, that he had said to her on that first visit to this beautiful place, "It is, but this work of art is only half finished. You are about to see something special. For, in front of you, lies the power of Mother Nature! And when she joins forces with the magnificent sun, that ball of energy, the powerhouse of this planet, then and only then will you see and marvel at the ultimate beauty."

As the eagle listened to the girl, he realised that she had clung to that memory so desperately over the last week, staving off the ever-encroaching fear of insanity, which had so threatened her, he could not help but marvel at her inner strength. As the last sounds fell from her lips, the majestic sun appeared above the horizon, and its golden rays spread across the plateau.

As the first rays struck an ice column, piercing it with its golden light, the light sprung out the other side in a rainbow of colours, and as it did, the column groaned as it expanded with the heat. Then the golden light hit the second and third columns, and so on, like a chain reaction. As the majestic sun's rays hit each stack, they creaked in a crescendo of sound echoing across the Ice Plateau. The sun rose higher, and a tidal wave of colour began to sweep over the terrain. The professor ran down the small hill into the plateau of ice stacks, running along with the tidal wave of light, amazed at its beauty and enthralled by its science. It raised so many questions for him to answer. His well-ordered mind took in both the visual and tactile information and within that unique intelligence he measured, calculated, hypothesised and stored all of the answers he had so meticulously worked out.

Borrack lowered his wing. He looked at Mermosia.

"Shall we?"

She nodded with an air of excitement and climbed aboard. The creature powered up his wings and soared high into the sky, almost vertically, then turned, swept his wings back and dived. The girl screamed with delight as they plummeted towards the ice stacks. He tucked his wings in tight to give him more speed. The Plateau rushed towards them. Mermosia held her breath as the mighty eagle spread out his huge wings, tilted them and, with expert accuracy, swept round horizontally with the Plateau, flying at tremendous speeds between the ice columns. He chased the tidal wave of light until they reached the crest of the wave, and then, once again, he angled his huge appendages lifting them upwards.

He shouted to Mermosia, "Hold on tight!"

She did as she was bade, then, he did a complete somersault bringing them back just behind the tidal wave of light. They swept, zigzagging through the ice stacks, on the crest of the wave, allowing the light to sweep across them in a kaleidoscope of colour.

The girl sighed with delight, and for the next two hours they flew around, zigzagged, swept upwards, dived, charged and confronted that tidal wave of light, and Mermosia screamed, laughed and cried with happiness. It was to form a lasting memory but, like Borrack, she sensed her waking hour was close at hand.

The eagle flew back to the small hill at the periphery of the plateau. There, he circled and landed. He lowered his wing and the girl slid down. She looked across the field of ice stacks, watching the tidal wave sweep across them. Mermosia turned and looked at her friend, her confidante.

"Will I ever see you again?" she said, though deep down, she already knew the answer.

The eagle smiled with his eyes, "No" he said in a caring way. "But you, like all the other innocents that have come into my life, will always be part of my family, as I will be yours."

She then threw her arms around his neck.

"Thank you! Thank you so much, you have given me my life back!"

Professor Conner Flynn, who was walking back through the dormant part of the Ice Plateau to the small hill, stopped and looked up to see Mermosia and Borrack talking. He realised that the girl was near her waking hour, so he rushed back.

She heard him coming, as the crisp, white snow crunched under his feet. Mermosia ran up to the professor and threw her arms around him.

"Thank you," she said.

The professor pushed her away with his hands, at arm's distance, and smiled at her.

"It's been my pleasure. In any case I will see you to——-" then stopped, looked at his watch and corrected himself, "This afternoon with Doctor Erick Ashoona."

She turned and looked back at Borrack. Tears welled up in her eyes as she ran back to him and threw her arms around his neck and said lovingly, "I will never forget you."

Then she vacillated between her two worlds, from her dream reality to her new life. A life without fear, a life built on hope and confidence. Both Borrack and the professor watched her go, as every cell in her body randomly disappeared. For a while, they remained quiet, both watching the tidal wave of light disappear into the horizon and, in a way, saddened by the girl's absence. They had been with her through her darkest hours and shared her fears, as well as her hopes. It had left them feeling empty, and, as they stood next to each other, they knew each was feeling the same way.

The eagle broke the silence, "I guess it's time to go."

Professor Conner Flynn nodded in agreement.

"So, I'll take you back to the hill overlooking Coral Harbour, shall I?" Borrack said.

The professor turned his head and looked sharply at the eagle, "No! Native Point! I've got to pick up my car."

"You can't call that thing a car," the eagle replied with a glint in his eye.

"I'll have you know that's my lucky charm."

"And you a scientist!" the professor laughed, and with that, the mighty eagle lowered his huge wing, and Conner Flynn climbed aboard. He powered up his wings, creating a vortex under those huge appendages, sending the soft, white snow into a frenzy. They soared upwards over the ice plateau and chased the tidal wave of light as they flew southeast toward the Artic Ocean and Southampton Island. It was well over an hour before they reached Native Point. The regal sun hovered between the horizon and its apex, a ribbon of cloud sat lazily across it, almost defying the sun's awesome power. A warm breeze blew in from the bay that flowed into Foxe Basin, and above it the gulls dived and squawked, looking for food. The eagle circled, braced his talons for impact, and landed. He lowered his wing and the professor dismounted.

"Well, my friend," the professor said, "What is your next adventure?"

Borrack smiled with his eyes, "I have a little time to spare, I thought I might seek out my paternal father's friend. I know he moved to the New World, and I would love to find out more about my paternal father. Then, I am going back to the homestead to be with Zackery and Maley for a while. What about you, Professor?"

"Like you, my mission has finished here, although I might go back to the crystal pool of personal history. With a bit of luck, I might be able to learn a lot more about the Sallirmiut and their history."

"Well, Professor Conner Flynn, I suppose this is good-bye then?"

Conner Flynn winked and said, "Maybe for now! But I am sure our paths will cross again."

The professor patted the huge eagle on his neck, turned, and walked to his car, then turned again to face Borrack, "Before I go, you were talking to Mermosia on the hill overlooking the ice plateau; is everything alright with the girl?"

"She's fine, just a little haunted by a black raven called Erigal! But that will go."

The name Erigal and black raven echoed around the well-ordered mind of the Professor, which sent alarm bells ringing. Within milliseconds, he had retrieved reams of information on the subject from the thousands of pigeonholes that stored and collated his vast encyclopaedic knowledge. Nearly all of which would be irrelevant to the mighty eagle's predicament. For instance, he could have told him that the black raven was the symbol of deceit and death for ancient tribes the world over. Indeed, Erigal is the name of the black raven that has haunted the tribes of Europe for thousands of years. Legend has it, the creature was hatched on the slopes of Mount Erigal in the northwest of Ireland, and that its sight is the harbinger of death to any one close to the recipient of that vision from that deceitful creature. But to the eagle at that moment in time such information was superfluous.

The eagle had seen the professor's expression change, "Is there something I've missed about the girl?" Borrack said in earnest.

"No! My friend, have you seen this creature in your dreams?"

"Why! Yes."

The professor looked down at the ground, then lifted his head and made eye contact with the eagle.

"Why did you not mention this before?"

The eagle looked confused.

"It didn't seem relevant."

"No! You're right, it was not relevant to the girl, but it is to you. The black raven, Erigal, is a messenger of death, and, unfortunately, the henchman as well. I honestly believe that someone close to you is in serious danger. True, these are only legends, but as I have said before, there is always an element of truth in them."

The eagle looked apprehensive.

"I sincerely hope you're wrong, but in view of your past record, I think that unlikely. From what you have just said, I must get back to my family and fast. Thank you for your help and friendship. I hope that our paths do cross again someday."

Professor Conner Flynn nodded, and Borrack flapped his huge wings, creating a cyclone of dust and debris and soared high into the sky. He flew southwest over Native Point towards Foxe Basin, over the Hudson Bay and towards home.

The professor watched him go, and in his heart, he hoped he was wrong about the black raven, Erigal, but in his head he knew it was too late.

CHAPTER 6

Retribution

The Labyrinth of Golden Dreams, hidden deep in the Black Mountains, waited and planned for that day when that emotion of adoration would once again adorn its great presence. It knew nothing of pain, love, compassion and hate; it was unaware of right or wrong. These emotions played no part in its existence and even if they did, they would be consigned to the dustbin of history. Its only desire was to have those lesser beings that shared this planet with itself, to once again pay homage to its great divinity.

* * * * *

The mighty eagle flew for what seemed an eternity. The majestic sun rose and fell, in all, four times in the length of his journey. He travelled through a myriad of weather systems, from scorching sun to powerful storms, and everything in-between. He flew across the Atlantic to the northwest of Ireland, and on towards England and the North Sea. In all that time his mind was so engrossed on the professor's prophecy that he didn't notice the events that had surrounded him.

And as each second passed, so his concern grew into a crescendo of fear. As the sun rose on the fifth day, casting its golden light across the planet, Borrack passed over the fjords of Norway. In a fleeting moment, he looked down at Mother Nature's splendour, and for a millisecond those fears evaporated. As he marvelled at that beautiful work of art, that which lay below him in such splendour, but as the moment passed, so the fear returned with such ferocity. The mighty eagle's wings cut through the air with such awesome power, moving even nearer the homestead and the dread that waited for him.

He flew over the pine-clad forest that surrounded Zachary's home, and in the distance, he could see the homestead. His eagle eye focused on the small chimney that served the building, and in an instant, he felt physically sick. The tell-tale signs of life were gone. The smoke that had wafted from that stack day and night, month on month, year on year, for as far back as he could remember, was absent. The giant eagle poured more energy into his wings in the futile belief, that his arrival would somehow change the course of events.

As Borrack scanned the clearing where the homestead stood, he saw Maley. The curse of the Labyrinth of Golden Dreams hung heavily around her. (The monster beyond imagination.)

He looked beyond what it evoked, and there he saw her kneeling next to a pile of stones, sobbing. At that moment, the realization hit home. Zachary had gone, his adopted father was dead, murdered by Erigal, the black raven. If he could have screamed, he would have done, and its sound would have reverberated far beyond the pine-clad forest, such was his grief. He spread his huge wings out to slow his descent, braced his talons for impact and landed.

Maley, turned, stood up, and ran to him, her face contorted with grief. Tears ran down her cheeks from her crystal blue eyes. She threw her arms around the eagle's neck. Borrack shook his huge head in uncontrollable anger, and the girl fell to the ground in a heap. She looked up at him confused and scared.

"I could not help it! It was the black raven; he fell upon Zachary with such evil contempt," Maley sobbed uncontrollably, "I so tried to help your father, I so tried to help…"

"How long ago?" the eagle replied aggressively. His anger consumed him; he knew deep down it was not Maley's fault; the truth was that he was responsible for his father's murder. He had had the warning signs since Poutia, and his first taste of humanity, in the form of a dream, but he chose to ignore it, instead blaming it on Mermosia's illness.

"How long ago?" the eagle repeated loudly. Maley, still confused and scared, looked down at the ground, her tears falling onto the sandy soil and being absorbed by the parched land.

"Yesterday evening."

"Which way did the creature go?" Borrack replied, his tone still angry. Maley lifted her head to face Borrack and pointed towards the Black Mountains and the Labyrinth of Golden Dreams.

The eagle flapped his huge wings and soared upwards, Maley watched him go, quietly pleading for him to stay and sobbing uncontrollably; she felt so scared and lonely. Maley wished at that moment in time that the parched earth would consume her as it had consumed her tears.

To the west, the Ice Blue Wind sensed the return of her adversary; she busied herself in preparation for his arrival. Once again, she would do battle with him and, like the last meeting, it would be another victory for her. The eagle flew towards the Ice Blue Wind; it took a little over an hour to reach the wall of dark blue sky and there he hovered.

He had seen this sight so many times in his life and the tell-tale signs that the Ice Blue Wind knew of his arrival were all too obvious. The flashing white streaks of lightning as it flitted from one side to the other, and the rumbling of thunder shook the ground below like an earthquake. Borrack hovered and waited patiently for the Ice Blue Wind to make her appearance. He did not have to wait long, as the translucent face appeared, followed by the two translucent hands. The three-dimensional apparition undulated as its fluid form washed from one side of the face to the other. The ugliness in her soul still played out in her angry expression.

"So, Borrack, you have come back to be humiliated again?" she said with an air of victory in her grating voice.

The eagle's anger still ate away at him.

"I'm not interested in your petty squabbles. All I want from you is some information, and then I'll leave you to stew in your own self-pity."

The Ice Blue Wind's face contorted with anger, as Borrack's insult registered.

"Why should I help you?" she retorted venomously.

The eagle was tired of her procrastination.

"To be honest, I don't care if you do or you don't, I will still complete my quest. It may take a little longer, but I will see it through to its conclusion and nothing will stand in my way. So, I will ask you one question. It is up to you whether you answer it or not. Has a black raven passed here?"

The Ice Blue Wind sneered, "You mean Erigal?"

Borrack was taken aback by her retort, "So, you know of him, then?" he said with surprise.

"Borrack you're so naïve," and, as she said it, a smug look appeared across her fluid face. "To answer your question, he wanted safe passage to the Labyrinth of Golden Dreams and, as always, I denied it, so he flew off towards the northwest."

The eagle did not bother to answer; he angled his wings and followed the direction given. As the Ice Blue Wind watched him go, she felt dejected; the truth was, that in her angry, lonely state, she needed any interaction to lift her sprits.

Borrack flew northwest; every so often he would stop, hover, scrutinize the surroundings, looking for the black raven, then move on and do the same. This went on for some hours, the eagle would not abandon his pursuit, and he owed it to his father, Zachary.

All the time he was looking for Erigal, his mind would keep harking back to the Ice Blue Wind's words: what did she know that he didn't, why was he naïve? The whole thing disturbed him. After what seemed an age, he caught sight of a large black object. He focused his eagle eye on the object. It was the black raven, Erigal. The creature was almost as big as himself; it sat perched on the large bow of a tree. Borrack hovered there for a while, deciding on his strategy; he had the element of surprise on his side.

He made his move; very quietly, he went into freefall. Diving towards the creature in total silence, just the sound of rushing of air as it passed over his body. He swept his wings back to increase his speed. The eagle was moving fast towards the black raven; he was less than thirty yards away, twenty, ten, five and then three. At that moment Erigal took fright, falling off the bow of the tree. He plummeted towards the ground and then, with the prowess of his acrobatic agility, he spread his wings and powered them up and flew vertically upwards. Borrack was stunned by the raven's actions. He quickly stretched out his wings to slow his descent, but it was too late, he hit the bow of the tree and plummeted towards the ground.

Confused and disorientated, the mighty eagle ploughed into the land. He let out a mighty squawk as searing pain ran through his whole body. Borrack lay stunned for a few seconds, and then gathered his thoughts, and watched the black raven flying west. The mighty eagle powered up his wings and went into pursuit.

The sky was like Borrack's mood, grey and angry. The eagle poured more power into those magnificent appendages, and within no time he was on the black raven's tail.

Borrack climbed up a little higher, pouring more power into his wings, until he was just above Erigal, his talons open, ready to clamp onto the raven's back. The shrewd Erigal dropped like a stone, just as the eagle made his move. The raven with his acrobatic quickness, turned vertically, powered up his wings, climbing at speed and rammed his bill into Borrack's underbelly.

The eagle was winded and plummeted to the ground. Borrack blacked out and only just regained consciousness before he would have hit the ground. He spread his huge wings, angled them and then turned almost vertically, scraping his talons across the rugged terrain. He flapped his wings again and went in pursuit of the black raven. The eagle realised that he had underestimated the raven's intelligence and agility. His acrobatic prowess he knew he could never equal. But the one thing Borrack knew he had an abundance of, even though he had been flying for more than four days and nights, and the black raven could only dream about, was his ability to out-fly the creature.

He had time on his side; he would pace the raven, keep up a steady pressure on Erigal until he tired, then he would go in for the kill. To Borrack, it did not matter if it took one hour or forty hours. The eagle had the tenacity, resolve and overwhelming desire to catch his father's murderer.

The angry daylight hours gave way to the night. The heavy, angry cloud thinned, allowing the Great Pretender to illuminate the area with its hazy silver light, revealing both the hunter and its prey in their life and death battle.

Fifteen hours into the pursuit, in which Borrack had been formulating his tactics, he could see the black raven faltering. The eagle would give it a little more time. Another hour went by, and then the mighty eagle went into attack. He poured more energy into his wings until he mimicked his last attempt at capturing the raven, and as hoped, Erigal copied his last ploy to the letter. He fell from the sky and plummeted to the ground. Borrack quickly retracted his talons, swept his wings back and went into a dive, plunging past the back of the cunning Erigal.

At a distance below the tumbling black raven, the eagle spread out his huge wings and hovered, watching and waiting for Erigal to make his move. As Borrack had foreseen, the creature too spread his wings out, sweeping almost vertically. As Erigal climbed to attack his foe the realisation that he had been duped fell upon him, but it was too late. The mighty eagle was flying vertically in front of him.

Borrack clamped his open talons across the black raven's breast. The creature screamed with pain as the claws buried themselves deep into Erigal's flesh.

The eagle scanned the terrain; to the left, he saw a sheer rock face with a ledge protruding outward from it, big enough to land on. He flapped his wings and headed towards it. The black raven limply hung in the majestic eagle's talons, unable to move and in incredible pain.

Borrack circled the ledge, spread his wings and landed with exacting accuracy, the black raven sandwiched between the eagle's talons and the rock ledge. Borrack looked deep into the black menacing eyes of the creature.

"Why?!" he said angrily, "Why did you kill my father?"

The raven replied coldly, "I was ordered to by the Labyrinth of Golden Dreams."

"What do you mean 'ordered to'?"

"It was an execution, and that is my job."

The eagle felt physically sick, shocked and unable to comprehend what he was told, by the raven's callous confession.

"So, you killed my father because you were ordered to do so by the Labyrinth of Golden Dreams?"

"Yes."

"Why did the Labyrinth of Golden Dreams want him murdered?"

"You broke your promise," Erigal replied arrogantly.

Borrack looked confused; he stumbled over his words, "Pro…. Promise, what promise?"

"Let me jog your memory. You took two children to see the Labyrinth of Golden Dreams. I believe their names were Jay and Gemma, is that correct?"

"Yes," the eagle replied cautiously.

"And did you not promise that if the children were reunited with their parents, and Melvin the King penguin was released from his purgatory as a chimera, you would destroy the Ice Blue Wind?"

Borrack's anger deepened, "So the Labyrinth of Golden Dreams had you kill Zachary on the strength of an impossible demand. The Ice Blue Wind, like me, is a chimera, and, as such, only that heartless lump of rock or the demise of this planet can kill us."

Erigal's black, menacing eyes seemed to relay a cold dismissal at Borrack's explanation.

"Why," the eagle continued, "Did the Labyrinth of Golden Dreams not kill me instead?"

The raven croaked, "Your ignorance is unbelievable; you have no idea, do you?"

Borrack looked confused,

"No idea about what?"

"That heartless lump of rock, as you put it, believes you are in some way his protégé. He has earmarked you for great things, but, like you, he is short-sighted and stupid. The Ice Blue Wind was a test; he knew you could not destroy her; the problem was you didn't even try. So, he's punishing you, until you submit to his will, your fate."

The eagle reacted defensively, "Fate, there is no such thing; our lives are not mapped out for us to follow like sheep. We have freewill."

The raven scoffed, "Listen to yourself, you'll buckle to his will eventually."

"How is that heartless lump of rock going to make me?" Borrack retorted angrily.

"It's simple: you've already lost your adopted father, and there are many more friends, and those you've helped, that could easily go the same way as him," Erigal said threateningly.

The eagle's eyes widened, he could feel his rage building, and he squeezed his talons into the raven's flesh. The bird cried out in pain and shouted at Borrack.

"You can hurt me as much as you like, but you can't kill me, because, like you, I'm a chimera."

The eagle released the pressure.

"You see, like you, I have human parents," Erigal continued, "I grew up on Mount Erigal in northwest Ireland about fifteen hundred years ago, give or take a century. I was young, and like all young humans, I wanted adventure and wealth. I had heard about the huge riches in the Black Mountains, and that's what I wanted, so I went for it and this is the result. The Labyrinth of Golden Dreams has turned me into one of his foot soldiers. I am now his chief executioner, which is my fate."

Borrack looked down at the creature he pinned to the stone ledge. The silver light of the moon reflected back in the raven's eyes.

"You said foot soldier?"

"Yes, foot soldier, there are many of us, all over the world."

The raven stopped and looked deep into the eagle's eyes.

"You don't know, do you?" Erigal said and squawked in disbelief, "You really have no idea, do you?"

Borrack replied in an agitated tone, "No idea about what?"

Erigal's pitch changed, he spoke with an air of sarcasm, "Let me ask you a question: what emotions does the Labyrinth of Golden Dreams possess?"

The eagle paused for a while; the answer was too easy. It was as if the raven was laying a trap.

"That heartless lump of rock has no feelings, except adoration."

The raven seemed to smirk with his eyes, "And since the evacuation and destruction of your ancestor's village, who now adores the Labyrinth of Golden Dreams?"

"Well, I guess, no one."

"Do you think that heartless lump of rock can live with that?"

Borrack mulled over the question for some time before answering, although the question was obvious from the start.

"No."

"So, what option has he?"

The eagle knew the answer and mumbled, "He wants to expand his influence."

Erigal squawked, "At last, yes! He wants to expand his influence. And, somehow, he believes you can be his general, and lead the thousands of chimeras that live outside the Black Mountains."

The raven noticed the look of surprise in Borrack's eyes.

"Did you honestly believe that you, Maley and the Ice Blue Wind were the only chimeras outside the Black Mountains? That's just unbelievable."

The eagle did not respond to Erigal's goading.

"As I was saying, he wants you, his general, to lead his army of chimeras, to force the leaders and their citizens, from the world over to come and pay homage to his egotistical beliefs."

For a minute, Borrack was dumbstruck, then he retorted angrily, "I won't join his band of thugs; I'll have nothing to do with it. He has no chance, the Ice Blue Wind, that chimera that he created will stop those who come to worshi…" Borrack stopped as he realised that the Labyrinth of Golden Dreams had set the trap for him, "That heartless lump of rock knew that I couldn't destroy the Ice Blue Wind; that was just a show. But, if I had shown more enthusiasm, that heartless lump of rock would have destroyed the Ice Blue Wind, and I would've been given the credit for it, giving me power of authority," the eagle mumbled.

"At last, Borrack, you have finally seen your fate."

The eagle irritably answered the black raven, "I don't believe in destiny. I have freewill, and I will not be dictated to by anyone, and certainly not the Labyrinth of Golden Dreams."

The raven seemed to smirk again with his eyes, "It doesn't bother me whether you do or you don't. In fact, if you don't do the Labyrinth of Golden Dream's bidding, it leaves the door open for me to become his general. As for those you have helped, well, they will meet their doom at my hands, for that is my fate."

Borrack's anger boiled over, he dug his talons deep into the black raven's flesh, "You talk of fate, Erigal, but that's just a cover, a cover for your own psychotic tendencies; it is not fate or duty. You enjoy goading, bullying and killing."

Although the raven was in extreme pain, his black, menacing eyes expressed his arrogant superiority, and, as Borrack peered into them, he knew he had lost the argument.

Erigal screamed as the pain seared through his body, "The truth is, Borrack, you may be bigger and stronger than me, but you're the one that has fallen into the Labyrinth of Golden Dream's trap, you're the one who has to choose between your principles or the fate of your loved ones, and although you would like to destroy me, you know you can't."

The eagle knew he was right. He flapped his huge wings and released the black raven from his talons. Erigal fell from the ledge, powered up his wings and flew off squawking with the air of victory.

Borrack swooped down, turned, and made his way back home. The misty night fell away as the majestic sun rose, but a thick, grey overcoat of cloud shrouded the one, true, material god. The skies again matched Borrack's mood; he was laden with doom and disappointment.

The eagle's mind was tormented by Erigal's revelations. If he followed the path of the natural laws of justice, which his philosophy demanded, his friends and family would be destroyed. If he did not, he would become no more than a lackey to the Labyrinth of Golden Dreams, becoming party to a tyrannical dictatorship and opening the doors to humanity's greatest weakness, greed, and, with it, the death of innocence. He felt the two bookends of future events were crushing him.

CHAPTER 7

The Pursuit of Natural Justice

Borrack arrived back at the homestead late evening. His eagle eye caught sight of Maley. The Labyrinth of Golden Dream's curse (the monster beyond imagination) enveloped her in a cocoon, as she knelt over Zachary's grave.

The eagle looked passed his fears to see the girl sobbing with grief. He spread out his wings and braced his talons, glided down, and landed. Maley looked up from her squat position, she jumped to her feet, and ran to greet the majestic creature.

Borrack's yellow eyes met hers. She stopped in her tracks, paralysed in one position. Maley looked deep into his yellow eyes, her heart sank, for there she saw unforgiving anger, and, in her paranoia, she believed it was aimed at her. Borrack shut his eyes and thought of Zachary, his father. A searing pain shot through his body, as he visualised his now deceased father and, as he changed from mighty eagle to man, his human stature seemed to shrink to half the man he was.

He walked, stooping, as though he was carrying a heavy burden. Borrack averted his eyes from Maley as he passed her and headed towards the mound of rocks that marked Zachary's final resting place. There he sat, his chin resting in his hands, staring at the pathetic pile of stones that covered a giant of a man. A man of great of wisdom, and humanity, a man who had taught him right from wrong, a man who had shown him the great worth of natural justice. There, Borrack sat, haunted by the fait accompli that had been thrust upon him by the Labyrinth of Golden Dream's messenger, Erigal, which was a contradiction of everything he had learnt from Zachary.

Borrack the man stared at the pile of rocks, trying to resolve the insurmountable problem he had been handed. For two days and nights, he did not move. just stared at the grave. Maley, in all that period, ran around him plying him with food that he did not eat, drink that he did not drink, covering him with blankets when the night fell, removing them when the overcast day appeared, and, in all that time, he did not once respond to her.

Halfway through the second day, Maley sat down next to Borrack. She turned and looked at him. A single tear rolled down her cheek. She made no sounds of distress, just looked at the man next to her.

Maley's heart ached so much, she had fallen in love with him on the first day they met, and, as each day had gone by, her love had deepened, even in his absence. But now she felt heart-broken; in her mind, she believed that Borrack blamed her for Zachary's death. She could not live without him and yet he would never forgive her for something she had no control over.

Maley believed that Borrack was about to exile her, sending her far away. She could not stand the thought. She would once again be as alone as she was when her parents died, alone with only her curse. It was too much for Maley; death would be her only way out. But, even that was barred from her, for she was a chimera, and only the Labyrinth of Golden Dreams or the demise of the planet could grant that wish. She put her head in her hands and sobbed quietly.

The heavy cloud that had hung over the area for the past two days and nights thinned, allowing the majestic sun's hazy outline to show through. The ball of energy lay low on the horizon, ready to relinquish its hold on the present day. Borrack lifted his head and stared at it for minute.

"I have decided," he said confidently. Maley looked up nervously and turned to face Borrack, with paranoia in her voice.

"No, no, please don't send me away. It wasn't my fault, I tried to stop the raven, but I couldn't. He fell upon Zachary, I just couldn't do anything," she said, sobbing. Borrack turned his head in surprise,

"I'm not going to send you away; whatever makes you think that?"

"Because you blame me for Zachary's death, don't you?"

Borrack smiled at her in a caring way,

"Of course, not! If anyone is to blame, it's me. The black raven, Erigal, has haunted me for some time. In my naivety, I believed it to be related to the young girl, Memosia. I have been so stupid, and this is the result," Borrack said, as he looked at the pile of stones in front of him. The girl moved over to him and threw her arms around him.

"Thank you," she said, her love for him even deeper than ever before. Borrack was oblivious to how Maley felt about him. To Borrack, she was just another person who he had helped and cared for.

"What I was going to say, was that I'm going to destroy the Labyrinth of Golden Dreams."

"How?" she replied, "how can such a thing be destroyed?"

"When we first met, I told you that the Labyrinth of Golden Dreams was just a heartless lump of rock, and you replied that it wasn't heartless, that, in fact, your parents had discovered its beating heart, behind one of the golden mirrors, I believe, and that because of that knowledge, they cursed you to stop them divulging the information."

Borrack glanced at Maley, waiting for her confirmation of the fact.

"Yes, yes," she replied, "They told me it was the second mirror from the left."

"Well, that's its Achilles' heel, and that's what I am going for," Borrack retorted

Maley's expression changed to one of concern.

"Have you thought through the consequences? What will happen?" Borrack butted in before she could finish.

"To be honest, I don't know, but I think it goes much deeper than that. It will impact on all the chimeras in a negative way."

Her expression remained the same, "I know you have, for a long time, wanted to destroy the Labyrinth of Golden Dreams, but why now?"

Borrack dropped his eyes to the parched soil beneath his feet; he dragged his fingers through the dry dirt sieving it between his fingers.

"Because of what Erigal has told me."

Borrack then repeated the black raven's prophecy. He told Maley of his journey to the Labyrinth of Golden Dreams with Jay and Gemma, their confrontation with the Ice Blue Wind, the meeting with the Labyrinth of Golden Dreams. The promise he had made to the heartless lump of rock for the children's dream to be realised, and the freedom of the King penguin from his purgatory. He told Maley of the fight with the Ice Blue Wind, and his subsequent defeat, and how the whole charade had been an elaborate trap to snare Borrack into becoming the Labyrinth of Golden Dream's stooge.

He told Maley of how the heartless lump of rock sent out his henchman, his executioner, Erigal, the black raven, to murder Zachary, and with a chilling message. That unless he submitted to the Labyrinth of Golden Dream's will, the same fate awaited all those that Borrack had loved or helped. And then he told Maley of the heartless lump of rock's desire to compel humanity to submit to its omnipotence, as if the Labyrinth of Golden Dreams were a god, a god of greed and adoration.

"So, you see Maley, I have no choice, if it means the destruction of me or —"

Then Borrack stopped. He looked at Maley, and in his eyes she saw the awful truth.

"… Or all chimeras? So, in the morning, after I have eaten and slept, I must fulfil my duty and destroy the Labyrinth of Golden Dreams."

The sun had long since disappeared behind the horizon, leaving the jealous moon to fill its place. The quicksilver light pierced through the hazy cloud, outlining the contours of the cloud with its light.

Maley turned to face the silver edged clouds and said in a quiet, confident manner, "I'm coming with you."

"No, Maley, it's too dangerous," she turned her face back to Borrack.

"I'm not asking. I am coming with you."

Before he could answer, she retorted angrily, "As you have said, if you're successful, the chances are that all chimeras will no longer exist, and I don't want to die alone. And if you go, you will never leave the Labyrinth of

Golden Dreams alive, and I refuse to live for an eternity alone, with only this godforsaken curse to keep me company. Anyway, I love you too much to let you…"

Then she stopped in mid flow, her face coloured as she realised what she had just said. Borrack was surprised but said nothing; he had no wish to embarrass her. He looked at her beautiful face with those blue eyes. He realised he had been so involved in his need to help others he had overlooked this beautiful, young lady. Borrack smiled at her.

"OK, if you want to come, we leave early in the morning. But you can only come as far as the cave entrance, is that clear?"

Maley nodded, although she knew she would not be content with the cave entrance. Her intent was to follow Borrack to the heartless lump of rock, and she would exact her revenge on the Labyrinth of Golden Dreams, for all the suffering she and her parents had endured, and, at the same time, she would be with the one she loved, no matter what the consequence.

"I'm quite hungry, I haven't eaten since…" Borrack stopped and contemplated, trying to remember the last time he had eaten in the last four or five days; the whole period seemed a blur, "Well, sometime ago."

Maley smiled and disappeared into the log cabin. While she was gone, Borrack wrestled with the problem of the Ice Blue Wind, especially with his new passenger, Maley. Then it came to him: Maley's curse! 'It could be the ideal distraction for the Ice Blue Wind, and maybe allow enough time to break through her defences,' he thought.

Maley returned with the food, and the two of them sat at the bench and ate while Borrack outlined his plan.

The cloud that had hung hazily across the moon cleared, leaving a clear bright night. The moon gently caressed its silver light across the landscape. Borrack and Maley sat quietly, looking up into the clear night sky. The stars littered the heavens as if suspended high up on invisible wires, like thousands of bright, sparkling diamonds.

Then Maley saw a shooting star arcing across the sky, "Look! Borrack, look!"

Borrack looked at Maley's facial profile as she spoke, the moonlight embraced her features, and he could not help but admire her. He had little interest in shooting stars, they certainly could not match her beauty. Maley sensed that Borrack was studying her. She turned her head to face him, and he quickly turned away in embarrassment. He looked up at the shooting star as it disappeared into the abyss of space, hoping that Maley had not sensed his wonder at her beauty, but knowing that deep down she had. They sat there quietly both aware of each other's embarrassment.

Borrack broke the silence, still staring up into the celestial heavens, "It's going to be a long day tomorrow, and I think we should get some sleep, don't you?"

Maley replied self-consciously, her voice barely audible, "Yes."

Both of them walked back to the door of the homestead awkwardly, trying not to look at each other, but knowing deep down that the kindling of love had ignited.

As the majestic sun, the one, true, material god appeared on the horizon, Borrack awoke. He dressed in his fine suit of golden-brown feathers. He made his way outside the building and walked around it. He knew, whatever the outcome of future advents, he would never return to this place.

Borrack knelt down next to the pile of stones and placed a large rock at its head. He smiled inwardly, a tear rolled down his cheek as he thought of his adopted father, Zachary, the wise, old man of the north, and he muttered, "What I do now is for you, firstly, and secondly, for humanity. I do not take this action lightly; you have taught me to be true to the laws of natural justice, and I will not let you down. That which threatens that philosophy must be destroyed, regardless of the consequences, and that is the responsibility I must bear alone. Thank you for your care, love and, above all, for your wisdom. Goodbye, Father, you're always in my thoughts, and my love will always be with you."

As his last words left his lips, that single tear dropped from his cheek onto the grave of his father and there it shimmered, as the sun's rays caught its fragility.

From behind, Borrack heard a noise. It was Maley. She carried in her hands two plates.

"Breakfast," she said, as she plodded over to the table. Borrack joined her and there they sat in embarrassed silence, staring at the pile of stones. Maley broke the silence,

"Will it take long to get to the Labyrinth of Golden Dreams?"

"No," Borrack replied, "Providing our tactic works on the Ice Blue Wind. In fact, I think we should make a move."

"OK, let me just clean the plates," Maley replied, and disappeared into the homestead. Borrack looked at Zachary's grave and filled his mind with his father's image from memory. The emotional pain seared through his body as he thought of his mentor, his role model and his friend, then he metamorphosed from Borrack the man to Borrack the mighty eagle.

Maley came out from the homestead, and Borrack lowered his wing, which she climbed up. Then, once again, the mighty eagle turned his yellow eyes to his father's grave.

"Goodbye, my old friend, you will always be in my thoughts."

Then he flapped his huge wings, lifting them high into the sky. He circled and flew in the direction of his destiny.

The Ice Blue Wind raced up and down the entrance to the Black Mountains. She sensed the return of her adversary, and, in her own insignificant world, she believed that once again she would defeat the mighty Borrack. Her excitement was profligate, as the Ice Blue Wind poured her boundless energy into the corridor of sky she controlled with lightning and thunder, and hail stones the size of rocks. To the Ice Blue Wind, Borrack's subjugation would be her crowning glory.

As the mighty eagle and Maley flew towards the Black Mountains, they could see in the distance the angry skies of the Ice Blue Wind. Borrack had seen it all before, to him it was nothing more than bravado, a show he had little time for.

Maley watched with fear. She had been sheltered from such anger, first, by her parents, and then by her curse. Maley's innocence had never been challenged, but now it was.

The eagle sensed her anguish. He shouted, "It's nothing more than a show! If we stick to the plan, we will have no trouble passing through the entrance to the Black Mountains. Tuck yourself down into my back; do not let the Ice Blue Wind see you, until I give you the signal."

Borrack reached the small mound that overlooked the deserted village, and the outer edges of his adversary's domain. He edged forward until he was just shy of the boundary and hovered, waiting for the Ice Blue Wind to make her appearance.

He did not have to wait long, for her excitement had got the better of her. First, her fluid face appeared, undulating, as its washing about distorted her features, surging from one side of the face to the other in a frenzy of aggression. Then, her fluid hands materialized, in direct proportion to her face.

She screamed at Borrack, her voice screeching and cackling like a witch, "So, at last you've come to meet your ruination, your destruction at my superiority?"

Borrack smiled with his eyes; it was an expression that conveyed an air of control.

"No, I have come to defeat you for the last time."

With that, he called to Maley. She raised her being so that the Ice Blue Wind could feast upon her curse. The Ice Blue Wind froze in fear as Maley's curse engulfed her.

The fluid hands rushed forward to cradle the fluid head, the inexplicable love and fear that had evolved deep down in the Ice Blue Wind's psyche, after so many millennia, was too much for the chimera. As love, anger, hate and fear of her father burst forth into a cauldron of emotion she was unable to control. She cried out her father's name, "Protness, Protness!"

The mighty eagle, seizing the opportunity, powered up his huge wings, pouring all his energy into them, and bursting through the Ice Blue Wind's boundary, towards the Black Mountains. He was nearly two thirds of the way across before the Ice Blue Wind realised the betrayal. Her fluid hand went into action, as they tried in vain to swipe at Borrack and his passenger, but it was too late; the mighty eagle burst out the other side of the Ice Blue Wind's domain.

Borrack did not stop. He, and his passenger, flew on towards the entrance to the Labyrinth of Golden Dreams. The Ice Blue Wind's anger knew no bounds. She cursed at her adversary. The eagle caught the last remnants of her tirade as he flew out of range.

"I'll get you, you devil, on your return, and be sure, I will show you no mercy!"

Borrack smiled inwardly. He knew, whatever the outcome of his mission, he would never face the Ice Blue Wind again as Borrack the mighty eagle.

The sun flooded the outer edge of the Ice Blue Wind's reign of terror. Both Borrack and Maley could feel its gentle warmth, as they were drawn towards it. The journey was short to the entrance of the Labyrinth of Golden Dreams. As Borrack peered downwards at the entrance, he hovered for a while, soaking up the last, wonderful moments of his freedom, the freedom of flight. Borrack knew he would never see the world again from this perspective, and it scared him a little, it was a sea change, the end of an era. But it was a sacrifice that was for the greater good, and he was ready for it.

Maley, too, felt the anxiety of change and the fear of the unknown. Her mind raced with the possibilities of future events. Would she survive or not, and, if she did, what life would she lead? Would it be with Borrack, or without? The last thought was unthinkable; she blocked it out from her mind.

The mighty eagle gently spiralled down to the barren and arid landscape, and, deep down, he was angered by the heartless lump of rock that imprisoned an army of humanity in the guise of chimeras to live an eternity of purgatory, for their basic instinct of greed.

Borrack braced his talons for impact... Thump! He was down. He lowered his wing, and Maley slid down. The eagle panned the vista; his eyes were drawn to the entrance of the Black Mountains, and the Ice Blue Wind. Her anger ravaged the skies; she had been humiliated by Borrack's tactics. In some ways, Borrack felt for the creature, but his actions were necessary, and he comforted himself with that thought. He thought of his birth parents, and their journey at the bequest of the Labyrinth of Golden Dreams, and it only confirmed his mission, the destruction of that heartless lump of rock.

He thought of Zachary for a second. It felt like a knife had been plunged into his chest, as he visualised his adopted father, then he changed from eagle to man. He looked at Maley, and then at the cave entrance.

He returned his gaze to Maley, and he smiled nervously, "I guess it's time to get the deed done?"

He proceeded to the cave entrance. Maley followed, but, as he heard the footsteps behind him, he turned and looked at her.

"I'm going alone."

"No," she replied, "I'm coming too!"

"But, you promised," Borrack urged.

"Did I?" she replied contemptuously.

"Please," he said, "It's too dangerous."

Maley looked at him implacably.

"I'm coming with you; I need to lay my ghosts to rest. The Labyrinth of

Golden Dreams has had a devastating effect on my life and that of my parents. I, like you, need redress, and that can only come with the destruction of that thing in there," she said, pointing to the cave entrance. Borrack could see her anger building.

"I know you're angry, but let me deal with…."

But, before he could finish speaking, Maley strode in front of him and through the cave entrance. As she passed over the threshold, she stopped and gasped.

"It's magnificent!" she said, as she panned the vista. Maley had long dreamed of this day, but she had never imagined that it was so beautiful. She took a deep intake of breath and the sweet smell of honeysuckle coursed through her very being. She turned to Borrack and looked up at him.

"It's hard to imagine something so beautiful could be so evil, isn't it?"

"Yes," he said, realising he wasn't going to change her mind, "Beauty can be deceptive."

Borrack took the lead, and Maley followed to the centre. She saw a beam of light, Maley followed it with her eyes to its source high up in the apex of the vaulted ceiling, she followed the light back down again. Beyond that stream of light, in the blackness of space, thousands of specks of light danced around in total disarray, mesmerising her. Then, she caught sight of the stalactites and stalagmites. She stood still for a while, watching as the brilliant light bounced off the objects and diffused into a myriad of colours.

Borrack walked off ahead, then realised that Maley was not following. He turned, and, from a distance, he could not help but admire her unique beauty as the light playfully danced across her face. She sensed his curiosity and faced him. He smiled, slightly embarrassed. He nodded towards the gallery, and Maley followed.

They walked side by side through the gallery. The warm wind gently swept across their being, filling them with the sweet aroma of honeysuckle. As the warm wind weaved in and out of the clinging vine dressed with such delicate blooms, it created a sound, like panpipes.

Borrack and Maley stopped in front of the last chamber. Borrack looked down at Maley, and she responded. Their eyes met. Both felt the anxiety of future events, the uncertainty – this was their fait accompli. There could be no going back. Maley clutched Borrack's hand. He smiled into her crystal blue eyes and whispered.

"It's time."

She nodded. They walked into the chamber, still holding hands. The brilliant, crisp light surrounded them, clinging to their bodies. They reached the white stone platform and stopped. They peered around nervously. In front of them stood the highly polished golden mirrors hewn into the vapid red rock. Borrack focused on the second mirror from the left and squeezed Maley's hand; she nodded the confirmation that that was their target.

At that moment, lights flashed across the huge chamber. As it became animated, a voice boomed out:

"Do you come in friendship?"

Borrack stayed quiet for a while, considering his options. He could have strung the emotionless entity along, and then go in for the kill, or get straight to the point. He decided on the latter.

"No."

The lights flashed vigorously and stopped.

"Is that Borrack?"

"Yes," Borrack replied, "Why did you have Zachary murdered, my adopted father?"

The lights stayed static for some time, and then flashed once, and the voice boomed out:

"For your place is at my side. You were born from my power, from my flesh. You are to be my general, and, between us, we will subjugate humanity and bring about lasting peace, and they will pay homage to my magnitude, my omnipotence."

Borrack laughed out loud, "You've got carried away with your own narcissism, and humanity will never bow to your so-called omnipotence. You are nothing but a heartless lump of rock."

The lights began to flash violently, stopped and started again and then stopped. The voice boomed angrily:

"You will bend to my will or I ..."

Borrack shouted over the booming voice, "Or you'll do what?"

The lights stayed static and the voice remained quiet.

Borrack looked at Maley and said, "That is the first time this thing has shown any emotion."

He then looked around at the ground, looking for a weapon. To the right of Maley, he saw a rock, large but not too big to throw. The voice calmly boomed again:

"The creature next to you, I know of her. She too was born from my power, my flesh. She is the product of the explorers."

The voice stopped, the lights flashed vigorously then stopped and remained static. Borrack felt uneasy, every nerve and sinew in his body was heightened for danger. The booming voice returned.

"The creature next to you is a hazard! It must be destroyed."

From Borrack's peripheral vision, he saw the materialisation of concentrated ball of light. His body went into overdrive, as he dived at Maley, pushing her off the limestone platform, as a white-hot thread of molten energy shot out of the ball of light.

Borrack rolled to one side, as the molten energy hit the limestone platform, splitting it in two. Borrack grabbed the rock and jumped to his feet. Maley regained her equanimity, she looked up to see another concentrated ball of light behind Borrack, she shouted. He dived to the left – at the same time, he threw the large rock towards the second golden mirror from the left.

Both Maley and Borrack watched in slow motion as the actions of past events unfolded. Maley looked on as another molten spear struck Borrack's foot. He screamed in agony, but never took his eyes off the flying rock as it homed in on its target like a missile, smashing into the golden mirror and shattering it into a thousand pieces.

Maley turned to face the commotion from behind, watching the shards of glass fall in slow motion like leaves falling off a tree in autumn. Suddenly, the chamber filled with a blinding light, and both of them shielded their eyes. It lasted less than a few milliseconds, only to be replaced with a myriad of balls of light ready to rain down molten spears on them.

Borrack shouted to Maley, "I can't walk, you must finish the job."

She leapt to her feet and ran towards the shattered aperture, all the time molten spears of light hitting the floor as she danced around them. Borrack rolled into a crevice, trying to protect himself from the Labyrinth of Golden Dream's attack.

Maley reached the orifice left by the shattered mirror. She peered inside and retched. The sight and smell were disgusting. The green mass of flesh throbbed, and every movement it excreted slime that immediately evaporated into a pungent gas, with the odour of rotting flesh.

She withdrew her head; it was spinning from the nauseous sight. Maley caught sight of another molten spear, she rolled away, cowering behind anything that would give her sanctuary. The Labyrinth of Golden Dreams now concentrated its defence on the open aperture; its weakness had been exposed, and the desire for self-preservation kicked in at the expense of all else.

Borrack shouted to Maley, "I'll try to draw its fire! Our only chance is its destruction!"

Borrack pulled himself out of his temporary bunker and moved around the edge of the chamber, in the direction of the shattered aperture. The strategy worked. The Labyrinth of Golden Dreams responded, and turned its attention to Borrack, pouring its energy into his extermination.

Maley jumped up from her defensive position and ran to the orifice, stooped down and picked up a shard of glass in her hand, which dug deep into her flesh allowing her blood to ooze from the self-inflicted wound. Then she lifted her arm high with the dagger-shaped shard of glass and brought it down with a vengeance on the green, throbbing mass of flesh.

As the shard of glass pierced it, the creature screamed, and a purple liquid spurted out. Maley lifted her arm again and again, each time bringing it down on the beating heart, and each time the creature screamed, and the purple liquid spurted from it.

Maley's strength was waning, but she summoned her last bit of energy by concentrating on her parents, and, as she brought the dagger-shaped shard of glass onto the Labyrinth of Golden Dream's heart she shouted, "This is for my parents and Zachary!"

The shard of glass buried itself deep into its flesh. The Labyrinth of

Golden Dreams screamed so loud that it reverberated around the chamber along the gallery to the exit and echoed around the Black Mountains. Maley covered her ears to protect them. The whole chamber become bathed in a brilliant white light. She swung her head around, looking for Borrack but he was nowhere to be seen.

Everything fell silent. The brilliant, white light dimmed, until it was swallowed up by the blackness of space.

Maley called out after Borrack, but there was no answer, just a deadly silence. She tried again, but nothing. She tried a third time… then a sound, nothing tangible, just a mumble, an incoherent sound. Again, she called his name. This time a reply, weak, but a reply.

"Yes, Maley?"

"Are you OK?" she pressed.

"I've been hit a couple of times, but I'm still in one piece. I am by the entrance."

The darkness surrounded them like a shroud of death.

"I'll make my way over," Maley replied.

She moved cautiously to the left, using the wall as a guide, placing her hands on the rocky surface. The wounds on her hands throbbed as she used them to feel her way, and the terrain beneath her feet was rugged; on more than one occasion, she lost her footing and stumbled. All the time, Borrack kept talking, both in encouragement and as a guide. It was some time before she reached him. When that moment arrived, she fell into his arms exhausted.

They sat there quietly for a while, in a state of shock. Borrack broke the silence.

"We're still here! We destroyed the Labyrinth of Golden Dreams and we're still here!"

"Yes!" Maley said and laughed.

Borrack followed suit, and they both sat in the pitch-black laughing with relief. They could not believe their luck; they had survived against all the odds.

But their consolation was short lived. From below, in the depths of the mountain, they felt a rumbling. The whole floor shook, and where once the limestone platform had stood, a fissure opened up. An orange glow emanated from it, followed by a tidal wave of hot gases. They covered their faces as the choking gases swirled around them.

"We've got to get out now!" Borrack spat.

The orange light illuminated the chamber. From the far side of the chamber, an explosion occurred as the remaining golden mirrors imploded.

Borrack pointed to the exit. Maley stood up and helped her companion to his feet, she helped him hobble to the entrance. As they moved through the gallery, another gush of hot gases washed over them, burning the vine and its fragrant blooms into oblivion. The sweet smell of honeysuckle was replaced with the acrid smell of sulphur.

They moved as fast as they could, even though Borrack's wounds slowed them down. They had reached the end of the gallery when they heard and felt another rumbling, much more powerful than the first.

Maley looked behind to see a crack appear in the floor and watched as it spread the full length of the gallery and into the antechamber. The whole structure shook violently, stalagmites keeled over, hitting the ground with incredible force, and the stalactites fell from the ceilings like huge thunderbolts.

Borrack and Maley kept close to the edge of the chamber. They reached the cave entrance, but, from behind, Maley heard a noise. She turned, and there, rushing towards them, she saw a huge ball of molten rock.

She pushed Borrack through the exit and followed. Once outside, Borrack pointed to a culvert in the rock. They dived for its safety in the nick of time, as the ball of molten rock exploded outwards.

The whole mountain shook for what seemed like an age. An avalanche of boulders and rubble plunged down the mountain side, just missing the pair. It took an hour before the mountain's anger subsided, and then it all went quiet. In all that time, Maley had clung to Borrack out of fear. The air was thick with dust, but, as it thinned, the sun's watery image burst through. Borrack heard something far off in the distance, the sound of bird song.

"Listen," he said, "Can you hear?"

"What?" Maley replied.

"There it is again, bird song."

"Yes," she said, smiling. Borrack looked at Maley, something was different about her, he looked at her again then he realised what the difference was. Maley's curse, that the Labyrinth of Golden Dreams had bestowed upon her, was gone.

He smiled at her, "It's gone. Your curse has gone."

She looked up at Borrack, and she too smiled, "Your eyes, they have turned green, and your hair – it's black."

They both burst into laughter out of relief.

As the dust settled, Maley helped Borrack to his feet. She helped him hobble over to the edge of the cliff. They stood and gazed at the vista. The majestic sun was bright and only just past its zenith. Borrack focused on the abandoned village, pointing it out to Maley. It nestled in the bright sunlight, no longer at the mercy of the Ice Blue Wind; her curse, too, had been lifted.

Borrack smiled at her, "I think it's time we went home."

"Back to the homestead?" Maley replied.

"No!" Borrack said, "Now Zachary's gone, there's nothing left for us. I mean, Poutia."

Maley questioned with her eyes.

He laughed, "Let me tell you of Poutia as we walk."

Maley helped him as they descended the mountain, and he told her of Poutia and the family connection.

Epilogue

At the time of the Labyrinth of Golden Dream's destruction, Erigal had been on another mission for the master he so despised.

He was flying high over northern Europe, when his curse evaporated. He changed from raven to man, and plummeted towards the ground, tumbling head over heels as he did. The ground sped towards him, and just before hitting it, he blacked out.

Many hours later he woke, on his back, groggy and confused. He tried to move but was unable to; he was paralysed. Far above him, the sky was blue, with the sun laying just above the western horizon. His vision cleared, and there above him flew half dozen buzzards. He knew he was their victim, and when the time was right, they would fly down and peck at his eyes, and rip the flesh from his bones until they were left dry. His cunning mind went into overdrive; he was not prepared to give up his fight for life. To Erigal, this was just another challenge; true, it looked bleak, but only the march of time would judge the outcome.

As Maley helped Borrack down the Black Mountains and towards its exit, they were not alone, for everywhere they looked, people (mostly men), moved about aimlessly, some on their bellies, some crawling, and some walking, but all mindless, naked and without hope. Maley looked at Borrack.

"Yes," he said, "You're right. They are the Labyrinth of Golden Dream's victims; chimeras."

"What will happen to them?"

Borrack shook his head, "Most will starve to death, and maybe some will survive. Perhaps, the only benefit is, with the destruction of that heartless lump of rock, that soon their purgatory will be over."

Borrack looked down at the ground. There he saw a small sapling bursting through the barren soil. He pointed towards it.

"Look Maley, Mother Nature is taking back that which is rightfully hers, that which was stolen from her by that malevolent being, the Labyrinth of Golden Dreams. Do you know, sometimes Mother Nature has a cruel sense of justice, for, within all of this futility and death, new life and hope emerges?"

High on the plateau, surrounded by the black granite cliffs, the Matriarch sat in her dwelling. Her empathic powers had long since told her that one of Poutia's sons was coming home for good, and with him he would bring a partner, a wife, and from that union they would bear children.

That son was Borrack. Borrack the man. She looked forward to his arrival, for the Matriarch was feeling tired. Although her mind was still strong, her body was weakened by age. She needed to rest, to retire, and the Matriarch saw and sensed within Borrack the gift of leadership. He would become the Patriarch and take the society of Poutia to a new level, because, within this man he had the greatest of all traits: his understanding of children and their potential, humanity's greatest gift.

The Matriarch knew that he would exploit this trait to create a fair and just society on the small Island of Poutia, which would become a beacon for the rest of the world.

Borrack, with Maley's help, hobbled into the derelict village of his parents. No structure had been left standing after the Ice Blue Wind had poured her rage down upon it all those years ago. All that was left were the footprints of the buildings.

Borrack pointed to one of the sights, "Do you see the foundations of that building?"

Maley nodded.

"That was where I was born," then he dropped his head, "And where my mother died."

Maley could see his pain. She patted his arm.

Then Borrack turned, a tear in his eye, "Over there," he pointed.

Maley helped him to his chosen destination. They both stood and looked down at the two mounds of soil.

"It looks as though they have been tended recently, I wonder who by," Borrack said inquisitively.

"I think it may have been Zackery," Maley replied.

Borrack looked at her, waiting for an explanation.

She looked up into his green eyes, "When you were away, just before the black," then she stopped and checked herself, "Well, you know…"

Borrack nodded and sensed her anxiety.

"Anyway, Zachary said he had an important job to do and disappeared for the whole day."

Borrack smiled, "Yes that sounds like the sort of thing he would do."

Borrack saw a bunch of wildflowers gently swaying in the breeze. He nodded towards them and Maley helped him over to pick them. Then he split them in two and laid a bunch on each grave.

"I know I never met you, but I have always loved you, and I'm immensely proud of you both."

Borrack could say no more, his words lost in emotion.

They stood there for a few minutes, and then moved off southwards.

Maley helped Borrack through the derelict village, still supporting his arm to help him to walk. A little beyond, they heard a scream. It was like a banshee from behind! They turned to see a small, dishevelled woman running towards them in a hysterical rage.

She pounced towards Borrack. With a single swing of her arm, Maley knocked her flying, and the small dishevelled woman ended up in a heap on the floor. Borrack immediately recognised her; it was Berlice, (the Ice Blue Wind), her face still contorted with the bitterness of her history. She jumped to her feet.

"This is not over, Borrack, you will never enter the Black Mountains again, at least, not alive."

Then she turned and ran off cackling as if she still believed she was the Ice Blue Wind.

Maley looked at Borrack, and he at her. Both knew in their own minds that Berlice would live for the rest of her life in a state of mental torture, unable to recognise her true reality.

Borrack and Maley resumed their journey a little further, and then decided to rest. The majestic sun was setting in the west, and the Great Pretender would soon take its place. Maley checked on Borrack's wounds, they were only superficial and would soon heal.

Professor Conner Flynn sat in his office. In less than an hour he would present his paper on the tribes and customs of the Americas, to a packed audience of eminent scientists.

There was a tap on the door.

"Enter," the professor said, lifting his head from his work. From the other side of the door a tall, bony man appeared.

"Ah! Marris!"

Marris Eliss was his assistant.

"What can I do for you?"

"Professor, the dean has sent me; have you read the papers today?" Conner Flynn shook his head. "Well, it seems there has been some serious seismic activity in an area considered to be stable; it certainly does not sit on any fault lines."

"Where?" the professor asked inquisitively.

"A place called the Black Mountains in northern Europe."

Within milliseconds of hearing the name of the location, the professor had drawn all the relevant strands of information from the thousands of pigeonholes that were part of his well-ordered mind.

"I suppose the Dean wishes me to go and investigate this anomaly?"

"Yes," Marris answered.

"Tell him it is unusual, but it will never happen again."

Marris Eliss looked at the professor; he was confused by his response.

The professor smiled, "There are some things, Maris, that are best left; this is one of them. I'm not saying there isn't a scientific answer, because we both know such a theory would not hold water. But in this instance, the answer would shake the scientific community out of its comfortable dream.

It's best left alone."

Maris Eliss went out the door even more confused.

As for the professor, he thought of Borrack, and had already theorised the likely outcome of Borrack's return to the homestead, and the subsequent altercation with Erigal, the black raven, and the connection with the Labyrinth of Golden Dreams, and, within that theory, he had surmised that Borrack was still alive and well.

Borrack and Maley had been travelling for just a month when they reached the shores of the Mediterranean Sea. In that time, they had learnt the skills of ordinary folk. They had thumbed lifts, taken on casual work to pay for food and transport, and lived rough. But, at last, they were at the shores of the Mediterranean.

The sun had long since dropped below the horizon; they were both tired after the day's journey. They sat on the edge of a cliff. Beneath them, that sea of antiquity, that sea of so much history, that sea that had seen so many empires come and go, the Mediterranean. Above, the moon was full and brimming with confidence, its light shone down upon the sea and land, bathing it in its quicksilver light.

Maley looked at Borrack and Borrack looked at Maley. Over the month together, their awkwardness had disappeared, and, in its place, their love had flourished. Borrack put his arm around her, Maley responded by bringing her head into his chest. They turned their gaze to the sea, and sat watching its majesty, its beauty, highlighted by the quicksilver light of the moon.

Far to the south, on an island that sits on the equator, and deep down within its bowels, an old man, tall, pale faced with pale blue eyes, bloodshot and red rimmed, sat at his desk, busy shuffling papers around. There was a rap on the door.

"Yes?"

The door opened.

"What is it, number two?"

"Sir, over the past month, the names of people we had lost track of through the aeons have begun to reappear."

The Accountant of Life sat bolt upright, "Go on, please."

"Well Sir, at first, it was just a trickle, but now, well, it's as if the floodgates have been opened. There are names from all over the world, but the greatest concentration is from the Black Mountains in northern Europe."

The old man got up from behind his desk, "Let's take a look," he said, "Lead the way."

The midget did as he was told; they both climbed the first scaffold. This layer was where the first ever registration of humanity was documented. Within this layer, a few names of history past had disappeared, as if they had never existed. As they climbed further up the tangle of scaffold, so many more names appeared, until they reached the archives covering the Black Mountains. From nowhere, midgets arrived with parchment files containing the names of those that had disappeared into the history of oblivion.

Other midgets were arriving with a list of names of those that had at last surfaced from that oblivion. There was a frenzy of activity, as each missing name was matched with one that had just recently surfaced. The Accountant of Lives watched with satisfaction, for, at last, the accountant's books would balance.

He smiled, "Good work, number two. I must leave you now, I have something I must attend to."

The Accountant of Lives made his way down the scaffold and followed the well-trodden path that led to the exit. He passed through the portal and walked until he reached the beach. It was quiet, the only noise was that of the ocean, in an almost perpetual rhythmic sound, lapping up against the beach, pulling back that fine sand, almost white in colour, and returning again for more. As if its mission was to wash that very sand away and regain that small desert island and return it to its own watery empire.

The moon was high, casting its quicksilver light across the endless Ocean, the night was balmy. The old man smiled to himself as he thought of that fine young man, Borrack. It was clear he had destroyed the Labyrinth of Golden Dreams, and freed the thousands of souls from their torment. The old man cupped his hands around his mouth and shouted.

"Well done, my friend! And now, live your life in peace with those you love! Good luck!" Then he turned, and went back through the portal to his work, his life and his office.

Borrack lifted his head. He heard a sound on the gentle breeze.

Maley looked up at him, "What?" she was just about to say, but Borrack smiled at her, put his finger vertically across his lips. She understood the signal and remained quiet. Borrack strained his hearing as the sound on that gentle breeze formed an audible statement. He spoke the words quietly.

"Well done, my friend! And now, live your life in peace with those you love! Good luck!"

Maley's expression was one of curiosity.

Borrack laughed, "It's from an old friend, a friend who understands the value of life. I think he is telling me that this is our time."

As Borrack looked into Maley's crystal blue eyes, he knew the Accountant of Lives was right. This was the start of their life together. He gently lifted Maley's head with his hand and kissed her.

The End

BV - #0039 - 120422 - C0 - 229/152/11 - PB - 9781914002052 - Gloss Lamination